THE YEAR WITHOUT SUMMER

Also by Guinevere Glasfurd

The Words in My Hand

Praise for *The Year Without Summer*

...listed for the HWA Gold Crown Award 2020

'Rich in voice, beautifully told, and with a
chilling sting in its tail'
Historical Writers' Association

'... a stay-up-all-night page-turner ... a beautifully
...en, angry, unflinching and unforgettable novel'
Financial Times

'...asfurd is a strikingly sharp and subtle writer
...finds beauty in the bleakest situations. She has
...re ability to conjure characters vividly in a few
...rokes and the gift, rarer still, of making us care
...bout them ... an angry and tender interrogation
...tangibly real lives ... Glasfurd's hard-hitting
admonition deserves to find its mark'
Guardian

'...Guinevere Glasfurd's follow-up to her 2016
...ta-shortlisted debut *The Words in My Hand* is
... superb saga, rich in both historical detail and
... interest ... [Glasfurd] combines her intricate
...ne with an impressively realised sense of a
...rld being dragged into the modern age'
Observer

'...ll-written, and entirely convincing work of
...ction. Each story adds a dimension to the
exploration of climate disaster across social class and
geograp... ...In *The Year Without Summer* we are offered
both ... ...re'

Guinevere Glasfurd

The Year Without Summer

First published in Great Britain in 2020 by Two Roads
An Imprint of John Murray Press
An Hachette UK company

This paperback edition published in 2021

1

A CIP catalogue record for this title is available from the British Library

Paperback ISBN 978 1 473 67233 8
eBook ISBN 978 1 473 67231 4
Audio Digital Download ISBN 978 1 473 67232 1

Typeset in Albertina MT by
Palimpsest Book Production Limited, Falkirk, Stirlingshire

Printed and bound in Great Britain by Clays Ltd, Elcograf S.p.A.

John Murray policy is to use papers that are natural,
renewable and recyclable products and made from wood grown in
sustainable forests. The logging and manufacturing processes are expected
to conform to the environmental regulations of the country of origin.

Two Roads
Carmelite House
50 Victoria Embankment
London EC4Y 0DZ

www.tworoadsbooks.com

for
Damian

and with thanks to the
MacDowell Colony Foundation
for their support

Contents

Foreword

IN APRIL 1815 Mount Tambora erupts on Sumbawa Island, Indonesia, then under British rule. Aboard *Benares*, ship's surgeon Henry Hogg sets sail to investigate, little suspecting what lies ahead.

After an unusually stormy winter, 1816 opens with hope for better times ahead. The newspapers are filled with reports of a royal wedding and the country is at peace after years of war. But this peace masks deeper divisions. Food prices are rising while wealthy land-owners and farmers enact laws to protect their interests. Common land continues to be enclosed.

As temperatures drop, John Constable is on his way to East Bergholt to visit his ailing father. Mary Wollstonecraft Godwin, together with Willmouse, her infant son, her stepsister Claire and lover Percy Shelley have set sail for France. In Littleport, on the Fens, Sarah Hobbs has had enough of working all day and always being hungry. Hope Peter, a soldier returning from the Napoleonic Wars, is headed to Corringham, Essex, to find what remains of his family home. And in Vermont, Charles Whitlock sets off on his pony to preach his ministry to anyone who will listen at the farms scattered about.

Unknown to one another and connected by an event they have little or no knowledge of, this is the story of the Tambora eruption and the tumultuous year that followed.

1815

Henry

Dearest Emmalina,

I write in haste as I have been called to the seas south of Makassar once more to investigate rumours of a disturbing nature. Very distinct reports, like cannons, were heard last week in Ternate, five hundred miles east of us and not easily reached. Pirates were suspected, but none found. Then, one night ago, more explosions, this time sufficient to shake our ship and the houses around the harbour, even though we were moored and Makassar peaceful. Yet more talk of pirates, who must be close at hand, if so.

I have had Susilo sharpen my short sword should I need it. I am as prepared as I might be in these parts. But I ask you please to pray for my return with my sword still safely sheathed beside me.

Pirates notwithstanding, I shall be happy to be at sea again. The air here is at its oppressive heaviest, some days it is as if mercury has been poured over us; I have never known it so stifling hot. Even the birds seem afflicted and have lost the will to sing. An eerie stillness hangs over the town and makes the most relaxed man uneasy. Perhaps one of their gods has taken a good breath in and is about to blow us off our feet.

You are a sweet sensible thing to stay in England.

So wish me a fair wind and a safe return, my darling. We sail when it is light.

Your ever loving husband,
Henry

Surgeon aboard the Benares

12 April our year of the Lord, 1815

Dearest Emmalina,

I am writing this by candlelight though it is not yet midday. A little after 8 a.m. this morning it was apparent we had sailed into what I can only describe as an extraordinary occurrence. To the west and south of us, the sky had assumed the most dismal prospect; the sunrise seemed smothered: a deep red glow that refused to brighten. By ten in the morning, I was certain night had been returned to us. I could scarcely make out the shore, and our ship was but one mile from it. I felt something brush against my skin, with the softness of snow. Snow? Imagine my confusion! What snow could survive this hostile clime? I touched my finger to it, incredulous, until I saw that it smudged. Ash. One question had been answered, but many more took its place. Within an hour, the sky, from horizon to the heavens, was filled with it. It fell in heavy showers with a soft patter, coating the deck then forming a thick layer. And now we have reached a truly awful and alarming state: a darkness as total as at new moon.

The ash is still falling as I write. We are working in shifts to sweep it away, such is its weight. And now the captain is calling me to help rig an awning, presumably to keep it off the deck. I do not know how we will rig anything when one cannot see one's hand in front of one's face. Darkness or not, I must go.

I shall write again later. Until then, I am
Your loving husband,
Henry

Surgeon aboard the Benares

13 April our year of the Lord, 1815

Dearest Emmalina,

I know not if this is night or day, though by the hours that have passed it must be morning once more. The captain's awning was a dismal failure and we have all been put to the broom in an attempt to keep the ash from reaching perilous levels. We are now sweeping it overboard else it will add many tons in weight to the ship. Wherever one sweeps you can be certain that behind you the ash will have heaped up readily to depths of a foot or more. The further south we sail, the grittier it becomes. The air is foul with it; every breath is a half breath and all on board are wheezing. The queue of the poorly lengthens to my door.

Forgive me, I am unable to write more. Exhaustion has felled me and my hands are blistered.
    Your loving husband,
    Henry

Surgeon aboard the Benares

                                18 April our year of the Lord, 1815

Dearest, dearest Emmalina,
    Forgive my silence, but I have been unwell, a consequence, I think, of ash having found its way into our drinking water. My blisters, I am relieved to say, are improved.
    My darling, I wish I had never seen this day for I am struggling to find the words that can adequately express it. Daylight is returned but, oh, for the darkness we had five days ago in favour of what I can now see.
    We have arrived off Bima on Sumbawa, which we believe almost certainly is the source of the 'cannons' that disturbed our peace in Makassar. This island, once a green gem, is now a hellish scene, to rival any produced by Breughel. The mountain Tomboro, sometimes called Tambora, is gone. Gone! But where? If I had not climbed it last year, when I was the guest of the Rajah here, I would scarce believe it were possible. I knew of the volcano beneath it, but had no reason to suspect an eruption. I am yet to find the Rajah among the few survivors we have met. I hope he lives. I will venture out tomorrow to find him.
    But I am ahead of myself. Let me tell you first of our

awful approach. We sighted Sumbawa yesterday. Then, still some distance off, the sea became sluggish, thickened with ash in a grey soup. I was below deck, assessing our water supply to determine what portion was spoiled, when I heard a cry go up from above.

I popped my head through the hatch, but it was impossible to make out what was being said. A sailor held out his arm, and pointed, then flapped up and down in a most peculiar manner. Already, he had a small crowd around him and they were similarly vexed. I heaved myself up through the hatch and elbowed my way through the commotion. I took the spyglass from one of them and looked.

That wasn't water ahead, but <u>stone:</u> a sea, made entirely of stone! But stone that undulated gently.

Bump, bump, bump went several pieces as they knocked into the hull. The bosun, hearing it, took a net and scooped up a small amount. He turned what he had out on deck and we stared as though at strange, dead specimens from the deep. I poked at one with my foot then reached down to pick it up. Stone, now cinder, and pocked like a sponge. The stone had no weight — so that was why it floated. The bosun ventured it was pumice.

<u>*Pumice?*</u> *Of course. I went to the port side and looked over. Pumice in every direction, the sea thick with it and as far as I could see. Although we had a good wind behind us, the ship had slowed and struggled to make way. It must have been many feet thick to slow us like that.*

And that, my dearest, is how the sea becomes a mountain and the mountain becomes a sea. There are riddles everywhere, it seems . . .

Henry put down his ink pen, unsure of how to end the letter. The point about riddles seemed flippant; he could see the frown on Emmalina's brow as she read it. But riddles interested him. Snow that was ash, a mountain that was the sea – it seemed to capture something of the extraordinary event he was bearing witness to. He shifted in his seat as he re-read the letter. He thought about crossing out the boast about himself and the Rajah, the story of them climbing Tambora together. If he did, it would mean writing the letter again and he hadn't the appetite for that. Besides, the story was true in that it wasn't a lie – only it was his captain's story, not his. The captain had often talked fondly of his time on Sumbawa Island last year. Emmalina, who had remained in England, would never know how Henry, with a few slight exaggerations, had made these stories his.

He considered the small pile of letters he had written to her. An absurd thing to do when he had no means to post them until he was landed again in Makassar. He would send them in intervals so she would receive his news over a period of time and have the anticipation of a story in parts, well told. The pumice stone sea had been true. He would remember that sight to his grave. Something like that deserved skilful telling. And if he did not tell it, who would?

He would go ashore in the morning and would write to her again after that. Going ashore was a prospect that filled him with dread. Their vessel was anchored some distance off as the bay usually used for anchoring had been changed beyond recognition by the eruption. A new promontory had formed a barrier across it; breaking waves revealed shallows where once there had been water, fathoms deep.

Survivors, if any, he knew not of – be that the Rajah or anyone else – their fate wouldn't be known until they had explored inland. A cursory glance through the spyglass had revealed a blasted world that bore no resemblance to the captain's stories. The captain, when he had looked too, had steadied one hand on the rail and visibly blanched.

Tomorrow. Tomorrow. He would make himself useful. What would he need to do that? His leather bag of surgical implements and his cabinet of medicines too. Poultices, bandages, a saw. He grimaced. Burns were a grisly business and difficult to heal; impossible in this climate. He would take what he had and it must do.

An image of pirates came suddenly to him. And he realised then that he had sheathed the truest part of himself in his letters as carefully as his sword. He was no warrior. He wasn't brave at all.

1816

John

CORNY-FACED FERRET. SOWPIG. *High-shoed prig. Parish prig. Maggot.* Though no one could hear, John looked about to be sure. 'Limping Jesus,' he muttered. 'To the devil with him.'

His thoughts turned from Reverend Rhudde to Farington, to their last meeting. As his face pulled into a scowl, his mother's voice came to him, chiding: *No scowling, John. Scowling suits no gentleman, least of all you.*

The rain came down, a drenching rain that seemed stalled across Essex, as though drawn in a line, purposefully so, along the length of his journey. He had made several such journeys from London to East Bergholt recently, riding at the back of the coach, but none as dismal as this. A sharp, spring shower could be expected at this time of year, but not rain so brutally blunt. It came at him and, hours later, at him still; an insult of rain. He felt the tug of mud under the coach wheels and their uneasy slither as they came free. He clenched hold of the bracing bar to his left, to prevent being pitched sideways off the coach. Up front, he heard the coach driver, by turns soothing and alarmed, guide the horses through the thickening mire. At one point, remembering him, the coach driver turned and called over his shoulder, 'All right back there?' John raised one hand to show that he was, though, in truth, any old fool would see he was not. The rain had come in at his collar, a cold, wet necklace that quickly saturated his shirt. He felt its clammy touch across his shoulders and down his back. The seat of his pants was soaked too. But there would come a time, and he looked forward to it, when he would have sufficient of that necessary evil – *money* – and could afford a seat in the dry. He did the sums in his head. On his father's death, a sixth part of his property, amounting possibly to four thousand pounds. Add to that two thousand from an aunt in Nayland, perhaps. That was enough, was it not, to marry? And yet, worry reached ahead of him and behind. Towards Suffolk, the worry of his ailing father; in London, the worry that was Farington. Neither had met the other and yet they seemed tied together as if on a loop of string: two beads he worried endlessly back and forth. He closed his eyes, if only to stop himself cursing again.

Oh, how that last meeting with Farington chafed. John had done his best to pry the old goat open; had invited him to his lodgings, spent what little he had left of his allowance on a new ruby port, setting it on a silver tray with a pair of bright crystal glasses. Neither this, nor his new canvases that he was submitting to the annual exhib-ition and which he had placed prominently on display, seemed to impress: *The Wheatfield* and *A Wood, Autumn*. Farington, blast him, drank four large glasses down straight, but neither comment nor compliment on the work was forthcoming. Instead, he had rubbed his eyes and squinted at the canvases as if he'd just noticed them. He'd cleared his throat, perhaps to pass judgement, but whatever opinion he had of the work he kept to himself. Not a word was said on it, nor, by implication, on John's suitability as a candidate to the Royal Academy this year. His candidacy last year had received no votes at all, not even from Farington. It had stung bitterly. John kicked one heel against the coach step. He needed Farington's support, for what success could he have without it, without the Royal Academy's approval? He'd be left painting portraits of Suffolk farmers' wives and their preening, ill-tempered daughters. Or, worse, the farmer's prize cattle. A poor prospect that.

Six thousand pounds. With careful, cautious investment it might, with luck – a vague and unknowable quantity, he knew – yield an annual return of four hundred pounds. That was more than the one hundred pounds allowance he presently had from his father, but he only had himself to keep on that. *Allowance?* John gave a bitter laugh. It neither allowed nor afforded for much.

The only other way to have more would be for him to earn it, through commissions or sales. He slumped at the thought of it, as the bald facts of his position presented themselves yet again. It was like watching a series of dishes paraded before him, grandly described, but then finding them made of the most meagre ingredients – he was a man made of morsels, if he was honest.

Bachelors happily made palaces of their scant accommodation, but he could not expect Maria to lodge in some miserable room and be content with it. Oh, she would tell him she could bear it, that she would bear anything for him. Even if he did not doubt her, he would hate to bring her so low. He had written once that she deserved a better fate, referring to the dreadful longing he felt for her and which he knew she felt for him in return. Fate? He saw a deeper meaning now. She deserved altogether better, a fate better than him. How could he expect her to marry him as he was?

The thoughts circled about him as the coach made its way through Marks Tey, with another hour ahead before they would reach East Bergholt. He could not take out his watch for fear of wetting it but knew from the mutterings of the driver that they were running late. John glanced up, one cheek angled against the rain, hungry for the first signs of Suffolk and the small comfort that recognition brought. He saw a gang of men in a field, huddled over a plough, scarce quarter of an acre turned over before the work had been abandoned. A strange time of year to be ploughing, he thought. He raised one hand as the coach passed by, to these men who seemed halfway made of mud, but not one returned his greeting.

John knew hard work too. Not ploughing, true, but he'd worked long summers, shouldering sacks of corn from cart into the mill. It had made him strong and proud to be so, and admiring of the tan on his arms. Dunthorne had only laughed at him. 'Just because you're in the fields, that don't make you no farm labourer, Constable.' So they'd tested it out, there and then, one against the other: an arm wrestle to see who was the stronger. John had won easily. 'Even so,' Dunthorne had said and had tapped his head in a way of saying that he knew who was right and that the loss of this wager mattered little to it, 'that don't change a thing. The fields of the father go to the son.'

John had never before seen himself on the opposite side of the fence to Dunthorne. Theirs was an unlikely friendship. Dunthorne, a plumber, painted too. But painting did not place Dunthorne on John's side of the fence either. One thing they did agree on, the enclosure of the East Bergholt common was a wretched development: field laid to field, fencing it into smaller plots. Among a few, he'd noted an extreme greediness, an ugly rapaciousness; among the many, a sense they'd been fleeced, of having lost what was theirs by right.

If he saw Dunthorne this time, he would avoid him; he was the one person Maria and Dr Rhudde's opinion had united on. An atheist, destitute of religious principle, they said. Worse, they'd heard, if worse were possible, a radical, infected with revolutionary ideas.

John realised that thinking of home was making him anxious in ways he'd not felt before. Bergholt, beloved Bergholt. Was it him that was changing, or it? He saw the men in the field fall into the distance, as the road took him ever further away from London and his Maria. A sadness at the gulf between them rose in him and something else too: a tide approaching, which he could not outrun.

The coach made East Bergholt a little after three and pulled up just beyond the church. The ground steamed in the sudden sunshine. Every bird in Suffolk seemed to be singing at once.

The driver pitched John's bag down to him. 'Home, is this?' he asked in a way that suggested no reply was expected.

'I am. Home at that.' John nodded in the direction of his father's house, meeting the driver's eye and noting his surprise.

'Well, you'll dry out soon enough.' The driver touched one finger to his cap. Perhaps it was sight of the house that made him seem hopeful for a tip.

'I suppose I will.' John's hand went instinctively to his trouser pocket, before he remembered his purse was empty. He gathered up his bag where the driver had dropped it. 'A beer, later, if you are stopping at the inn . . .' But the invitation was vague and he knew it.

'This is the *Ipswich* coach, in case you were forgetting. Now, if you were after accompanying me there . . .?'

When John didn't reply, the driver gathered up the reins and with one sharp flick set the horses neatly on their way.

John stood for a moment as if unsure which way to go. He turned away from his father's house and faced Dr Rhudde's church. He walked up to the gate to a view he had sketched many times. If he had thought Dr Rhudde would find those sketches pleasing, or to have been in any way flattered by the gift of them, he was mistaken; a mistake he had learned early on. He had learned also that a man who might be so fulsome in his consolations on the death of his mother and his father's faltering health, could just as easily become a cantankerous old gager, threatening his granddaughter, Maria, with disinheritance should her father ever agree to their match. On matters of money, Dr Rhudde was always right and mostly indignant. He would neither countenance John as suitor nor accept his *pictures*, as he called them, as prospect.

John considered the church. Dr Rhudde might be rector of several parishes around, but here, in Bergholt, he was rector of this: a church without a spire. It never failed to amuse John. Even today, with his father so dangerously ill, he managed a small, bleak smile as he assessed the church in its lopped-off glory – a man's pretences, cut down to size.

He found his father asleep in a chair, pooled in sunshine, light haloed in his thin white hair. The chair had been angled into the light and set by the large drawing room window, placed to give him a view over the back garden. John swallowed as he remembered his mother: the garden was hers, but tended for them all. His father had had this house built. The brickwork still looked new-fired from the kiln, not weather-worn or damp as so many of the village dwellings were. But now, with his mother dead, and his father certainly soon to follow, the house would be sold. John had few prospects without it. Dunthorne was wrong. The fortunes of the son were not the same as the father.

He saw his father's arm, newly bandaged from being bled, hang limply over the arm of the chair. The simple curve of his hand, relaxed in sleep, filled him with a love that made his chest ache. A memory came to him of his father delving a hand into a sack of wheat, to bring up a handful, then letting it run freely through his fingers. He knew the quality of the grain just from that, from a handful lifted and let fall again. He had taught John the colour to look for: not yellow, nor green, nor in any way speckled black or white with must or mould. But if John had learned the colours it was only so he could paint them better and the business had passed to Abram, his younger brother. To this day John could not say what set one good bag of wheat apart from another and the dust in the mill made him cough.

As John turned to go, his father awoke and blinked several times to focus.

'*John?* My honest son John come home to me? You are my good boi, come home.' And with that, he reached out a wavering hand, his eyes suddenly bright.

John took a seat by his father's side. Nothing further was said, nor was it expected. He waited until his father had dozed off again then took a couple of shillings from the desk. He needed that drink after all.

'Aye, Constable,' said Harold the publican in greeting. He reached for a tankard and filled it with ale from a barrel, kept on the bar.

John drank deeply, with relief. 'Quiet for this time of day,' he said, as he turned to Harold. The men should be in from the fields by now, but he was the only one there.

Harold took down a tankard from the shelf and rubbed at it with a cloth, though to what end was not clear as it was neither dirty nor wet. 'The rain has kept a good many home.'

John frowned. Just then, he heard a sound and turned in its direction. At the far end of the room ran a narrow corridor that led through to a room at the back but the door to it, usually left wedged open, was closed. He heard cheers erupt from behind it, followed by a hammering of mugs on the tables.

'That meeting's not for you,' Harold said in warning as John took a step in its direction.

Before John could protest, the door was flung open and

people spilled out – not just men, but women and children too. Half the village seemed to have crammed in there and many were still caught up in the matter of their debate and remonstrating loudly. But as they spotted John, a hush fell upon them all. They hurried past, out the door, not stopping to say hello, nor even to raise a cup with him.

Here, at least, he had expected a welcome. And now even Harold would not meet his eye.

Sarah

IF I'D KNOW'D it were wrong, I'd never have done it.

Weren't anything much anyhow.

Mairster Benton had sent me away from his farm that morning with nothing and it was then that I catch'd up with Tessie and I guessed he'd sent her away too.

'Mornin',' I said in greeting, as is only polite and she's my elder by four years.

'Mornin',' she said back, not looking at me, as if I were the slummocky one though she had the same lack of shoes on as me.

'Where are you oft to?' I asked, polite as I could, enquiring.

Her striding on, head in the air, as though making for Norwich.

I asked her again and tugged on her sleeve to get her to say.

'Never you mind, Sarah Hobbs,' she said and shook my hand free.

Hobbs, was it? I didn't know Tessie so well, but we'd worked the same fields last year, 'cluding Benton's, and we were only two alleys apart when we were home so there weren't need for talking to me as if I were up on high with the rectory folk.

'Did he not have work for you then either?'

'What's that?'

'Mairster Benton.' Of course, Mairster Benton. Who else did she think I meant?

Her shoulders went up and down as though she'd been bumped over a tussock.

On we went like this, me asking and her not saying, though me knowing she was in the same such difficulty as me. I'd walked three miles already from Littleport to Benton's farm and now here we was, halfway through walking those three miles back again. I hadn't done it for the good of it and neither I knew had she.

'Are you going home?' I asked. The path we were on could take us on further, if we decided we wanted to.

She shrugged again. All that shrugging. She'd only herself to blame if her arms shook off.

'Because I was thinkin' of going on to Cook's farm. To see what's likely there.' Well, I had her attention then, I could tell. By this point, we'd reached the edge of Willow Row and were walking along a ditch. I noticed the sparrergras they'd planted alongside were shrunk up as if shy of the light, as if it'd changed its mind and had turned its way back to the earth again. The thought of no sparrergras was a miserable thing. It weren't the only miserable sight. A mizzlin rain had started, cold as frost.

Tessie's eyes redded up and not just from the cold and I saw she was crying.

'Tessie?' I said and this time when I touched her she stopped with her long striding ahead. Her name, me saying it, brought from her such a shudder. She was crying the way you cry when there's not anyone for miles to see. 'Tessie, Tessie,' I said and I rubbed her back. I hadn't expected this.

'How can I marry now?' she said.

There weren't no place to sit but she sat down anyway and I sat down beside her. I'd have pulled at the cotton grass but there were no grass to pull, nor anything much else come up green. Spring had passed us by without resting. I felt the rain, prickling, on its way to snow. No wonder the sparrergras wanted none of it. Still, Tessie and me both had our bonnets on so at least our heads could keep warm, after a fashion.

Tessie cried for some time. It were best to let her be and maybe she would tell me what were wrong but maybe she wouldn't.

'He's a bastid,' she said at last. 'If I were a man, I'd take up a gun an' I'd shoot him, I would.'

'Who?'

'Mairster Benton, that's who.'

It was shocking to hear it, so strongly said, though I knew no one around had a good word for him.

'You'd not!' I imagined her with a gun, taking aim.

'I would!' and I saw then that she meant it.

'They'd hang you, Tessie. By your neck.'

'Don't care.'

You would, I thought, but I kept that to meself. 'What's he done? He turned you away too?'

She nodded and dipped her head down. I knew she was trying not to cry again even though her bonnet had her hid.

'I don't know what I'll do . . .' She wrung her hands, despairing.

'He didn't want me either.' Small consolation to her, adding my own misery to hers, no help at all, in fact. So I put on my Mairster Benton voice: '*Employ a girl like you when*

I have my fill of good men?' Sounded funny how I said it.
Hadn't been funny when he had.

'Bastid,' she said again and this time I agreed.

We sat for a while in the prinkling drizzle. I tucked my
feet into my skirts to keep the worst of the cold off.

'He hadn't work for Thomas either.' Thomas was her
sweetheart, I knew. 'Says he now has a plough this wide.'
She stretched her arms open as far as she could. 'Would
plough a field as wide as from here to Littleport. No need
of Thomas with a plough like that. He said if I wanted to
pick up stones he'd pay me half what he did before, elsewise
he could get a man who'd do the same for what he paid
me last year, only a man would pick up twice as much. He
had a choice of fine men, good strong soldiering men more
deserving of work than me, he said.'

'Why'd he not take Thomas on then?'

She looked at me as if I were slower than a snail on dry
sand. 'Thomas told him straight he'd not pick up stones
for a girl's wages. That it weren't right to put a man to such
work.'

Well, yes. If I were a man, I'd be thinking it weren't fair
either. I never liked picking up stones anyway.

'Benton told him beggars could not be choosers. And
Thomas called him a bad 'un and damned him and his new
plough and that's when Benton told him to be gone and
never come back.'

'Bastid!' I clapp'd my hand over my mouth.

Tessie pushed me on the shoulder and though she were
not happy, she gave a small smile.

*   *   *

Now that we were on swearing terms together, we carried on our way in better cheer having decided we'd go on to Park Farm after all and ask after work there.

It was a fair traipse to the farm in the rain. We passed two men dragging a contraption by hand. So beggardly muddy they were, they'd not even the breath to call after us.

'Irish,' she whispered and we hurried on by.

I couldn't say it, but perhaps the thought was too noisy, chattering away to itself there in my head because then Tessie said, 'I don't have no hope we'll be welcome at Cook's farm.'

It was proper blowy when we reached the farm's fence, there being nothing on the Fen to keep the wind from blowing how or where it wanted. I was relieved of it raining; there'd be a choke of dust otherwise. Through the gate, the track went on out to a farm at the end. Simple enough to walk down there to the door in a straight line like that. There were straight lines everywhere now since the Bedford Level lot had put in their ditches. Not all the land was fenced off like here at Cook's farm, with a farmhouse plonked down in the middle of it, but that didn't give us the say-so to walk over it. Tessie and I stood there, our feet mired in mud and it had me thinking about the differences between straight and simple.

A notice had been fixed either side of the gate.

> **POACHERS BEWARE**
> Let it be known
> that any such person found without permit
> or any Foul Poacher caught on this land
> will be punish'd severely or shot
> & no mercy show'd.
> Mr Cook Esq, Park Farm.

> **REWARD**
> to the BREAKING down of FENCES
> or DRAINS or SLUICES
> ONE GUINEA Apply:
> the Bedford Level Commissioners.

'What's they say?'

Tessie shrugged. 'Summat else they got to shout about, I suppose. Never could read.'

She gave a look same as to say *come on then* and reached for my hand.

We'd gone no more than halfway down the track when I stopped and pulled out what I'd had in my pocket all the while. Tessie's eyes opened up wide when she saw it.

A penknife. Handsome carved, with initials too. I turned it over in my hand and pulled out the blade.

'That's never yours . . .'

'It's Mairster Benton's.' Pride swelled my voice; I'd fluffed out fatter than a dandelion clock.

She looked at me full agog. 'How did you come by it? *Did you steal it?'*

I pretended not to hear. One puff of wind would have shivered me all away. Truth was, he'd dropp'd it without noticing and I'd covered it with my foot and whipped it up quick when he looked the other way.

'Finders keepers,' I said and skipped ahead. Weren't much use other than for whittling that I could see, but he weren't having it back.

And that about served him right.

Mary

THIS TIME THEY would go by a different route, from Paris towards Troyes and Dijon and thereby reach Geneva. Although filled with the hope of a journey newly begun, they would need to make their way carefully; tempered, if not by caution, then by what they had learned before. And Mary did want at least to have a chance to unpack her books before they returned home.

They were a family now. She had Willmouse to carry and care for – love and worry utterly inseparable. Space had needed to be made in their small portmanteau for his clothes, which meant less room for books and an argument as to what must be left. Shelley insisted that Voltaire, Lucretius, Pliny's Letters and Virgil must come, leaving several sorry discarded volumes on the bed. A small complaint, no complaint at all.

Mary's thoughts turned briefly to Fanny. She would miss her. And yet it would be wrong to suppose her too sober or sorrowful on Fanny's account, and the excitement at the thought of quitting England and leaving certain vexatious matters behind – of which, she admitted, her sister was one and her father another – was impossible to suppress. Besides, she had promised she would write and rather than the brief, lived moment, Fanny would have the pleasure of those letters again and again. So, yes, excitement, of course excitement; how could they not, why should they not, deny themselves that? Claire, giddy with it, leaned over the ship's gunwale to wave goodbye to anyone who was watching. As the boat got under way, she took a huge gulp of air and threw her arms wide to the wind, as though reaching with one hand to catch it and with the other to prevent its escape. Claire, Claire. Her ready, simple delight was infectious. Shelley, who had been watching, laughed. Mary felt a flicker of envy. Quickly, she swallowed it. What was there to be envious of? The freedom to stand at the gunwale and behave like a loon?

After a short while and now soaked with sea spray, Claire came back to where Mary was seated and slumped by her side. She pulled at her skirts, the fabric stiff with salt. 'These skirts will never dry. See how the salt has chafed me?' She held out two pink wrists as proof and examined them with sullen reproach. 'Could we not afford seats in the dry?'

Her question went unanswered. How young she seemed suddenly, Mary thought – though only a few months separated them – and this journey, so impelled by her, a reckless one. Nowhere was possible without Claire, it seemed. She had accompanied them on their last tour to the Continent too. Runaways three they had been then, though left to Mary to write to Papa with their apology, explaining their flight. No need for that this time. Yet Godwin's disapproval still trailed after them like a storm cloud, ready with rain. Well, goodbye to that and for however long they would be gone. Perhaps they would never return. So be it. To summer and happier times.

Claire held out her wrists for Shelley to inspect but he'd withdrawn into his thoughts and he gave them, and her, barely a glance – anxious already, she supposed. Mute with nausea, Mary had no words of consolation for Claire either, nor comfort for Shelley. The sickness rose and fell in her with the increasing squall. She hugged Willmouse close, brought her head down to his, her world become a small muffled place, the smallest place possible for Dormouse, her, and Willmouse, him, to be. Willmouse, darling boy; her newborn babe and none more precious.

He let out a wail. She didn't think he could be hungry again. Could a baby be seasick too?

'Hush, hush now.' She rocked him in the hope he would sleep.

From time to time she looked up and her eye roved across the passengers huddled along the opposite rail. She was the only one travelling with an infant that she could see. Still he cried. Perhaps she should feed him after all. She quickly dismissed the thought, it was too exposed on deck. Nor could she risk going below for fear she'd lose her footing. Had Shelley not considered any of this when agreeing their fare?

Doing her best to ignore Willmouse's cries, she watched two deckhands struggle to reef the sail. When they were done and the boat brought back into the wind, she felt it fall into a trough and then lurch forward as a wave surged under them. Wave after wave crashed over the bow and sent sheets of spray high into the air and down on to them.

Shelley turned up his collar against the buffeting. 'The child is hungry, Mary. A feed will quieten him.'

'It's not an hour since he was last fed—'

'Can you not at least try?' said Claire.

'I do think you should,' said Shelley.

Mary looked from one to the other and blinked away a
sudden, ridiculous urge to cry. Stung, she brought
Willmouse under her cape and held him fast in the crook
of one arm. With her other hand, she fiddled to free her
breast from her dress. By now, he was a bundle of howling
protest and at risk of wriggling free of her grasp. She
brought her elbow in to her side to prevent his escape. At
last, her breast was bared and she desperately directed her
nipple to his mouth, if only to silence his scream. 'Take it,
for goodness' sake, William,' she scolded, 'take it.'

Oh, dear God. Her stomach heaved and a prickling cold
ran across her. Then a violent gust of wind caught under
her cape. It billowed about her like the wing of some
deranged bird, tugging at her neck where it was tied as it
tried vainly to take flight. She caught the eye of an older
woman and her husband as she fought to cover herself
once again. The woman tutted and turned away, but not
before she mouthed *fool*; the man pursed his lips and blew
a kiss.

What idiocy this? Bringing a babe, not yet six months
old, on such a journey? The woman's disapproval was a
familiar one and if Mary bent to it, she would never venture
anywhere. It was not easy to travel with a child but neither
was it impossible. Her mother had managed across Europe,
on her own, with Fanny. Mary felt her courage reassert
itself. This would not be her first time in France, but her
second. Her second time in Switzerland too. She was a
seasoned traveller. She knew what was needed: the mules
required; the cheating *voituriers* and other loathsome
creepers on the way; the asses and ponies – old nags, if she
was honest – that gave up after the first week and stubbornly

refused to be led. No amount of cajoling or goading or whipping had encouraged them. She remembered how one, with only their small portmanteau to carry, had folded forward, as if hobbled, on to its knees. Oh, their talk might have been of Napoleon, but it was thoughts of Albion and strong English horses that had carried them on their footsore way.

Extraordinary, she knew, to be in possession of such experience and not yet nineteen. She lifted her chin in defiance, then felt an immeasurable relief as the milk in her breast let down and Willmouse began to feed.

They approached Calais at dawn; a struggle at first to distinguish the thin line of cliffs from the grey drizzle. All went quiet as the skipper brought their vessel into a channel, there to be left to settle in the mud on the falling tide. Even as the anchor fell, there was a scrum to the ladder, bundles and baskets aloft, in a rush to be the first off.

'Back, back,' shouted the bosun as he herded them into a bad-tempered line. Then began the slow spill of English tourists and their effects into the row boat that ploughed the passage between ship and shore.

'Here,' said Mary when it was their turn. She handed Willmouse down to Shelley in the boat below. As she seated herself next to him, she linked her arm through his, her happiness impossible to contain.

'La Belle France!' he said and kissed her.

Belle? Oh, she hoped so. With the interminable war behind them she was hopeful for signs of recovery. Such wretched places they had passed through two years ago, she could scarce bear to remember it: the rotten meals they'd been served, the filthy hostelries, the foul linen. A people so sullen, and their discontent worn in abruptly hostile ways. If those had been the strong, then what of their children?

She saw them running over the dunes before they reached shore. Then came their cries: *Un sou, un sou! Pour l'amour de Dieu . . . un sou!* As Shelley clambered out of the boat, they clustered around him in a great tumult. *Mon roi! Mon roi!*

King? Shelley recoiled. If king he be, then King of the Urchins. One man, hearing Shelley's accent – *un moment, s'il vous plaît* – spat at his feet. Shelley threw a few small coins on to the beach and the children scattered after them. In the bedlam, a little girl fell down in the shallows. Claire ran over and helped her up again.

'Whose child is this?' She cast about her. '*S'il vous plaît? Qui sont les parents de cette fille?*'

She crouched down in front of the girl and smoothed her hair across her brow. '*Tu habites près d'içi?*'

The girl gave no reply, no indication that she had either heard or understood.

'*Et vous,*' Claire said to a man standing nearby, '*vous êtes le père?*'

'*Moi? Non, non, madem'selle.*' The man backed away.

'Well, she must belong to someone.' Claire turned to the girl. 'What a little kitten you are. Shall I put you in my pocket?'

'She isn't a stray you can carry off with you,' Mary said, alarmed that she might do just that.

'Then let's set her down there.' Claire took an apple from their provisions and led the girl over to a grassy mound. '*Mange, ma petite.* Someone will come soon. *Ça va mieux?*'

The girl sat with the apple in her lap and cried. On seeing the basket of food, more children came running. Shelley lifted the basket above his head with one hand, leaving him the other to defend his pockets from attack.

'*Une pomme! Moi, je veux une pomme!*'

'*Désolé, désolé,*' he said. '*Arrête! Arrête!*'

'Yah!' came a cry, scattering children left and right. Cutting through the crowd came several dealers with long sticks, herding asses and mules for sale.

The woman from the boat approached with her husband. Mary watched them agree quickly on an ass and lead it hopefully away.

'What do you think to this one?' asked Shelley. 'Sturdy enough to carry you and Voltaire both?'

'Plenty, I should think, and that one there.' Mary pointed to a mule that stood a hand taller than the rest.

So it was decided, and once they had loaded their portmanteau and several baskets, they could go.

Mary gave a last glance back to the beach. 'It looks as if someone has claimed her.'

'Who?'

'Your girl, silly. She's gone.'

Claire cast a look briefly back in the direction that Mary pointed. 'Oh? Good.' She turned back to the mule and tugged at its reins. 'This mule needs a name. What shall we call him?'

Shelley thought for a moment. 'Rowley—'

'Ha!' laughed Mary.

'Georgie?' Claire clapped and gave a skip, the child quite forgotten. 'Non, trop anglais.'

'Diderot donkey?'

'Montesquieu mule . . .'

If they gave the mule one name, they gave him twenty, and so it went, along the road to Calais. Shortly, they came upon the couple from the boat, trying and failing to get their recalcitrant beast to move.

Mary waved as they went by. 'Bonne chance!' she called out. She reached forward and patted her mule. *Who was the fool now?*

If nothing delayed them, they would make Hôtel Sécheron in Geneva in ten days, there to await Lord Byron. Mary worried about Claire. These past few days, she had risen with a dragging reluctance, as though weighted. She was tired, that was all, she said. It made for a peculiarly quiet journey. No sudden exclamations of how beautiful any place was, or exhortations to *let us live here!* Mary wasn't much given to chatter. If she did not remark on what she saw, it did not mean that it went by unnoticed. Impossible, of course, to note anything down on the back of a lumbering mule, nor did she attempt to. Now and then she would close her eyes, recalling details, so as to fix an image more firmly in her mind.

She was struck by the lack of enclosed land. Whole tracts of countryside untilled; livestock allowed to roam where-soever it pleased. It was wild in a way so little of the English countryside was any more. It caused a sudden yearning in her, a desire to reach their destination, to be *there*. They were delayed by floods near Troyes, the remains of which proved a nuisance to navigate and blighted an otherwise charming view. In places, where the water had stood a while, it had formed into green lakes, thick with hovering flies. Further on, they came upon a drowned wood. The unfortunate trees should have been in full leaf, instead their bare branches thrust up from the water's surface. It was quite the most disconsolate sight and not one to linger by. She wondered why it affected her so. Then she realised. A man, given warning, could flee, but no tree could make good its escape. It must either withstand the storm, or fall. It had the luck of high ground, or must be consumed utterly on a lower plain. Poor trees, she thought, as she kicked her mule to get it to move again.

They were several days out of Paris and on the road to Champagnole, when a storm came upon them. Their destination still lay some hours ahead, the village buried in the depths of the mountains and reached only by an exceedingly steep, serpentine road. Hidden in the ravines that fell away to either side came the deafening roar of mountain streams. It was not just the sound of water, but of boulder thrown against boulder and it filled her chest with thunder. But even this tremendous noise was at times overcome by that of the wind. It bore down on them and brought their mules to a standstill. Mary sheltered Willmouse as best she could and if there was a means to have gone back, to retrace their steps, she would have insisted they did. But they had come too far. The only way was ahead. It was midnight when they arrived at the hostelry, exhausted and shivering, cold to their bones.

Mary fell into bed, not caring for its state. Then, *oh darling girl*, there she was. *Only cold, only cold. Light as frost, no weight at all. To the fireside with her, quick, to warm her, warm her; kiss her cheeks until they are pink. See? She lives.*

Mary woke with a howl, as her cry wrenched her to the surface of her dream.

'*Mary?*'

She shuddered violently as Shelley gathered her to him. 'Why now, why come to me now?'

'Who?'

She turned to him, astonished he did not know. '*Clara.*'

'Oh, Maie.' Shelley held her to him and kissed the side of her head.

'She was too small. What could I do? What could I do?'

'Nothing, Maie, nothing. She came too soon, dearest girl. Of course you remember her, as do I. Shh, now. You must sleep. We have a long and arduous day again tomorrow.'

But sleep that came so easily for him would not come for her, for the memory of their first-born child would not leave her. Clara, Clara. Clara. Mary nursed her sorrow for her lost babe into the grey dawn light.

The morning brought snow. To go further, with Willmouse in her arms, they would need the protection of a carriage. Impossible to negotiate when their needs were so obvious, and the mules were sold for a smallish sum and a carriage purchased for considerably more. Yet the expense, though they could ill afford it, seemed to renew their resolve. With no reason to delay, they pressed on.

They still had higher to go, climbing through dense pine forests of impenetrable thickness that threw down snow from their branches in heavy, stinging swipes. Suddenly, briefly, the sun broke through and Mary saw what had so far been hidden: green-black trees, pressed against the precipitous cliffs as though afraid they too would fall. Soaring above, a dizzying sky of the clearest azure blue.

The spring, they learned, was unusually late. The cold seemed sunk fathoms deep into the ground, from which all life had been lost and seemed irrecoverable. Could anything survive beneath it? Only life in its fiercest form.

They pressed on to Les Rousses where they took on four new horses and a team of ten men, hired to support the carriage where needed. Not able to face another miserable night's accommodation and so close to their end point, they continued in the direction of Nion. As the moon rose, it illuminated a great white plane of snow. What stillness; as if the storm, in its fury, had exhausted the wind. They crested the hill. There below, their destination: Nion and beyond it, Lac Léman, silvered with moonlight. *There is eternity in such moments.* Mary heard a small cheer go up from the men as they began their cautious, careful descent.

And finally, finally, as though only now were it possible, she allowed thoughts of the summer ahead to approach. She knew her plans were vague and ill-formed when placed alongside those of Shelley and Claire, but much of what they hoped for depended on the fourth member of their group – *Byron* – a man whom she doubted had similar concerns or need for reliance on them. She thought of the books they had brought and imagined lazy, lie-abed days with Shelley; days when they'd read to one another; idle days of love. She'd have him fetch her bread and sultanas and fat slices of orange-rinded cheese. Oh, she would have climbed into that bed at that moment and stayed there a week without rising if she could.

Shelley rested one hand on her lap. Claire, seated opposite, slept. Her head nudged gently against the headrest as the coach rocked.

Mary frowned. Was it only at these times, when Claire was asleep and they were not, that she and Shelley could be alone and be entirely free of her?

'If this adventure with Byron does not fare well' – Mary straightened, surprised by her sudden vehemence – 'I shan't have her say what we do; nor when we return, not this time.' She dropped her voice to a whisper: 'Ridiculous for us to have made that journey as we did, to have come all that way, at such expense – *your expense*. We had so little to begin with. And then to return home, no sooner than we arrived. Not this time. That is all I have to say.'

He lifted his hand away. 'That was then. We scarcely knew what was needed.'

'You're making excuses.'

'Pecksie Maie . . .'

She wanted his hand back but folded her arms against him. 'You would forgive her anything. Allow her anything.'

'Mary . . .'

This time, she heard the warning in his voice. She didn't want to be thought a wearisome scold before they had even arrived. 'It's our summer. Ours. It belongs to us all.'

'Of course it does. And it will be marvellous. Really, such a drama over nothing.'

The snow had started again. It pressed against the carriage window, coating it white. Never was a scene more awfully desolate. Then the view, brief as it was, was gone.

John

A WALK TO Dedham along the river would do him good. He would call in to the mill on the way. Abram had returned from business in Manningtree and would be expecting him. But before that, John had letters to write. To Maria. To Fisher. To Farington, if he could bear it.

All this writing had improved his style, but he had written more letters to Maria than he had been able to prevail upon himself to send. Timidity apart, one happy consequence of all this was that he was becoming less prone to anecdote or abrupt ending. He knew he still had a tendency towards complaint and sarcasm, against which he needed to guard. There were times when he thought he had been at his cheeriest, only for Maria to find *grey clouds* had cast long shadows across the page. His boasts, she gently rebuffed. His recent, seriously meant tease, in which he had imagined a blue or red riband presented to him by the Prince Regent for his 'very excellent landscapes', she ignored. She had seen through it for what it was: vainglorious posturing. She would, he thought with relief, be the making of him.

What we have we do not value, and what we have not, we want, she wrote to him in reply.

I love you entirely, he had answered, words spilling out of him in a panic, as though she were water cupped in his hands. *We can never be rich, but we can have what riches cannot purchase, and what enemies cannot deprive us of . . .*

Enemies, enemies. Perhaps it was a little strongly put, but he let it stay. The time had come for a more robust vocabulary.

Seven long years had passed since he had declared his love and he had waited with patience and fortitude he believed few men capable of. Honourable qualities, he thought; qualities Dr Rhudde had scant regard for and valued not. Indeed, John feared that the reverend was entirely inveterate against him and he knew that in writing to Maria and she to him, they had been making themselves happy over a barrel of gunpowder. *My dearest*, she wrote. *My dearest love*, he wrote in reply, never more acutely aware of the barrel under them and Dr Rhudde standing ready to light the fuse. Any slight provocation and John knew it could yet explode, blowing hope for their union sky high. What a worry it was. And that only worried him more. He would keep this letter to her brief. He summarised the parlous state of his father's health in as few words as possible and avoided description. Earlier that morning, he'd found his father slumped forward in bed and had rushed to him, thinking him fatally collapsed. By the time he had roused him, his father had pissed the bed. No need to tell Maria that.

In his letter to Fisher he set out his worries. *Damn it.* He wanted nothing more than to marry, but perhaps it was best he remained single for Maria's sake? Fisher was a good friend, the best since Dunthorne, and he trusted his advice. His only friend, he supposed, but the right kind. Fisher occasionally bought a canvas off him and John valued his opinion on his work. More encouragingly, Maria approved. *Reverend Fisher and he,* she said, *were friends befitting one another.* On matters of marriage, or rather, *proposals,* Fisher would know what to do.

To Farington, he hinted at new work: a Wivenhoe commission; enough, he hoped, to pique Farington's interest and secure an invitation to tea on his return to London.

When he was done, he sealed the three letters and pocketed them. He would post them when he reached Dedham. The morning's rain had cleared and following through after it, a fresher day, with a bright, cold edge. Another shower looked likely, but he would take his sketchbook and pencils with him, just in case.

At the mill, he found Abram upstairs in the accounts room, sitting at their father's battered oak desk. So covered in papers was it, that none of the surface showed. Ledgers, agricultural almanacs, invoices and receipts; a book of tides for Mistley and Manningtree; wheat prices from corn exchanges in Cambridge and Ipswich. To the left, a set of scales; to the right, a velvet-lined weights' box. Where one was worn, the other was bright: the velvet had scuffed away over the years, but the brass weights gleamed from being handled.

'Abram . . . ?'

At the sound of his name, Abram was up on his feet, one hand outstretched to take John's. He patted John on the back, cleared more papers and a cat from a chair, and showed John the empty seat. 'Sit down. Sit down.'

Although Abram was the younger and he the elder, John felt their reversal keenly whenever he visited. Abram had shouldered the responsibility of the mill; without him, his dedication, it would already have had to be sold. He should be grateful to Abram, he knew, and he was. But in some peculiar way, his annual allowance, paid by his father but drawn from the mill's profits, made him feel in his brother's employ; it was a feeling he had never managed to shake.

'Keeping well?' Abram asked.

It was an invitation to talk wider, but John did not take it. 'I am. And you? How's business?'

Abram lifted his hands and let them fall. He looked tired, John thought, with the paleness of someone kept indoors too long.

Abram turned back to the desk, searching for a document among the pile of papers. 'Here long?' he asked, without looking up.

'A week or so. It depends . . .'

'And Father? You've seen him?'

'Yes.'

'Had a chance to talk?'

'I have.'

'Good.'

More turning over of papers. What wretched thing was he searching for? John suspected it was a way to avoid looking at him directly.

'You know the mill will be coming to me after? Has Father said yet?'

It was more an interview, this, John realised, and an abrupt one at that. 'Yes. Yes, he has.'

'You're not minded?'

Now it was John's turn to shrug. The matter of his annual allowance hung between them, unsaid. 'The mill has kept us well these years.'

'The house will be sold too, of course.'

At this, John said nothing.

Now his brother looked up. 'Is the suggestion disagreeable to you?'

John thought for a moment before he replied. 'What is necessary is not always agreeable.'

Abram stared at him, unblinking, until John dropped his gaze. 'The sale of the house will give you what you need. Until, well, you know . . .'

'Yes,' said John. He knew. Until his work started to sell.

'Still have hopes for Maria?'

John flushed. Abram was blunt in ways only a brother could be. 'Yes. I do.'

It was impossible to tell what Abram thought of her and John did not much care to discover. 'And you? No farmer's daughter caught your eye yet?'

'No time for that kind of thing.' Abram swept an arm out to one side in an ill-tempered gesture, scattering several papers to the floor. 'Married to this.'

John raised his eyes, but held his peace. There, on the wall, a dusty painting of his; an early work he had gifted to his father. Its naivety made him wince. It had been placed in line of sight of any visitor to the room, but at his father's back, out of sight. What was he to make of that? Even this most basic of questions had him foxed. It seemed fraught with a meaning he could not fathom, like standing on the edge of a conversation at the Academy, mumble, mumble, nod, nod, nod, and not catching a word of it.

That the painting was on display at all was likely because his mother had insisted.

From deep within the building, John heard the groan of the mill, the dull rumble of the millstones as they ran over each other, the rush of the water through the millstream. He closed his eyes. In a week, he would be back in London, to the ghastly business of courting Farington's opinion once more. An image came to him of being swept away down the river and out to the sea.

John walked away from the mill, all thoughts of a river walk to Dedham gone. He cut across the fields, away from the Stour. As he made his way up, he saw four men and a boy struggle through a gap in the hedge and then come down the path towards him. The man in front tipped his cap to John. 'Constable,' he said, not stopping to chat.

'Afternoon.' John recognised him as one of the wheelwrights who serviced the mill's several carts and ploughs. The men murmured their greetings in turn as they passed by. One had an axe over his shoulder, the other men carried bundles of sticks; the boy had two small dead rabbits and a hare, tied by their hind legs to a stick. Was that a snare he was attempting to tuck inside his jacket?

'Only small 'uns, Mr Constable, sir,' said the boy. One of

the men cuffed the top of his head to shut him up. A sharp smell of sweat hung in the air.

John raised one hand to show he wasn't minded. Might have been nerves, but the lad laughed. Not much of a meal in those rabbits anyway, from the look of them. John's father was known as a fair man. As long as they kept to the edges of the fields and did not trample the wheat, they would not be accused of trespass. He'd not have minded a couple of rabbits gone in the boy's direction. The hare was another matter. John watched the group hurry away; the boy stumbled as he looked back. John wasn't certain, but he thought he was the smithy's lad. The smithy's lad? And the wheelwright? What need had they to resort to hunting? John frowned. Another man might have called for them to come back and account for themselves. Abram would. But by now it was too late – they were gone. Would they take his acquiescence – for what else was it? – as kindness? Or would they have him marked down as a soft fellow and speak of him later with scorn? Would they be back again tomorrow, emboldened?

Two rabbits. A hare. For God's sake. He wasn't the bloody gamekeeper. John hunched into himself, head down, and carried on his way.

At the top of the path, instead of heading straight back to Bergholt, he took a right and followed a track overhung with mature ash trees. Up ahead, he saw a notice had been pinned to one of the trunks and he crossed the path to take a look.

~ PROCLAMATION ~

Whereas it has been humbly represented to his Royal Highness the Prince Regent, that a great Number of Persons have, for some Time past, unlawfully assembled themselves together in diverse Parts of the Counties of NORFOLK, SUFFOLK, HUNTINGDON and CAMBRIDGE, and have circulated Threatening letters and Incendiary Hand Bills; held Nightly Meetings; and set fire to several Dwelling Houses, Barns, Outbuildings, and Stacks of Corn; and have destroyed Cattle, Corn, Threshing Machines, and other Instruments of Husbandry –

A sum of ONE HUNDRED POUNDS,
for each and every Person who shall be convicted of any of the aforesaid Felonies. The said Reward of One Hundred Pounds to be paid by the Lords Commissioners of His Majesty's Treasury.
SIDMOUTH.

Had similar been posted on a London street, John would never have had cause to pay it attention. But in Suffolk? Down this muddy track? What sorry state was the world coming to?

He wandered a little further on then stopped and sat down with his sketchbook balanced on his knees. Before him, the track was deeply rutted with thick pleats of mud, making lines of pleasing diagonals; a lozenge of field

behind provided a focal point. In the summer, with the sun
flat on it, the wheat would blaze golden. Even today, when
the field was little more than a grey-brown smudge, he
found the view compelling. He felt the lift of an idea for a
much larger work that had been tugging at him for a while.
He knew Farington disdained these images, finding them
parochial and lacking narrative. A touch of Turner's
flourish, or Gainsborough's majesty, might help *elevate* his
work, Farington had once suggested. It had taken all John's
control to stand where he was, head inclined as if listening
intently. It would never do to swear at an Academician.
Or, worse, question his opinion.

He noticed the wind, high in the trees, as it often was
before a squall. The air, on the point of rain, charged with
restless energy. He stared at the blank sheet of paper. He loved
this moment, the moment before his pencil touched the page.
With all that there was to draw, why this? This track, these
trees, the field beyond? He leafed quickly back through his
sketchbook, looking at what he had drawn. Men at work:
digging, scything, boat-building; men with shovels, men
leading horses, men atop hay carts, men fishing. Sketches of
a water wheel, a sluice, a post. Dock leaves, dogs. Children
at play. Women with children, women gleaning. He was
neither swaggerer nor show-off. He admired Gainsborough,
but Turner's bravura – *his audacity* – frankly appalled.

He turned the page over to a blank sheet and sketched
quickly, bringing the pencil lead flat to the page, laying
down a number of rapid, broad lines, pressing harder where
the shadows were darkest. *Majesty?* Here it was. Here, in the
mossy stone he was seated on; or, there, in the ash tree's
rutted bark; in the arch of a man's back as he shouldered

the weight of a sack of corn from off a cart and into his father's mill. It was just a matter of persuading Farington and the Academy of the same.

He continued to sketch, never before so possessed of his purpose, or determined, or certain, even as the first fat raindrops started to fall.

He saw Dunthorne before Dunthorne saw him. There was no way to avoid walking past him. He registered Dunthorne's surprise: a moment of unguarded pleasure from an old friend before a look closed over it that was altogether more reserved and composed, hostile, even. There was a time when John would have written to Dunthorne to let him know of his visit, so they could have made arrangements to paint together. Those days had gone.

'Constable,' said Dunthorne.

'Dunthorne.' John went to continue past. The rain came down steadily now and he had no desire for a soaking.

'Wait . . .' Dunthorne ran to catch him up. 'I'll walk with you.'

John nodded his assent, though Dunthorne's company was the last thing he wanted. He could feel his good mood from sketching evaporate.

The common was abustle with fences going up. Cattle that had been given free roam were confined to a smaller area; one mooed mournfully as John approached.

'World's changing, Constable. And not for the better.'

This was something they could agree on. 'Indeed,' said John, but not wanting a discussion of it.

'I heard you got a plot of land off the enclosure?'

'A small parcel up by the windmill. No use to me. Will pass it on to Abram.'

Dunthorne shook his head, as if John's answer had confirmed an obvious point. 'To them that have already—'

'Oh, I see what this is. Several here have profited well from the enclosure. But I am not one of them, Dunthorne.' His allotment could have fitted inside his bedroom, but he wasn't going to tell Dunthorne that.

Dunthorne made no challenge. He nodded to the sketch-book under John's arm. 'Are you here to paint it then?'

'I beg your pardon?'

'The common. Before it is gone.'

'I've painted it before. Many times,' John retorted, bris-tling like a hedgehog that had been poked with a stick.

Dunthorne turned to face him. Here it came. Whatever it was he was determined to say.

'But never like this. As it is now.'

'Now?'

'With the fences. Are you blind?'

John gave several exaggerated blinks. 'No. I am not.'

Dunthorne did not rise to the taunt. He kicked at the verge with his boot. 'You only see what you want to see. A comfort to you, I suppose.'

'Whatever is the matter with you, Dunthorne?'

Dunthorne gave a bitter laugh. 'Your sort don't suffer. They never do.'

'My sort?' John's blood was up and his voice had risen with it.

'Your father still a director at the Tattingstone workhouse,

is he? Still fetching folk off there, is he? Out of sight, out
of mind. Then there's that brother of yours—'

'*My brother?*'

'Yes, your brother. Abram. When a quartern loaf is
twelve pence and wheat is up eighteen shillings in three
weeks, then it's profiteering, that's what it is. That's how
your brother, *how your lot*, get rich. They should open up
the grain stores and bring in the wheat that's needed. That'd
fetch the price down.'

'Well, Dunthorne, I did not have you down as an economist. But if you're trying to blame the state of things on
my family – next you will be telling me the fences are my
fault.'

'Aye, well. High prices. Fences. Suits you just fine.'

Maria was right, the man was a rogue; with all his ranting
and raving, he'd not even had the manners to ask after his
father's health.

When John made to push past him, Dunthorne gripped
his arm. 'Paint it then, why don't you?'

John shook his arm free.

As he walked away, Dunthorne called after him, 'The
only thing you're after protecting is yer'selves. And you
know it.'

Sarah

MAIRSTER COOK WOULD take me on but not Tessie so she had the long walk back to Littleport to make on her own.

'Mardy bitch, that one,' Mairster Cook said to her back as she walked off.

I kept my attention fix'd on the ground but he lifted my chin to get a better look. I didn't like being considered in that way so I kept my eyes off of his. I smelled him though, onions and shit and didn't like that either.

'So. *Sarah*. What work will we find for you?' He walked in a circle around me and after him belted his hounds. 'What do you reckon, Pearson?'

Pearson, I'd learned, was the overseer. He had mutton chop whiskers that near met in the middle of his nose. I was sore missing Tessie right now.

'The piggery?' suggestid mutton chops.

'The piggery?' Mairster Cook rubbed his chin, thoughtful like. 'What are you good for, girl?'

'Picking up stones and weeding.' Over his shoulder I saw a sad-looking mare, tied up to a post by the stable. 'I'm good with an 'oss too.'

'Good with horses too?'

What an echo there was out here, bad as in any church, but I minded my lip on that. I nodded.

'Then we should put you to work in the stables. Have we a pitchfork short enough, Pearson?'

I heard mutton chops snicker. 'I'll see if we have.'

'You do that.' Mairster Cook took hold of my chin to get me to look at him. 'You follow Mr Pearson now. He'll give you a fork and your instructions.'

He looked at me some more and then he let go. I walk'd over to the stables six steps behind and wiped my chin on my shoulder as I went. I glanced up at the farmhouse. Queer place it was, built of hard brick, neatsome new. But no curtains or vase or any kind of decorating ornament suggesting of a Missus Cook.

I badly regretted coming this way after all.

I worked the morning shovelling shit and not a drop they brought me to drink. Then, when my stomach got to burning hungry and still nothing, I put down my fork and went to the house. I hadn't anything with me but the knife in my pocket, not even a crust. At Mairster Benton's, they had a kettle broth brought to the fields on a cart; a gotch of beer sometimes in summer. Weren't much, but kept the starving out of us.

The door were open so I knock'd on it and waited. Pretty soon Mairster Cook came out. He had the scruffed-up look of someone broken from sleep.

'You finished yet?' he asked, thinking I was done.

'No, not the all of it.'

That didn't please him none. 'Then what do you want?'

'Summat to eat.'

'Summat to eat?' he said.

There was that echo again, this time wearing my voice. He looked at me and I looked at him back.

'Well, I've nothing for you,' he said and shut the door flat in my face.

All farmers were bastids, and that was a certainty. I kicked at a stone then hopped up and down as the pain of it shot up to my ears and back to my toes. I went back to the midden, cussing as I went. I'd finish it then ask for my payment and be on my way. I'd started at the outside edges of the midden, where the straw was thickest and the shit had dried in big lumps. And now there was no avoiding the middle, where the shit was as slippery as ice. I hoiked up my skirts either side and took a step into it, feeling it come up between my toes.

When I came out of the midden again, the day had left the sky. I took a deep breath and stood in the yard, breathing and breathing and breathing and seeing my breath come out of me and go up to God. I was grateful to God for the good air taking the place of the bad air that I'd had in me before.

But it was too cold to stand there for long being thankful to God and I was desperate hungry for something to eat. Some days, I was so made of hunger, I imagined a stone in me that started as grit then got bigger and bigger till it felt like I had the whole of Ely Cathedral in there. When I got to feeling like that, I had to bite on my knuckle for it to stop.

There was no light showing in any of the windows and the door was still slammed shut closed, but on the step a plate with a penny coin on it. Weren't no one else it were for, I could see. A penny? Were that it? I slipped the coin into my pocket then was walking out along the track, past the post with the two notices on it, over Wood Fen in the direction of home, the coin clinking against my knife and the shit between my toes forgotten.

When I was home, I placed the coin on the table for my ma, and when it was morning, I got myself up and went back to Park Farm. This time I took bread.

It went on like this from Monday to Saturday and Monday to Saturday again, two times over, and always the same: a penny in my hand at the end of it. It weren't just me working like that. Others came too. Some turned up, worked a week, and then they were gone. Some, just for a day and we were no names together and paid by the day. Some I knew from Littleport, but most came in from other directions, places I'd heard of but had never been. It were like the farm were a great big pond and we were lots of little ducks flying to it and Mairster Cook deciding which he wanted and which he did not. For ten of them days it never stopped raining, so truly it was the best place for ducks for miles around.

One day he had a grut big contraption delivered and it must have been special because it went straight in a barn that six of us had just swept out.

'Know what that is?' said a boy who'd been sweeping with me.

I shook my head.

'It's a threshing machine.'

'What's it do?'

'Thresh.'

All this said in whispers as though scared we'd wake it.

Another day, I gets there and the yard is full of us standing about in the puddles. Mairster Cook making himself tall on the top step while mutton chops prodded us into lines with a stick. From each line he chose a master. Men, not girls. We were each given a shovel or a rake and told to shut up.

'It's been a bad wet start to the year. Winter was short, but spring has not advanced as it should. The cole seed we planted is not up. It is not just this farm that is suffering. There are reports of similar troubles affecting all parts of the land. Acres washed away. Floods beyond recollection.'

There was an unhappy murmuring at this.

Mairster Cook raised a hand for us to hush. 'Our farms fed us through the war years and gave us a glorious victory at Waterloo . . .'

Cheering at this and a couple of hats lobbed in the air. 'Pay us for it then, pay us for it,' came a shout from the back, before being told to shush.

'Yet more and more farms stand empty because of the burden of taxes upon us and many a farmer's investment ruined.'

Some booing, but mostly we was silent. Most of us knew the size of our bones, but none had seen a thin farmer yet.

'I do not intend to join their ranks. It leaves me no choice but to burn the Fen again and rake in the ashes. I'll put in cole seed and wheat after. Them's that want work will be paid by the acre, not a day rate, which in my opinion only encourages laziness and sloth. Them's not happy with it, leave by the gate.'

We all turned as mutton chops opened the gate and swept one arm out of it. There was muttering at that, then quiet lay over the hush that was there. We looked at our feet. No one moved. I appraised the gang I'd been placed in. Gave me no cheer to be the only girl there. That's how pennies become ha'pennies, I thought.

'How will we light it?' shouted some clever spark from the back.

'*With big fucking fire, you shanny fucking bugger!*' Mairster Cook roared and that set us all roaring too.

All that day we dug and raked, dug and raked, bringing the peat into heaps, lining up the heaps alongside the furrows. On account of the acreage pay, we all work'd double hard to cover as much ground as we could as quick as we could. It were usual to leave the peat to dry and then to set fire to the lot, but we hadn't time for that so added in a good deal of straw to get it to start. Even so, the fire underneath was slow cold and smouldering. Smoke lifted in a thick choke. From out of it flew birds in a terrible shriek and hares came running every which way, but, seeing us, stopp'd and ran back the way they'd come. Slowly, slowly the smouldering took hold and the heaps dusted over with white ashes. We stood ready with our rakes. These ashes were why we were doing it, needed for the crops that would come out of it after, but if anyone would have asked I'd have told them it was a bad way of doing and were just for the farmer's convenience, to hurry things up. Sometimes, the Fen would burn for weeks and there was no putting it out. From my pa, I knew the proper way of growing was to put shit down, then to be patient. But here we were, our know-how not asked for nor wanted, so we set to digging the ash in, throwing to one side all the poor creatures that hadn't escaped the smoke. Weren't a quarter way done with it when the rain started coming down in gushes. Any fire that were left burned out and the ashes got washed away. Not a chance the land would even grow paigles.

Mairster Cook was in a miserable hard mood as a consequence and sent us away with nowt. There was much complaining and calling him names to his back and me as angry as the rest of them as I slodged through the mud. Then, from behind, came a shout, 'A bit less fucking rain would be appreciated.'

'God will sort out nowt if yer swear like that.'

'Get him to sort out Cook while he's at it,' someone else muttered.

'Aye. There'll be a reckoning, all right. God has his eye on Cook, same as he has the rest of us.'

One of the men in the gang I was in gave a sharp laugh, like he didn't believe a word of it. He'd come down from Lincolnshire way, after ditching work, there being nowt to be had up there. He lived in a huddle of rough huts with the Irish on the far side of the Littleport Field.

'Why wouldn't God not?' I asked.

He looked at me then, with a look that said he knew more than he would say. 'Ah, now. Questions like that are best left. I'm just a *tattie spailpeen*, here to dig ditches. And you' – he reached out and drew back my sodden bonnet so he could look at me better – 'you've got too many thoughts in your head. I'll wager you this – the only one sleeping in a warm bed tonight is that bastard Cook. And if you want it any different, it'll take more than what's going on in there to make it happen.' He rapped my head once with his knuckle then lifted his hat to me and bade me goodbye.

I watched him walk off, him with his thoughts, me with mine. And it made me wonder, how did anyone get their thoughts out of their head so as to make anything different?

I got home that night smudged up with soots and soaked to my skin. I was more tired than I'd ever known and I have known tired times. My eyes, my nose, my throat – any part of me the smoke had been in to – felt like needles had been sharpened against it. My hands had bubbled with blisters though I'd bound them up with dock leaves. True, I did not know what to do with m'self right then.

When I turned the corner into my road, I saw Tessie waiting there. When she saw me, she came running.

'Shh,' she said and pressed a finger to my mouth and she pulled me in the direction of the Globe.

As I went into a room in the back, a sea of faces greeted me, most I knew, some I did not. I got handed a mug of beer and someone else pulled me out a chair.

'Sit down, Sarah,' said Tessie. No more encouragement were needed and I did what she said. Her Thomas came up and brought an arm around her as loved ones do. But he had a serious sad look to him. And Tessie had too.

'We're after knowing about Mairster Cook and Park Farm.'

Folk pushed in closer, gathered up tight to the table.

'He's a bad 'un!'

'A right bad 'un at that!'

Thomas shifted his chair in closer to me. 'Tell us, Sarah. Tell us what you know.'

I looked at him, then at my beer. Before I could say anything, I needed a drink.

Mary

'THERE IS NO honey to be had anywhere,' said Claire, coming in. She clattered the door shut behind her. 'No honey in Cologny. No honey in Choulex. No honey in Meinier or in Annemasse.' She wrenched at her hat ribbons, but only succeeded in pulling them tighter. 'I promised I would find some.'

Honey? Mary had no need to ask who for. 'There are hives all the way up the hill to Diodati. I should think he will have honey enough—'

'Of course there are hives. I do know that. And every one of them empty!'

'Well' – Mary had to choose her words carefully, aware of how easily Claire was given to affront – 'I am certain he will appreciate your effort.'

'Oh, it was no effort. No effort at all. He did not *make* me go. It would have made a nice gift, that is all. And now I have nothing to take him.' Even if there were fifty hives with honey enough to last the year, Mary thought, Claire would make herself bee so as to be useful. Claire gave up with the ribbon and stamped her foot. 'Ugh! Help me, someone.'

'M'selle?'

Claire turned to face Elise and angled her chin so she could reach the knot. As the ribbons loosened, Claire yanked the hat free and dropped it to the floor with her shawl. She slumped in a chair, thrust her legs out in front of her and smoothed her skirts flat. 'Why did we have to choose this house? I cannot tell you how much I dislike it. I dislike it immensely. It is always so dark in here.'

Claire would blame everything on their little house. Her moods came at it like hail against the window.

'We need a bright day, that is all.' But Mary did not feel confident for such. The few bright days in May that had greeted their arrival seemed long gone and the season had fallen in on itself like discarded bagpipes dropped to the floor at a party's end.

Claire rested her hands on her stomach. A frown gathered on her brow. 'It isn't what I'd hoped for.'

Elise scooped up hat and shawl from the floor. She shook the rain from them and placed them over a chair to dry.

'Elise, *merci*.' Mary accepted her small curtsey with a nod. She did not know who was the most uncertain, her or the maid. Her eighteen years made her no mistress, she knew, but Elise seemed accepting of this pretence of theirs. She had hardly a word of English, and Mary, little French. Claire translated – useful, ever useful Claire. What fictions did she spin, Mary wondered, the times when she found them, side by side at the basin, and Elise's eyes, wide in surprise, like two new moons filled with the wonder of the sky?

'Has he been down already?'

'Briefly, yes. With Polidori.'

'They've taken themselves sailing, I suppose?'

'Yes.'

'We'll go up after dinner. So I'll see him then.'

'If we are invited.'

'*If* we are invited?' Claire mimicked Mary's voice with mocking precision. 'We're always welcome. He said as much. The invitation is an open one.'

'For Shelley, I think.' He had been twice before to breakfast, but on both occasions had waited for an invitation to be sent down with a servant and had gone up the hill very hungry indeed.

'You didn't go sailing with them?'

Mary shook her head.

'*Not invited?*'

She felt a nip of anger and gave Claire a sharp look. She simply could not resist a provocation.

'I have William to care for.'

'You have Elise for that now.'

'Indeed.' It required effort to keep her voice steady. 'In which case, I might go out on the lake later and Elise can have him.' Mary ignored Claire's smile. There would be no other boat trip later, nor opportunity to do so.

'You won't go.'

'Why not?'

'Because they left you behind and you are cross about it. You're like a mouse here, trapped under a cup.'

'I am not!'

'Reading, reading. Dormouse, Mary.'

'Claire!'

'*Dormouse!*' Claire feigned a mouse, timid and cowering. 'Not a peep. Not a squeak. A very long way to come to read books. Might as well have stayed at home.'

'Then that makes us mice together,' Mary retorted, though at that moment she pictured her as a rat.

'I'm not!'

'Good mousey.' Mary held out the palm of one hand and with her other mimed a mouse running across it. 'Find me some honey, mousey.'

It was into this row that the men came. Shelley first, then Byron, followed by a wan-looking Polidori.

'What have we to eat, Mary?' asked Shelley, 'The water was wild out there. Poor Polidori has been sick. He needs something to fortify him. And a cloth to dry him. Cloths for us all, in fact.'

Claire jumped to her feet. She took Byron's outer coat from him, which he held out. 'We have bread. I'll get it.'

'Bread?' said Byron. 'The man needs meat!'

Claire went to the crock pot where the bread was kept. She took out a crust and examined it. 'Is this all there is?'

Mary nodded. The bread was obviously stale and needed soaking in milk to revive it, but they had no milk either. Everyone looked at Mary as though this sad state of affairs was her doing.

Claire handed the bread to Polidori. 'Oh well. Here you are.'

'Eat it up!' said Byron. He slapped Polidori on the back, 'Always the least well among us, Polidori. What use a sick physician? If I have to nurse my doctor, who will nurse me?'

Polidori took the bread and nibbled it, doubly wretched from the sickness and the teasing. He wasn't an easy man to feel sorry for, but at that moment Mary did. A man so desperate for attention and only finding it when it could not have suited him less.

Alone among them it seemed at that moment was Claire,

who had gone to Byron's side. She reached for him, in a shy approach, but he slipped his hand into his pocket and took a step back, away from her. Mary saw her stiffen and blink rapidly.

Oh, Claire. She would have gone to her had Willmouse not cried out from his cot. When Elise went to fetch him, Mary shook her head and got up to go instead. It was with relief that she headed upstairs, glad to be away from them all. They were, together, too many people in one room.

The next morning and quite ashamed for their lack of supplies, Mary went with Claire into Cologny for bread; she left Willmouse in Elise's care. They had been confined indoors by the unseasonal weather for days and Mary was desperate to step out. They only had a short distance to go, but they walked briskly even so, fearing a shower could come upon them at any moment. They arrived at the shop giddy and out of breath.

'*Bonjour!*' said Claire to the boulanger.

It was a wretched little place, truth be told, and their smiles quickly faded. Four small loaves were arrayed on a dusty shelf; a basket of eggs on the counter, most dimpled or cracked.

'*Combien pour les oeufs?*' asked Claire.

'*Dix sous.*'

'*Pour un?*'

'*Oui.*' He folded his arms. '*Pour un.*'

Claire gave a bright laugh. '*Et le pain?*'

'*Quatorze sous.*'

'*Quatre?*'

'*Pas quatre. Quatorze. Quatorze.*' He held up ten fingers, then four. He counted these last four off, slowly as though Claire were an idiot, '*On-ze, dou-ze, trei-ze, Quat-or-ze.*'

'How much?' whispered Mary.

'Fourteen sous.'

Mary counted the coins she had. She felt a rush of panic. 'I haven't the money for that. Twelve is all I have, twelve. I thought that plenty.'

'*Douze?*' asked Claire, hopeful.

'*Douze,*' Mary echoed. She held out the coins to show him.

The boulanger shook his head. '*Quatorze.*'

'*Voleur!*' Claire said. 'He's a rogue and a thief. A loaf was four sous last week. He knows we're English. Well, we shan't be taken advantage of—'

The boulanger shook a floury fist at her then banged it down on the counter. '*Fourteen sous or fuck off back to England with nothing!*'

'Keep your rotten bread then!' Claire linked an arm in Mary's and turned towards the door.

For the want of two sous, and the short walk back to fetch them, they could have had a loaf of bread to take home. Instead, they left with the insults of the local boulanger battering their ears. Outside, children clustered around them, attracted by the row. Their hands came out, then a familiar jostling.

'*Non!*' said Claire and pushed them away. '*Nous n'avons rien.*'

'I cannot help,' Mary said, 'I'm sorry.'

A large number of beggars had gathered by a nearby water pump. Some drank deeply, others attempted to wash themselves and their children. She caught the eye of a young mother and her child and looked away. She knew what was there without needing to look longer: hunger, keening and unguarded.

The boulanger came out after them. 'Vermin! Rats!' he shouted. He grabbed a man in a tattered shirt and gave him a shove, sending him tumbling into the road. The shirt rent apart, leaving the boulanger holding a rag which he threw down in disgust.

The man staggered to his feet. He clutched his shirt at his shoulder. 'You bastard. Do you own this road? Is it yours? Is it for you to say where I can stand? No.'

The boulanger raised his fist. 'Be off with you.'

'Be off where?'

'Think I care? You're not welcome here.'

'You owe me a shirt.'

'Ah, fuck off with you.' The boulanger went to go in then turned back. 'Geneva's that way. Try your luck there.'

Mary looked in the direction the boulanger pointed. She leaned in to Claire. 'What is he saying?'

'That Geneva's that way, that they might have better luck there.'

A woman approached from the crowd. She reached out and touched Mary's skirt, running the cloth between her fingers.

'Tellement jolie,' she said. 'J'avais la même avant.'

'We should go, Mary,' said Claire.

As they set off, so did the man with the tattered shirt with the others trailing behind by a short distance.

When Claire and Mary reached their cottage, they found Shelley gone, out on the lake most likely. Quickly, they bolted the door and drew back into a corner of the room with Elise and Willmouse, out of sight. There they remained, huddled in silence for some time, and it seemed to Mary that, truly, they were mice under a cup: a cup they had willingly hidden beneath. But the knock they expected and were guarded against did not come. The group of beggars must have passed by and carried on along the road to Geneva. Then, stiff from sitting on the floor, they got to their feet, eased out their aches and went to their various tasks. But each movement seemed wooden and made of exaggerated gestures. Mary sat by the window with a book, looking up frequently as though yet expecting an interruption. Although she turned through several pages, if she had been asked, she could not have said what she had read. The relief she felt gave way to a gnawing unease. She placed her book to one side. The mountains with the sun falling on them were so beautiful, so sublime; the sky, a heavenly blue. If that were all she paid attention to then, yes, she could say this was paradise. As she brought her eye down, she could just make out the last of the beggars on the road in the direction of Geneva: grey and slow-moving. But what was it that disturbed her? The beggars? Or her fear, her disgust?

'In future, I think Elise should go for bread,' she said.

'Yes,' said Claire. 'He wasn't so very friendly, that boulanger. Ten sous for an egg. Think how much an omelette would cost.'

Their diet was simple and plain, necessitated, in part, by the scarcity of the most mundane ingredients and their galloping expense. A struggle to find cheese and the milk was seldom fresh. Their local market was full of extremes and oddities: a surfeit of lettuce but no fruit. There was only so much salad Mary could eat.

Now that they and Byron were neighbours – he at villa Diodati, they at humble Chaphuis – they fell briefly into the conventions expected by their proximity. They dined together twice then abandoned the idea. Byron was a picky eater and largely ignored what they served him. In turn, he was dismayed by their refusal to eat the meat his servants had gone to some lengths to procure. As host, he appeared oddly aloof at his own table and showed little interest in what was served, so the dish was given to Polidori, who ate it with great gusto.

Thereafter, they met at Diodati, after making their separate arrangements. Elise stayed behind to care for Willmouse, and Shelley, Claire and Mary then made their way up the path that linked their separate houses: a steep climb that took ten minutes. They were here together in Cologny, but it was Byron who looked down on them from the hill; all other society he rejected. He turned his attention on them in ways that were generous and disarming. Not dissimilar, Mary thought, to being dazzled by the sun.

The lord on the hill, and Mary had taken to calling him Albé.

Diodati, like its lord, was all shoulders. A four-shouldered house, with an imposing, square aspect and a balconied terrace, supported on columns: a choice of rooms, and yet most evenings they found themselves in the drawing room on the first floor. From there, they enjoyed a view over the lake to the Jura Mountains beyond.

Mary felt less cowed by the view than she did from their small house by the lake. The elevation in some way seemed to raise her up to it, to meet the mountains with a level gaze.

Between the two windows stood a large glazed door that opened out on to the balcony. A table and chairs had been set there, which they immediately made theirs. It was a house built for summer, for long summer evenings spent outside on the terrace, drinking wine and watching swallows and swifts cavort above.

They managed one much longed-for evening like that, sitting out in their summer clothes, maintaining a defiance against the undoubtedly chilly wind. Then, too windy for candles, which burned down in minutes, they hurried indoors to their clumsy fire-making, giddy with cold and shivering. The grate was a monstrous affair, made of forged iron, twisted and pinned, and set in a cavernous fireplace; the chimney, like some huge throat, swallowed any heat for itself. Once they had managed a fire, they drew ever closer to it, half in the fireplace itself. They turned their faces to the flames and were silent, lost in the need to be warm.

Such evenings suited the men well. Albé and Shelley and Polidori had what they wanted. Claire seemed content. Mary sat apart and listened. The easier the men's company became, the more reserved hers seemed to be; their talk of Plato, Rousseau and Wordsworth did not exclude her, but encouraged no place for her either. It wasn't that she had nothing to say, but what use standing as a shadow at the feet of the altogether more vivid and vibrant discussion that was theirs? Although she was mute, her mind ran riot.

So engrossed were the men, they did not once question her reticence. Perhaps they saw her silence as repose, or dreaming or demurring, when really the opposite was true.

Shelley and Albé had their writing. Claire made fair copies of it all. Polidori sent hither and thither, endlessly on errands and returning with every detail of his encounters. Such quantities of the English about, he said, clearly forgetting he was English too – speaking amongst themselves, arms by their sides, mouths open and eyes glowing; he might as well have made a tour of the Isle of Dogs! Everyone occupied apart from Mary, it seemed. What was she to do with herself?

'Keep a journal,' said Shelley, when she confided in him one night. He ruffled her hair as though this most obvious advice had been there under her nose all the while.

'He thinks you very clever, you know.'

'Oh,' said Mary, at a loss. It did not flatter her to know she had been talked about. It was astonishing how such a remark could make one feel so wretchedly stupid.

'He says he will never return to England.'

'I thought him a little bored already.'

'You do? How so? Is this you speaking, dearest Pecksie? If so, be honest.'

Why every question had to be turned back to her in this way, she did not know.

'I am perfectly happy here. But the weather is limiting.'

'I think it suits him well. We must make the best of it. Besides, I think the reverse is true. If he were bored, as you suggest, he would be unable to work.'

Perhaps, from now on, they should all stand out in the rain to write.

The next day brought fairer weather, and the men went sailing. Mary thought of them out on the water, their excited return, the evening ahead which would progress in the same way.

She opened a notebook she had bought in Geneva, picked up her pen and dipped it in the ink.

I was his inestimable treasure, she wrote. *But a treasure, much looked at, becomes an ordinary thing and a treasure ignored, is most easily forgotten . . .*

Mary looked at what she had written. Was she no different to Claire in her hat, with ribbons drawn ever tighter about her in knots?

She crossed the words out angrily. Whatever she was to do with herself, this was not it.

John

'HE'S NOT WANTING anything dark now, my boi. Or showy. Francis is not a showy man.'

John tried not to let his discomfort show. He would not be made to force a bright day from a grey one. But neither had he a desire to argue with his father, who had shown some small improvement overnight.

His father, sensing his reserve, grew irritable. 'Make it cheerful, son. He's paying you, don't forget. You've got to give him what he wants. I showed him the garden pictures you did when he was here. Said he liked them a good deal; liked how they made him feel. But he wants summat wider, as much of the park as you can get in with the house prominent in it. A house like that has to be seen. I told him you could do him that. A picture fit for his drawing room. You can do that, can't you?'

'I can. Yes.'

'Good, good. And I said so myself.' He dropped his arms with relief, as though for these past few minutes he had been made to hold up an anvil. 'He'll pay well. I told him not to expect favours on account of our families being on friendly terms. Business is business. He knows that.'

'Thank you.'

In truth, John had been dreading the discussion about terms: payment, how much and when due; all necessary, but distasteful. He would have liked to know more of what his father had said to Francis Rebow but decided against asking, wary of what might be revealed and knowing full well how delicate his father's approval was. The worth of his work, its value: the two were inextricably linked, yet separated by a chasm he needed to bridge. An image of a bridge came to him, thin and sinuous, made of rope and him stranded midway. This year, he was determined to cross it. If he were to marry Maria and to provide for her and the family they planned, he could not continue in this way. He would be forty this year: an alarming thought, which chastened him beyond measure.

'Anything been happening in London? What they been learning you there?' His father brought his hands together on the blanket covering his lap. He leaned in towards John to hear.

'Well, Pa . . .' John faltered, uncertain where to begin. In previous years, these stories, his news, he had relayed to his mother without difficulty, leaving her the task of passing it on to his father: stories of Farington, anecdotes of dinners he had attended, portraits he was working on. Even the most mundane detail seemed to delight her and came away brighter in her hands. She could buff pewter into silver; brass into gold. Since her death, that task, the truth or otherwise of it, was his. He had to face his father himself.

'I've two paintings in the Royal Academy Exhibition this year.'

'Two?' His father sounded disappointed and sat back.

John drew breath and steadied himself. 'The Wheatfield and A Wood, Autumn.'

'Got a look at them, did I?'

'Yes, Pa. I showed them to you before I took them back to London with me. Do you not remember?'

He gave John an affronted look. 'Think I'd remember if I had. London continues the same, I take it?'

'Cold and wet.' The news from Maria was of horrid black, cold, raw, easterly winds.

'And the Bicknells? What of them?'

Before John could answer, his father moved on, 'How old is she now?'

'Maria? Twenty-nine—'

'Twenty-nine? She'd be stupid to refuse you. Have you asked her yet?'

'I—'

'Ask her!'

'I am thinking of it.'

'Thinking? Thinking? Nothing ever got done just by the thinking of it.' He took a sharp, shuddering breath and coughed it out. Then another breath the same. Coughing, coughing, until something seemed to slacken in him and give way, like wind knocked from a sail. He screwed up his eyes and grimaced. 'Just do Francis a good painting, won't you? If you've any sense, you'll listen to what he says and give him what he wants. All else will follow. Now be a good boi and let me be.'

The newspaper on his father's lap slipped to the floor. As John picked it up, he saw circled in his father's unsteady hand that week's prices from the Bury St Edmunds Corn Exchange. Wheat was trading at forty-four shillings per coomb sack. He'd never known it much above twenty shillings before. Barley, oats, butter, malt: all the same and soaring in price. The cost could be passed on and he felt relief at knowing it. An uncomfortable prickle ran across him as he remembered his spat with Dunthorne and what he had said.

As John made his way upstairs, he realised he had forgotten to tell his father of his return to London at the end of the week. He'd had word that his paintings in the Annual Exhibition had not been well displayed.

London. London. Hooves skittering on cobbles, the stink of shit in every alley. A hackney coach horse, if it knew of the Bergholt common, would never go back to those streets. Wasn't that what his mother had hoped, that Bergholt would bring him home again and return him to her?

He felt in his pocket for the letter he had received from Maria earlier that day:

Spring Garden Terrace, London

My Dearest John,

How heartened I was to receive news of your return. If my eagerness appears selfish, then I beg your forgiveness — I know how your father treasures you and how pressingly short your time together is . . .

Alas, I continue with my dreadful cold, which has not been eased by this ceaseless damp. London draws its long grey coat around us most days. If it is meant to warm us, then it certainly does not. I am so envious of your Bergholt, as I ever was, that steals you away and makes blue eyes at you.

Father has indicated he would welcome a visit, so do, please, consider yourself welcome, <u>be encouraged</u>, and visit.

I remain ever yours,
Maria Bicknell

Bergholt's blue eyes? A tease, he knew, but the line and its inference of infidelity made his heart lurch. There, as well, an invitation to visit. Finally, a break in the fence that the Bicknell family had erected around their daughter. A longing for Maria flooded him. He took the stairs to his room, two by two, and brought his case out from under the bed, ready for his departure.

The morning of his return to London, he rose early. The overnight rain that had kept him from sleep had cleared; a strengthening wind promised more later. He had not yet had the chance to walk the river towards Dedham and was eager to do so, to carry some part of that wind-tossed day back with him to London. He pulled on his boots, buttoned his coat, slung his paint box over his shoulder and set off.

Crows tipped and tilted above him in raucous delight as he made his way along the towpath. He held his hat flat to his head to stop it being blown into the sky after them, shouldered himself against the wind and pressed on, paint-brushes rattling in his paint box with every step. It seemed remarkable that all of who he was, all he hoped to be, could be contained in so few things: in a half-dozen brushes, and a rag to clean them, and a small number of paints and a palette he'd fashioned himself from an off-cut of wood.

As John neared Dedham lock, he stopped and took out a sheet of paper barely ten inches across and pinned it on the inside of his paint-box lid. He took in the view of the watermill. Saturated by days of rain, the warm ochres of the brick buildings and clay tile roof had stained a deep red. Water gushed volubly through the sluices into the shallower basin near where he stood, overflowing the bank and seeping into the field behind. The sluices were only usually opened in winter, when winter storms threatened floods. John pushed the thought away. It wasn't his concern.

He painted quickly. Sketching with oils was a technique he was still trying to master: it needed him to let go, to become what he saw, so that eye and hand were one, no thinking space between them. *Damn*, but it was difficult. Doubly difficult with cold hands. He studied what he had put down: he had the shape of it all – practice had brought him that much – but each part: mill, trees, pond in the foreground, church tower to the back, seemed oddly estranged. And although green came at him from every direction, the finished result – the tone – was too dark.

He threw his brush down in disgust. Who was he if he was not one thing nor the other? Neither miller, nor artist? Not of country, nor of town? But for a pair of wings, he'd have taken to the sky with the crows.

Sarah

I WENT TO bed with sparrows in my ears and woke the next morning with crows. A sad sorry Sarah I was and no mistake. Every step set the crows bickerin'.

When Ma saw me, she gave me a scolding look. 'Don't expect me to feel sorry for you. Where's your penny from yesterday?'

'Didn't get one.'

She looked at me like she didn't believe it. Like I had a pennyworth of beer in me instead.

I broke off some bread from the loaf to take with me to the farm, but she took it right back.

'No penny, no bread.'

'Ma—'

She broke the chunk in two and gave me the half of it then sent me out the door. 'He owes you tuppence. Don't let him tell you otherwise. He'll make beggars of us all.'

'He knows the parish pays the rest.'

'The rest? The rest? A pittance! He should pay you proper for the work you do.'

Ma's words rested heavy on me as I made my way off. Weren't my fault some in these parts had no care for the *shoulds* in life. Out over the Fen I went, cussing, the sun ablaze on the reed tops, like one cross look from me had scorched them up. I lifted my face, glad of the warm. I needed that warm more than anything; first morning like it since I'd started at Cook's farm. A good thing the sun was not under his say-so and I thumbed my nose in his direction for that. Then, there on the path, a badger and a cub. Had God stuck out a foot in front of me, I could not have stopped up more quick.

The badger lay dead on its side, done in with starving, thinner than a fox. A cub clambered over it and chittered for milk. All I had with me was my bread so I sat down where I was and broke it into crumbs.

But the cub wouldn't take none. It chittered and chittered, frantic for its ma. Me, on my useless bum, with a handful of crumbs.

'Well, I can't sit here all day.'

That made no difference so I scooped the cub up and dropped it in my apron pocket. 'You'll have to come with me, is all.'

I weren't the first to arrive and I weren't the last either. More folk here than there was work for and more arriving all the while. Didn't they have farms to go to of their own? Mutton chops was vexed, I could tell, running about like the chickens were out of the coop. He swung the gate shut to stop more folk getting in and hollered at those who tried to clamber over it.

A young lass, not even up to my shoulder, stepped up beside me.

'Hello,' she said.

'Hello,' I said back.

'I'm Kate.'

'Sarah.'

'Sarah. What's it you do here then, Sarah?'

'The midden.'

Her eyes widened up at that.

'Can I do it too?'

I gave her a look up and down. But the thought I was thinking was she'd take a ha'penny for doing the midden if they asked her. It put worms in my tummy and they were doing a jig.

'What you got there?' she asked when she saw my apron pocket wriggle.

I pulled the pocket open so she could see. 'A baby cub. It needs milk.'

Just then mutton chops came along the line. 'You and you,' he said and nodded to two lads. Next he came to Kate and me. He stopped, looked me over and rubbed at his chin, making a show of deciding.

Without saying more, he turned to Kate. 'What's it you do?'

Quick as you like, she said, 'I can fetch milk,' and she peeked a look at me and winked.

Milk was the last thing that needed fetching and if I'd known she'd say that, I'd have told her – there was no dairy on the farm.

'A milk fetcher?' mutton chops roared, before the smile fell off his face. 'Got no need for that.'

'She can do the midden with me,' I said.

His mouth pinched in like he'd been hung on a hook. 'Finding the midden a struggle, are you? I can always find someone else.'

'No—'

'Well, off you get to it then.'

'What about me?' cried Kate and made after him as he walked off. 'I can fetch what you like.' She tugged on his arm to get him to stop. 'Please, mister, please. I can scrog beans. Anything—'

One swipe of his hand sent her clattering across the yard with a yelp.

When he saw me still stood there, he shouted, 'Off to the midden, I said.'

And so – and this were the shame of it – that's what I did.

About mid-morning, mutton chops come in. I'd picked up the shit and was putting down straw.

'Morning, Susan.'

Suppose he thought it funny, calling me that. But I weren't stupid. There were things for complaining about and this weren't one. Meant I got to keep my own name for myself.

'You done fart-arsing around?'

'I've the water yet to fetch from the pump.'

'When you're done fetching it, you're to come over to the barn.'

And with that, he were off.

I felt for the cub in my pocket. Heavy and soft as a pup it was. 'Oh,' I said, as it sucked at my finger. It sore needed milk but I had to finish up with the water and hurry across.

'Did you fetch the horses?' he said when I got there.

There I was, and not a horse in either hand. I turned on my heel and went back to get them.

'And the others,' he said, when I had brought them, so that then we had four.

The barn door had a new beam fastening across it and took some effort to lift. In we went, me, him and the horses. It were dark until my eyes adjust'd. The barn had no windows, but light came in through the cracks in the roof. Stood in the middle of this, the threshing machine, covered over with a big cloth.

He kept his eyes on me as I looked.

'Know what it is?'

'A threshing machine.'

That made him snort, that I should know. 'Seen one before?'

'Only this 'un.'

At that moment, Mairster Cook came in. In along with him came two other men, one dressed up fancy in a waistcoat. Two women who'd got took on that morning were made to stand over with me. Also with him were other farmers: Mairster Benton for one, and Mairster Martin for another. Mr fancy waistcoat clambered on top of the contraption, untied the cover and threw it down.

The man nearest Mairster Cook explained, 'The corn gets fed in here, at the top. From off of a cart, or from a haystack out in the field.' He walked round the machine to the far end. 'Chaff comes out here.' He took up an empty sack and tied it to a funnel in the middle. 'Grain comes out here.'

Mairster Cook wore a look that said he knew this without having needed to be told, that this was for the benefit of

the others. A more pleased with hisself man, I never had
seen. Wasn't just the cat with the cream. He lit up, like cats
and cream were a new-found thing and only he knew they
went together.

The man walked over to the far side of the barn where
a spindle had been set on a wooden cradle, like a wheel
laid flat on its side but raised up. Across the spindle a beam
had been set and it stuck out a way. By means of this,
anyhow, and a pole and long belt, it all attached up to the
thresher.

'Here,' the man said and beckoned to me. 'The horses,
bring the horses.'

I led my two over and he fastened them by a harness to
the beam. Then mutton chops brought his two and they
were fixed on the opposite end of the beam. One 'oss threw
a wild kick as if it knew its days being outside were up.

The man looped a belt on to the threshing machine and
stood back, admiring of his work.

Daftest contraption I'd ever seen. Dafter than Mairster
Benton's seed drill, which lastid a week.

The man took the reins of an 'oss. 'G'up!' Off in a circle
they went, round and round. The spindle turned the pole
and the pole turned the wheel and the wheel turned the
belt. Such a rattling set up then from inside the contraption,
like someone had been made to sit inside it clattering pans.

The man sat on top, pretend'd to throw in corn. One of
the women got sent over to where the bag was attached
and the other told to stand by the chute. They stood there
and gived each other worrisome looks, afeared of being
shouted at, not knowing what it was they were supposed
to be pretending to do.

The man with the 'oss said, 'You need one man to oversee, for the heavy work. Women can tidy the chaff and tie up the bagged corn.'

'You, girl,' he called to me and drew his 'oss to a stop.

I went over to him and he handed me the reins so then I was leading it round. Round and round and round and round. I reached a hand to its flank to soothe it and felt a shiver under my touch, a fear trying to escape. *There*, I whispered but I shivered too, that contraption being a violence brought down on me too.

'See,' said the man. 'No skill required.'

He stepped up to Mairster Cook's side. 'A threshing machine is as necessary to a farmer as a tithe barn to a rector. It puts an end to the evil of gleaning, when the poor are generally a nuisance among the sheaves. It protects the farmer's property, regulates labour supply—'

'And its cost,' piped in Mr fancy waistcoat from on high. 'And, not forgetting, the income to be had from hiring it out to neighbouring farms.' He gave a nod in the direction of Mairsters Benton and Martin.

Mairster Cook smiled his fat cream smile. One man, two women and me were doing the work of a gang of men, any fool could see that. Weren't so much corn Mairster Cook was bagging, but pennies, bright as gold.

And then I realised one more other thing. I'd said to Tessie and Thomas that I knew nothing much about Mairster Cook's farm, that all I did was gather up horse shit and had a penny for it at the end of the day. But going in circles changed all that. Nothing was not nothing after all.

For leading the horses so well, I were given a penny extra. Tuppence, in all.

'An' as for yesterday? Am I not still owed for that?'

'Tuppence is plenty enough for it all. And what is greed rewarded with?'

I looked at my feet and waited for him to tell me.

'Nowt, that's what. *A greedy man stirs up strife . . .*'

That were that. He were off on one, harrying God to his side. I closed up my ears to the rest.

On my way homewards, I placed the cub back with its ma. My little cub was dead for want of milk and I was done in with it all. Such a sadness heaved up in me then. I'd had care of it but hadn't put a stop to it dying. Not even tuppence could cheer me. I wiped my eyes dry on my arm but more tears came. Never thought I'd be so sore afflicted by a little scrap of fur.

Reverend Vachell was vicar and magistrate and that's why, on Sundays, the Globe was a throng and his church was not. Word was Littleport folk were godless and being godless weren't no good. But what did they know of how or when or where we prayed? Well then. If they'd ever of asked us, they'd of known.

Thomas was the first to speak. 'Here's a young man, four shillings a week, by gravel. What do we think of that?'

'Damn shame . . .'

A man got up and hushed us with his hands. 'They do as they like. They rob us of what's ours, plough the grass up that God sends to grow, that we might neither feed a cow, pig, horse nor ass. There is five or six of them have gotten all the whole of the land in this parish in their own hands and they would wish to be rich and starve all the other part of the poor of the parish. The commons were a poor man's heritage for ages past. They took away the land, ours by right. Are we to accept it?'

'No, no!' A volley of tankards battered down on the tables.

'Look at us. Have you ever seen poorer?'

'The Irish?'

Laughter and boos at this.

'I tell you, even Irish slubbers have it better. We reside in miserable huts. Wretchedly bad. Tell me this: for whom are we to be sober? For whom are we to save? If I am diligent, shall I have leave to build a cottage? If I am sober, shall I have land for a cow? If I mind my pennies, shall I ever have enough for half an acre of potatoes?'

'No! No!'

'They stole the land from under us!'

I leaned over to Tessie and nudged her. 'Who is it there that's speaking?'

'Tom. He's come over from Downham Market this morning by horse. Same's happening there, he said, with the price of bread and the farmers paying sod all. But they're raising a bustle about it and he reckons we should do the same here.' She leaned in close as though to tell a secret. 'He was at Waterloo.'

'*He was?*' My eyes went on stalks for him then.

'How are we to feed ourselves with wheat up twenty shillings in a month?'

'We can't. We can't. We're starving . . .'

'We want a cheap loaf, cheap bread and provisions cheaper!'

From the back came a song, quiet at first then louder as we all joined in.

> *The law locks up the man or woman*
> > *Who steals the goose from off the common*
> *But leaves the greater villain loose*
> > *Who steals the common off the goose.*

All of us singing. I hadn't known the words before I went in, but they were fixed pretty straight by the time I came out.

I crossed the street, humming the tune and the thought of a good roast goose dinner in my head. I'd have it with sausages or a thick slice of bacon. I didn't mind. *Bacon.* My tummy near collapsed at the thought. And peas. All the peas I could eat.

It was punishing to think of.

All the singing in the world couldn't hide a thing. I was hard hungry. And I was no nearer to being fed.

1815

Henry

THE FIRST DIFFICULTY they faced was how to reach shore. Although morning had broken, it was not light; ash continued in the air, fine as dust, stealing away the horizon and the shadow at Henry's feet. He'd noticed that the ash formed a tenacious mud when wetted, as those who did not piss accurately overboard soon found out. The lower slopes of the mountain smouldered and gave off a considerable quantity of leaden clouds. Every now and then, a flare of orange cut through the grey gloom that shrouded it. Whatever remained underneath, its condition could not be judged from their position – to determine that they would have to land, that much was certain. The heat from the land came at them in waves, carried across by the wind. It dried the words in his mouth and dessicated his thoughts.

On his previous visits to Bima, the captain had always anchored in the bay, but now as he stood on deck and considered the aspect, he looked bewildered, like one arrived somewhere uncharted. He had commanded the ship be anchored a good distance off, in what could only be described as a *wary position*. When Henry enquired if they might not move the boat closer, the captain left him in no doubt as to the risks. Did Henry not know the obstacles that might lie below the water's surface; the lava that likely had thrust into it? One wrong manoeuvre, even that most delicately undertaken, risked disaster: being grounded on a reef; the hull, holed; shipwreck, even. First observations through the spyglass revealed shoaling water where before an anchorage many fathoms deep had been available; the entrance to Bima choked off by a thick raft of pumice. The mood among the men was subdued, then fretful; a feeling exacerbated by the constant sound of pumice as it ground against the hull, as though the sea would yet devour them. As Henry lay in his bunk, he imagined the hull by his ear worn thin as paper and the planks giving way suddenly and a violence of water coming through.

'Could we not walk across?' came a suggestion.

Several men nodded and shrugged, in a way that suggested they'd considered it too.

The captain gave a look that would have felled a great oak. 'I'll be in my cabin.' He beckoned to the ship's boy. 'Alfie, boil a kettle for tea.'

It was decided to launch the largest dinghy and take supplies for a short exploratory expedition inland. The captain selected six of the strongest crew, and they, together with Henry, clambered over the rail and down into the boat where the oars were handed to them, one by one. Slotting the oars into the rowlocks and eight men manoeuvring around each other in order to be seated would normally result in the dinghy being tipped perilously this way and that, but the pumice held them alongside the ship, stationary, as though clamped in position. Once settled in place, the men pushed off a short way. They pushed off again. Their first attempts at rowing sent the oars scudding across the surface and threw several pieces of pumice into the air.

'Dig the oars in,' shouted the captain. 'Put your backs into it. *Pull!*'

Their progress was slow, pitifully so, but gradually the distance between them and the ship widened. It was the damnedest sensation: to know one was moving, but yet to feel as if one were not. If Medusa had risen out of the sea before him, Henry would not have been surprised.

The oarsmen rowed with grim determination and within a few minutes were sweating. They came upon an area where the pumice was littered with timber, as though whole forests had been ripped up and thrown out to sea. Tree trunks, broken and twisted, shivered to pieces; vast spears of wood, jagged and splintered as though a giant had snatched up the island's forests in great handfuls and tossed all away in a furious temper.

'One moment.' The captain raised a hand to stop the men rowing and pointed to the port side. 'There.'

In among the shattered trees and pumice floated a blackened cinder ball, the size of a large dog. As the dinghy came upon it, the oars were raised and two of the crew lifted it into the dinghy. They passed it forward to the captain, where it was placed at Henry's feet.

'There's more, there,' said one of the oarsmen.

Henry took out his pince-nez from his waistcoat pocket and adjusted it on his nose. He crouched forward to examine it then shook his head, as though struggling to accept what he was seeing. A childhood memory came suddenly to him: a game of hide and seek and him finding his sister behind a parlour room chair, curled quite as tightly as this, ten pink toes sticking out from the under the hem of her dress.

He took off his pince-nez, folded it and placed it back in his pocket.

'A child. Eight or nine years old.'

He heard the men murmur, and several of them shifted uneasily where they sat. Those nearest took off their caps.

'Are you certain?' asked the captain.

Henry nodded. He pointed to a line of pitiful bumps. 'Vertebrae.'

'Boy or girl?'

'No way of knowing.'

The child had curled in on itself, as tight as it could. Henry had seen burns plenty in the war. But in all those years, nothing compared with this. Even during the bombardment of Copenhagen, when thousands of cannon-balls and barbed iron rockets had been launched at the city – he'd seen at first hand the injuries such weapons could inflict. But this was different. He looked at the cindered child and shook his head. The child's essential form was intact. He saw at once its awful fate: incinerated as it had tried to shelter. His hands shook as he cast about for some-thing with which to cover it. Another memory came to him, of a cadaver on the dissecting table at London University: a young woman, found drowned in the river. Her nakedness before them had been the cause of much tittering among the assembled students. Once the butchery was done, Henry had removed his apron and covered her as best he could. That the dead deserved dignity had since been a principle of his.

'There is no need,' said the captain. 'I shall note it in the record.' He gave a curt nod and, with that, the child was set back over the side among the pumice again. A prayer was said. The men lowered their oars. They did what they could to steer between other cindered forms, but there were too many – many too many to count and impossible to avoid. Each thud against their boat a sickening rebuke.

Henry checked his pocket watch. By his reckoning, they had been rowing for fifteen minutes; the shore could now be made out clearly without need of the spyglass. The captain guided the boat into a small bay. An oar was dipped over the side, to ascertain depth, and when it was shallow enough, one man slipped over the gunwale. One by one, the men went in after him, chest-deep in thick, ashy water, and hauled the dinghy towards shore.

Henry delayed leaving the boat for as long as he could, supervising the passing of his medical bag along the line of men. When that was done and he the only one left, the sailor nearest him reached up a hand for him to take. A helpful gesture and impossible to ignore. And then he too was over the side and struggling to find his feet.

He came out of the sea, heaving for breath, like some stinking, floundering beast, dazed by the weight of water in his clothes. He ran his hands along his arms, disgusted, to remove what he could of the sludge that coated them.

What godforsaken place this? Land, certainly, but not of

the living and utterly devoid of life. Neither tree nor plant of any description could he see. Neither mammal, bird, beetle nor fly. Such stillness. No leaves for the wind to move through; no branch from which a bird might sing. Was this the end of the world and they the only ones in it?

Here the accumulation of ash was to some depth and made what they had encountered thus far appear a light dusting. The land seemed made entirely of it, heaped up in dunes, in huge drifts. Impossible to tell what lay beneath. With each step, more and more of the wretched stuff adhered to Henry's boots. The captain lifted a handful and weighed it in his hand. A terrible dread overcame Henry – that if he did not keep moving he too would ossify and his arms and legs would petrify into the branches and trunk of a stone tree.

'Ailing for summat, Doctor?' asked one of the men.

Henry shuddered as though to free his shoulders from an unwelcome grip. 'Perfectly well, thank you.'

They unloaded the supplies they had brought with them – enough for three days. As to what would happen next, Henry had no idea; the captain had not said. Never a happy day was built solely from conjecture. As medical officer, surgeon no less, he felt he had sufficient station, a right, to know. So when the captain stepped away to consider their position, Henry saw his opportunity.

'Might I enquire after our route?'

The captain turned and considered Henry with cold regard. He gestured to the landscape before them. 'Would you like me to draw you a map?'

Henry swallowed. He lowered his eyes. 'I'm sorry. The question was foolish.'

The captain made a gruff sound in reply, but seemed placated. Sometimes, in situations such as this, one had to assert one's inferiority, Henry knew.

How devilishly tricky this man was to meet on a level, he thought. He suspected him of being one of those who had been promoted quickly through the ranks by the necessity of war. But Henry had known worse. Medical school had provided him with training aplenty in the handling of ego and ambition.

The captain grew thoughtful. 'Bima is two miles, no more, as the crow flies. But as we are not crows we can either follow the coast round – which leaves us exposed to rock falls – or make our way inland a short way and approach from that direction.'

Much as Henry did not care for the thought of rocks on his head, the prospect of a climb did not encourage him either. The choice, it seemed, was between having the devil for a brother or for a friend.

The captain called for one of the barrels of water to be carried over and, once seated on it, he took out a pocket-book and sketched the scene before them.

'Any experience of an eruption before, Hogg?'

'No, sir. None. And you?'

'Not at such close quarters.' The captain held out the sketch at arm's length and seemed pleased. He snapped the book shut. 'Well then, we should make a start.'

The heat was devilish, the stench of sulphur overwhelming. Henry bound his neckerchief around his face to cover his mouth, but could taste the ash through it even so. They had brought a supply of water with them, but with such a small crew, it meant several forays, forward and back, to stage the barrels ahead. All had to help, Henry and the captain included. And all this wretched, filthy business was carried on over the worst terrain. They mounted a series of dunes, only to face a much steeper climb over far rougher ground. Huge boulders blocked the way. They would need either to scale them, or find some other way around. Each handhold risked laceration; each loose stone, a broken ankle. The climb was doubly arduous to how it had appeared at sea level looking up. One step felt like twenty and sent a trail of skittering stones down on the man behind. And the heat, the heat. Nothing had prepared Henry for it. His feet throbbed painfully in his boots.

Finally, after several hours' walk, back and forth to carry their supplies ahead, they crested a hill. There below, Bima. Or what remained of it.

'See there? That's where the Resident's house stood,' said the captain as he made another sketch.

Henry followed the line of his hand, but saw only stumps: the remains of trees, shattered to the ground. He saw a boat snagged in one, like some bizarrely placed ornament and then noticed several more, or rather the fragments of them, similarly placed. He closed his eyes as he imagined what had happened, how the sea must have pulled away and run at the land again, gathering all in a fury before it: boats, huts, carts, and hurling them inshore.

Then, as he opened his eyes, Henry saw a flicker of movement.

'There!' he cried, making all around him startle. 'There! See? Dear God! I do believe I saw someone!'

Then he was off down the hillside at such a rate he was at risk of falling. But he knew what he had seen: two, maybe three people, quite as grey as the ash. He shouted now, so they would hear him. The thought that there was life here after all surged in him.

His breath knocked from him as he ran. 'We're here. *We're here!*'

1816

Hope Peter

IF THE WAR had taught him one thing, it was this: no one could come home and expect what he'd had before. Home: like the letter he kept in his pocket, took out and considered, folded, refolded, till the words had near rubbed off and the paper fell apart at the creases. His homecoming being delayed, he knew not if his mother lived, or, if she did, what would be his welcome. No matter. That he'd survived these past years and had returned, upright, neither leg made of wood, an arm either side of his ribs and both eyes in his head – when he had last counted – was miracle enough. He wasn't about to get particular with his demands or to want things just so. It had never been his way to be godly, so why he had been deserving of the Lord's mercy when so many had perished, he could not say, but he worried, as the fortunate sometimes have sense to, that whatever had favoured him might just as quick be taken away.

'Watch it,' he shouted to the driver as the cart jolted into and out of a rut and knocked him hard against its edge. He'd survived the war – all of it, end to end. How many could say that? Cannon, sabres, muskets and knives; the creeping sickness that could cut a man down in hours: none of it had touched him. What certain insult would it be, if on this last mile to Hadleigh Cross his head got stove in after tumbling from a turnip cart, or if death by a thousand bruises did for him instead?

Willie Hutchen, a spry small boy, eyes quick-moving like a mouse looking for escape, had been his only companion since Billericay. Something about the lad suggested he'd be in and out of his pockets and off with the contents before he noticed – if only he weren't so busy asking questions. Seemed he had a hundred and ten such tucked behind his ears and wasn't afraid to ask.

'Did ya see him? Napoleon?'

'No, can't say I did.'

'Pop a shot at him?'

'Would be tricky that, not having seen him . . .' Was the lad daft?

The boy shifted and gave him a frown. 'Kill a Frenchie, then?'

'I did.'

At this the boy cheered and sat upright. 'Did yer?'

'Aye. I did.'

'How?'

He held the boy's eye. How old was he? Ten, maybe eleven. Fair; freckles the colour of chestnuts. Wasn't any of the lad's business, nor a pleasant story should he tell it. He stabbed a finger in the boy's soft gut. 'With a blade, like this.'

The boy folded up so sharp it was a wonder the freckles stayed stuck to his nose. 'Oof,' he said but soon recovered. 'How many Frenchies d'ya kill?'

He shrugged.

'Tell me then!'

'Three or four.' A lie, if ever, but he'd no stomach for the truth. His thoughts were ahead of him, halfway home now, desiring to be as far away as possible from the memories that trailed behind, busy hanging their sorrows on every hedgerow, gurning at him if he chanced a look back. Look too long in a pastwards direction, that's how scarecrows got fixed in your head.

'Three or four?' The lad sounded disappointed. 'Bet you showed 'em, even so.' He opened his mouth as if to say something more, but shut it again.

Let the lad be quiet and be glad of it. Silence, peace: times were he thought them gone from the world. When the fighting was done for the day and they fell to their knees, too knackered to stand and gripped by the mud, what he remembered most of all was how the small sounds came back to him: leaves rustling, grasses stirring, the creak of a branch in the wind; birds returning, twos and threes of them, dipping through the carnage in short, startled hops; clustering in bickering groups, as if laying the blame for the grim scene around on him. But no slaughtering had started on his say-so, and he'd have told them, if he could. Not for king, not for country did he kill. He wanted to live. And once in the thick of it, killing was the only damn sure way of that. Thoughts like that were best kept to himself. Men had had their knackers kicked in and were run through or shot for less.

Sparrows, greenfinches, blue tits. Same birds at Waterloo as at home. Might have consoled him but it did not. Instead it had filled him with sickening shame, with dread. Every day, the same sombre reckoning by those, like him, who found themselves not yet shot and on their feet: corpses counted; grievously wounded horses – and no one with the strength or will to kill them – chased away into the trees. Days had come when even the hardiest soul caved in and would have fled that damned place with the horses if they could. When he saw the birds look down from their branches, he threw his arms in the air to scare them away.

When news of victory had finally come, he'd felt relief, knowing it was ended. But if this was victory, it was not his. Neither honour nor glory attached to him. War had used up the young man in him and spat out the leftovers.

'Yeah,' he said, not looking at the boy but down at his hands, 'I showed them.'

At Hadleigh Cross he asked the driver to halt and got out. He could have continued on further, but needed the walk.

'What's yer name, mister?'

He looked at the lad. Been a while since anyone had asked him that. He liked him then, a little, for being a kid and asking.

'Peter,' he said.

'Willie Hutchen,' said the lad.

He checked his pocket for his purse, to be sure he still had it, then held out his hand. The lad, having got over the belly poke, took it and shook it between his.

'Well, take care of yourself, Willie Hutchen.'

'I will.' He grinned and flushed pink; a lad, after all.

Peter watched the cart shamble off and when it was gone from his sight, he turned in the direction of Corringham and the place he called home.

* * *

Peter. It wasn't the name he was born with. His father not surviving to the time of his birth, his mother had christened him Hope.

Fair to say he had begun life hopeful. Then, in his eighth year, he'd started at the tide mill at Oil Mill Farm. Wasn't much to it. Dangle on a rope, try not to cry and keep the race clear of whatever the Thames flushed into it: drowned fowl; great turds; a turmoil of dead fish, white bellies twisted skywards; these he had to get to, quick as he could, before they dashed on the railing and split open, spilling their gut stench through the mill. The men did the heavy work: cole seed was brought in and the oil was taken out; in summer it ran clear and golden, like honey; in winter, cloudy as tallow. When the tide turned and ran out, they hauled him back up but sometimes they forgot and he'd be found cold and snivelling hours later when the tide was on its way in again. It wasn't all bad. Between times, he could do what he liked. If the afternoon was ahead of him and it was fair, he followed the tide out over the salt marsh. He did it for the feel of the turf under his feet, for the warm mud that sucked at his toes. On he went until the land ran out and the Thames stretched wide before him: to his right, upstream, London; to his left, the yawning mouth of the sea. He'd watch the boats and wonder where they'd come from or where they were headed and when he was finally bored with that he found oysters in great clutches and he'd fill his pockets till their weight near dragged his trousers down.

That's how his first years had passed, with him growing taller and stronger, no longer crying but keeping the race clear and doing it well. He fetched oysters most days to take home and when his mother said she'd had enough of them, then he brought them with him to the mill instead. From then on, never once did they forget to haul him up. When he got too big for dangling on a rope, he was made to lean over with a great pole and keep the race clear that way. *Them's that fall in have to get themselves out again*, he was warned. They were appreciative of the oysters, but only to a point.

He was fourteen when war came and he was old enough to take a shilling off the King.

'Your mother meant well, but Hope's no name to be going to war with,' said old Jack, one of the men he worked with, shortly after he told him he was off.

'How come's that?'

'Courting fate. May as well dance a jig for the devil.'

'*Hope*,' said Boyce, earwigging, in a voice that set the others elbowing each other in the ribs. Way they laughed made him think his name had given them cause for merriment before. 'Godfool name for a boy.'

There was more laughter at this.

'Leave off the lad,' said old Jack.

'What am I to call myself then?'

The men looked at each other. Not one of them had anything else to suggest. They sat there a while, scratching and jiggling their balls.

'Peter,' said old Jack and he slapped one hand down on the table as if that decided it.

Peter? He said it aloud and pulled his shoulders back, as though trying it on for size.

Old Jack thumbed in the direction of a heap of oyster shells. 'Fisherman of sorts, ain't you?'

'Unless you'd rather be called Pearl,' quipped Boyce.

Pearl? The others told Boyce to shut it. So, Peter it was and from then on he gave up on Hope as his name.

—terpeterpeterpeter!

Peter turned, he lifted one arm as though expecting a crow to come at him, only then seeing Willie, the boy from the cart, making his way towards him, half at a hobble, half at a run. The lad, not the fleet-footed mouse he'd taken him to be, moved with a limp, and a bad one at that.

'Mister Peter!' he shouted. 'Wait!'

He slowed until the lad had caught up to his side.

'Can I walk with you?'

'No law says you can't.'

'Where are you off to?'

He pointed at the track ahead. 'This ways.'

'Which way is that?'

He lifted his hands then dropped them. This lad and his questions. 'Homewards.'

'Can I come with you?'

'Nothing stopping you from going where you like.' That wasn't true. He could have picked up a stone and shooed the boy off. They walked on, at a slow pace so the lad could keep up.

It was his turn for questions. 'So where are you off to?'

Willie shrugged.

'No home of your own?'

At this he grew vexed. 'Have so!'

'Where's that then?'

'Manchester.'

Manchester? A good way north. Willie explained, though no one had asked, how he'd taken lifts wherever he could, as long as they were headed south and he hadn't had to pay for them.

'So, how far south are you headed, Willie Hutchen?'

The question lifted a sudden smile from the lad. 'To London, of course!'

And it seemed at that moment that if he could, little Willie Hutchen would have skipped.

On they walked. The lad's condition was a sore hindrance to begin with, but after a while Peter got not to mind.

'Know any songs, lad?'

'Hymns.' Willie opened his mouth to sing.

Peter covered his ears and gave the lad a nudge that near sent him flying. 'Save it for Sunday.'

'What about you then?'

'Nowt I can hold a tune to.' He thought for a moment. 'Here then. Learned this in France. There's no tune to it though.'

And did those feet in ancient time . . .

He glanced at the lad. He felt awkward of a sudden, like a boy who had stuffed his mouth with conkers to see how many he could fit in.

'Go on then,' urged Willie.

Walk upon England's mountains green:
And was the holy Lamb of God,
On England's pleasant pastures seen!

As the words came back to Peter, it raised a longing in him he could not explain.

'What comes after?' A surprise the lad was still listening. Now he had to think. The first verse, he had off pat, but as for remembering the rest – it was like pulling the words up, one by one, from out the mud.

And did the . . .
Shine forth upon our . . .

clouded hills?
And was Jerusalem . . .
builded here,
Among these dark Satanic Mills?
Bring me my . . .

He scratched his head. Ah, damn it.

Bring me my . . . Bow –
Bow of burning gold:
Bring me my arrows of desire:
. . . O clouds unfold!
summat summat.

Then the rest of it whipped into him like wind into a sail:

I will not cease from Mental Fight,
Nor shall my sword sleep in my hand:
Till we have built Jerusalem,
In England's green and pleasant Land.

Willie blinked. 'Did you write it?'

'Did I write it?' Peter laughed, though something of what the lad had said touched him. 'Don't be daft. They're the words of a poet.'

'A poet? What's that?'

'Someone with different eyes in his head to me.' He lifted Willie up on to a wall. They looked out over the bareworn land. A fatstock bull, bare able to stand, lifted its head and snorted.

'It don't look green and pleasant.'

'No, lad. It don't.'

And, with that, Peter lifted Willie back down and they continued on their way.

Charles

CHARLES NO MORE thought he could be a preacher than he thought he could be God. As a boy, nothing stood out about him to suggest he was destined for anything other than a job skulking at the back of his father's store. His manner was set somewhere between shy and scornful: shy of what lay beyond him and scornful of what did not. Shy, perhaps, in the watching way the avaricious have. He prayed, ardently some said, for God's forgiveness when he'd done wrong and as he had been taught. He learned when he should drop to his knees and when he need not. When he had gone barrelling through Joe McGovern's hay field, flattening a good portion of it, he was sorry, truly, for that; he was sorry too for calling Mary Ann a *fiddler's bitch* – language unbecoming of a young man aspiring to a higher calling, even though he thought her deserving of it, devil's butterfly that she was.

It was said of his father, Jonas Whitlock, that he spent Monday to Saturday in prayer but only on a Sabbath did he pray and only on his deathbed did he mean it. That some questioned his daddy's fervour was troubling. P'rhaps it was simple jealousy on their part.

Many were the days when Charles felt he looked out at the world from inside the whale's belly. It was only when his daddy died that he was, to all intents and purposes, *spat out.* He forsook the store, sold it up, and bought himself a stout pony, fit for the ups and downs of the trail. He called her Thistledown for no other reason than to mark a Scots heritage his mother had mostly neglected to tell him of. Next, he decked himself out in a suit of black wool cloth. The fashion was for a wide-brimmed hat to go with it and though the one he tried in Boston suited him well, he left it behind unsold. *Awake, O north wind; and come, thou south; blow upon my garden . . .* Let it rain: Charles wanted to see where he was headed.

He paid rent on a room in town where he was to live. His intent was to preach outside, whenever God called him to it. He did not expect folk to come to him, but he would go to them. Then out he went, into forest and field and up the mountain too: Charles Whitlock, *preacher,* Bible clutched in one hand to his chest. Clip clop, clip clop. *Oh Lord, convert their Soules that they may prais thee.*

It was a tall order, for sure.

He'd been on a preaching circuit in Vermont for near five years. It took him from Bethel in the north to Londonderry in the south and most places between. Five years was plenty enough to learn where he was welcome and where he was not. Bit by bit, folk came round to his way of preaching but some did not, their being either doubting, or stubborn, or plain numb-skulled. As most folk were in the town, he hired a room for meeting there, but it stood empty month after month, a steady drip-drip drain on the money he had. Most took against the idea pretty strong, believing God should be met in the open. But Charles had his shop years behind him. He knew that a four-squared room, covered over with a roof, was the way the years would bend round to in time. Folk wanted communion together and he – secretly – not to have to struggle to be heard above the honking of geese or the tomfool antics of chickadees in the bushes.

So when the Reverend Jeremiah Scott, Baptist, took a fit and fell down dead, a whispering set in that came to profit Charles. The manner of Scott's death – to be struck down, mid-sermonising – encouraged questioning thoughts and uneasy conjectures on past behaviour. Unfortunate, yes; suspicious, for certain. Scott's congregation drifted more and more Charles's way. He grew respected, if not for his oratory, then for his dogged persistence in keeping up that room of his. People stepped over his threshold and with it came the grudging admiration from the ordinary man and then the patronage of some wealthier townsfolk. That all were equal before God in Charles's eyes did nothing to erase a stubborn fact: the funds he had, which had whittled down some, now began once more to swell. It set him thinking. An idle thought. Perhaps from that one room, he could build a church.

For those who could not or would not make it into town, he rode out to them on Thistledown. When he thought of the paths he and his pony had made connecting up the farms scattered about, it did make him proud that by his own efforts he was drawing the souls around him into true ways. Pride, he knew, should rightly be damned, but this pride of his seemed stepped to the side by several degrees. Pride, if it were for God, could be defended some. This congregation of his was hard won.

The town afforded no curiosity; no minerals of consequence lay about. Neither visitors nor prospectors came
by. The women he had an eye for were all married. His first
wool suit wore through at the elbows and knees so he
bought another. He saw his life laid out in that manner: a
new wool suit, every other year; life's milestones lived
through his ministry to others and in a lengthening bolt
of cloth. Laurel Gray, for whom he might have an affection
should she allow it, called him a miscreant, Wesley's weasel,
and would have shooed him off with her broom had her
father, Seth Gray, not had it off her. It made for awkward
times, as it was Seth he came most to visit. At dinner, she
served them a single slice of meat and a potato each, rattling
their plates down in front of them. They sat there when
they were done, which never took long, but neither plate
was cleared nor pie nor sweet fancy offered after. When
time came for Charles to go, Laurel would stay in the back
room and would not come out to bid him goodbye as was
polite.

'She feels these things strongly,' said Seth. 'She'll come
round.'

'God willeth all men to be saved,' Charles had replied.
Scottish Presbyterians too.

Universalists, Episcopalians, Baptists, Congregationalists,
Presbyterians. It was his duty to exhort their every one,
else by his neglect they would be condemned.

*Praise the Lord to distroy false Doctrines and stop blind guides.
Amen.*

But his stomach had growled, as though to dispute it.

* * *

One morning, he had come by the Green Mountain to visit Seth as he'd heard in town that he was abed with a fever. As he approached, he saw Laurel working a patch of ground to the side of the house. He raised one hand to her in greeting, a greeting she did not return.

He slipped one leg over his pony, dismounted and threw the reins loosely around a gate post to secure them.

'A good day for it, Laurel,' he said. It was too hot for a black wool suit and he was prickling up inside in a sweat. Perhaps more minded of his appearance and not looking where he was going, he turned his ankle sharply on a rut.

'Is it?' She bent back to her work and hoed at a thin row of seedlings. Dust rose up around the hem of her skirts.

He watched her for a while. 'Corn?' he asked.

'Pardon me?'

'Is that spring corn coming up? That you're hoeing there.'

'No, it is not. The corn grows over there.' She pointed vaguely to land behind the house. 'Leastways, it tries to.'

'Ah. I see.'

'You do? Good.'

She stopped what she was doing and wiped her brow, showing the red palm of her hand. The sight of it was both troubling and arousing. When she noticed him still there she said, 'Can I help you with something?'

'I have brought a sermon to share with your father.'

'A sermon?'

'I heard he was unwell. I thought a sermon helpful.'

Her laugh came at him like a hazelnut flicked at his brow.

'You think yourself so holy.'

'Most certainly, I do not.' He flushed. Of all the things she could have said this was the most unjust.

She fixed him with a hard stare, not about to give an inch.

'Charity. Isn't that what your lot are good at? Tell me one good charitable thing you have done today.'

His mouth opened and closed, like a fish hooked out of the pond on to the bank.

'This week then . . .' She lifted one hand and chewed at a nail. 'Hmm? This month?'

'I ride out in God's ministry most days—'

'You ride out in God's ministry?'

This came at him in a singsong voice he didn't care for at all. These were the most words he'd had from her in as long as he could remember, none being what he'd imagined she might say to him and they were sore stinging to hear.

'The only charity you know of is the charity you have off others.'

'I—'

'Do you know the dinners I've fed you these past years? Do you?'

He realised she was waiting for a number and that he should suggest it.

'Fifty or so?'

'Fifty, or so?'

Her derision made his toes curl. He should have doubled it and then been on her right side and some.

'Uh-huh.'

'Four hundred and sixteen.'

He glanced down at his belly as though disbelieving so

much could be fitted in there. So many? She'd counted them? And yet, in all that time, he had still failed to convert her? It made him more admiring of her than ever, seeing the same stubbornness in her as he saw in himself.

'Some weeks, you ate here more than once. And many were the weeks you did.'

What was this hippety-hoppety way with his heart when he was with her? He straightened himself and kept his voice gruff, for it not to show. 'They were?'

'And what charitable thing did you do for my daddy, or for me, in that time? *Or Mary Ann?*'

He swallowed. 'Mary Ann?'

'You were terrible unkind. P'rhaps you don't remember? Mary Ann was my friend.'

'I do remember,' he said, quite unexpectedly contrite. He remembered them, as girls, coming into his father's shop; sisters he'd thought them at first.

'You are a hypocrite, Charles Whitlock. *Let not mercy and truth forsake thee; Write them upon the tablet of thine heart.* I know my Bible too.'

And with that, Laurel dropped the hoe to the ground and turned on one heel and left him where he stood. Her words weren't just written on his heart, she'd scored them into him with a chisel.

He untied Thistledown and led her up to the paddock where Laurel's pony, Bella, was kept. Bella ambled over, heavy with foal. This foal would be a first and from how Seth had talked of it was looked forward to with the same hope as any of the infants born in the town.

Charles reached for some grass and pulled up a thin handful. 'Here you go, girl.'

At least his pony and her pony did not object to each other. He stood between them a while, soothed by their agreeableness.

Back at the house, Charles saw himself in and went to Seth's room. Seeing him there, tucked up in bed, the shallow dimple left in the pillow as he raised himself up, caused a sharp pang in Charles's chest. Plain to see, the old man was ailing.

'How are you today?' Charles asked.

By way of answer, Seth hacked up a rattling cough that had Charles reaching for a glass of water on the table. Leastways, that's what he thought it was; it had a cloudy quality, like milk that had been let down. Seth took a sip, grimaced, and passed the glass back.

'Stop your frowning. I'm not dead yet,' he muttered.

'That's exactly how we want to keep it.' And with that, Charles felt for his sermon and flattened out the creases.

Later, as he made his way off their land, he noticed the gate he had spent five years coming in and out of was half fallen on its side. It had sat that way so long the brambles had grown through it, died back and grown through again. He pulled away at the tangle and located it back on its pins. It was a deal heavier than it appeared; no doubt why it had been left.

He wiped his hands clean, sucking blood from his thumb where a thorn had snagged it, and swung the gate shut behind him. A little grease would stop the squeak and he would fetch some next time.

Wasn't much in the way of helping, but it was a start.

*   *   *

Back in the town, the talk was of sunspots. Albert Taggart, barber and surgeon, lifted Charles's chin with a finger and tilted his head back, the better to get at his neck. He dabbed and dabbed until he had built up a thick lather of soap.

'Sunspots?' First Charles had heard of such a thing. The thought the sun might have contracted something, that it too ailed in some way, disturbed him. He'd had measles as a child and the memory of it made him itch.

'The season is very backawards. Never been dry like this. Some says sunspots is to blame.'

'Sunspots?'

'They have a cooling effect.'

'Ah,' said Charles, in a way that kept his view on the matter open.

'Keep leant back.' Albert nudged his head back further. 'Soon have you tidy agin.'

Charles was happy to do as he was told. Being shaved made talking difficult. Usually, he spent the time in agreeable silence, mindful of the risk a bobbing Adam's apple presented to a razor. Suffice to say, Albert had conversation for two.

Dry it had been with little rain for months. It gave Charles no cause for complaint and had made the path of his ministering easier, it not being the usual muddy mire. On his travels about he had noticed how the peach and pear trees were late to flower and in field after field the seeds that had come through were stunted and straggly. His heart contracted as he remembered Laurel scratching at the ground with the hoe.

'Some says it's the devil's work.' Albert ran the razor up

Charles's cheek in a single deft swoop. He wiped the blade clean on a cloth.

'I don't know about that.' Charles felt the blade press to his cheek once more.

'How'd they get there then?' Albert lifted the blade away again so Charles could reply.

'I'm sorry?'

'How'd the sunspots get up there without' – he lowered his voice – '*them being put there?*'

Charles frowned. Many were the times, he felt, when his message had been taken up too earnestly, some being intent on out-devilling the devil. But if the devil's hand were so obviously in everything, what room was left for God? It was another of the questions that vexed him. God's intent could not be understood in simple terms. Caution was needed and conclusions best not jumped to.

'Well, as neither you nor I can look at the sun—'

'They've been seen through a telescope,' said Albert, cutting him short. 'Franklin has seen them himself.'

'Where d'you hear of it?'

Albert's mouth set in a straight line. 'Carter mentioned it, when he were in last.'

Patience, Charles, patience. 'And where had he got it from?'

'Newsprint.'

Charles gave a laugh. Another Boston habit, which would pass soon enough.

Albert lapsed into a silence that bordered on sulking. When he had finished up he placed the razor back on a shelf.

Charles felt the need to offer some conciliatory words

to close off the conversation. It was not the Bible that came to mind, but a passage from an Annual Almanac which, back in his shop days and half dumb with boredom, he would thumb through with endless listlessness. 'A forest path is colder than one that crosses the meadow – cut the forest, clear the land and sow it with grain. So the land warms and is bountiful.'

'Way I see it, an open field gets frosted up hard,' said Albert, still piqued. 'But what do I know? My work is whiskers. I'll leave planting to those who knows what they're doing.'

Charles paid up and went to the door. As he opened it, the sun fell in, dazzling bright. He screened his eyes against it. Too bright, of course, to look at directly. Sunspots or no, all passed by along the street in its usual way. The rain would come again. The land would provide. The burden would ease.

Seen in this way, even Laurel's assessment of him stung a little less. He would try harder and be the better man he knew he could be. As the land gave to those serious in their husbandry, so, with application, might he not find his full measure too?

Let us praise the Lord from every quarter.

Amen.

John

ON REACHING LONDON, John wasted no time. He headed straight for Somerset House and the Royal Academy Exhibition where Sam, the porter, met him at the door.

'Sorry to say, Mr Constable, sir, they've put you in a peculiar place.'

Sam stopped in front of a canvas, a ghastly tangle of cherubs, pink nipples and pouting lips. He pointed upwards.

There, indeed, it was. His poor *Wheatfield*, mounted as high as was possible without it being nailed to the sky. John took a step back, dumbfounded. He needed a spyglass to see it. 'How anyone can see from this distance—'

'I told them they should have put your painting in a more appreciative place, where it could be seen and better shown off, but they don't take advice from me. Nearer to God, if it's any consolation.'

John kept his reply to himself. His mind was already turning through a list of those whose decision it had been to place it there and what he would say to them when he saw them next.

'I got a good look before it went up.' Sam gave a cough, in admission. 'I worked a farm once. Never made it to head of the harvest like you got there, but I can still handle a scythe as good as any young man.'

'Did you? And where was it you worked?'

'Outside of Hadleigh.'

John turned and regarded Sam anew. 'Well, that would have made us near neighbours.'

Sam gave a nod. 'Where's the painting of, if you don't mind me asking?'

'East Bergholt. One of my father's fields.'

'Ah, a Bergholt boi? Thought that was Suffolk in your accent. I did not have you down as being from farming folk, Mr Constable.' Sam took a step back, perhaps realising he had spoken out of turn.

'Hardly. My father has two mills. Some land. Most corn he fetches in by boat through Manningtree.' Realising his tone had been abrupt, he turned to Sam. 'Do you still call Hadleigh home?'

Sam shook his head as though he thought the question daft. 'Nothing for me there any more.' He turned to consider the painting again. 'I saw you had put an inscription on the back.'

'I did. Robert Bloomfield, *The Farmer's Boy* – do you know it? *Nature herself invites the reapers forth; No rake takes here what heaven to all bestows; Children of want, for you the bounty flows!*' He saw Sam frown. 'You think Bloomfield meant different?'

'*Midst air, health, daylight, can he prisoner be? If fields are prisons, where is Liberty?* That's the Bloomfield I know.'

John blew out his cheeks. *Dear God.* If that didn't put a stop to it. He was relieved when Sam finally had reason to go, turning away to scold a boy for touching a finger to a painting to see if the paint was still wet.

After he had gone, John watched people move through the gallery. Most showed interest in what was before them,

the canvases at eye level. Less frequently did anyone turn
their attention to what was above. Of course, there was a
huddle around Turner's latest, the discussion quite as
animated as the work. A bitter thought rose in him: that
one deserved the other. He would not go over and join
them, being in no mood to acquiesce and smilingly accept
his position. He wanted no part of that circus.

And then he could bear it no longer. Even his brief
conversation with Sam seemed now to turn back towards
him with sly intent. If there had been a ladder handy, he
would have climbed it and taken his painting down.
He left, as he had come, no less burdened with doubt.

Outside, he found the nearest bench and sat on it. He
picked up an abandoned copy of *The Times* and, shaking it
open, glanced at the headlines. Most of it was taken up
with reports of the wedding of Princess Charlotte to Prince
Leopold. Rumours that Lord Byron had quit England for
Switzerland had now been confirmed. *Good riddance!*

John turned the page. As he scanned across it, his eye
was caught by a headline:

DREADFUL ERUPTION

*A volcano broke out at the mountain of Tamboro, in the Island of
Sumbawa, near Java, in April 1815, the eruption of which was by
far the most violent that ever happened in the history of the world,
far exceeding in the extent of its effects, any of Vesuvius, Etna or
Helca . . . At Ternate, 700 miles distant, the explosion resembled
a firing at sea, so that a vessel was ordered to chase in the direction
of the sound, to discover its cause. At Batavia, 600 miles off, the
sashes of the windows were so shaken, that they required to be*

fastened. At Makassar, the company's cruiser Benares *had some part of her decks covered a foot thick with ashes. The quantities within a hundred miles of the volcano were most tremendous: covering up forests and towns and filling up deep valleys; even the contour of the coast being altered by them.*

At Sangier, a town about 15 miles off, men, horses, cattle, houses, extensive forests and whatever came in the way of the whirlwind occasioned by the eruption, were carried into the air, and never more heard of . . .

Volcanos? There was a subject for Turner! John snapped the paper shut. Was everything in the world determined to taunt him?

Two letters arrived. One from Maria, cancelling the visit she had so recently encouraged. She was sorry to be such a feeble wretch but she continued unwell. A second letter brought confirmation that the Rebows would be happy to welcome John to Wivenhoe Park in August. They were happy, too, to advance payment, which he could expect in the coming weeks. It was all he could do not to leap in the air at the news. He hadn't the funds yet to buy Maria a ring, but he could at least go and see and determine the cost. He grabbed his coat and once out on the pavement, he raised one hand to hail a cab: 'Hatton Garden.'

A journey that should only have taken minutes soon had him at a standstill. When John peered out of the carriage window, it wasn't cobbles he saw, but a lake. He could just make out the horse up front, standing knee-deep in water, and water had started to seep in around the bottom of the carriage door too. John lifted his feet up and out of the way.

'Can you not turn us round and take us another way?' he called forward to the driver.

'Ain't the room to turn here.'

It was true, the street was too narrow. 'And if we just continue on through it?'

'With the water rising as it is? Who knows what's underneath? I cannot risk my horse's legs.' The driver jumped down and waded back. 'I'm sorry,' he said, as he opened the carriage door, 'you'll have to get out here.'

'Here?'

The driver shrugged. He went back to the horse to uncouple it from the carriage. 'My horse is my livelihood. Sit it out if you want to, but you'll not stay dry for long if you do.'

John sat there a while, contemplating his options, but all that thinking only led to the same, inescapable conclusion. He eased himself down from the step and into the water. He grimaced as he felt the cloth of his trousers grip his legs. Inch by inch, he made his way forward, doing his best to dismiss thoughts of the vile matter floating about him. He was about to berate the driver again, but what use that? All along the street, as water poured into cellars and ground-floor rooms, people emptied out of them, heaving their belongings with them in sodden bundles. He saw an infant, in a wooden crib, set afloat like Moses.

A spring tide, no doubt – which, with all the rain, had conspired to push the Thames over its banks. John huddled into himself like a jilted lover. He turned his back on Hatton Garden, all thoughts of a wedding band gone.

On his return to his lodgings, he found a letter from Bergholt waiting for him. He recognised the hand – Abram – and frowned as he broke the seal.

> *I am sorry to tell you that since you left, Father is much worse. We were at his bedside last night and he said that if it be the will and pleasure of God, he was ready & wish'd to be released. The doctor has been and has told us to prepare. He is gradually sinking and is near death . . .*

John brought one hand up to his forehead. It was news he expected but now that he had it, it did not make it any easier to bear. He crossed the room to the window where the light was better.

> *There are reports of barns alight and riots in Needham Market and Bury St Edmunds – Father, at least, will be spared this worry, but as you can appreciate it is further concern when I have plenty.*
> *We were very glad to see you when we last did, John.*
> *Respectfully, your brother,*
> *Abram Constable*

Then, the next day, came the news his father had died. *We await your return, if you are able.*

Able? He knew what was meant by that. He had missed his mother's funeral less than a year before; he was not to miss his father's. In his reply to Abram, he said he would take the first available coach to Colchester in the morning and would need collecting from there.

Next, he wrote to Maria, to share the unhappy news. *A week, my love, no more. I will hope to see you then.*

Hope Peter

WITHIN A SHORT while he had Willie Hutchen hoiked up on his back as he knew he would: all things in life being just a matter of when. What the lad lacked in speed, he made up for in chatter. There was more to be known about Manchester than he'd ever thought was in the world to know. He wasn't complaining, was glad of the company in many ways. The lad wasn't much of a burden and he lifted him with ease.

'When'd you eat last, Willie Hutchen?'

'Yesterday.'

'And before that?'

'A couple days back.'

'Hungry then, are you?'

'Some.'

Some. He'd have given the lad clover to suck on if the fucking sheep hadn't nibbled it flat. A number of their idiocy had escaped a field. They ran ahead, zigzagging across the path, hemmed in by a fence on both sides. It did little to calm the swill of nerves that had sloshed in him since leaving the cart at Hadleigh Cross. Ten years of slosh and swill, that's what coming home felt like. A long time to be gone. In some ways, he and Willie Hutchen were alike; journeying wasn't easy for either of them.

His war years felt like they had fifty wrapped up in them; that he had lived up the life he had. When he got to thinking like that, he had to give himself a shake. He was young enough – not yet twenty-five and the war behind him. *Git yourself straight*, he told himself, *else you'll end up twisted for good.*

The letter in his pocket was a consolation. He could say what was on it with his eyes shut:

> *My Dear Son – If you are surviving this bl--dy War then*
> *this house will be yours and if you are not then it is for*
> *Lizzie's boy as he has a family now.*
>   *I hope to see you returned home again*
>   *X The mark of Peggy Dunn*
> *& put into words on her behalf by Rev Cruikshank*

If Peter closed his eyes he could hear her voice in them, same as she was standing by his side.

Like all the places built on the edge of the marshes – Fobbing, Heards, Warrents – Corringham was little more than a huddle of dwellings either side of a track that continued on over the marsh until it reached the Thames. Not a face he recognised among the fewsome people they had met on the road, which surprised him. On reaching Rookery Hill and the turning that would take him to his mother's, he felt a change in the wind, the warmth robbed out of it. He could smell the river on it too – the tide was on its way in. One simple thing come back to him. It lifted his spirit, knowing he wasn't a stranger after all. Taking a breath, he lifted Willie higher. 'Not much further now,' he said.

The stories he'd spun on the way had shot off away from him as if a salmon had been hooked to the end of each of them. He needed to reel them back in again. He'd not want the lad disappointed. The memories that had bubbled to the top were those he remembered with most affection. What point dwelling on the slurry at the bottom?

'Has she chickens?' Willie asked.

'Yes.' This much was true.

'So there'll be eggs!'

'I'd say so. The best eggs ever.' This much was true too.

'And what's her cow called?'

'No, well, it's not *her* cow—'

'Thought you said it was.'

'She gets a share of the milk for the cider apples she grows.'

'Cider?' Willie dug his heels into Peter's ribs, urging him on.

Just the mention of it had set Peter's mouth watering. He quickened his step. He passed by the church and the Hall, the wealth heaved up at that end of the village. Thereafter, the houses were little more than mean huts. He'd always known that were true, but seeing it now had a cold sobering effect.

Peter stopped and seemed lost. Where his home used to be, stood a fence. He could still make out a path on the other side of it, but there was no gate to go through, no way to follow it further without clambering over. He eased Willie down off his back.

'What is it?'

Peter turned in a circle, for a moment unable to speak. 'It's gone . . .'

'What's gone?'

'Where I lived.'

And now Willie was turning in circles too, as if the cottage had up and offed and settled itself down somewhere near at hand.

Peter gripped his head as the insult of what had happened became clear. It was into this general confusion and consternation that an elderly man came wandering.

'Jack?' said Peter, thinking he recognised him from his time at Oil Mill Farm.

The man squinted up his eyes as if he had the sun in them. His eyes were so milky it was a wonder he could see at all. 'Peter?'

'It is. The same.'

Jack brought one hand flat to his chest and held it there. 'You've given me a shock. I thought you was dead.'

'Well, I'm not.' Obvious to say with him standing there, but he could not hold down the feeling that coming home had thrust him up into the world anew.

'I was looking for my mother.' He looked at Jack, whose mouth had now fallen open.

'She died. Did you not know, lad?'

Peter felt his breath lock in his chest, a struggle to get the next words out. 'When?'

'Michaelmas last. I'm sorry that you should find it out like this. It happened sudden.' Jack shook his head at the memory, then softened. 'Well, well. Look at you standing there.'

'Where's her house? And the others that were here?'

'They all got took down.'

'So whose fence is this?' Peter gave one of the posts a sharp kick. He wrenched at it, but it had been fixed in deep and budged not an inch. 'Them bastards up at the Hall, I'll wager.'

Jack laid his hand on Peter's shoulder. 'I'd not bother. What's it matter whose fence it is? It's not yours.'

'The cottage was.'

'The cottage was tied. Same as they all were. You knew that.'

'Tied? Even so, it was mine to come back to. Ma said as such. She got the reverend to write it down.' He took out the letter. 'Here.'

'Ain't no good showing me that. I can't read. Where's it say the house was yours?'

Peter stuffed the letter back in his pocket. 'It just does. That's how it always was.'

'All the huts here were cleared out the same. John Simpson, the Carters, Arthur Brown and his father. All of them, out on their ear. The next big storm would've carried half of them off anyhow, the state they was in. The reverend, may God bless him, put in a good word on everyone's behalf. But a good word never paid the rent.'

'Where did they go?'

'John Simpson is in the workhouse. Everyone else headed London way. Nothing for it. Half the village has emptied out that way. A bad business for you to come back to. How old was your ma?'

'Fifty, thereabouts.'

'Well then. Not such a bad age, lad.'

At that, they both hushed up. If that was supposed to give him consolation then he wanted none of it. He wanted to be placed in a barrel and tumbled about with his grief. He felt for the letter in his pocket and screwed it up in his fist. 'Ah, fuck it.'

'What are we to do now?' asked Willie.

Jack rested his hand on Peter's back. 'Get yourselves a room up at the inn for the night and sleep on it. It's getting late to be heading off elsewhere and it looks like weather's setting in. Terrible the wind we've had of late. Brought down such a number of trees. Branches bloody everywhere, but will the bastards let us have a stick of it?' And with that, Jack left them and went off muttering.

Peter did as Jack suggested and settled Willie at the Bull Inn. Though the rate was halved on account of him being returned from the war, he needed to mind every penny now and he took one room between the two of them.

The bed was little more than a wooden bench and shoved up against one wall with a blanket straightened over it. He'd sat on more comfortable pews in his time. Fortunate the fellow who would get a wink of sleep on that.

'Where you off?' asked Willie when he saw Peter fasten the buckles on his boots.

'Never mind about me. I'll be back by the morning. You're to stay put, you hear? No shifting from this room until then. There's cider in the jug to keep you happy and a pot under the bed to piss in.'

'But—'

'Never mind, I said. You do as I say.'

At this, Willie pinched up like an oyster soused in vinegar. Peter had not meant to be sharp, but hadn't time for the lad's questions. 'If I'm not back, you're in no worse of a spot than you were before. And you'll have had a bed for the night and a belly full of cider to thank me for.'

From the inn, Peter headed in the direction of Rookery Hill until he was standing outside old Jack's house. The seething in him at what had happened twisted so hard it was a wonder he wasn't in knots. He gulped back the night air but that did nothing to calm him. Stealing up to the window where a candle burned dimly, Peter peered in. He rapped a knuckle on the frame.

Jack pulled back a piece of sacking that part-covered the window. 'What's it you want?' His tone was guarded with none of its earlier welcome. Folk needed good reason to come knocking at night.

'Do you still have your hunting nets, Jack?'

'What's it your business to know?'

'I need use of them, till morning.'

Jack's eyes narrowed up, appraising him anew. 'If I did, they'd be well hid.'

Peter nodded. 'I have need of them. You could go look.'

'Aye. I could, I suppose.'

So off Jack went to look. Peter blew on his hands and shook them to ease the stiffness out. Christ, it was cold. His coat was poor match for it.

'Here goes then,' said Jack, coming back. He held out a sack. 'If they catch you, there's no mention of me.'

Peter nodded and lifted the sack over his shoulder. 'They'll never have me. I'll be back before dawn.'

'If I'm not here, leave the sack inside the door at the back. There's hares a-plenty other side of Northlands' woods. Plenty enough just to be scooped up off the ground by their ears. Mind how you go. You might be home, but them fields is theirs . . .'

'I can mind myself.' And with that, he was off, the cold in him forgotten as his purpose took hold.

He followed the track out of Corringham and north towards One Tree Hill. He could feel thunder gathering; a distant rumble confirmed it. He hurried on, head down, glancing up to a sky bruised over blue and black. He'd be lucky to catch anything, what with the wind throwing his scent every which way. From One Tree Hill, he headed leftwards, crossing the fields in front of Northlands' woods. Here, on the open, untilled field, he had to be at his most wary. He stopped, his mouth gone dry as he struggled for breath. Fear had set something loose in him. As he set off again, and giddy with nerves, he skidded on a patch of ice. Thrown headlong, he slapped a hand over his mouth to shut up the shock that jolted through him. Ice? Was everything in the world arse over tit?

On through the woods he sped. As Jack had said, there were trees down in some number, a struggle to make his way over them in the fading light. Birds' nests littered the ground, soft as moss underfoot. But it wasn't the nests he worried about. There could be mantraps – one wrong step and he could lose a leg. He heard thunder again, closer this time, and the wind flew about him as if not knowing which way to go.

And then, with relief, he was out of the wood and looking on to a narrow open field: a finger of land, banked and hedged on the far side. A strip of about an acre, he reckoned, and perfect for hares. His years in Spain and France had taught him what signs to look for. He could just make out a honeycomb of old rabbit burrows from where he was, but with all his galumphing about any living creature for miles would likely have scarpered. But give it time to settle and they'd be out, and out in some numbers. Funny how the same such hunting skills – so necessary for their survival at war – could put his life in such peril here. But it wasn't funny. He knew the risks. The men who had lorded it over him there had been happy to eat the game he caught. But the self-same self-righteous bastards would have him in chains, soon as they could, if he were caught with their game here.

He brought out a net from the sack and teased it apart, running it through his fingers to check for tears. He had to think where best to stake it, with it set in such a way as to anticipate the track a startled hare would take. He spotted a gap in the hedge where the blackthorn had been cut back hard and the new growth had yet to come through. Gathering up a net, he made his way over and strung it tight across the hole.

And then it was done and it was just a matter of waiting, keeping himself well hid and figuring which way to leg it should anyone come on him in surprise.

Snugged down in thicket at the edge of the wood he supposed he must have slept because then he heard a terrible shriek, worse than any alarm. He was up on his feet and running and pulled out a knife as he did. Ah, hell, three of them, leaping and struggling. He had to kill them quick but they would fight him before they'd die. They kicked and scratched with furious might. Two he despatched quickly, slipping his knife in at the neck. But the third kicked so hard it knocked the knife from his hand. He wrestled the animal with one hand as he tried to locate his knife with his other.

'Fucking die, will you . . .'

He took a nasty scratch before his fingers found the knife

again. He clutched it in his hand and killed the hare with a single, sharp thrust, and it too lay limp in his hands.

He tried not to think on what he was doing, only that he must do it well. He wanted the skin to come off with as few cuts as possible. Not mangled and torn, head half garrotted from the struggle. He made a cut in the belly, bringing the knife up under the skin on either sides of the ribs. He slipped his fingers underneath to force a gap between the skin and the spine, then down each of the rear legs. Once this was loose, he slipped out one leg, then the other, and brought the skin up and over the hare's head as he might when lifting a shirt over his own. And when all three skins were off, and panting hard, he stuffed carcasses, nets, all of it back into the sack.

As he made his way back across the field, he heard a lapwing's call, shrill and mournful, as if to damn his bloody business from on high.

Once back in Corringham and along Rookery Hill, he hurried down the track to where his home used to be. Over the fence he went, through the apple orchard that had once been his mother's and on towards the Hall behind. He grabbed straw from a small barn and stuffed it into the skins, to make each plump again. The front legs he stiffened with sticks.

What ghoulish sight would greet the household when they opened the door that morning. Three hares, they'd think, sitting on the step. Then a moment or two more to realise what else was there, pink and still and laid down next to each: a carcass, as if each hare had jumped out of its skin with fright.

He turned his back on the Hall. Jack was wrong. It did matter whose bastard fence it was. He spat on the ground.

Charles

HE WOULD DEDICATE himself anew to God's service. He would make himself more humble and faithful and be truly useful to all he served. When he next visited Seth he took grease for the gate and two apples towards the making of a pie.

He found Laurel out in the yard as he arrived. She was on her way over from a small barn at the back and headed towards the house.

'Hello, Laurel.' Oh, what a joy, even to say her name.

'Hello.' Her reply, the tone of it, suggested the joy was his alone.

'How is your father today?' he asked, as she drew alongside. Although he wore his sombre-best look, inside he was all sparks.

'Same as before. No better.'

'I am most sorry to hear that.'

To this, she gave no reply. He followed on behind until they reached the house.

She'd been hoeing again but this time she left the hoe propped by the door as they went in.

Laurel, Laurel. No, he would never tire of saying it.

'I wanted to ask you something.' It was a question he'd had for a while.

'Oh?' She took up a cloth, spat on it, and rubbed at her

hands. She frowned at the state of her knuckles. She sucked on one and rubbed again.

'About your name.'

On she went rubbing, a friction that rose a heat in him too.

'*Laurel*,' he said, as though needing to remind her. 'It sure is unusual . . .' It sure does suit you, is what he wanted to say.

She put the cloth down, despairing of it or him he could not tell. 'I will tell you now it isn't the name I was born with. But it is the name I have took for myself.'

'It is?'

'Laura was how I was baptised. But I liked Laurel better, so have settled on that instead.'

'And your pa was agreed on—'

She cut his question short, ignoring it. 'Have you something to say?' She wore a severe look, as if anticipating and guarding against his disapproval. She had a way of looking at him straight, so that he looked down first.

He should not approve, he knew, with Laura being her baptised name. But at least Laurel wasn't frivolous, or French, or Catholic. An honest mountain name: *Laurel*. Same as the bush that blossomed pink in spring. It wasn't flowers he was thinking of, but her arms, bared to her elbows; the palms of her hands opened to him as she broke from her work. She was laurel-like, he decided: strong and hardy; just what a man these parts around needed. A Laura, on the other hand, would want to go to Boston, read books and drink tea. When it came to it, her name could be – if not overlooked exactly – then not examined in too close particular detail. *Mrs Charles Laurel Whitlock*. He liked how it sounded. Had said it aloud in his room when no one else was around to hear.

'No, no. I've nothing to say on that.'

She gave a small smile, clearly not believing him.

'Here . . .' He reached into his carry bag and brought out the apples. Sorrowful specimens they were, wrinkled with age, but not beyond use. 'Guess they need eating up.'

'Guess so.'

As she made no move to take them from him, he placed them on the table.

'Last there is. Until the new season.'

He flushed. Why did he say the things that he said when he did not know what to say?

She crossed her arms. Whatever conversation could be had between them was not going to be continued by her. Her gaze rested on the clock on the mantel, where the hands were stuck three hours ahead, then she stared out the window unblinking. If the clock had been working he might have noticed a tick; instead what came to him was the distant lowing of a cow from out in the barn. Even allowing for the clock being ahead, it was past milking time. Laurel bit her cheek.

'Something troubling you, Laurel?' he managed at last. 'More than your father?'

She stiffened as her attention came back to him.

Try again and this time be useful. 'I brought grease for the gate . . .'

And now she blinked, a couple of times, quickly. 'I saw that you had placed it up straight. Thank you.'

Thank you. And he heard that she meant it sincerely.

* * *

It was worrisome to see Seth still abed. As Seth went to sit up, his nightshirt slipped at the shoulder. His every joint pressed against his skin; where there'd been muscle, skin hung loose instead.

'Easy does it,' said Charles as he helped ease him forward.

Seth winced as he took his weight on his arms. He tried to shrug Charles away, but hadn't the strength for that either. 'No fussing. I can manage.'

Charles wasn't so sure but made an agreeing sound and drew up a chair by the bed.

Seth was sore with complaint; his mood pricklier than cocklebur. The only way out for it all was through his mouth. It was the same for most folk, Charles had noticed. It wasn't enough to turn their worries in silence until they had the answer, or part answer, what mattered was the yawing. And who else did they know who they could yaw at, who had a ready ear and the time to listen? So that's how the best part of the morning passed by. Seth listing his complaints on the lack of rain. It was a story Charles was well familiar with but Seth did not know his was not the first telling. Charles nodded as Seth talked, one ear listening out for any sound indicating Laurel had come back to the house. If anyone had cause for complaint, it was her.

In the end, all that talking plain wore Seth out. They prayed together and when they reached their *Amen*, Seth shook his head with the same sad resignation as when something is broken and can never be mended. Leaving Seth to rest, Charles went downstairs. He found the apples where he had left them, not even close to becoming pie. Nor, he realised with a sinking heart, was there any other smell of anything else baking or boiling or in a stew. The door stood open and he saw now how loose it was held in its frame, how any knock of the wind would carry it off the latch.

The sound of lowing came again from the barn, this time more urgent. Charles went out of the house and crossed over the yard towards it. Truthfully, he did not know the telling apart of a happy from an unhappy cow, but this cow had news it wanted announced. It took some moments for his eyes to adjust to the darkness when he went in. He was surprised to see not one cow, but three skinny ones, tight together in a stall. They eyed him with a doleful expression.

He reached towards the nearest and scratched it on its nose. By his feet, the water trough stood empty. 'Thirsty, are you? Don't you worry none. I'll get that fixed.' He scouted about for a pail and then went to find the well.

What folly this, he thought, as he hunted about, turning in circles, not finding the well. He could just as easily have told Laurel about the cows' need for water. But she was as elusive as the well and nowhere to be seen. He was about to give up when he saw her coming down the slope towards him with a milkmaid's yoke across her shoulders. Although doing her best to make her way carefully, water sloshed out with every step.

On reaching him, she looked at the pail in his hands. She gave a nod in the direction she had come from. 'The well's up behind me a-ways if you're wanting to help.' And with that, she carried on by.

Yes, he could help. Wasn't that what he was already doing? He hurried up a rise and down the far side, to a small opening where a well had been sunk.

The first time he drew the pail to the top, it came up near empty. The second time the same. The third time the water he raised up was brown. He grimaced and threw it away. By the time he had raised the pail a fourth time, Laurel had returned. But the fourth pail had come up even muddier than the third and he cast it away too.

As he did, Laurel grabbed the pail off him. 'What are you doing?' Her neck flushed red as she struggled to contain her anger. 'It's all the water we have.'

It took a moment for him to understand what she'd said, leastways what she meant by what she'd said. And now that he did, he hoped he had managed to mask his disgust.

'It settles out fine,' she said, then, 'Yes, it is what we drink, before you ask.'

She went to the well and dropped the pail down. And then, without warning, she closed her eyes and brought her hands together to pray.

Although they were not the exact same prayers as the ones he favoured, he was moved beyond measure at the sight of her. He reached a hand for hers when she was done but she looked at it as though it were a strange thing and brushed at her skirts instead.

'You need know that when Pa is stronger, we're moving ourselves to Ohio. We've made up our minds, so there's no point in you trying to change them again.'

Ohio? He spent all that week thinking about it but found it no less of a tomfool, reckless idea than he had at the start. He didn't know what was in Ohio that made it so

desirable, didn't much care to know either. He did try –
with as much sympathy as he could muster – to understand
what had brought them to that way of thinking. To look
at it as he might one of his sermons, appreciating the
strengths, the flaws, from every which direction. He was
full aware of the difficulties they had. The skinny cattle,
the dry well, Seth's complaint. Hardship abounded at
present, no denying. But what could be harder than starting
from scratch – with no farm, no cows, no well? In Ohio?
He would put these three same points to Seth when he
next saw him. He would try not to labour it, or show hurt
that the old man had not confided his plans to him.

Vermont. A blessing to farm here, was it not?

But Seth would have none of it and the three points
Charles had were three too many. 'It's been a hard couple
of years, no denying, but this season has done for us.
Everything we put in has withered up for lack of rain. And
now the well is about dried up too. Ain't never happened
afore. I've not the strength to bear it.'

'A shower of rain will put it right—'

'It'll take more than a shower of rain.'

'You have a good farm here—'

'Once had,' Seth corrected.

'A crying shame to give it up—'

'Would be, I agree. But it's been getting harder a whiles
now, that's the truth. The Dunbars says they're going.
Spaldings says so too.'

The Spaldings? Charles tried not to show his surprise.
Not a word had come back to him about that either. He
swallowed as he thought of his congregation deserting him,
scattering westwards like frightened sheep. What rankled

more than anything was that no one had seen fit to tell him. He felt the momentary triumph of the aggrieved – yes, they should all be ashamed – before it fell back in on him with a crushing melancholy.

Whatever alternative Charles put forward, Seth knocked the corners right off it, finding some other objection to add, thus frustrating any reasonable proposition that might have them stay put. This way, that way, whichever way Charles suggested, it ran into thickets that he struggled to cut a clear path through.

That night, he went to bed more troubled than he could remember. His panicked heart thudded the same it had when, as a kid, he had just managed to jump out of the way of the Boston stagecoach as it thundered past. Yes, no denying, it had been an unusual dry winter and spring. But if everyone with a dry well moved on, Vermont would empty out. Charles tossed and turned, unable to find rest, until quite exhausted by it he finally became still. Moonlight spilled in through his window, like a white coverlet thrown over the bed. He took a deep breath and let it out again, the fervour in him releasing with it. Patience and fortitude were what was needed. Patience and fortitude and belief. He would broadcast it loud and wide, starting on Sunday with his next sermon.

'Be patient therefore, brethren, unto the coming of the Lord. Behold, the husbandman waiteth for the precious fruit of the earth, and hath long patience for it, until he receive the early and latter rain.' He heard disgruntled muttering from the back of the room,

'Any rain would do.' He didn't catch who said it, but gave a stern look before he continued. 'And God said, "Behold, I have given you every herb bearing seed, which is upon the face of all the earth, and every tree, in the which is the fruit of a tree yielding seed; to you it shall be for meat."' If anyone quoted Deuteronomy back at him, he was ready. He delivered the sermon with command, he thought, being sure to meet everyone's eye. He ended with Romans 5: 3–4: 'And not only so, but we glory in tribulations also: knowing that tribulation worketh patience; And patience, experience; and experience, hope.' At this, one woman held a hand to her chest and closed her eyes. Several others nodded their solemn agreement. The rest sat without expression and could be said to be thinking on it. As much as it was possible to say so, the sermon was a success. But if he thought any deeper, all would be doubt.

Two days later, it rained. And not just rain, but a deluge of rain. A mighty storm that came in from the west and washed Nathan and Peggy Townsend and their pony and trap clear off the track. Tree roots came exposed, like gnarly old knuckles; sheep huddled in sodden flocks, too soaked to scatter anywhere. When Charles next rode over to see Seth and Laurel, he did so with resolve in his spirit and fire in his heart: Then I will give you rain in due season, and the land shall yield her increase, and the trees of the field shall yield their fruit. His midnight fretting had delivered him a plan that would keep them where they were. He, Charles Whitlock, would dedicate himself to the farm until Seth was back on his feet. Seth was too ill for any journey yet, least of all to Ohio, and he would tell him so. And if that failed to persuade him, as perhaps it might, then he would make a proposal. Of marriage. Laurel was a fine woman but it was apparent she did not have suitors queued at her door. Would Ohio provide an abundance of such? He doubted it. Her manner was abrupt but it was a manner that he had come to understand, even to accept. She might not at first be agreeing to it, but nor was she any fool. They were not a bad match. He was not a farming man, but they knew that. He'd learn quick; between them this farm could yet be made something of. One season would bring them straight.

Yes, he would be frank. The conversation was long overdue; he regretted not having it sooner. They would prevail. No need for rash thought or flight. It gave him great heart to see how confidence had grown in him. The stronger the faith, the stronger the man.

Sarah

'SO THEN. ARE we to go there one night and see what's to be had?'

'Are we to go where?'

Tessie tapped her knuckle to the side of my head. 'To Mairster Cook's.'

That had me listening at last. 'We couldn't do that.'

'Couldn't we not?' She twisted away from me with a wink that said we could.

We were walking along the Ten Mile Bank in the direction of Southery. It was Sunday, so no working allowed and that included being out with a dog, dogs being a matter that vexed Reverend Vachell a great deal. *Thou shalt not walk thy dog on a Sabbath* was not a commandment I knew of, but he took dogs as a sign of enjoyment in life, and that was sin enough. Whatever his reason, we wasn't to do it and it was a shilling fine if we did. It made for miserable Sundays not only for Littleport dogs, but for any of us needing seven days' work in order to eat.

'I'm not suggesting we do anything. You know my mind on that. Even if it is what he deserves.'

She was right. He did deserve it. There had been trouble all over, from Norwich down to Ipswich then over Huntingdon way and a good many places in between. So much hay put to the torch, the cattle would be lucky if they had gleanings to eat come winter.

'He must have summat going spare. Farmers always do.'

I had no sympathy for Mairster Cook, or for his larder, but what was the point of us going to see? All we'd dare do was take a nibble for the risk of it being discovered and the trouble it'd fetch down on us. And we'd be just as hungry again the next day.

'He'll have his larder locked up, for certain.'

'What is it with you? You're in a right maudlin mood. I was only suggesting.'

I gave a shrug. I wasn't myself and I knew. So I told her about what I had been thinking. 'Did you never wonder, Tessie, how you got to be you and I got to be me? Do you ever think if it could have been otherwise?'

'Otherwise what? I have my mother and father and you have yours. How can we be otherwise?' She squinted as she thought. 'We can't be. There's no changing our parents.'

Nowt to be said to that. But I hadn't meant about mothers and fathers.

'You're a right one, Sarah, you are.'

'Do you reckon the King thinks on it? Why it is he is the King and not someone else?'

'Don't be daft. Who put these funny oddities in your head?'

'See, that's what I get called – daft. For having thoughts in my head.' I wrapped my arms about me tight as I could and stamped on ahead without her.

Then I stopped and held out my hand. Because there coming down through the air, through all that sky, tumbled a snowflake. I looked at Tessie from over it and she looked at me. Her nose was red and she sniffed. A line of ducklings darted out of the reeds, banking the Ouse, then thought better and darted back.

I gave a hard shiver and dropped my hand to my side. Hard enough to be hungry and now I was cold. I hadn't the words for what I was feeling. Everything inside of me and outside of me was wrong. Winter had come upon me in spring.

'If I had summat to set fire to now, I'd burn the bloody lot of it, I would.'

And, with that, Tessie linked her arm in mine and pressed in close, so as we could both be warm.

By the time we got back, the church folk had come out and were standing about. They looked to be waiting for summat to happen. From the looks we usually had off them, they didn't want us anywhere near. But today, summat was different. One girl skipped over, ribbons flying from her bonnet and her hair tied neat in plaits.

'You're poor, aren't you?' she said and held out her hand.

From around the side of the church came two men, carrying a table between them and Mrs Vachell, the reverend's wife, shooing them along. Behind her came her maid, carrying a pot with a ladle. Behind her, another maid, with bowls stacked up under her chin. When it was all laid out, the church bell set to ringing, slow and steady, as when someone dies.

'There, there. Good,' Mrs Vachell said as she tidied us into a line.

And when it came my turn, I looked at what I'd been given. The peelings off their potatoes. Any thinner, the broth would have been water. As the bowl was handed over to me, Reverend Vachell held one hand up and thanked God.

'Amen.' He waited for me to say the same.

They looked at me and I looked at them. And I knew what their look said. That I should be thankful and I should be grateful and I should take what I'd been given quietly away.

'No, thank you,' I said, and handed Mrs Vachell her bowl back. And with that, I turned and walked off.

That cross I was, I could have kicked over the gate; I could have wrenched the post it was stood on, clean out of the ground. Just a whisper from me would have broken all their windows in a shatter and knocked over their chimney pots too.

But when I was home again, I told Ma there was soup to be had up at the church because I knew she was as hungry as me.

'I'll not go begging to them,' she said and crossed her arms in front of her.

And we sat there, the both of us, nursing our hunger, a sore ache that only summat to eat would ever put right.

Mrs Vachell. I shook my head at the thought of her. Well maybe one day she'd lift her pot lid and find it empty, same as the rest of us.

'Come on, Tessie, then,' I said. 'If we're to get going, then we need to get gone.'

I had taken the loan of a pony from off the common and was stood there with it at her door. Night had come on.

She took one look at me and it and said, 'Not Mairster Cook's then?'

'No. *Benton's.*'

Her eyes flashed bright, as the thought took hold. She shot back inside to grab her shawl then was up on the pony behind me.

Benton's place was a hard enough hike in the daylight, but I hadn't a brave enough heart to walk it in the dark. The moon showed barely a quarter, its face hid behind cloud. It was so dark and never more so once we were out on the Fen. Gradually, my eyes adjusted and I could just make out the line of the path, and the tufts of the sedges and reeds that marked where the riverbank was.

'How will you know the way?'

'If I've forgot it, then we'll go back.'

'What will we do when we get there?'

'Oh, summat.'

I already had a fair idea. Benton kept cows and had a dairy. And in that dairy was cheese. When I'd worked there, I'd seen it. Rows and rows of it on shelves. He'd turn it and sniff it and pat it and look pleased. He showed more kindness to those cheeses than he did to any of us. We wasn't to go near. One boy who had touched one got brought out into the yard and was flogged.

'What happens if the bog dog comes after us?'

'There is no bog dog, Tessie.'

'How do you know that there's not?'

I stopped the pony up. 'Listen,' I said. 'Do you hear a bog dog barking?'

She listened a while then meekly shook her head.

'Well then.' I giddied up the pony again, so we was at a

trot, and though it half shook me to bits, it did at least shut Tessie's worrying up.

We got to the farm a good time later, late enough for not a candle to show. We left the pony tied up at the end of the lane so as to sneak up as quiet as we could. I remembered where the dairy was and we made our way over the cobbles towards it. Each step placed down so careful as though expecting the cobbles to crack. Tessie lifted the latch, one hand placed over the other so it would not come up with a *clack*. And then we were in, and our breath coming hard and fast. My heart was fit for bursting with the fear that it held.

Oh, the cheese that was there. The fresh, sweet tang of it. I took a step towards it, eager, as to embrace a long-lost friend. But as I did, my foot hit a bucket. The clatter of it over the stone floor – how could one small bucket make such a din?

A dog set to barking, worse than any bog dog could. Tessie grabbed a cheese and so did I and we were helter-skelter out the door and over the yard without stopping.

The farmhouse door flung open and out stepped Mairster Benton in a daze of candlelight. But we had the dark on our side and he stood there blinking. That did not stop him raising his pistol in the direction we was running.

'Fuckers! I'll have yer!'

Then an orange flash as he fired. How he did miss us, I do not know. I did not dwell on it for he was loading his pistol again, only stopping to hoik up his britches.

It was his modesty that saved us because a full cheese is a hard thing to carry and we were labouring to make progress away. Too heavy for one person to run off with in the dark. Tessie dropped hers first and I dropped mine after.

It never was stealing because we never took that cheese, leastways not far. And then we were up on the pony and giddy-gaddying back as fast as we could the way we had come. And though we had nothing to show for it, we had done what we had intended.

And in the morning, that's when it come to me. *That's how the thoughts get out of your head.*

Hope Peter

HE SHOULD'VE UP and offed and been over the field and far away by morning. But there was something in him wanted to know, like the devil had him held by the ankles and would not let him go until he did. By his recent arrival, anyone with a half-ounce of sense would suspect the bloody business was his. To flee would only confirm their suspicions. How far would he get, with Willie hop-hobbling by his side, if the hounds were sent after them? Best brazen it out. *Christ, no.* And so it went for hours, as his thoughts chased from one side of his head to the other, knocking against the sides of his skull.

Back in the inn, he'd found Willie asleep and the cider all supped. Peter slumped down in the chair with his legs out in front of him. He inspected the sorry state of his boots, caked with mud from the field, stuck at the end of two – if he were to be kind to himself – beanpole legs. He'd closed his eyes, feeling the great heaviness of the night come upon him and then its miraculous release. So it was, and that decided it: the blind relief of sleep kept him fast where he was. Next thing he knew, he was startled awake by a kerfuffle at the door. A furious whispering, a shuffling, then a sharp rap. He looked about, no idea what hour of the clock it was. The knock came again. He would have to answer it, the window being too small to climb out of. His heart seemed to stop, as if it had heaved up its britches and was about to take off without him. *Shit*, the state of his boots. He kicked them off and threw them under the bed, kicking away the trail of dried mud with his feet. As Willie stirred, he gestured to the lad to keep hushed.

'Who's that there?' Peter flung back the door, so as to keep the surprise on his side. 'And what hour is this to come knocking?'

Ah, they did not expect that. At the door, the keeper of the inn and his wife, who had at the same moment the door was flung open elbowed her husband sharply in the ribs.

They blinked. 'It's past the hour of eleven,' said the woman as she gathered herself quick. Her tone left no doubt that, paying guest or not, he was a lazy lie-a-bed.

Though it was she who had spoken, Peter looked to the husband for reply. 'Well?'

The man was sore embarrassed, regretful already. No man – least of all a soldiering man, new back from the war – should be roused from his sleep in this manner. Hadn't the inn few enough paying guests without harrying away the two that they had? All of this Peter tried to convey in a grave expression which he held until the innkeeper reddened and looked down.

'Sorry to disturb your peace. . .' He straightened, perhaps skewered by his wife's furious glare. 'But there's been a to-do at the Hall.'

'A to-do?'

'A vile, unspeakable act,' interrupted the woman. 'With hares.' Her gaze snagged on Peter's unbuttoned shirt.

He saw her swallow and her attention fix on his shirt.

Only then did he think to look too. Across either side of it, where he had wiped the gore from his hands, were brown smears of dry blood.

'You wouldn't know nothing about it, would you?'

'No.'

'See,' said the man and turned to his wife, 'didn't I say as much?' He brought his hands to her shoulders and turned her away. He gave her a sharp nudge in the back to get her to move. 'Women,' he muttered and gave an apologetic shrug.

Peter wasn't sure who was more surprised at this development, him or the innkeeper's wife. What was he to make of it, the innkeeper's reluctance to press him further on the evident point of his shirt?

Clearly his wife thought the same. 'But—' she protested. But whatever was said next, Peter did not hear, it being lost in the clattering of clogs on the stairs. The innkeeper followed for a couple of steps, then turned back. He dropped his voice to a whisper.

'Whatever gripe it is you have with them at the Hall is your matter. But the constable has been called for. I thought it only fair to warn you.'

'The constable?'

'Johnson. A right bastard. Way he sees it, the law's only there for his own benefit and reward. He'll pull any wrongdoing over your head till it fits, snug as Wellington's hat.'

When Peter went to protest his innocence, the innkeeper hushed him. 'I don't want to hear it. He will be looking for anyone likely. Chances are, he'll come for you anyway, knowing what went on with the cottagers down Rookery

Hill. Afore you know it, you'll find yourself shipped off to Van Diemen's Land.'

'For three hares?'

'Yes, lad, for three fucking hares. And for the fright you gave them up at the house. Get yourself gone. And cover up that shirt before you do.'

Peter nodded his thanks.

'Aye, well,' said the man, 'I got no sympathy for them at the Hall either. But my wife thinks different. She'd flay me if she knew what I'd said.'

Peter could still feel her eyes on him. She knew what he'd been up to as surely as if she had stood by his side on the field and handed him the knife to skin the hares.

'Get yerselves to Tilbury and catch a corn barge up the river, is my advice. Should get you as far as the docks.'

Peter closed the door and rested back against it. The constable was serious business and not one he wanted to be close witness to. Down on his hands and knees by the bed he went and felt about blindly for his boots, dipping his hand in the piss pot as he did so.

'Ah, bugger it. Come on, Willie, let's be off.'

A good two, three hours of walking would get them to Tilbury, he reckoned. But wouldn't a constable expect them to head that way, out on the road? Thinking of it set a fear in him, loose and rattling. How could he know that the innkeeper's advice wasn't a trap? It was a risk he was not willing to take.

As they set off from the inn, and taking Willie up on his

back, he turned, not in the direction of the Tilbury road, but so that he faced the river. Down the track they went, past Oil Mill Farm and over the marsh beyond.

Shell Haven Creek, that's where they were headed, towards a memory of oyster smacks, by the dozen, leading him there as if by the nose. He could see them, clear as if it were yesterday, the boats as they tacked up the channel, tan sails fit to burst with the wind. As the memory sharpened, he saw how the boats came in from all directions, but on leaving they always tacked starboard, for London. Of course. *London.* Peter quickened his step.

On reaching the creek, he was relieved to see they had not missed the tide, but his relief was sharply curtailed by the sight that greeted him. Not the dozens of boats he had expected, nor even a single dozen. Two lay at anchor in the middle of the channel, but neither had sign of life aboard. On a third, moored closer in, he saw a boy on deck, sorting oysters into baskets and, there, heading towards shore in a small row boat, came a man. Peter raised a hand to get his attention. He helped steady the boat as it drew alongside and the man clambered out.

'Are you headed to London on the tide? We're after a lift that way if you are.'

The man eyed him, but said nothing.

'Here,' said Peter, as the man went to shoulder a sack of oysters on to his back. 'I'll pass the sacks down to you.'

The man was of few words but Peter knew he was being taken in even so.

'Used to come here as a lad,' Peter went on, needing to speak for the both of them and frustrated that his helpfulness had not softened the man any. 'Changed some since then. Full of boats it was, water near over the gunwales of some they were so weighed down.'

The man gave a sharp laugh. *Aye well*, that laugh said, *those days had long gone*. Finally, the man spoke: 'A shilling each and I'll fetch you up to London.'

'A shilling, the pair of us,' Peter countered. 'Look at the lad, there's nowt to him. He takes up no room.'

'A shilling for the each of you, and that's it.'

Thieving bastard. What was Peter but a fly, trapped under a glass, that this sly bugger had his hand clamped down on? He shook his head but held out his hand so they could agree it.

Once on board, the man, who it turned out was the skipper, cheered. He broke open the seal on a bottle of rum and passed it between them. Oh aye, all hale and hearty he was now, with the generosity of a man with two shillings in his pocket he'd never expected to have at breakfast. Rum wasn't a drink Peter cared for, but he took a long sup. He'd paid for it, hadn't he? He was desperate to be off, but the skipper was biding his time and would catch the tide on the flood. At least the lad was occupied. He was sitting on the foredeck with the ship's boy, who was showing him how to tie knots.

'Queer way of getting to London. Did you not fancy the road?' The skipper offered Peter the bottle again.

Let him root, thought Peter. 'After the rain we've had? Reckon there's more water on the highway than under your boat.'

True, Peter knew nothing of the state of the road towards London but the route to Hadleigh Cross had been badly bogged down.

The skipper's interest in the roads thereabouts being either satisfied, or limited, he turned his attention back to matters on which he could hold forth. *Oysters*. 'They aren't here the same as they was. Gets worse each year. Boats are going further to fetch them, some as far as Friesland and Scotland, after the oysters there. Bigger boats has the advantage, being more suited to offshore. There's a chance of fetching taters from St Malo way. But that's just for the season and been no call for it so far this year.'

'Taters? New kind of fish, is it?' Peter joked, only half listening by now.

The skipper grunted as the cheer of the rum wore off. 'We still get oysters up but they're not the same as they was. I never take the tiddly ones. Others aren't so fussy that way, they'll land whatever they lift. But even the fat ones that are keepers' – he gripped his stomach in both hands – 'they're not such good eating.'

'But you sell them?'

'Course I do. How can you know from the outside which is bad? What would you do? Chuck 'em back overboard? Now then, look. See how the tide is running? Make yerself useful and hand me that line.'

And then, with the mooring let go, they were under way – carried out of the creek and into the Thames. Mostly, they were quiet apart from the skipper telling him the names of the bends in the river as they tacked back and forth: *Gravesend Reach, Northfleet Hope, the Rands*. Peter nodded but the names were lost to him, soon as he heard them. What need to remember if he never did intend to come back this way?

Little else marked their journey upstream except for the gradual narrowing of the river. A great number of willows hid the view on both banks and with nothing else to note and wary of being drawn into idle chatter and its likely casual drift, Peter fell into silence, happy to be left with his thoughts.

It was only when the skipper pointed ahead to where the crumbling bank gave way to a wall of warehouses that Peter was jolted out of his reverie. 'East India Docks. And there, beyond it, the entrance to West India Docks, just coming into sight.'

The skipper nudged the boat in alongside a number of others that had been rafted out from the bank. Their two-shillings' worth was up. 'Off you get here and safe as you go.'

Peter and Willie clambered over the rail on to the fore-deck of the boat alongside. Over that foredeck they went and three more besides before their feet were finally on firm ground again. He raised a hand to bid the skipper farewell.

And then he and Willie weren't alone any more, but in a scrum of people, mostly on foot, some with carts, some riding ponies; and black polished carriages with bright gleaming horses and drivers in top hats, tilted this way and that. Blue, yellow, orange, green, like a rainbow had been tipped out of the sky and had dropped down upon them. And women wearing bonnets with feathers, and ribbons fluttering in the wind, and he and Willie in the middle of it, gawping, as though they'd been trussed to a

May pole. They'd made it: *London*. Peter's shoulders dropped with relief.

They followed the road along the river until they reached Billingsgate, just a short walk further on. What wasn't given away by the smell was given away by the noise. Peter had never heard a clamour like it: *Live eels! Crabs! Fresh Cod! Oysters-oh!*

Oysters might be scarce in Shell Haven Creek, but he'd never seen such fish as he did that afternoon. Fish in baskets, spilling over the top, carried away and more baskets filled after. Herrings in barrels, each barrel the size of a man. Barrel after barrel hoisted on to carts, stacked in pyramids and then driven off. Brown crabs, pitched in a boiler then fished out pink. Oysters, piled in grey heaps and those that weren't being sorted into baskets were shovelled into sacks. As fast as the men shovelling could go, more were offloaded and tipped out on top so that the heap never did grow less. And as one boat emptied out and moved off, another came in and on it went. It was the first fair day in weeks. Such a press of boats, desperate to offload their catch.

He watched lines of women gut fish the size of a man's arm: one swift movement – cut and twist, cut and twist – done in a blink, and the fish dropped into baskets to one side and the guts tossed away in the river. As they worked, the ground about them grew slick and slithery, everywhere crusted with fish scales, bright as frost.

He saw a boat flying the Spanish flag. He saw a French flag too, but it felt queer to see it.

They stayed so long at the market that the tide turned again and the sun had started to set. The sky blazed the deepest red he had ever seen and bled across the Thames. Every window looked hung with red curtains. Red gulls tilted above the rooftops, coming down to rest on the water. Peter closed his eyes, exhausted, but saw only red there too.

If those fucking hares were looking down on him from on high, he had no doubt they were dancing.

Charles

MIRACLES WERE GOD'S holy work. And he, Charles Whitlock, being God's humble servant, was but clay. But in a quiet moment, he felt a certain knowing: that his sermon had been heard and God had listened. That rain was a divine gift. Not just *a* divine gift, but *their* divine gift. God's benevolence. It wasn't pride Charles felt, but a great peace; a fathomless peace, as wide as it was deep.

He shut his ears to the nay-sayers, to those who said it would make no difference, that the ground was too hard and the rain had run off or was too late anyway for anything much of use to grow; that weeks of rain were needed for the earth to yield and be fruitful again. But, by Charles's reasoning, if the rain ran off, it had to run someplace. And wherever it ran to, then that land would surely revive.

In spite of this, all Seth would talk about was of leaving. Ohio. Ohio. Ohio. It inflated in Charles's mind like a giant gurning balloon. He had no pin long enough to pop it. The peace, the steadfastness he had felt began once more to ebb. Charles was at a loss to know what to do to staunch it.

And now when he visited Seth, he looked about the room with an urgency at what was there, as though at any moment it might be taken off him. An embroidery sample in a rough frame on the wall; a sturdy chest of drawers on hand-carved feet; a plain, three-legged stool, richly burnished from years of being sat on. The furnishings were simple, each object a treasure to him, so bad did he covet it. In his mind, he saw it all being loaded on a cart, tied up with rope and Seth and Laurel trundling it off. He saw himself, standing there, watching them go, nursing his hopes like a songbird in his hands only to find it had given up the last of its song.

Next time he visited, he found Laurel at the table, mixing water into rough meal.

'You're in a sorrowful state.' She gave him a sideways look; a frown deepened her brow. He longed to touch it, to smooth it away. A small kiss would do it.

He was sore lovesick, no denying. He watched her knead the meal into a dough. It stuck to the table, then to her fingers for the want of flour. In the end, she gave up and flattened it on a skillet with the heel of her hand and set it to the side of the fire to cook. She pulled away what she could of the dough still stuck to her fingers.

'Would you?' She nodded towards a pitcher of water.

He sloshed some into a bowl, mindful not to waste it. He clasped the jug to him while she washed and then poured small amounts into her cupped hands when she offered them to him.

Such a small thing to do, but that his days could be filled with the same.

'You are in a strange peculiar mood, Charles Whitlock. Has God deserted you?'

He knew she meant it as a tease, but he raised his eyes to hers without smiling.

'I want you to marry me, Laurel, that's what I want.'

Where the daughter was resistant, the father was not. Seth agreed theirs was not such a bad match and he would look forward to their union – on them reaching Ohio.

'Ohio?'

'Ohio.'

And he'd fixed Charles with the self-same hard look his daughter was in the habit of giving him.

Charles ought to have been happy. He'd got what he wanted, hadn't he? Instead, he went on his way, cussing under his breath. All he wanted was Laurel as his wife, the farm as his home and the congregation he had worked so hard for to gather round him and continue with him here. *In Vermont.*

The Dunbars could not be persuaded from leaving. They had gotten land in Upper New York State and would take their chances with that. After that, Charles was in no certain hurry to reach the Spaldings on the next farm over, to restate arguments he'd already failed to find a sympathetic ear for. So he let his pony clop along at her own pace and pull her head down to graze as she went. It made for slow progress, it being mostly dry grass and thistles.

It was as he expected. The Spaldings provided no kinder audience for his pleading.

'If the Israelites made it to Egypt, I can't see why we can't make it to Ohio,' was Teddy Spalding's certain opinion on the matter. Of the arguments Charles had expected to find arrayed against him, the Israelites were not one of them.

Teddy had taken on the farm after the death of his father. Six years had passed since then. Unlike Seth and Laurel, Teddy had the help of his siblings: two brothers and their wives. But with all those hands had come other problems besides that Charles had not foreseen.

'It's a heavy responsibility. All those mouths to feed.' It was a rare admission of Teddy's. In the years they'd known each other, he'd never had cause to be so frank with Charles.

'It's one of the best farms around, Teddy.' Charles knew that Teddy was not a man to be wooed with false praise but he meant it, and he hoped to appeal to whatever fond memory Teddy might still have of the farm. But his opinion was met with silence. *Think, Charles, think*, but the more he did, the more his thoughts scattered.

'Tell me . . .' He looked up to make sure he had Teddy's attention. 'Would your father have wanted you to go?'

He saw Teddy slump under the weight of his father's memory. Teddy blew out his cheeks. 'Well, no. No, I think not.'

'Your father knew some lean years, did he not?'

'He did some at that.'

'And he got through them?' That made Teddy flinch, but Charles was unrepentant. He would wait as long as it took for Teddy to reply.

'He did,' Teddy said at last.

'And what would your father think to your selling up on that? On all he went through? To move to Ohio?'

Teddy shifted uncomfortably. Charles felt the pull of the hook, as of a trout in the stream.

'Would you get his approval on it?'

Teddy brought one hand to his brow. Charles's level gaze was waiting to catch his as he looked up.

'No. I would not.'

Charles raised his hands as though the answer were there should Teddy want it. No need to appeal to scripture, all he'd had to do was to remind him of a son's duty to his father. Even so, Teddy seemed not yet convinced.

Time to try a different tack. 'I do have my own news. Laurel and I are to be wed.'

'You are?' If Teddy's surprise was evident, he swallowed it quick. 'Well, there's news indeed.'

'Commitment and hope, Teddy. Commitment and hope. We need to remember that in hard times.'

No mention need be made of Seth only agreeing to their union on condition Charles moved to Ohio. An omission was an omission. It was not a lie.

By now, Teddy looked full chastened. 'Perhaps I've been rash.'

A small shudder ran through Charles – a mixture of triumph and relief. For better, for worse, we are all our father's sons, he thought as he bade Teddy farewell. He tried not to think of his daddy as he went out and what that made him. Charles turned his pony back in the direction he had come. 'Giddy-up.' He kicked his heels into the pony's flanks to get her to move. Belly full of thistles or no, he had places he needed to get to. Ohio? No one was going to Ohio or any other place for that matter. If he could change Teddy Spalding's mind, then he could change Seth's too.

It was not the news Seth expected. 'Well, well,' he said. 'Well, well.'

'I'm not much of a farmer, but let me come work for you. You tell me what to do and I'll do it. Another pair of hands must surely help.' Charles held out his hands to show he meant what he said sincerely.

He saw Laurel take a look at him and shake her head. And he saw her every memory of him standing, looking back at him too: her with the hoe in her hand, him chit-chatting away.

He knew it wasn't what she minded that mattered, but what Seth thought. But Seth wasn't to be hurried and it was some time before he could be parted from his opinion, which seemed held fast in his fist.

'Help sure would be appreciated.'

'*Daddy*—' Laurel shot Charles a furious look.

Seth held up his hand to quieten her. 'If the Spaldings are prepared to see the season out then so can we. Let's see where we are at the harvest . . .'

'No.' Laurel spun away and slumped on a stool.

'Now then hush. It's decided. Ohio ain't going nowhere.' Seth turned to Charles. 'And that set me thinking further. If you're to help, you will need to live here. But I don't want gossip. This needs a proper arrangement behind it. You two will need to be wed just as soon as you can.'

Seth might as well have kicked Laurel for the yelp she let out. Charles looked at his feet, lest the shame he felt show itself more.

Scant two weeks later and they were wed: 8 June. A date forevermore carved into his heart. The ceremony was short and everyone remarked how much better Seth looked, a wedding being much needed by everyone.

Charles kissed Laurel on the cheek, relieved she would let him do that. And even if she did take her hand from his as soon as she could, he knew in time she would come round. But if he hoped that that night might have been time soon enough, he was sore mistaken.

'You got what you want, now let me be.' Laurel turned from him, tucking the sheet tight between them, so that he was presented with the curve of her spine.

But in the night, she drew closer, as did he to her, both of them stricken with cold. He brought one arm in under the covers, then the other. He inched the covers up to his chin, then to his nose. And when she gave a sudden violent shiver, he whispered, 'Are you cold too?'

He felt her nod. 'Yes.'

He sat up, swung his legs out of bed, stumbled to the dresser, goosebumps rising all over him.

'Bottom drawer, is the winter quilt,' said Laurel in an urgent whisper.

He brought the quilt back to the bed and was under the covers again, and oh the relief to have the weight of it on him. He sat up again as he remembered Seth.

'Your father . . .'

Laurel told him where a second coverlet could be found and he took it through.

'Thank you,' she said as he returned and clambered back in beside her.

'Uh-huh.' He drew close to her back, one shy arm over her, before sleep fell upon him hard and fast once more.

As he blinked awake in the morning, he came aware of the quilt over him. Its deep warmth comforted him back to dozing until, part dream, part memory, it pulled him to the surface once again and he remembered how he had fetched it in the night. He gave a yawn, surprised to see a cloud of breath as he did. Cold pressed against his cheeks. His eyes stung and he blinked. From where he lay, he could see out through the window. At least, he should've been able to. He cocked his head and frowned. Across the surface of the glass – oddly shrouded now that he noticed it – stretched a fan of ice.

A strange quiet hung in the air. Not the peace of a summer morning on waking before dawn, but the deep, hard hush of winter when every bird is stunned into silence. Beside him, the bed was cold too. Laurel had gone from his side.

1815

Henry

BANDAGES, SPLINTS, SUGAR of lead – woefully inadequate and all used up in hours. He'd brought what he could of the ship's medical supplies. His immediate regret was that he had not brought more. But the supplies they had set out with from Makassar were barely sufficient to treat other than a portion of the crew in a combat situation. He was, after all, only one man, one pair of hands. A limit, therefore, to the number of limbs he might set in an hour, to the wounds he might cauterise and bandage. It all came down to a simple mathematical sum; a rational amount. A ration, then. He had never questioned it before.

'A wretched state of affairs,' said the captain as he surveyed those waiting to be seen. Many were suffering festering wounds or the effects of ash inhalation. All were starving.

'You have what you need?'

'I hardly think—'

'You must do what you can.'

The captain turned away, neither wanting nor waiting for Henry to elaborate. His way of command was to listen with barely contained patience to the first few words of whatever was being said before dismissing or accepting it, then turning to the next matter, then the next and the next.

Although Bima had escaped the direct impact of the

eruption it had been considerably damaged by the ash fall.
Survivors from across the peninsula had trudged in the
town's direction, desperate for help.

Henry had to remind himself, lest despair overcome him,
that he was as prepared as he could be; that he could not
have foreseen such a catastrophe, neither the scale of it nor
its sheer unending misery. But as the day wore on and his
supplies ran out, and still people came to him in desperate
need, he grew first to question then to despise his excuses.

They'd sailed south expecting pirates? He shook his head
at the idiocy of it. How stupid, how *infantile* that assumption
now appeared. No intelligence had suggested pirates
anywhere around. An assumption – one that he, Henry
Hogg, might have challenged, but had not. Could he truly
say therefore that he was without blame? Any fool might
suppose the source of the explosions as natural. A volcano.
Of course a volcano. A child could have reached that
conclusion. Volcanos everywhere in this part of the world.
If they had thought more, had used some plain common
sense, they might have set sail better supplied: not just with
medicine, but food and drinking water too. Instead, here
they were, with strictly limited sufficiency of any such item
and no useful means to relieve the suffering of those who
waited for his attention.

He'd discarded his small bundle of surgical implements
almost immediately. Their bright varnished handles, blades
yet unblemished, were as much use as a Chippendale *chaise*
in this foul clearing – chosen for being the least foul of
foul places around for the purposes of consultation and
surgery. What he needed, that most basic and necessary
of supplies: *water*, to rinse ash from the wounds so he could

at least inspect them, was mostly being kept for drinking. This infernal ash stuck to everything. And the heat, the heat. Like being tossed in a cauldron. It wasn't just hellish. It was hell.

'Here.' Henry beckoned to Alfie, the ship's boy who had been assisting him. 'Hold this.'

He passed a basin to the boy and dabbed a rag in the grey water then turned to the young woman before him and the infant she had on her lap. 'I'm sorry.'

The woman stared at him without blinking. He dropped his eye from hers, appalled by the trust she had placed in him. 'Hold the child, tight as you can.' He made as if he had hold of the child and brought his arms into him to show how she should hold the infant to her, one hand at the head, the other under its bottom. He tried not to think on what they had been through, their suffering, pressed as he was into the moment by the urgency of the child's condition.

As the woman drew her baby to her, he touched the rag to the wound. Such a howl came from the child, he pulled away as though he too had been scalded.

'I'm sorry, so sorry.' He touched the cloth to the wound again in quick, soft dabs, and hoped the woman did not notice how his hand shook. He did his best to shut his ears to the infant's screams. Little by little, the ash lifted away, exposing livid red flesh beneath. It needed a barrier ointment of wax and oil, bandaging with soft lint to exclude air and provide comfort, and for all of it to be soaked in a tincture of sugar of lead so it would cool. Then for it to be kept that way until the wound had healed.

But his supply of bandages was completely depleted. He

had neither salve nor ointment and no means of covering the wound. There was nothing he could do to alleviate the child's suffering. He dropped the rag into the bowl and shooed Alfie away with his hand.

And though no word could pass between them, he saw the woman understood. Two tears tipped from her eyes. As she stood up and turned to go, an elderly man took her place. A burn ran the length of his left side, where his arm was fixed in a scalded hook. Behind him stretched a ragged line of thirty of forty more souls, huddled and silent for the most part. From among them came the pitiful wails of children.

In all his years of training, he never thought he'd be presented with anything like this. The hours he'd spent sitting on the hard bench at Great Windmill School in London, under the direction of William Hunter, then Charles Bell, his bottom grown as numb as his attention. The specimens that would be passed around, marvelled at and discussed. The drawings made from wax models, to train hand and eye – learning by handling, by seeing, by discussion. He'd made a particularly good copy of a femur, snugly located in its hip socket, and could still feel the warm flush of Hunter's approval on him as the drawing was held aloft for all to appreciate. If nothing else, he was a remarkably adept illustrator, it seemed, at least in his ability to copy what was before him. Another – this time a drawing of the nervous system of a leech – had been similarly admired. If asked to reproduce it now, he was certain he would still be able to make a fair copy. The training was supposed to provide insight, *in sight*, a way to see into. But, and he suspected it was the same for many seated on the bench with him, their knowledge seemed stuck resolutely to the surface of the paper and went no deeper. For a pencil was not a scalpel. And paper was not skin.

He lifted fragments of cloth from the edge of another wound and grimaced. He should have accepted his limits and stuck with illustration instead.

That night, he fell into sleep as if pitched into a cave. He felt himself falling, falling, only shuddering awake to a hand on his shoulder, shaking him.

'Dr Hogg, Dr Hogg . . .'

Henry reached for his glasses, an automatic gesture with little purpose, it being so dark.

Alfie brought a candle up to Henry's face and he shielded his eyes against it.

'The Rajah is here.'

'The Rajah?'

'Of Saugur. Captain sent for me to fetch you.'

Henry levered himself up from the ground and stumbled after the boy, bewildered, like a moth pitching after a candle's flame. Beyond the feeble light of the candle's halo, bobbing ahead of him, darkness pressed in on all sides.

Within a short distance, he and Alfie found themselves in another small clearing, where the captain had established his accommodation: little more than a rough patch of ground and a straw mat salvaged from God knows where. Several wooden cases, emptied of their supplies and upended on their sides, served as seating. The captain was seated on one crate and a man, whom Henry took to be the Rajah, was seated on another. On the mat lay a young girl. Two women knelt nearby.

'This is our doctor,' said the captain, as Henry arrived.

Henry bowed. 'Your Excellency.'

The Rajah turned to Henry, his mouth set in a grim line. He covered his eyes with one hand. 'My daughter. I ask for your help.'

Henry was struck by the Rajah's English. He should not, he knew, be surprised. He knew from the captain that the Rajah spoke not only English but Dutch and French too. He had need to. These islands had passed between many avaricious hands in recent years.

Henry had nothing with him. Nothing other than who he was. Never had he felt so exposed. He went over to where the girl lay and knelt down by her. He eased the blanket down. A blessed relief to see she was not burned, but a shock to see how emaciated she was. Her skin felt clammy to the touch; a sour smell of diarrhoea hung about her. The women by her side had the drawn watchfulness of those who knew death was near.

'Her mother and aunt,' explained the Rajah when he saw Henry look.

The women watched as Henry felt for a pulse. 'How old is she?'

'Five,' replied the Rajah.

'Has she eaten?' As soon as Henry said it, he realised how foolish his question was.

The Rajah swept an arm out to one side, barely able to contain his contempt. 'Eaten? What do you suggest she eats? Papaya stalks?'

'Forgive me.' He lifted his hand away. It was no use.

There was nothing he could do. 'Perhaps she will take some water.'

The Rajah's eye came to rest on the barrels they had brought with them from the ship and which were guarded by the crew. 'You have water?'

'Yes.' The admission, if not reluctant, was cautious. The captain beckoned to a guard and whispered an instruction to him. Water was fetched in a cup and shared between the Rajah and his family, but the child was beyond taking any.

The captain reached in a satchel by his side and brought out a notebook. 'I have a duty to account for events in our territories. Will you tell me what happened? You were witness to it?'

'*Witness?*' The Rajah's hand trembled as he held out the cup for more water.

The captain nodded his assent for more to be brought, then sat poised, ready to make notes. When nothing was said he prompted again: 'Yes. Timing, duration, such forth.'

The Rajah cradled the cup in his hands. 'Then tell your King this. It is gone. All of it, gone.'

'The volcano?'

The Rajah looked up. 'No. My people.'

The captain scribbled a note. 'The eruption – could you be more specific? How did it begin? When?' He shot Henry an anxious look but there was something in his manner, a narrowing of his eyes, that suggested irritation.

'The mountain had made complaints for a while. But none expected it. Not this. It was evening, when three columns of flame burst from the mountain. *Boom!*'

The captain jolted as the Rajah threw his arms in the air.

'Each column went up to a very great height then joined in the air in a terrible confusion. The whole of the mountain next to Saugur came down, running like water in every direction, the sky all fire. Furious, raging. Then darkness . . .'

The captain paused to dip his quill in the ink. 'Darkness? Had night fallen by now?'

The Rajah shook his head. 'No. A darkness of stones. Very thick at Saugur – large as two fists, hammering down, they beat everything flat. Papaya, plantain, all gone. Then smaller stones, smaller, then ashes, then the wind. Such a violent wind. It blew down nearly every house in our village, carrying the tops and light parts away with it. In the part of Saugur closest to Tambora everything was carried away. It tore up our trees by their roots, carried them into the air together with men, houses, cattle, anything within in its reach.'

'That accounts for the immense amount of timber we saw floating at sea.' The captain caught Henry's eye once again. They both knew they had seen worse.

'And the sea,' continued the Rajah, 'it rose very much higher. Higher than ever before. All the rice lands in Saugur, completely destroyed – houses, everything, drowned.'

'This continued until when?'

'Until the morning; explosions all the next day too.'

'And survivors? How many do you know of?'

'Tempo, with about forty villagers, is the only village remaining on Tambora. No house is left in Precate.'

'Forty? How many inhabitants were there before?'

'In Tambora and Precate? Twelve thousand. More.'

'And, all dead?'

The Rajah slumped. He covered his face with his hands.
'Yes.'

The captain put down his quill, stunned finally by this.
'A shocking event. Most, most shocking. Unlike any I have
had to account for before. Your testimony has been helpful.
Thank you. I am sorry for your people, for the loss . . .'

At this, the Rajah stood up. He went over to the captain
and took his hands in his, clasping them tight. 'Please, the
children, take them with you.'

As the captain pulled away, the Rajah tightened his grip.
'The children. How can they survive? You see how
everything is poisoned. Take them. I beg you.'

'I cannot—'

'No one else. The children, that is all.'

The captain's notebook tumbled from his lap as he struggled to free his hands from the Rajah's grasp. 'No. No. I
simply cannot.'

'No?'

'On our return to Makassar, I shall request a supply ship
is dispatched. As a matter of urgency.'

Nothing was said then. Such a journey would take ten
days, at least.

'We cannot live where nothing grows.'

'A supply ship, as I said.'

The captain picked up his notebook and dusted it off,
but did not note anything further. He walked over to where
the water barrels were stacked and passed an order to the
men on guard. They straightened their shoulders and
brought their hands to rest on the hilt of their swords,
ready to draw if commanded to.

* * *

The Rajah's daughter died in the night. The little girl wasn't his to grieve but Henry felt the hood of despair pull over him even so.

The following morning, with his record of the eruption completed, the captain gave orders for them to leave and ordered half the water be left behind.

'Let no one accuse me of not being a reasonable man,' he said, as the remaining barrels were shouldered back to the ship by the crew.

1816

Sarah

MY LIFE WEREN'T all tiptoeing about the threshing machine at Cook's place, hands in my apron pockets like I had the answers to Thomas's questions stuffed in there, tight in my fists, case they had the idea of hopping out and scarpering off. Answers like that had a holler to them and no doubt about it. Would bellow their way cross the yard straight into mutton chops's ears.

With mutton chops about, I had to be careful. Hard to know what kind of careful I needed to be, or what the usual way for me to be was. The more usual I tried to make myself, the more odd-ways I seemed. Bumping into all and every and tripping over my own feet after.

Mutton chops had took to lolling at the midden door, watching me a while, until beside bored with hisself, off he'd skulk. Never a word.

Until, one day, 'Susan,' he said, his voice sneaking out wearisome, like a dry tongue bristling up my arms and the back of my neck.

'What?' I said.

His eyes had a hard cold shine to them. '*What?* One of these days I shall learn you some manners.' He looked at me like I were a fluffed-up sparrow and he were the cat. 'Reverend Vachell and his wife will be paying us a visit this afternoon. You're to serve tea.'

As I made no answer to that, on he went, 'You know the good reverend?'

I gave a quick nod. 'I do.'

He drew back to consider me some more. 'Course you do. Obvious to me you're a good church girl . . .'

A fierce hot red burst across my cheeks. Had word got to him about me refusing the soup? But no one I knew had time for Reverend Vachell, or his wife, or went within a mile of any pew of his, not in Littleport, nor any place else. Most knew of him not because of the church, but because he was magistrate and the poor relief was his doing too. Had hold of all of our miseries together, he did.

Mutton chops gave a little snicker. 'Not a drinking girl. Not a rowdy girl . . .'

I went back to sweeping, hard as I could, till I had the straw bundled into a mound and a pile of it had fetched up at his feet and I could shift it no further. Would have swept him out of the door with it too, if I could.

'Not a girl given to singing, or bawdy songs.'

I stopped.

'Go to the Globe often, do you?' He rested one arm against the door frame. 'Now we all got to drink. But too much gets some folk fired up, resentful.'

'What gets folk resentful?'

'Ale, that's what. Have you not noticed? How folk get resentful?'

All I had to do was say no, but my breath had bundled up in my throat and was stuck there.

He waited for my answer, watching a feather drift down from the rafters while he did. 'You'd let me know, wouldn't you? There's all kinds of trouble about. Seems that Ludd is not done running about in his skirts just yet.' He spat on the ground and pulled at the neckerchief around his neck to slacken it off. 'A man in a skirt. Goes against all that is natural. A man like that is deserving of all that he gets.'

'Don't know nothing about a man in a skirt. Or songs and singing.' I said, as my voice found me at last. And if I did, I'd give a cheer for him and his petticoats and mutton chops'd be the last person I'd tell.

'A ruckus at Benton's place. The dairy broken into and several of his best cheese stolen. Not heard nothing about that either?'

'No.'

Though he must've heard me, he weren't listening, because then he said, 'Barns set afire, ploughs tossed into ditches. Threshers smashed to splinters. Know what that would mean for a farm like this?' He kept his level gaze on me and frowned when I shrugged. 'We'd be hard pressed to make it pay, that's what. How much is it we pay you, Susan?'

'A penny a day.'

'A penny a day?' Way he said it, you'd have thought that penny were made of gold. A slow smile snagged in his whiskers. 'I can see you think you're worth more than that.' His eye went down over me and up. 'But you know what's worse than a penny a day?'

Oh, I knew well enough, but I shook my head.

'No penny at all. No penny today. Nor the day after. Nor the day after that. That's what folk need to remember when they're singing their songs. Gets forgot pretty easy, how farmer Cook's pennies and shillings keep a good many off of the parish. You've seen what it's like in the mornings.

Them that come here from all parts around looking for work. Not enough work for everyone, is there? You've seen that. Mr Cook's got plenty folk to choose from. Plenty, plenty. An ample sufficiency, in fact. It's my good word for you makes sure you get picked every day. Makes you special. Had you not thought on that?'

That I had not. The thought fell in a shudder to my feet.

'But I got no time for troublemakers, *Sarah*.' He tapped the side of his nose and gave me a wink. And with that, he took the broom from me, rested his hand flat on the top of it, and toppled it over in the shit.

As was said, the Reverend Vachell and his wife arrived later by pony. He, like a sack of potatoes made to sit upright in the saddle; she, like a turkey tied to the pony's back. Mairster Cook had us line up by the gate and we had to drop curtsies or take our hats off and bow as they made their way by.

Once in the yard and clambered off, Reverend Vachell set his wig square. A box got carried over so that Mrs Vachell could clamber off too but we had to look at our feet while she did. After I tied up the ponies, I went to the scullery where I was to help. A strange thing to behold, how different a life could be. From one room into another and then a third. Coats on hooks, boots in pairs lined up underneath, like the men that had been stood in them had been vanished away. It wasn't the coats and boots, nor the great number of copper pans up on the shelf that took me, but the floor. Planks of wood laid flat, one to another, so the ground underneath was covered. Wood so smooth there was no risk of a splinter in my toe. Every step announced the sound of my feet. Mutton chops's shoes on it made for a sore creaking din. I was made to wash my hands and placed in a clean apron. Even so, what was I but a muddy clod served up neat on a plate?

Seemed Mairster Cook had china cups after all, which I fetched out of the dresser and rubbed at with a cloth to take off the dust. Why they'd been made so the cups rattled on their saucers when I carried them, I did not know. Mrs Vachell took a hard look at me, but if she remembered the soup, she minded that matter to herself.

When I went to pass a cup to Reverend Vachell, he drew back like a bee had come to sting him.

'Not like that.' Mrs Vachell shooed me off with her hand. 'On the table. Cups go on the table.'

I took the cup off of the reverend again, but he had it gripped tighter than the Bible at his own funeral and tea sloshed everywhere.

Mrs Vachell gave me a scolding look. She leaned in to Mairster Cook. 'You really should get a girl in from Cambridge. A Cambridge girl would know what to do.'

'Good advice. I should heed it,' he said. 'There's not much to be done with dumb stock.'

That made them laugh, it did, but I ignored it. A boggart was a boggart, even them dressed in fancy fa-lals.

'You're Hobbs's daughter, are you not?' said Reverend Vachell. 'Remind me what became of your father.'

'He got kicked by an 'oss.'

'Ah, yes. I remember. Left completely without capacity for a good while.'

Had he come here so as to try out his long words on me? I pointed to the cup. 'There's your tea, Reverend Vachell.'

'A nasty injury too, if I remember—'

Clear to me he did not.

'He got knocked down by Benton's stallion and trampled on bad. He never did recover. Ended up dead because of it.'

The reverend sipped his tea. 'Well, a shame. A waste of a man. What was it he did?'

'Harvested sedge. And laboured for Benton. Hand threshing in the winter. He was good with 'osses, best there was for calming any jiggety mare. He—'

'*Farmer* Benton, that is to you,' Mairster Cook interrupted, narrowing his eyes.

Mrs Vachell pointed her pointy nose my ways. 'Was he not able to work afterwards? Not even at some small task?'

What was meant by that? He was like a sack of broken-up brick after. 'Shelling peas?' Hadn't meant to say it, but there it was said.

She laughed, but her laugh was all prickles; how a thistle would laugh if it could. 'No. No. I'd have thought there was something he might do, *sitting down*.' She sipped her tea as she considered me.

I looked at her. She was the one sat down.

'Ah, I remember you now. You're the one who is fussy about soup.' She went to touch my arm but drew back. 'Some are deserving of relief, others are not. Most of this parish, even those unfortunately scarred by war, labour their complaint a little too loudly. They must put the horrors of the past behind them. They can and should work. Most are able but present with all manner of dropsical complaint. Workshy, is all. Loitering about.'

All this she addressed to me and the teapot, like we were the worst loiterers of all.

The reverend took another sip of tea. 'Indeed. God does not care for a lazy wretch.'

'Who shall teach them that but you, dear?' said Mrs Vachell.

Mairster Cook looked less pleased. He hooked his thumbs into his waistcoat pockets. 'I am certain the reverend does do his best. While one must keep in mind the need to be sympathetic, one must also be on one's guard so as not to be played for a fool and the poor rate set so as not to encourage indolence. Set it too high and what incentive is there to anything? Why work? Who would want to? A steady supply of labour, as required, is essential to the modern farming economy.'

'You touch on a profound truth,' said the reverend. 'A man must not only be eager to work, but to take such work as is there. I mean, whatever next? I will only work on Tuesdays in July?'

'But first I should like apple pie for breakfast,' said Mrs Vachell in a queer, high voice.

'Those that can work, must.'

At this, Mairster Cook lifted his cup to the reverend's, same as they were toasting the King.

'So how goes the season?' asked the reverend.

Mairster Cook blew out his cheeks. He shook his head. 'A slow start. There's time yet for it to come right, but if it continues this way . . .'

'You have made such great improvements. I've heard
excellent reports. That thresher of yours—'

'A thresher's no use if there's no grain in the field to be
threshed.'

The only sound then was the supping of tea. They had
their wood floors and china cups; stables full of ponies. It
all went their way and yet from how they put it, they had
the worst of all. Weren't right to say that folk didn't want
work, it was Cook and Benton and the rest of them that
decided when and if we could work and what for. But any
word of that and it would be the last of me standing there
with the teapot.

I remembered the ashes that had got washed away. It
weren't the thresher I was worried about. If nothing grew,
there'd be no harvest. No pennies in anyone's pocket. 'What'll
get the grain to grow then?' I asked, so caught up in my
thoughts I was and thinking they had no machine for that.

The reverend turned to me sharp, torn between chiding
and putting me right. 'What'll get the grain to grow?' Way
he said it, was plain no answer was expected off me. 'God
will, stupid girl. God will.'

After some talk about the desirability of Sunday school
for heathens such as me, their tattling turned to the Princess
Charlotte's wedding.

'Ten thousand pounds for the dress! It's stitched all over
with silver thread. A wonder she can stand in it . . .'

I cradled the teapot. I thought of Benton's plough and
Cook's thresher and how Thomas and the others had no
work. What Cook and the reverend thought right and fair
were made to blunt a bright edge, not sharpen it – folk
tossed away like old shovels into the ditch.

'Oh, I am partial to a little something sweet with my tea.' Mrs Vachell cast her eye around the room as though I'd a cake hid high up on a shelf. 'Don't you cook, girl?' she asked as her attention returned to me, like the glum lack of cake were my doing.

'I can cook.'

'You can?'

'Yes.' I went to clear up the cups, stacking them under my chin.

'And what is it you cook?'

'Oh,' I said, as I backed away, the cups in danger of toppling. 'Roast goose.'

And with that, I turned, but not before I saw her mouth drop.

Wasn't that I wanted to go to the Globe again, not with mutton chops's warning buzzing about my ears like a horsefly. The more I tried to bat it away, the more it pestered me. But I made myself go. I had to. Thomas would be after news of the thresher and it was only right to tell him what mutton chops had said.

When I got there, I found him and Tessie already seated and mole catcher George had joined them too. George worked all the farms around because moles liked nothing better than new drained land. Downham Tom was there and other folk I recognised from when I worked at Benton's farm. Ten of us, p'rhaps, in all, but when next I looked, there were twenty or more. After that I gave up counting. I was the only one from Cook's farm and that rested heavy on me.

I told Thomas the thresher needed horses to shift it, but six men maybe might roll it out the barn. What they'd do with it then, I couldn't imagine.

'When's Cook at home?' asked Thomas.

'Most days. Excepting when he goes to Ely market or Cambridge.'

'Who else lives in?'

'Just mutton chops does.'

'Mutton chops?'

'His name's Pearson. And he knows summat's up.'

'Such as?'

'Us. Being here—'

'Where else we supposed to go to get a sup to drink?'

'No law against it as yet,' George butted in. 'But give 'em time.'

'And he knows about us.'

'Knows what?'

'About us singing songs.' Sounded daft now, but it had given me a horrible feeling when mutton chops had said it. Same feeling that swilled about in me now.

'No law against that either,' said Thomas.

'Pearson can fuck off,' said George. 'We can sing what we like. When we like.'

'He's in with that bastard Robert Beville and the Bedford Level lot. They've been fixing up signs – no digging of turves or fishing allowed.'

Thomas turned back to me. 'Owt else?'

I shook my head. I didn't know what more to say. Sounded like nothing now.

'What you want to know about the thresher for?' I asked.

'What do you think what for? So we can smash it!' A

cheer went up as George lifted his cudgel in the air. He might have been stunted up shorter than me but that weren't no hindrance to him.

'It's made of grut thick planks! That cudgel won't even dint it.'

'We'll tip it over then.' George folded his arms as if that settled it. He had a stubborn set to him, same as a mole determined to make an acre of a half-acre field.

'And they'll just set it the right way up again,' I said straight back.

'So? We'll go up there one night and *steal* it off him,' he said, making it sound as if I were the thick plank. 'You're scared, is all.'

I was scared, it were true. There was plenty in my life I didn't care for, but I had never reckoned with breaking summat to bits. Not a thresher, leastways.

'If we get the thresher, where'll we take it to?' asked Tessie, catching on to my way of thinking. 'They'll have us for certain if we're caught.'

A right hush at this. Every track for miles round was soft mud just waiting for any daft plan to sink up to its axles in. Not liking that contraption was one thing, but getting rid of it were another. Though the room was now jam full, no one seemed to have thought of that. It were like a big hole had opened up and any plan we had was swallowed up into it.

'I've summat more I want to say.'

'Ah, shut it,' said George. 'No one wants to know.'

'Let her speak.' Downham Tom held out his hand, to get me to stand.

I pushed the stool back and got to my feet. All I had to

do was say what I'd heard straight, but my voice had took fright.

'What?' George cupped his hand to his ear. 'Can't hear yer.'

'Even if we took Cook's thresher off him it'll not change nothing.'

Well, the ceiling near lifted off over my head, such was the clammer. So I told them what had got said. That without a good crop, the thresher was good as useless.

'Boo bloody hoo,' said George. 'Should've thought of that before he spent his coin on it, shouldn't he?'

'It's not just the thresher. It's Cook and Benton and all the rest of the farmers round these parts. And the Bedford lot for stopping us from fishing and digging our turves. And the reverend. The lot of them. What Cook pays us for our work. What the reverend says we get when we can't. It's them keeps us poor.' I looked at my feet and the ground they was stood on. Same hard trampled dirt as at home. Dirt poor, that's what I was. What we all were. 'It's not right. And it's not fair.'

As I sat down, Thomas got to his feet. 'The farmers says they is suffering. Aye, well, some of them are tenanted to bigger rogues than themselves so are in a pinch too, there's no denying. Has that made them understanding of our plight? It has not. Families hoofed out on their ear along the Ten Mile Bank, not just here but in Hilgay and at Downham and what was done to stop it? Nothing. They took away our means so we could farm for ourselves and now we must work for them instead. We work for scraps because we've no choice. And they know it. Brute animals, that's what they think we are, to be treated any way they want. We'll show them different. We want higher wages—'

'Cheaper bread!'

Thomas leapt on to the table and clenched a fist in the air. 'Higher wages and the price of bread cheaper!'

'Higher wages and the price of bread cheaper!'

All our voices were as one as we jumped to our feet. A tankard got banged down and another and we were hammering our hands on the tables and stamping our feet, not caring if the windows rattled loose from their frames. Let the reverend walk by or Mairster Cook or mutton chops for that matter. Let them hear and damn the lot of them.

At the night's end a hat got passed round for the benefit of those in perilous need and to protect us in the time ahead.

I took out my penny and thought of the work in it. Oh, for the thread that held up Princess Charlotte's hem. Just one silver thread would see us right. I gave the coin a kiss and dropped it in the hat.

John

JOHN SAW ABRAM at the bottom of the garden, deep in discussion with Silas the gardener, and made his way down the path to them. At his approach, Silas looked up. 'Afternoon, John.'

'Afternoon, Silas.' John nodded to Abram. 'Abram.'

'John. I'm instructing Silas on readying the garden for the sale.'

It seemed an unreasonable haste so close after the funeral of their father, but there was sense in it. John knew Abram was not given to nostalgia or romance. He nodded his acknowledgement and took a polite step back so Abram and Silas could conclude their discussion. With no need to include him, he heard their voices drop to a murmur.

John wandered about the garden while they talked. A few bedraggled bluebells had pushed through along the westernmost edge, but other than that the garden was devoid of spring flowers. The fruit trees were only just coming into bud, the buds nipped tight as if not yet decided whether to open or not. Clods that would have been turned over weeks before in preparation for spring planting remained untilled and barren. That morning, first thing, looking out from his bedroom window, he had noticed a shimmer of frost across them. The garden had seemed in mourning, in quiet despair at its future.

'Good. That's that done.' Abram came up by his side with a brisk, businesslike manner that announced that matters had been discussed and decisions made. 'Shall we go indoors?'

John allowed himself to be steered towards the house as though he were no more than a visitor, to be shown through to the lounge where he should have the good patience to wait until Abram had tidied himself and Biddy the maid had fetched tea for them both.

On one wall hung two pictures of the garden, which John had painted for his mother. He must ask Abram if he could have them. Damn it, he thought. He would do no such thing. He stood up and went over to the paintings and lifted them from their hooks. They were his.

At dinner, Abram indicated that John should sit at the head of the table. Abram sat to his left.

They ate their soup in silence, with only the tick of the clock on the mantel for company. Biddy cleared the dishes and brought beef with boiled potatoes and gravy. The potatoes had a yellow-grey tinge to them and smelled of the sacking they had been stored in for months. John was well used to such stale fare in London, but here? How he had hoped for fresh-lifted, new potatoes with butter and a sprinkling of mint. His heart sank.

'So, what's next?'

The suddenness of Abram's question caught John off guard and he started, like a child caught daydreaming, unable, briefly, to reply. 'I'll return to London.'

Abram closed his eyes. 'Well, yes, I expected that. But in London. What's next for you *in London*?'

'Continue as I am, what else?'

John saw Abram's eyes flicker beneath his eyelids. He felt his brother's exasperation keenly upon him.

'I am trying my damned hardest, you know, Abram. Despite what you may think, I have not enjoyed generous support these past years. Nor would I expect to.' He lifted one hand, before Abram could object. He would not have his brother continue with the lecture his father had left unfinished.

At this, he saw his brother's shoulders go down. Grief weighed upon him too.

'I know that, John.' Abram reached over and rested his hand on John's shoulder, an uneasy truce established between them for now.

'After London, I'll be in Colchester. I have a commission in Wivenhoe at the Rebows, which will keep me there for several weeks. After that, I'd like to return here, if I may, for a short while.'

'It remains as much your home as it is mine, until it is sold.'

As they continued with their meal, Abram explained how the house had been placed with an agent in Ipswich. How the estate, once sold, would be split between them as set out in their father's will. The mill would continue as before under his charge and the annual revenue would be shared out equally. No differentiation. No favouritism. Their father was a fair man.

'Not a fortune, but sufficient. You will marry now?' The question was a tentative one.

'Yes. If she will have me.'

'You have reason to doubt it?'

John shook his head. 'Her fidelity I am certain of. The family is another matter. Dr Rhudde, as you know, is set against me and has sworn against our union.'

'Dr Rhudde. Dr Rhudde . . .'

Dr Rhudde was an intractable problem, to which he had no ready answer. John went to change the subject. 'I read in the paper of a corn mill attacked in Needham Market, rioters in Bury. Haystacks on fire all around. There's been no trouble here, has there?'

'Murmurings, I believe. If the bastards come anywhere near, they'll get what's what from me. I've a shotgun kept loaded for the purpose. Years of work to get the mill where it is, turning a profit. All our prospects are riding on it, do you think I would jeopardise that?' At this, Abram lifted his glass to John's. 'To the mill.'

'The mill.'

They drank back their glasses and, when emptied, Abram reached for the decanter and filled them again.

'Don't dress her in silver, is all I ask. Twenty years of good harvests would be needed to pay for it.'

'Silver?'

'Dear brother, she will need a wedding dress?'

'Yes.' John shook his head, baffled. What point was he driving at?

'Princess Charlotte? No? Well, here's to your continued good sense and modest habits. We can only hope your dear Maria thinks similarly and does not read *The Times*.'

* * *

In the morning, he stood at his bedroom window and looked out over the garden to the distant view of the common beyond. He watched a gang of men trudge out around the edge of a field to work. This would likely be one of the last times he could do this: stand at this window and take in the view. He thought of his *Wheatfield* and what Sam had said. *Can he prisoner be? If fields are prisons, where is Liberty?*

Prisoner? A field was never just a field, he knew, but when – at what point – had fields become prisons? He frowned as he realised that his painting, captured but a few months ago, had been a moment of looking and was already lost.

He'd been long enough a boy, for whom home is the world, knowing no different, caught in a naive and inviolable sense of self, as all children were. It had seemed to him this life would be his for ever – but everything must end, even this. Here he was, approaching forty – finally, unquestionably, a man.

He took a deep breath and closed the shutters on the view.

Mary

'DID I TELL you that I, too, am a writer?' Polidori's stride broke briefly into a skip by her side. 'At least, I aspire to be.'

Mary's hopes that he might tire of her company, or at least of her pace, which she had quickened since leaving the cottage, had all but faded. The man appeared utterly indefatigable. His cheeks wore the bright fresh pink of an eager man in confident pursuit of his aim. The walk was doing him good. He looked much the better for it, the healthiest he had in days. She thought of complimenting him, then thought better of it.

'What a glorious day. I should be happy to do this more often. As often as possible. Should you accept my company, Mrs Shelley. My Italian is passable. More so than that. Actually, I'm told I read it quite well. I could read some to you . . .' A furious blush spread across his cheeks, peeking out above the cravat at his throat.

Mrs Shelley? What game was this of his? To laugh would be unkind. A rebuke, especially of one so close to Albé, would not go unnoticed. Silence, perhaps, a better strategy. She should have, she knew, invited him to address her as Mary by now, but the prospect of him doing so galled her. *Mary, Mary*, he would say with lovelorn longing. *Mary, Mary.* He would be looping his arm through hers next. Indeed, he had an unpleasant habit of touching her whenever he could – resting his hand on the centre of her back or shoulder – an act of possession she had only managed to discourage by stepping determinedly away whenever he did. That she might have choice did not infer his suit was certain, a distinction he seemed incapable of grasping the subtlety of. Tedious man.

She stopped to lift Willmouse higher in her arms. Polidori, not realising, strode on several more steps before halting and coming back to her side.

'Something the matter?'

Mary ignored him. 'Look, Willmouse. Can you see the sail boats? See, there? Your father and Albé? Is that their boat? Or that one?' The morning's fair weather had brought several out on to the water, more than she expected. Journeys needed to be made, she supposed, beyond simple sport.

Willmouse was not in the least bit interested in boats or anything else. He reached out one chubby hand and grasped her nose.

'Ha! You rascal!' She kissed his cheek.

'Let me carry the boy,' said Polidori. 'If you are tired.'

'I am not tired. But thank you.'

Polidori, downcast at the refusal, twisted on the ball of one foot as though to crush whatever was beneath it. He might be two years older than her, but his petulance was wearing.

'I shan't drop him. If that concerns you. I am sensible, you know.'

The most sensible of all, he might have added, from the churlish curl in his lip. What would it be like to kiss him?

she wondered. She imagined not the soft, ever-hungry lips of Shelley, but something hard, dry and prim. A bit like kissing the Archbishop of Canterbury. She gave an involuntary shudder.

'Are you cold?' Polidori went to shrug off his jacket to give it to her. Mary held up one hand. How she wished he would not fuss.

Even for such a thick-skinned man, an awareness of sorts had started to dawn.

'I'm sorry. I am making a fool of myself.'

And now it was impossible not to feel sorry for him. 'My apologies. Please, let's continue our walk. As we do, you can tell me all about what you are writing.'

So, on they went and Polidori, having what he wanted, *her attention*, chatted brightly. Every so often, Mary nodded to show she was listening, but the rest of her, the most part, she held apart, in silence, for herself.

Even before they were home again, Mary felt the cold edge of a freshening breeze approach from off the lake; waves furrowed the surface, capped white where they broke. Her eyes streamed. She regretted refusing Polidori's jacket to cover Willmouse and he did not offer it again, but held it bunched up at his throat, his head angled down against the wind. It shook the trees with such violence, as though in their weeks of stillness they had been storing up the capacity for a furious outburst such as this. A capacity, God knew, she understood.

She heard a branch break and fall to the ground behind her. Leaves whipped through the air above. Then thunder fell upon her, occupying the space in her chest where her breath was held. Again it came, this time louder. The thunder, like some huge boulder, heaved to the highest hill and let roll down towards her. When it came again, she could not bear it. She ran.

As much as Polidori might have wanted it, there would be no walk the next day, or the day after. Such was the rain that came in behind the storm that it flooded the path between Chaphuis and Diodati. A fast-flowing stream took its place, which she, Claire and Shelley had to navigate with caution, choosing the least muddy route around its edge. After a week of this, the slope, which was steep, had become utterly slithery with mud. Impossible to climb without the aid of handholds, each step assisted by vine or post or any other likely means to brace oneself and prevent a dangerous fall. What had started out as a short ramble up the hill when they had first arrived, had turned into an unpleasant and bad-tempered slog. Water streamed down off every slope. The lakeside path she walked with Polidori flooded over. Elise came back with news of deluged streets in Geneva.

Nearly a month had passed since their arrival. The sun, when it shone, did so with sudden, shocking heat. But the ground was so saturated that even the few dry days they had were heavy and leaden.

Mary saw less and less of Claire. Several were the occasions when she and Shelley returned from Diodati to

Chaphuis without her. During those early weeks, she was to be found at Albé's elbow, or as close to him as he would permit, quietly and diligently making fair copies of his work. Her attention to him had a sincerely earnest quality. Another might have found this utterly endearing, but he gave no indication that he recognised or valued her effort. When Shelley arrived at the villa, Albé would turn to him, as a sunflower to the sun, abandoning Claire to her work, leaving her bent over the page in furious intent. As if to add insult, he flattered Mary with the attention that Claire so craved, asking her opinion and listening, hungering for her answers. What could such casual disregard be understood as, other than a form of contempt? Mary hoped Claire did not see it too.

'Are you happy?' Mary asked her after she found her alone once again, struggling to copy in the dim light.

'Happy?' For a moment, the question seemed to confuse Claire, as if happiness were neither expected nor required of her. Would one question the calling – of a nun's, say – by reference to such a trivial emotional state?

Mary had been about to apologise, to leave her where she was, when Claire retorted, 'Why? Does it appear I am not?'

Mary countered with another question. 'You don't regret our coming here?'

Claire's expression darkened. Her laugh was dismissive. 'Not for a moment. I know I am not half as clever as you, but I do what I do quite well.' She turned the page to face Mary. 'See? My hand is neat. Half clever and reasonably neat.'

'It is beautiful work, Claire,' said Mary, seeing the care

and love that had gone into it. Love could see love. But where it was not, all else was selfish disregard.

'So what do you say,' said Albé one evening shortly after dinner, 'to a reading?'

'A splendid idea! Will you read to us?' said Claire. 'How thrilling!'

'Mary?'

Mary looked up from her book and saw Albé was waiting for her reply.

'Forgive me. I missed what you said.'

'I propose a reading. What would you suggest?'

In truth, she would have been happy to continue reading her book. It had become a pleasant way to pass their evenings together, a way to avoid drinking wine all night with the men. The long summer evenings she had dreamed of, light until ten o'clock, wore an autumnal edge. She had heard a clock chime nine not long before and yet here she was, needing a lamp to read by and struggling even to do that. Rain clattered against the windows, the darkness fractured by lightning which sent sudden frightful bursts of light into the room. If he must read to them, then let it not drag on.

'Something to be read in one sitting. Something complete,' she suggested.

'Something complete? Well then. How about the *Fantasmagoriana*? Do you know of it? I fear this storm might upstage it . . .'

Without waiting for her reply, he went out of the room

and returned with a slim volume. He ran his finger down an index page until he found what he was after.

'Oh, my dear Mary, you are in for a treat. Now then, let's see. This, I think. *"La Morte Fiancée"* – "The Death Bride" – shall I begin?'

Mary placed her book face down on her lap and waited for him to start. The wine she had drunk earlier still had a pleasantly subduing effect. She took another sip and felt the warmth of it spread through her. A loosening. A feeling she liked.

'*L'été étoit superbe; aussi, de mémoire d'homme, jamais on n'avoit vu tant de monde aux eaux. Mais les salons de réunion avoient beau se remplir, la gaîté ne s'y trouvoit pas . . .*'

Oh, God, she thought, *French*, but smiled. She would get Claire to explain the gist of it to her later.

Albé read for a while and then paused. 'Here, continue, please.' He passed the book to Shelley. He stood up somewhat unsteadily and reached for a small bottle on the mantel, uncorked it, and spent some time counting out drops. When he was done, he offered it to Shelley, who took the spoon with a coy smile.

'*La noblesse se tenoit à part . . .*'

When Shelley had taken his measure, Albé measured more into the spoon. 'Mary?'

'What is it?'

'The lovely Lady Laudanum, come to say hello.' Again, that same smile, his eyes, heavy-lidded and so dilated they seemed black, though she knew they were not.

'It allows a certain . . .' He closed his eyes slowly as words seemed lost from him; as he opened them again, a steadier gaze returned. 'A certain *depth*. Here, try.'

Mary sat forward and took the spoon from him. She glanced across at Shelley, who had stopped reading. His head lolled back as his gaze fixed on the ceiling.

'Just a little, to begin.' Albé watched her bring the spoon to her lips and take a sip. 'There. Good. Is that better? Tell me it is.'

Mary closed her eyes as the feeling closed over her: a relaxation so profound, so encompassing, she felt suspended in water; in an ocean so deep there was no way of knowing which way was up and which way was down. 'Oh,' she said, 'oh,' as the feeling intensified. 'Oh, Albé, *it is.*'

Then laughter, Shelley's, she supposed, or Claire's. And a voice reading, but the words seemed now to stretch one over the other. As one sentence compressed, another seemed to shudder, to heave up, until the story had become a mountain, cascading with water and cut deep with gulleys and ravines into which the living might tumble.

Mary startled and sat forward, her eyes open wide. She gripped the sides of her chair, lest she fall off.

'*Un spectacle affreux nous attendoit dans la chambre nuptiale, où il me conduisit. Nous trouvâmes le duc étendu à terre. Il ne restoit pas en lui le plus léger signe de vie; ses traits étoient défigurés d'une manière effrayante . . .*'

At the story's end, Albé, who was reading again, let go of the book. She saw it fall from his hand and fall and fall.

'Oh, oh,' she cried, as she felt her chair topple back. And laughter again – *hers?* Every breath she took pressed into her as though she could only ever breathe in. And then Albé was beside her. He brought his mouth to her ear and whispered, 'We shall each of us come up with our own story, a *ghost* story. What say you to that, Mary, Mary, Mary? What say you to that . . .'

The next day, on waking, Mary sat up in bed. A sudden terror seized her: *Willmouse.* She flung back the covers but as she stood up, a rush of nausea rose in her. She staggered, as if at sea. Then, oh, there he was, darling boy, blissfully asleep in his cot. As her relief in seeing him washed over her, she turned to Shelley in a fury.

'You. You . . .' She could not even bring herself to say his name. 'How could you? How could you *abandon our child*?'

'Me? The matter is more how could *you*?'

'*Me*?'

'Yes. You. The child's *mother*.'

What outrage to have her accusation turned back in this way! Her mouth fell open, for a moment incredulous, then stunned by her own failure, her own stupidity. She thought back to the evening they'd spent at the villa but all detail of it was lost as though it had been painted over black. And Willmouse? Where had he been while she had been so keen, so eager, to forget? She'd abandoned him, that's what, and now she couldn't even remember. She scooped him up from the cot and held him to her breast as though last night's foolishness might yet creep up and steal him away. She slumped down on the side of the bed, her breath ragged with grief. 'I could not lose another.'

'Maie, Maie.' Shelley drew up behind her and kissed her bare shoulder. 'We left Willmouse under Elise's care.' He lifted her hair and kissed the nape of her neck. 'See, the boy thrives. And we shall have another strong boy. And another.' She felt his mouth open against her and his tongue touch her skin. His teeth gave a gentle nip.

'And another and another and another. Poor, disconsolate girl. Please, Maie. Don't scold me. If we cannot be free here, where can we be?'

Mary gave a miserable nod and her breath shuddered in her.

'Here. Put the boy in his cot. Come back to bed . . .'

But her thoughts, as she returned to bed and lay back, were not of their lovemaking.

It was so easy to die. So very hard to keep what you loved alive.

Hope Peter

'I'M SORRY, MR Peter, I am.'

'Nowt to be sorry for.'

'Willie nowt legs. That's what I am. Just a hindrance, in your way.'

'Enough of it.'

Willie thumped a fist against his thigh. 'Bloody useless leg.'

'Enough, I said.'

'*You* swear.' Willie shot him an accusing look.

'When you've lived through what I've lived through, then you can swear.'

'Well, it is anyway. *Useless.*'

'Tell me this, is that leg of yours made of wood?' Peter thumbed his knife at the lad's leg.

'No.'

'Can you stand on it? Walk?'

'You know that I can.'

'Then take it from me, it's a leg.'

Willie looked no happier. 'Got no family what cares either.'

You and me both, thought Peter. He lifted the pitcher of ale and filled up the lad's cup. 'Well then, you'll have to make do with me. Now drink,' he said. Only one thing to be done with moping and that was to drink your way out the other side of it. He pointed his knife at the herring on the lad's plate. 'You not eating that?'

'I wanted a chop.'

'A chop?'

Willie nodded.

'Then why didn't you say so?' He leaned over and took the lad's plate and tipped the fish on to his. He lifted one hand to get the serving lass's attention.

'Yes?' she said, and rested her hip against their table.

'What chops have you got?'

'Chops? You jesting me?' When she saw he was not, she called back over her shoulder, her eyes never leaving his. 'Oi, Betty, what chops we got?'

'Eel chops. Plaice chops. Hake chops. Cod chops. That do you?'

'There it is. Chops aplenty. You decide.'

Peter turned to Willie. 'Well?'

'Cod chop,' said Willie.

'You know it's not really a chop,' said the woman, leaning down close.

'I do. Don't like herring that's all.'

She straightened up and held out her hand. 'Who's paying?'

'I am.' Peter felt in his pocket for his purse. 'We'll have a dish of potatoes too.'

'Bread's a penny more, if you want it.'

'A penny? For bread?'

'You heard right.'

'A pennyworth of bread, then. And potatoes. Another pitcher of ale. And any sweet pie you have.'

'You two condemned?' she asked as she scooped up three

coins from Peter's hand. Then, with a wink, she was gone.

While they waited for the food to come, Peter looked about the inn. They'd fetched up at a tavern round the corner from Billingsgate and from the crowd that had gathered it was clear it was popular with fishermen and lightermen alike. He recognised a group of men he'd seen shovelling oysters. But no sign of any of the Frenchies who had moored up by them. What a world it was that could have men at each other's throats one year and drinking at the same table the next. Better that, he supposed, than fighting.

'Here you go, my lovelies,' said the woman, coming back. She placed a griddled cod on a platter in front of Willie, and the potatoes, scarce quarter of a loaf of bread, and the pie before Peter. 'I'll fetch your ale now.'

'You're to eat up,' said Peter after she had gone. 'Every last scrap. Even if it takes you till suppertime tomorrow.'

'I will.' Willie nodded. He picked at the skin on the cod, blew on his fingers to cool them, and scooped up a chunk of the steaming flesh and gobbled it down.

'After we're done here, I'm going to get us work. Likelihood is there won't be hot dinners for a while.' What he might have added, but did not, was that where they were headed there was a good chance Willie might not want to eat at all.

Peter had something else in mind too, something he'd not had for a while and might not again for longer. His eye had come to rest on the woman who had served them. When she caught him looking, she smiled. When she caught him looking again, she pushed her tongue into her cheek and winked.

Fuck the meal. 'You're to wait here a while until I'm back,' he said to Willie, getting to his feet.

Ten minutes later, he was in a back room with her.

She sighed as his hand found the warmth between her legs. Her breath went out of her and he felt her give against him as she opened her legs wider. That give of a woman. God, he had missed it.

And then he was on his back on some kind of sacking, arched up so she could pull his breeches down over his hips.

'No,' she said, when he went to bring her under him. She brought one leg over him, straddling him instead.

'God,' he groaned and pushed up into her, feeling her finally on him. What woman would do this to a man? Fuck, fuck. Thoughts of the home he had lost and the hares he had caught flashed through his mind. Then he could no longer think; no longer cared. All of him heaped into her, into that moment, into that one magnificent fuck.

'So it's you and the boy both, that's what you're saying? He's a cripple and you've never been fishing at sea in your life. Got that right, have I? Not missing any particulars, am I not? You'll be telling me next you were at Waterloo.' The skipper took the pipe out of his mouth and tapped the ash into the palm of his hand.

'I was. I've the strength of two—'

'I can see that.'

'I can tie knots,' Willie piped up. 'A bowline too.'

'A bowline is a fucking knot,' said the skipper. He turned to Peter. 'I'll take you, but not the lad.'

Peter looked down at Willie. For a moment, he was sore tempted to accept the skipper's offer. Then he remembered being Willie's age and his years working at Oil Mill Farm. It came to him then how he'd never had the chance to know what he was good at, that his life weren't made for him to know that. Any fool could be made to dangle at the end of a rope. Any fool could sign up for war. It took a real fool to lose his home, as he had. All of that foolhardiness had barrelled behind him and now here he was, fetched up in London. In a way, he envied the lad. Not his leg, but the chance of not being the sad accumulation of happenings that he was. But with that leg of his, it was all against the lad from the off. If nothing else, he would try and see him right.

'As I said, you need to take us together.'

'Ah, be off with you.' The skipper waved Peter off with his hand. 'Wasting my time.'

'He can bugger off too,' Willie muttered as they turned to go.

'On to the next one.' Peter squared his shoulders against the dismissal. He'd started off with the tidiest-looking boat. Well, there were fifty more. True, several looked to have bare reason to float, their hulls being half rotted at the water-line, stinking rotten, with decks sprung from lack of caulking.

'You're to shut up about knots and bowlines,' said Peter after they were turned away from five more boats. 'They don't want to know.'

'What's it they want to know about then?' Willie countered.

Peter shrugged. He'd not got that figured yet. He'd expected they'd find work, with a choice of offers they could take their pick from and would have been long gone and out to sea by now. What chance then of any constable finding them?

Every eye he met, he regarded with suspicion. The worry that word had got out – from the innkeeper or his wife – gripped him. A terrible churning gripe clutched his bowels at the thought a constable had caught the next tide down after them. But he hadn't expected so many others to be looking for work too. Any number of men were there for the choosing and were chosen before them. Many as weathered as the rope they carried in heavy coils over their shoulders; their hands so salt-hardened their tattoos seemed to suffice for gloves. And such a quantity of beggars, squabbling like seagulls over the fish scraps. With his purse near empty, if Peter didn't find summat soon, he and the lad would be joining their bickering ranks.

As they stood there, considering what next, a man came by, dressed to his toes in black with a Bible clutched to his chest. When he saw Peter and Willie, he stopped, held up one hand to the heavens and closed his eyes fast.

'*And the prayer of faith shall save the sick, and the Lord shall raise him up . . .*'

'Oh!' Willie took hold of his leg.

The man opened one eye to check he had their attention.

'Thank you, but the lad's not in need of your priestcraft.' Peter stepped in between so Willie was shielded.

The man had opened both eyes now. He blinked quickly, steadied his hand and tried again, 'Jesus said to the cripple—'

'I told you, no. Take your ministry elsewheres. You're just after tapping me up.'

The man shrank back. He pointed to Peter then Willie. 'Those who do not willingly come to God are for the devil to take . . .'

Willie flinched as though God might reach down, grab him by the scruff of his neck and give him a good shake.

Peter gave the man a shove. As he dodged to one side, Peter went to kick his arse. 'I said, leave the lad alone.'

'God never forgets the face of a sinner.'

Peter reached to the ground. He ferreted out a loose cobble. 'And you'll not forget this if it catches your head.'

At this the man turned tail, black skirts flapping either side of him as he fled.

'What are you looking at me like that for?' asked Peter as he turned back to Willie.

'He'd have fixed my leg . . .'

'It was Jesus made the miracle, not him. You think a few words passed over you will get you standing right again?'

'I'm not stupid.'

'Am I saying that you are? There's a difference between stupid and daft.'

Anyone could promise anyone anything these days and folk would believe it, so desperate were they for any small improvement to their lot. He dropped the cobble back at his feet.

His gripe with it went deeper. War had knocked God out of him, he knew. Suffer the meek? Far as he could see that only benefited the strong. If God had made the world and everything in it and made it for man, then how come only scraps ended up on his plate when others got to heap their plates high? The hares apart, he did try in all he did to be good. What in his life had made him so undeserving?

* * *

They slept that night in the porch of St Magnus's Church, but time and tide cared not for their rest and even before dawn lifted, dank and cold, Peter heard the unholy row of fishing boats, vying again to moor up.

As Peter went to wake Willie, the lad clutched to him in a violent shiver. He rubbed the lad's back, to get some warmth into him. 'Come on, rouse yourself. We've work to find.'

But although the tide had brought in many new boats for them to choose from, no skipper seemed to consider them with any brighter favour. The nub of the matter was this: a fishing boat needed not just a man with the strength to haul in a net but also the ken to cast it overboard, a skill that, if done wrong, imperilled the vessel and all aboard. It needed a man not just to have sea legs, but the stomach to work at gutting fish, in all weathers, hot and cold.

'You think you can imagine it, but you can't,' said one skipper, taking pity enough on them to explain. His was one of the smaller boats, the *Florence*, a fishing smack that worked the east coast herring fisheries between King's Lynn and Grimsby.

As he described the stench of it, the slither of fish guts and oil, Peter felt his stomach heave. The skipper, on seeing him pale, gave a laugh. 'Ain't never seen a man get seasick just from the thought of it before.'

'He weren't sick on the oyster boat,' said Willie, in hopeful defence.

'Likely not,' said the skipper. 'But with a following wind up the Thames, you would have sat flat on the water. My little *Florence* cuts in, like this.' He brought his hands together to make a v. 'Sleek as a stoat and as fast. Can outrun a customs and excise cutter, not that I have need to,' he added, 'in case you were thinking. Herring's my business. And the odd sack of French wheat. Stand in one place long enough, someone will have you.'

So, that's what they did. Stood there, looking likely. But by lunchtime and hungry again, all they had succeeded in getting was a drenching. Peter was like a weather cock spinning round, but no matter what direction he faced in there was no interest from anyone.

'That skipper's a niffling lying pig,' said Willie. He rubbed at his leg and sat down in a puddle, past caring. 'Ain't no one needing crew. You never should of lifted that cobble to the priest.'

'He weren't no priest.' Peter turned his collar up against the rain. 'If we can't get work in London, then we can't get work anywhere.'

As he weighed what was left of his purse his attention was caught by a man, standing on a box, addressing a huddle of people. A number had gathered about to listen and more were approaching all the while. Behind the man hung a banner.

The brave soldiers are our friends. Treat them kindly!

Peter frowned. Whatever was he to make of that? The words had a pull to them even if he couldn't quite make out their meaning. He took a step closer to hear what was being said.

'Was there ever a more calamitous time in this country than at present?' the man on the box shouted. On his head, a hat. And on the hat, a tricolour cockade in red, white and blue.

'No, no. None worse than now!' called a man from the crowd.

'Are we to go on, from year to year, crying to the father of his people, as he is called, in vain, for redress? We have been placed in a state of bondage for years . . .'

Murmuring and shuffling at this.

'It is not only this country that has been thus oppressed – our sister in Ireland has shared in our misfortune. Though many starve, they are ignored or told to bear their misfortune. Easy for them with food on their plates to say that—'

'Tá sin fíor!'

'Ah, we have brothers from Ireland here.' The man made a fist in the air. 'How, then, are we to be restored to our rights? Not by talking, not by long speeches.'

'Aye, well,' muttered a man next to Peter, 'best get on with it then.'

'Not by petitions, for our petitions are not heard—'

'Weren't learned to write anyhow!' came a voice from further behind.

'Will Englishmen any longer suffer themselves to be trod upon, like the poor African slaves in the West Indies?'

'No! But they starve us to death instead,' shouted a woman. She wore a tricolour cockade too, fastened to her breast. 'Where is the relief? They give us pennies but we need pounds!'

'Indeed we do.' The man turned from her to address the crowd again. 'And if they will not give us what we want, *shall we not take it?*'

Peter elbowed his way to the front. It was true, he'd known little kindness since his return. He wanted to know more about what was meant by the banner.

'Please, please. Any soldiers here, come forward.' The man held out his hand as if to invite Peter and the six or seven other men by his side to join him but there was only room for one on the box and he made no move to step down.

'Is it right that you have come home to this? Your bravery rewarded with poverty and despair? A year since your return and no end to your suffering?'

'What is that to you?' said the man beside Peter. 'Easy enough for you to get folk riled up and knock a king off his throne. Then what? Start another war? And who'll you get to fight it for you? Me? Summat has to change, on that we can agree. Question is – what? Can't say the French had it right. Look at the sorry mess that has occasioned.'

'Change is coming, whether it is wanted by you or not, brother.' He spoke over the man's head to the crowd behind. 'This man asks, what next? Why, we start again, that's what! Long live liberty!' As he lifted his arms high, a roar erupted around him. Then, as the tumult died down, he grew serious and turned back to Peter and the men by his side. 'Who among you are soldiers still?'

Peter shook his head, but three of the men raised their hands.

'I must ask you this. If these good people around you were to rise up in a mob, and if you were commanded to do so, would you turn your fire against them?'

The woman who had spoken earlier brought her shawl tight round her. So thin she was, she could have fastened the spare in a knot at her back.

'Well, would you?' she asked. Her look was guarded, her eyes filled with mistrust.

'No,' said one of the men. 'I would not. I am in as much need of a loaf as anyone here.' He looked to the others. At first, they said nothing, taking sudden interest in their feet, but when pressed again they agreed that they were in sore need of a big loaf too.

Behind them, the crowd had started to drift away. The fire had gone out of them, like cinders kicked from the grate.

The man furled up his banner and tucked it under one arm. 'We meet at the Cock on Grafton Street for those who would join us.'

A couple of the men nodded, before they too wandered off to find shelter. And soon it was just Peter and Willie left and the pissing rain. He stooped down and picked up a ribbon that had been dropped on the ground. The colours were different: red, white, green.

'What do we do now?' asked Willie.

'Ah, the hell with it.' Peter closed his hand over the ribbon. He turned on one heel, away from the fish market, away from the Thames and away from any prospect of work aboard any boat that was there.

John

FINALLY WORD CAME from Maria that she was well enough to see him. Enclosed with her note was an invitation from the Bicknells, who would be delighted to have his company for dinner at Spring Gardens. Formal attire. Eight p.m. He chose the shirt he kept for best, sent by his mother the summer before. Over it, he wore a black frock coat with a white cravat knotted at his neck. When he caught sight of his reflection as he walked past a shop window on Oxford Street, he stopped and pulled his shirt cuffs down so that they showed. He supposed that was how they should be. How cuffs were worn at the Admiralty.

To his surprise, when he knocked, it was Maria who answered the door. As he came in, he saw the maid step to one side, uncertain what to do now that her role had been usurped. Maria flushed and widened her eyes. 'Look how bold you have made me.' She reached for his hands and pressed them between hers. 'Love, my love.' She stole a glance left and right and, ignoring the maid, went on to tiptoe and gave him a kiss.

The maid, finally finding the courage of her voice, stepped forward. 'Your coat, please?'

John had no waistcoat underneath and would appear underdressed in only his shirt. All he could hope was that a fire had not been set in the dining room.

'I shall keep my coat with me, thank you.'

Clearly it was not the reply the maid expected, but she took his gloves and hat and dropped him a small curtsey.

Maria looped her arm into his and steered him away. 'This way. Come, sit down. You're expected. Everyone is waiting for you.'

She led him through into the dining room where Mr Bicknell and an elderly woman – introduced as Maria's aunt – had taken their seats. The conversation cut off as he and Maria came in.

'Constable!' said Mr Bicknell, with exaggerated surprise, as though John were the prodigal son returned not once, but twice. 'Please do come in.'

The elderly aunt half rose from her seat, then seated herself again. It was only a little while later that she remembered to smile, a smile that was to stay oddly fixed through the evening as though he'd come not to dinner but to paint her portrait.

This was not the first time John had met Maria's family, but the formality of this dinner was new. Encouraged and somewhat emboldened, John drank an aperitif and accepted a second. Amontillado sherry. Delicious.

The meal began with a consommé, then came fish, accompanied by a dry Riesling.

Mr Bicknell poked at the fillet of fish with his knife. 'Plaice?'

'Yes, Daddy, plaice,' answered Maria. 'We are eating more fish so as to diminish our usual order of beef.'

'Why ever should we want to do that?'

'Increasing the supply of fish to wealthy tables decreases the demand on butchers, thus reducing the price of meat to the inferior orders of society. Everyone is doing it.'

'Doing what?'

She gave her father a look of pure exasperation. 'Eating fish, Daddy!'

'Are they indeed? Only on Fridays, I'll wager. And whose jolly idea is it to press a midweek fillet of plaice on the population?'

'The London Association for the Relief of the Labouring and Manufacturing Poor.'

'*The who?* Is our diet to be decided by the whim of some association economist with pescatarian tastes? I shall eat beef if I want to, the consumption of which, I'll hazard, makes not a whit of difference to the status of the labouring poor of this country.'

Maria brought herself straight against the back of her chair. Father and daughter glared at each other before hunger nudged both into grudging submission and their attention returned to their plates.

'Thank you,' said John to the maid as she topped up his glass.

He could smell Maria's perfume. Orange water with a touch of spice. Cardamom? Clove? Being welcomed into their home in this way, to the point of being witness to private family bickering, was as good as being married, was it not? A great contentment settled over him. He reached out a hand, rested it on Maria's and squeezed gently.

Mr Bicknell stiffened. 'Sir, if you were the most approved of lovers, you could not take a greater liberty with my daughter.'

The rebuke was so little expected, and Maria's kiss still so vividly imprinted on his mind that John's reply was out before he could contain it. 'And don't you know, sir, that I am the most approved of lovers?'

He felt a sharp kick on his ankle and glanced at Maria. Her eyes widened with caution.

'If you two continue like this, I shall have to ask you to sit apart.'

'My apologies.' John returned his hand to his lap. Although chastened, nothing could quash the elation he felt sitting by Maria's side.

'So where are you living now, Constable?' asked Mr Bicknell. 'Still in that place in Soho?'

'Daddy—'

Mr Bicknell ignored her. 'Pass the peas, would you?' He took a spoonful and another, until he had a pile of peas on his plate. 'Anyone else? No?' He clattered the spoon into the dish and mashed the peas with his fork.

John thought of his lodgings. He could never offer that as a home to Maria. She had visited once and been gracious, but afterwards he had worried that her demeanour had simply been a kindness to hide her disappointment.

'Are you working, Constable?'

'Daddy, please—'

'Maria. *Enough.* I must ask you to refrain from these interruptions. We are having dinner. I have questions. It is not without precedent to ask questions of one's dinner guests. At dinner. And besides, John is not simply our guest. He is your, your . . .' Mr Bicknell cast about, at a loss.

'*Suitor*,' offered the aunt, this being the first word she had uttered all dinner. She held one hand to her throat, as surprised as anyone that she had said it.

Maria returned her father's frown with a glassy stare.

'Thank you.' He turned back to John. 'You were about to tell me of your work . . .'

Was he? It was his chance and the best, perhaps only, chance he might have to boast of the upcoming Wivenhoe commission. And yet he hesitated to do so. However much the commission meant to him, it was, *he was*, still at the start of whatever it was he was trying to achieve. It might mean something. Then again, it might not. Mr Bicknell, he knew, was not a man easily impressed by mights and maybes.

At his hesitation, Mr Bicknell went on unabashed, 'And the Royal Academy? No news? I could put in a word for you. William Owen. He's an Academician, is he not? The man to go to, as it were?'

Go to? John did not like the sound of that. 'He is. But, no, please, there is no need.' In truth, the prospect appalled him. He swallowed. 'It's tremendously generous of you to suggest so doing, however I am confident this year the Academy will decide in my favour.'

Mr Bicknell gave a noncommittal grunt. 'What use bashfulness, Constable? Hmm? Bashfulness never got anyone promoted at the Admiralty, I can tell you that. Besides, generosity has nothing to do with it. I have an interest in your success. We *all* do.' He turned his fork over and scooped up the flattened peas and chewed them for a while. But the lull was a temporary one and if John thought the interrogation over, he was mistaken.

'I was sorry to hear of the death of your father. I assume your intent is to continue as you are in London with your, er, studies?'

John nodded, mute with worry that whatever he said

would further erode the small standing he had with his prospective father-in-law. Prospective? Even that seemed presumptuous.

'What might you expect on the settlement of your father's estate?'

John's mouth opened and closed at the sheer affront of the question, but Mr Bicknell continued with his meal unperturbed as if he had asked for nothing other than an opinion on the dish.

'Perhaps four thousand pounds.'

Maria blinked quickly and looked down.

'I see. That's it? The extent of it?'

'From the mill, perhaps an annual return of two hundred pounds in addition. But yes. That is the extent of it.' The second inheritance he had hoped for from a Nayland aunt, which might have yielded a further two thousand pounds, had not been forthcoming. She had not been so fond of him after all. He could see Mr Bicknell turning sums in his head, considering them from every direction and finding them lacking. He knew what he was thinking: not a great amount these days for a man with no other prospect and far short of what his daughter might reasonably expect.

'You must know what an invidious position this places me in.' Before John could respond, Mr Bicknell raised a hand to silence him. 'Before all this' – he waved his knife at John – 'Maria was in certain expectation of a generous inheritance from her grandfather. Your continued suit almost certainly rules this out. If you continue to press your hopes, to persist in this way, you will ruin her chances of securing a comfortable life. I have to be frank. Is that what you want?'

John's cheeks burned with indignation and humiliation. It was all he could do not to throw down his napkin and leave.

Mr Bicknell, taking John's silence as either contrition or submission, did not press his point further and the rest of the meal passed without further interrogation. Growing too hot, John shrugged off his coat after all and handed it to the maid, no longer caring for the lack of a waistcoat. He saw Mr Bicknell take a look and frown, but what worse injury could be inflicted on him than what he had already borne? And, as for the aunt, her only other comment was to remark that he had become quite pink. The wine, in part. John had drunk freely of that. But mostly it was pique. Mr Bicknell's blunt assessment caused an uncomfortable prickle whenever he thought of it. *Put in a word for him?* Had opinion of him fallen so low that it would need to be recovered by means of whispered intervention behind Academy doors or, God forbid, some other called-in favour Mr Bicknell might leverage on his account?

John managed to be agreeable when required to and when more wine was offered, he held out his glass and accepted. By the time it came to take his leave, he was quite tipsy.

Maria escorted him back out into the parlour. As they waited for the maid to fetch his things, he swept his arm wide, raising it to the chandelier and its furious glare as though it were the source of his plight. 'Forgive me if I cannot offer you this—'

'But I do not want it.' Maria's mouth pulled down and he could see she was trying not to cry.

Dear, sweet love. He could have swept her out the door with him then.

Maria reached out a hand to him. 'When will I see you again?'

John took his gloves and hat from the maid. 'Not until I am back from Wivenhoe.'

'Then write to me, write to me. Write to me every day.'

He brought her hand to his cheek and held it there.

She jumped back from him as Mr Bicknell shouted for her.

'Go, go!' She gave him a gentle push so that he was out on the step and then the door was shut after him, closing off both light and warmth in one.

The hour was late, almost midnight, but he decided he would walk. If he kept to the main thoroughfares, there would be less risk of incident. He dodged into a doorway for shelter as a light rain shower turned from mildly irritating to utterly drenching. Bedraggled bunting left over from the royal wedding hung in limp celebration, a line of water cascading from each flag.

'Spare me a penny, can you?' asked a young man, as he stepped out of the shadows.

John cast a wary eye over him and saw that one leg ended in a stump. There was little chance, at this hour, of a carriage to take him home, but it gave him reason to appear occupied and to look in the opposite direction.

'A penny, please, sir?'

'Sorry. No.'

'Gentleman such as yerself must have a penny to spare. I've not eaten for days. A little pity is all I ask. I lost my leg at Waterloo.'

John brought one hand to his forehead and held it there. 'Where would I be, if I was to give a penny to every man who came to me in the street, claiming lineage to Waterloo?' He was appalled to realise that the words might have come from Mr Bicknell.

The man did not shrink away from him as John had with Maria's father. With effort, he pulled himself straight. 'I don't need to prove nothing to you. Just a penny, is all.'

John was in no mood to listen. Importunate wretch. Did he not know when to back down? 'It'd be me in the gutter, that's what. Not a place I have intention ever of being. See this?' He pulled at one cuff. 'The only reason this shirt is not yet threadbare is because I take great care when I wear it. And as for my coat—' He patted his chest, only then realising he had been ejected from the house in such a hurry that he had left it behind. 'Its primary use is that it is thin and stands half a chance of drying before it gets soaked wet through again. And why might that matter to a gentleman like me? Well might you ask! Because a gentleman like me has scant means to travel about by carriage, though he might earnestly wish to do so. Indeed, he goes from place to place, doorway to doorway, from one drenching to another, day in and day *pissing* out.'

He stepped out of the doorway and wheeled about on the pavement. Lashing rods of rain stung his face; a headache had come upon him and he felt it press behind his eyes. A sudden feeling of vertigo seized him and he staggered.

'Because there are days when I am as skint as the next

fellow, that is why. Days when I've had precious little to eat. See, there,' he said, gesticulating wildly in the direction of Spring Gardens, 'lives the woman I want to marry. How will I feed her if not from the contents of my purse?'

'One miserable fucking penny . . .'

He looked at the beggar and the beggar looked at him – both of them drenched to the skin. What a pitiful place London was in the rain; clutched in every doorway, some penniless wretch.

'Here,' he said, disgusted at himself and sickened by the creeping humiliation he felt after Mr Bicknell's assault. He dug in his pocket and brought out a handful of coins, silver among the coppers. His hand shot out and he hurled the coins across the cobbles, as though broadcasting corn across his father's field, in hope of a good crop.

Fuck Napoleon, fuck Waterloo, and fuck the fucking Royal Academy too.

Charles

'LAUREL?'

Charles listened, but no reply came. All was still. Even the hermit thrushes had hushed their singing.

He lay a while in bed until by his reckoning he had waited plenty enough for a coffee pot to be filled and put to boil. So bad his longing, he could about smell it too. Charles kicked back the covers in frustration, reluctant to leave the warmth of the bed. The quilt sagged around his ankles, its feeble warmth exhaled into the room's frigid air. He sat there, sore with disappointment from the night before, a pool of Laurel's petticoats on the floor where she had stepped out of them. He picked them up, shy of them, and studied the lace at the hem. Cold and lifeless, even this simple garment seemed to rebuff him. She'd left her skirts, hanging on a hook on the door. Wherever she'd gone, she'd sure taken off in a hurry.

Getting up, he cast about for his shirt, as yet a stranger in this unfamiliar room. As he turned, he stubbed his toe on the dresser. A blinding pain shot through him and he fell back on the bed, his foot clutched in his hands, too stunned even to howl. He rocked in pain and frustration. This was not the wedding morning he had hoped and longed for. He could have wept.

Down in the kitchen, he found the door to the yard open

and a cold wind blowing in through it. Framed in it stood Laurel, wearing only her nightgown and her shawl drawn round her shoulders. Hearing him, she turned, worry etched deep on her brow. Beyond her, a day unlike any other. What hellish vision this? Summer and winter had been tipped from the heavens together and looked to have fought their way down from there.

He shook his head, as if that might fetch a summer's morning in its place, and stepped over the threshold into snow. *Snow?* Only a covering, but enough for him to feel it melt between his toes. A shadow fell over him and he looked up, seeing the sky bank over with cloud. The temperature dropped further as the sun was lost behind it.

'Bella's foal . . .' Laurel stepped past him into the yard, her boots unlaced.

Snow fell steadily now. Bella was pastured with her foal in a field, halfway to the well. Pastured? Was there ever a less likely word for a piece of scuffed-up ground?

'Wait, Laurel,' he called. 'I'll come with you. But we'll be needing something warmer to wear.'

Charles gathered his shirt at the neck as a shiver racked his chest. He shuffled from one foot to another; the pain from earlier became a burning cold in both feet. Whatever the urgency, it would be foolhardy to go further dressed only in their night garments.

So in they traipsed, in silence, his advice, sensible as it was, never likely to meet well with her. Back upstairs to their room they went, to find what they could that would keep them warm. His winter woollens were still in his room in town. He had been planning to move them up with his other effects, when needed. Having nothing more than the shirt he had married in, Laurel went to fetch him an old jacket of Seth's and came back with a threadbare and moth-eaten garment, a size too small. Now it was her turn to insist, to the point of helping him on with it.

'You're not off to church, Charles Whitlock,' she chided on seeing him frown.

Chastened, he allowed himself to be dressed.

In the short time it had taken them to do so, a blizzard had closed in. Never had Charles known such a day. There had been hard years, of course; hard, hard winters. Winters when a pie, hot from the oven, could be left out on the step to freeze and kept that way until spring. But winter thrown over summer like this? The season full turned on its head? He saw only the devil's hand in it.

The snow wasn't going to stop Laurel. Off she set and he followed after, out across the yard, over the hill in the direction of the well, until they'd left the farm behind them. They passed a line of hemlock pine by now so laden with snow their lower branches touched the ground. The trees creaked in protest as they went by. On past the corn field they went, where spears of young corn stood in rigid atten-tion, the green of them that could still be seen, a shock against all that white. Laurel snapped a cob off a stem and pulled away the husk to reveal its frozen core. She snapped off another and another and stripped them back the same, dropping them to her feet.

'No.'

Her distress sent a plumb line straight through him, carrying what hope there was for the crop with it. The tending it had taken – the graft, the slog of it, hauling water from the well to get it to grow in the first place. Laurel's work, not his. All of it taken away by this, this, this – he hesitated to use the word but what other word was there for it – this *abomination* of a day. He rubbed snow from his eyes and saw that their footsteps had already covered over; the path behind them, gone. Then, as he turned, his feet went from under him. He came down hard on one knee, twisting it as he fell.

He lay there with his head pressed to the snow, not able to get up. 'For the love of God,' he cried and beat his fist on the ground. He felt Laurel's hands under him, to get him to sit upright.

'Get up.' She tugged at his jacket, but hadn't the strength to lift him. 'Get up.'

What a fool of a man he was and she'd had it known before him. Him and his imaginings of being some kind of help to them; no place for that kind of folly here. With grim resolve, he pressed his hands flat and pushed hard as he could; his arms shook with the effort as he levered himself upright again.

Across the path in front of them trotted Bella. Laurel held out one hand to get the pony to come. 'Bella,' she called, gentle and soothing. But the pony wouldn't come, not even to her. Spooked, she backed away in skittish steps. Behind, the gate to the paddock stood open. Beyond it, a little way into the field, a mound, covered over with snow.

Laurel let out a cry when she saw. *The foal.*

Charles limped through the gate after her to where it lay. Laurel, ahead of him, dropped to her knees. She brushed the snow away to reveal its rich chestnut coat beneath.

Charles brushed at the snow too, frantic at first, then slowing as he realised the foal was dead. It was not yet a week old. Just yesterday, Seth had raised a toast to it, expressing an earnest hope for a child that would grow up with it and ride it one day, a suggestion that had caused many to chuckle and Charles to redden up. As he got to his feet again, a splintering pain tore through his knee. He staggered, but Laurel did not come to his help this time. No need for words, her look said it all.

A sin to waste good food, so they gave thanks for the foal and ate the meat that was on it, hushed over the table like condemned men at their last meal. Three days of frosts came after, then the weather warmed just enough for the meat that was left to spoil. Then the cold came again, unsparing. In the barn, the water in the trough froze over, the land beset with black ice. Branches, heavy with leaf, plain dropped to the ground under the weight. Birds froze on their perches and fell from the trees like stones.

Then a sudden thaw released them. But it was not with relief that Charles went with Laurel to look out on their land. For what emerged from under the ice was withered and rotted: a poisoned, blighted harvest, little of it fit to eat. As he went out again on his ministering, he brought his neckerchief up over his nose to stop the stench of it from reaching him as he whispered his song:

Depth of mercy! Can there be Mercy still reserved for me?
Can my God his wrath forbear, Me, the chief of sinners, spare?

Then the cold set in again, not as raw as had been, but deep-set and aching, like a sore tooth in no hurry to loosen. There'd be no corn, little wheat or oats or barley, no fodder to bring in for the winter, that much was clear. Their cattle ate up the hay stored for winter and the corn set aside for the next year's planting. When the pasture was nibbled bare, Laurel turned them out of it, to find what they could. At first they were reluctant to roam, shy of the freedom, then were into the woods and lost from sight.

The rain held away and the land dried more.

One evening, Teddy Spalding came by to visit. He greeted Seth and Laurel, but his eye passed over Charles as if he were not there. Charles had last seen Teddy on his wedding day. A distance, wide as Lake Champlain, now stood between him and it. The memory seemed set away from Charles as if he were an old man looking back on the long years of his life. He had not, he realised with a pang, had a day of happiness since. He spent more time looking down than up, as his thoughts weighed ever more upon him. He'd taken on a stoop which Laurel neither commented on nor sought to correct. All he wanted was a wife's gentle hand on his shoulder, for her to set him straight.

Seth pulled out a chair for Teddy to sit on but Teddy lifted one hand to refuse. 'Never been anything like it. Months of no rain, now this. Lost every spring lamb that I had. Twenty perished that first night.'

'I did hear of it.' Seth tucked the chair back under the table. 'Hearing it again pains me no less. It's been a terrible year. No year like it.'

'We lost Bella's foal,' said Laurel, without looking up. 'Turned the cattle out too.' She sat at the table, hunched over a whetting stone and ground the blade of a knife on to it.

They stood in silence and considered their losses. Teddy shot Charles a thunderous look. 'Have you nothing to say?'

'Now then, Teddy . . .' said Seth, in warning.

'No, Seth. Let him speak. It needs saying and he has come here to say it.'

Teddy folded his arms across his chest. 'Was you got us to stay. We were ready to leave. No saying what success we might have had from it, but we'd have taken our chances and done our best. Stupidest thing I did, allowing myself to be persuaded by you. God doesn't want us here. Seems he gave us fair warning on that months ago. To quit. A good year gave us little enough, but this? Scarce one tenth of the crop will be gathered. Orchards, empty. Potatoes cut off by the drought and the frost.' He turned to Seth. 'Genesee Valley where the Dunbars took themselves off to can still be had for two or three dollars an acre.'

Seth gave a low whistle. 'That is a good price.'

'Genesee Valley?' asked Laurel.

'Upper New York State. Might have afforded it but the last I have has gone on fodder. We've been made fools of, Seth, is my opinion. Gives me no joy to say it, not with us all suffering so bad.' He turned to Charles with ill-concealed contempt. 'Got a prayer that'll bring my lambs back?'

Charles blinked. Never before had he been so cut down and not a word from Seth nor Laurel in his defence.

'Thought as much.' And with that, Teddy tipped his hat to Seth and Laurel and went out.

1815

Henry

'WHAT VALUE A native account is to the record, I cannot comprehend.' The captain handed his *Narrative of the effects of the Eruption* to Henry so that he could check it for error. The narrative included his conversation with the Rajah. 'It should be sufficient to note our observations, the *facts* of the matter and be done with it. But if this is how we are to conduct ourselves now, to cloud the account with the subjective, then far be it from me to argue with our esteemed Lieutenant Governor Raffles.'

Raffles had wider ambitions in the region beyond his governorship of Java, Henry had heard. It wasn't for Henry to venture his opinion either but he suspected the eruption could not be seen as anything other than a setback. He kept his silence, tucked the captain's folder of papers under his arm and retreated to his cabin to read them. He promised to have them back with the captain by noon though there was no urgency that he could see. The *Benares* was still three days out from their home port of Makassar.

Henry's willingness disguised a terrible lethargy, for once he had reached the safety of his cabin and had closed the door he sat there incapacitated, not knowing where to begin. He had been like this ever since their departure from Sumbawa. Memories buffeted him from every direction, knocking his attention away from whatever task was in front of him. Since leaving the island, he had spent most of his time confined this way: seated at the tiny writing desk, staring into space. He could not forget so easily what he had seen, nor his inability to treat anything other than the most superficial injury.

When he went up on deck, the briefest of spells there rewarded him with a clutching anxiety. He'd search the heavens, alarmed to see the ash cloud following them north. Though he could no longer taste ash in the air, it hung in a greyish haze along the length of the horizon, reaching behind and ahead – an embrace from which there was no escape.

It was the ash that ailed him, he knew. His chest ached in the morning on waking, every breath seemed lined with lead. The last time he had felt so unwell had been in London, two winters ago, when weeks of fog had wrapped the chimney smoke into a choking black smog, staining London's fair-faced facades with dismal black streaks.

Here he was, lost in thoughts, again. Henry shook himself out of his lethargy. He turned over the first page of the captain's account, it starting with them leaving Makassar and sailing into the ash.

The appearance of the ship when day-light returned was most singular, every part being covered in falling matter – it had the appearance of calcined Pumice Stone, nearly the colour of wood ashes; it lay in heaps of a foot in depth in many parts of the deck, and several tons of it must have been thrown overboard, for though an impalpable powder or dust when it fell, it was, when compressed, of considerable weight; a pint measure of it weighed 12¾ ounces.

Henry broke off reading, baffled by the captain's tone. More extraordinary was the fact that in the nightmarish journey into the darkness of the blanketing ash, the captain had considered it important to weigh it.

On the 18th made Sumbawa; on approaching the coast passed through great quantities of Pumice Stone floating on the sea, which had at first strongly the appearance of shoals, so much so that I sent a boat to examine one, which at a distance of less than a mile, I took for a dry sand-bank of upwards of 3 miles, with black rocks in several parts of it.

Black rocks? Was that reference to the cindered forms they had found floating in the water? Then why not say so? Henry made irritable note of that in the margin and read on.

The captain described how the anchorage at Bima had altered; how they had found the island under a deluge of ashes, rendering many places uninhabitable. Henry cast his eye over the rest of the account. The bare facts of the eruption had been included: the columns of fire and flame, the fall of stones, large as two fists but generally not larger than walnuts – *walnuts?* Mention was made of the death of the Rajah's daughter. But nothing on the appalling condition of the survivors, nor the cowardly manner with which the expedition had quitted the place.

Henry yanked open a drawer, feeling for paper. He had a *narrative* and would tell it. But where to begin? Behind every thought lengthened the shadow of his failure. He coughed. A deep rattling cough that set his ears ringing. He banged his fist hard into his ribs to get it to stop.

He would write to his dearest Emmalina first:

*My Darling, Never have I felt at such remove from all that
is familiar and secure, from the home I love, and from you,
my dearest wife. Forgive this uncharacteristic outburst but
these last few days have taxed me greatly . . .*

Henry paused, caught between the release of writing
what was in his heart and the shame of revealing his
thoughts in such explicit, intimate form.

He closed his eyes, unable for a moment to continue.

*We sailed unwittingly towards an event of unprecedented
magnitude, utterly cataclysmic, wholly unprepared. I had
nothing that could help with the injuries presented to me:
the most terrible burns; people scalded inside and out; children, hair matted and fused, features burned away . . .*

He groped towards a comparison that might reveal the
scale of the disaster. No mountain in England could match
the geographical might of Mount Tambora. He estimated
its height at three times that of Snowdon, perhaps more.

*Do you remember our time together walking the lower slopes
of Snowdon? How disappointed we were that that magnificent mountain, so high in the heavens, was most often
shrouded by clouds? Imagine it, blown into the sky, utterly
destroyed in a matter of hours and the hellish force required
to do it and all that stone become dust; if you can imagine
that then perhaps you can begin to imagine the calamity
that has beset the island of Sumbawa and its people.*

*So many have perished, Emmalina. The population
swept away or buried. Thousands killed and more dying by
the day. The water is poisoned; the land choked with ash.
People, starving . . . I will carry my failure here ever more.*

*My darling, I can hear your objection, you were always so
good at seeing the best in everyone. But I know my failure is
manifest. I hope God will forgive me and that in the time
left to me I can forgive myself.*

He looked at what he had written. All that remained was
for him to sign it. He picked up the ink pen, dipped it, and
wrote with great care:

Your loving husband,
Henry

A cough started in his chest, deep and racking. He
pushed out of his cabin, still with the letter in his hand,
seized by a sudden claustrophobia, desperate for air. Up
on deck, he hung over the rail, gasping for breath. But in
all the free air of the ocean, it would not come. He pulled
his handkerchief away from his mouth, aghast at the grey
sludge he had brought up. The pain in his chest was
crushing as though his lungs had filled with splintered
glass. Then he tasted blood.

He staggered and fell, every particle of sky a weight of
stone upon him, pressing him to the deck.

The letter loosened from his grip and the wind snatched
it away.

1816

Sarah

THAT WERE IT. Wasn't wanted no more. Mutton chops waited till the end of the day then he came on over to the midden and told me to be off.

'I gave you plenty good warning,' he said.

'Warning for what?'

'Sarah. Sarah.' Lolling there by the door he were, loving being him.

'Off with you then.'

I waited for him to give me my coin, but he did not. Well, I weren't having that. 'I want paying. I worked for that coin. It's mine.'

'Fuck me,' he said, and threw his head back to laugh. With his mouth open wide like that, was like all the laughter in the world had been swallowed up in him and it could never come out. Then he stopped. He took a step towards me. Then another. Then another.

When he were no more than three, four steps away he leaned in and went, 'Boo . . .'

I jumped back, how could I not? My shoulders went up down in a flinch. My hand shot in my pocket for Benton's knife and I held it straight out at him. Oh, the look on his face. He weren't expecting that, he were not.

He looked at the blade then at me. 'What you going to do with that? Skin a mouse for yer supper?'

His hand came out and made a grab for it, catching the side of my hand and knocking the knife to the floor. I were out past him in a flash.

At the far side of the yard, I glanced back, saw him come out of the barn, stand there and fold the blade back into the handle. He turned the knife over in his hand and took a proper look. I remembered then how it had Benton's initials carved on it pretty.

'Well, well.' He wagged the knife in the air. 'Didn't have you down as a thief.'

And then I were off, over the Fen, faster than a hare with the hounds coming after it.

I was up the next morning before dawn and I went with Tessie and Thomas and the others, numbering twenty-two of us in all, to see what work was to be had. But Tessie weren't wanted, nor was Thomas and nor was I. Word gets round between farmers. Bad word gets stuck to you and the three of us were stickier than a tar man's brush.

'Now what?' said my ma in a voice that supposed the fault were mine when I returned home again.

I had to admit a penny a day was riches to standing where I was, with nowt.

'How did you come to lose the work that you had?'

I shrugged. 'Weren't nothing I did, Ma.'

'Were you cheeky, is that what it is? Did you not do as you were told?'

'I don't know what it was that I did.'

'What will we do, Sarah? What will we do?'

Ma went to fetch straw for the floor and I followed out after.

'Here, make yourself useful.' She got me to hold out my apron so she could bundle the straw into it. Then back inside we traipsed and she threw it down and trampled it so the mud got covered over. I trampled too. See, I always was helpful. Had not needed asked. The bright straw soon turned brown and matted, most of it stuck to me so I looked like I had hairy caterpillars for feet. It were a losing task, but we did it anyway. A drenching rain had come down that morning, up from the floor and down through the roof. But if the straw were soaked wet through to begin with, how was that supposed to help keep us dry? The way we was, the house would soon be trampled into a mound of mud with us sat in the rain on top of it.

Seeing I was ailing, Ma made poppy tea for us both. 'Have a sip of this. It'll take the cold out of you.'

What was we but Fen slodgers after all? I took a sip and another and the cold jumped out of me scalded, like I'd stepped on the sun.

We went to Stevens, the baker.

'Will you ask him?' Ma said as we stood on the step. Then, as quick, she looked ashamed she'd asked such a thing of me. She pushed the door open.

Well, Stevens did not want to know as I knew he would not. Them with a full cupboard were the worst, was my opinion.

'If it's a crust you're after, you've come to the wrong place.'

'I've always had my bread from you.'

'If you're after charity in return for it then you can take yourself off.'

Ma lifted her hands to him. 'Please, I beg you.'

A woman had come in behind us with her three children, each as pinched with hunger as it were possible to be. 'Bread is all we have and if we cannot get it we will starve.'

Stevens made a show of tightening his apron strings. 'Mrs Vachell makes a soup once weekly—'

'Soup? That what she calls it?' The woman gathered her children close. 'If I want a sup of hot water, I'll boil it m'self. I'll not be made to pray on my knees for it for an hour first.'

I linked my arm through Ma's and turned her away. 'Come on. You're a bad 'un, Mr Stevens, you are.'

Out of the door we went and on down the path and over Church Fen to the Croft river, the wind in our backs pushing us on. We soon found ourselves by a small plot of land that had once had our name on it to see what was there. Taters, perhaps. They often came up in daft places, least expected. Once was, most had a plot here where water could be got at easy, but the Bedford Level lot had took the most of the water away from the river with their designs. Besides, after Pa, we hadn't the rent for it to stay ours and had to part with it. Wasn't often I thought back to anything then, but now as I made my way over the furrows the memories hopped their way across to me. Me, Ma and Pa and the hard pelting rain and oftentimes wanting to cry because the work was so hard. But we got ourselves fed

out of it with potatoes and beans and peas. Wild strawberries grew up over the banks and the taste would pinch
up your cheeks same as a mouthful of sorrel. But one sweet
one, when you found it, was enough to turn cartwheels
all afternoon for. But the banks were bare of them too. No
taters, no duck taters either, which sometimes could be
had from the ditch. I closed my eyes, as sorry for myself
as it was possible to be at the thought I'd eaten my last
strawberry. I might have cried, so wretched I was, had I
not heard a voice.

'Sarah!'

And again, 'Sarah!'

We turned to see Downham Tom on a horse, cut across
from the Ten Mile Bank, come riding towards us at a fair
clatter. He brought the horse up sharp by my side. The
cantering still being in him, it took him a moment before
he had breath enough to speak.

'Downham's a—' He gulped his breath back. 'A *riot*! We
made the magistrate listen, we did. He's in agreement.
Work and two shillings a day! Fifteen hundred are out at
Brandon. Denver and Southery too. Folk won't stand for
it no more.'

'Two shillings? A *day*?' Oh, the coins that tumbled out
of my ears at this.

'Yes! And them that'd been had for poaching, he let them
go too.'

'He never did!'

'He did so. Weren't none too happy about it. If we got
that from the magistrate there, then we can get the same
here!' He reached down his hand for me to take hold. 'Are
you coming then?'

I turned to Ma and she nodded. 'You get yourself gone.'

So with that, I took Tom's hand and put my foot in the stirrup and heaved myself up in the saddle behind him. He turned the horse back in the direction of Littleport, gave a sharp kick and we were off.

I held on for the dear life of me, my cheek rested snug on his back. I whispered so only I would hear it, 'Oh, I am glad to see you, Downham Tom.'

When we reached the Globe, I went to get Tessie and her Thomas and as many of the others who lived nearby.

'We need to get more folk together so that they know,' said Downham Tom as we came back.

The landlord leaned over the bar. 'The church bell?'

'Vachell will strip the hide off our backsides and cover his Bible with it if we do.'

Robert Cornwall, one of Benton's men, had a seed drill spout he reckoned would do the trick. He went out the door and blew down the pipe, but raised only a squeak. Next, he took off into Stevens's bakery, two doors down, and come out again with a horn and Stevens at his heels after him. *Peep*, it went when he blew down it. He threw the horn away, gave Stevens a shove which I was not sorry for, then set off again, round the corner, out of sight. Finally, back he came, this time triumphant, with a horn he'd had off Burgess, the lighterman. He drew in a breath and blew hard as he could.

The sound that come out would have knocked the

tankards off the shelf and pictures off the wall had he not already been on his way out the door again.

As folk came out wanting to know what was up, Robert shouted, 'A cheap loaf, cheap bread and provisions cheaper!' Then off down the road he went, blowing the horn and Downham Tom and Thomas running after, knocking on doors, telling folk about the bustle that had gone on at Downham Market and elsewheres about.

Tessie elbowed me in the ribs. 'What we stood here for?' Off with a skip she went to join the back of the throng. 'Come on with you then,' and she beckoned with a swoop of her arm for me to come.

'A cheap loaf!' she shouted at me.

'And cheap bread!' I shouted back.

'And provisions cheaper!' came a cry from behind as more people joined us.

Mingay, the shopkeeper, shook his fist at us and got a stone through his window for his trouble. We went slow past the rectory to be sure our good Reverend Vachell got an eyeful. Mrs Vachell too. I saw her at the window, struggling with the latch. 'Be off!' she shrieked as she flung it open. 'Oh! You mind my pansies there . . .'

Tessie looked down at the scraggy plants by her feet. She ferreted out a handful and lobbed the plant at the window.

Mrs Vachell bobbed out of the way as it hit the frame. When she saw me, she pointed in horror. 'You, *you*—'

Yes, *me*. I stuck out my tongue and waggled my arms up and down same as if I had wings. 'Roast goose, roast goose!' and I gave a great, hearty laugh.

As we went on our way, plenty more folk I recognised joined along with us. William Beamiss, John Harris and

Francis Torrington, cordwainers all, came up by one side, and publican John Dennis and Thomas Hunt the tailor by the other.

'That Vachell's long been riding for a fall. Way he lords it over us,' muttered Beamiss and the others nodded and patted his shoulder to show they agreed.

We fetched up outside of farmer Martin's house, a new house with two stone lions at the gate. What were they there for? So as to scare us? I'd not worked for him, but a number of others there had. Clear from their grumblings, none remembered it well. When Martin saw us, he straight way started with his threats. If we didn't get ourselves gone, none of us would work for him again. From the cheer that went up, none was much minded by this. A man pushed forward, said he'd worked for Martin too, till he'd recent been let go.

'How's that new shirt of yours?'

All a hush as Martin touched his fingers to his chest.

'My shirt?'

'That's it. The very same.' The man climbed on a wall so we could hear him better. Up by his side clambered two others. 'He paid the three of us less than he pays for that shirt. Then says he can't afford us. My children starve and he dandies hisself up.' A low hiss at this and jeering.

'Shame on you!' I called out.

Martin swung round to see who'd said it. He puffed himself out, overfed moorcock that he was and said, 'You good-fer-nothing little runt of a girl.'

'I'm not,' I said, stung to my heart. Sick of it, I was. Of being treated like that, like I was nowt. Of work that was there one day and then was not. Of working all day and it still not enough at the end of it to keep myself fed. And mutton chops at the farm for pinching my coin and Martin with his dandy new shirt. Sick of the lot of them.

'You're a wrong 'un, you are! A right bastid, that's what,' I hollered, loud as I could.

It all went quiet for the shock that a girl like me could have a voice like that. Then, around me, murmuring, and pretty soon a clammer the like I'd never heard before.

Martin opened his mouth but must have thought better of it and clapped it shut it again. He turned on his tail and slammed the door shut behind him. There came such a crack as the bolt come across. Weren't much, the thought of him hiding, but we cheered at the thought that he was.

By the time we made it back to the the Globe there were many too many of us to count. Some banged pans, some shook sticks, others held pitchforks up high. William Beamiss had been in the butcher's and had his cleaver off him. Red in the face with shouting we were and our hearts full a-fire.

Then someone said Vachell had come out and read the Riot Act at them, and had gone to fetch his pistol.

'Are we afraid of him?' shouted Beamiss.

'No, no!'

'He's a wrong 'un, the worst of them all.' Thomas clenched his fist in the air. 'Bread or blood! Bread or blood! Bread or blood we will have this day!'

Mary

A LITTLE BEFORE midday, still rumpled with sleep, Shelley came downstairs. He reached an arm round Mary and pressed into her back. She felt his arousal nudge against her and elbowed him gently away.

'No. *Elise* . . .' she whispered.

That Elise was only by the hearth, clearing the ashes from the grate, seemed no discouragement. 'What about us does she not know already? *Nothing.*' He took her earlobe between his teeth and nipped it.

Mary pushed him once more, firmer this time. '*No.*'

Oh, the look he gave her, all sunny innocence, palms of his hands open to her, invitation all. 'Mary, Mary.' Eyes widening, *your very last chance.* A pause. A flicker. And then, just as suddenly as it had come, his good mood had gone.

Piqued, he took up the jug from the table and drew away the cover. 'Have we milk?' He sniffed and pulled a face at the smell. He turned through the apples in the dish, one by one, before choosing the least bruised. 'Sour milk, old apples. Riches, beyond compare.' He turned to her, gave a thin smile, and took a bite.

'So, have you a story yet?'

Would he not quit with this questioning of her? Every morning since Albé had made the challenge, the same. In part a tease, she knew, but he did appear to enjoy her discomfort a little too much.

'No. No story.' Mortifying to admit to, again.

Her embarrassment only seemed a source of further delight. 'What a reluctant muse you have. I should give her a kick if I were you. Throw her out, if she continues unwilling.'

'I shall,' said Mary, glad for her failure to be deflected elsewhere. 'And you? How does your story progress?'

'Albé and I have decided not to continue with it.'

Mary suppressed a smile. 'A pity. I thought Albé's idea dramatic and striking.'

'*Vampires?* You think?' Shelley gave a dismissive laugh. 'The difference as I see it, is this: poetry makes immortal all that is best and most beautiful in the world. A story is designed with obvious intent to steer the reader's mind in shallow and limiting ways. Amusing for a day or two, but a distraction.' He wagged the apple at her. 'Distractions are not why we are here.'

A distraction, was it? A story did seem like a silly thing when placed alongside a poem. Yet if it were so silly, why had it defeated her? How could something so seemingly trivial also be so infuriatingly tricky? Shelley and Albé had at least tried, whereas she had failed even to find a beginning.

Shelley crossed over to the window and peered out. 'What day do we have? Any chance of the sun gracing us with its presence? I had hoped to sail later.'

The rain had hung over the lake all morning. It fell with such intensity that the mountains were lost from view. Earlier, when Elise had taken the night soil to the lake, a journey of no distance at all, she had returned so drenched that Mary thought she had tripped and fallen in.

'A reading day, then. Shall we read together, you and I, and then *talk* about it? For hours? Would that please you, dearest Maie?' He was back at her side, his arm scooped around her waist, spinning her round with him.

Then they were off on a mad jig from one side of the room to the other, ducking under a line of limp washing, strung across their path in vain hope it might dry.

'Polidori has a story,' Shelley said as they came to a stop.

'*He does?*' She could not keep the astonishment from her voice.

'Perhaps he might be encouraged to share his approach?'

'Oh! You dare!' She fished up a bundle of wet cloths that had been left to soak in a bucket and ran after him, clattering up the stairs, until it was she who had him cornered, helpless with laughter at her approach.

After they had made love, Shelley rolled out of bed. He pulled on his britches and tumbled out the door as though late for an appointment elsewhere.

'And now, *I* must write.' And, with that, he blew her a kiss and was gone.

She should write too, she thought, as she lay there. She sat up in bed and reached for her notebook. *Everything must have a beginning.*

Everything must have a beginning.

Everything must have a beginning.

Indeed it must. But, oh, if hers was not the most stubborn, unwilling beginning of all. She could summon only a feeling of blank incapability; a dull, boring nothing. Characters from the stories she had read tripped through her mind and gurned at her. She dropped the notebook to the floor and flopped forward, face down. What misery it was to write.

The bed still held their warmth and she pressed her cheek against it. It was, at first, a comfort, then a provocation.

So what if Polidori had a story? She cringed at the thought of his company later. The bragging. What an importuning chancer he was. Hopeful, still, that she would submit. She shuddered. Oh, how was it possible *to be*? To love without loathing, without anger, without scorn? To progress in oneself, *for oneself*, without vanity, cruelty, or bitterness; without diminishing others? She frowned.

It did her no good either to think of her mother, of the advice her mother might have had for her. It was a strange loss she felt: an ache for a woman she had never known; for an irrecoverable other; tantalisingly close and for ever out of reach. Her mother's death had forged her life's consequent shape. It had made Mary who she was. She wondered what might have been if her mother had lived. She did not want to think of that, of a life without Shelley, without Willmouse, without Claire. No, she would not think further on it. She pulled her skirts straight, stood up and went downstairs. While she had been gone, the storm had closed in over them from across the lake. Rain beat against every quarter of the cottage. It chased under the door, coming in around the window frames and pooled in puddles on the sills. Shelley, oblivious, was lost in his work; Claire had risen at last and was combing her hair. Elise had Willmouse on her knee and sang French rhymes to him. Seeing Mary, he reached up his arms.

She leaned down and kissed his nose. '*Un moment, mon petit bébé.*'

She lit candles and lamps, all that they had, and banked the fire until it was roaring. She mopped up the water on the floor and the sills, stuffing cloths into the gaps to prevent further ingress. No matter the storm outside, the house would be lit and they would be dry and they would be warm. She turned to look. Their little home, bright lit in the storm, like a gold cup tossed out to sea. Precious, beyond precious.

That evening, she had not intended to drink but needed it to help her recover in some way. They had chased up the hill, in such imminent peril they had felt, with the storm behind them, heedless of the great gushing torrent that gouged away the path. A great clattering rain had come at them. It stung so hard, Mary had lifted her arm against it in defence. The wind seemed to fall from every mountain at once and met in a terrible tumult. Lightning fractured the heavens with such violence they had cowered from it, as though expecting the sky to fall down in great shards upon them. They tumbled into the villa, battered and breathless, and bolted the door behind them, gulping with relief. And now, with her shoes off, feet bared to the fire, sodden skirts hitched to her knees, Mary could still feel the storm's wild assault on her. She felt giddy, knocked askance, off-kilter. It had left her in mischievous mood. She drank deeply from her glass. The wine tasted, absurdly, of summer fruit, the startling incongruity of which made her laugh. And so, when Polidori came into the lounge to join their group, she was almost delighted to see him and it was she, not he, who broached the subject of Albé's challenge.

'You have written a story, I hear. A terrifying tale . . .' She leaned towards him, wide-eyed and tipsy.

'Oh, do tell us!' said Claire.

Poor Polidori. Even by candlelight, Mary could see how such meagre flattery made him blush.

'I do have a story,' he said, with painfully apparent pleasure.

Needing no further encouragement, he went on to outline a strange little tale, both stultifying in the telling and obvious in its plot. He soon lost Claire's attention and she drew her chair a little closer to Albé and Shelley to listen to them instead. It was a story, Mary had to admit, whereas she had none. So engrossed was he in the telling of it, that he did not ask about her progress. She would not remind him. When he was done, she turned with relief to the conversation of the others.

'. . . and if one were to think wider on this,' mused Shelley.

'It would not be too much to suppose, to imagine,' said Albé, picking up on Shelley's point, 'not *vorticellae*, nor a frog's leg, but the leg of a man, for instance.'

Mary was still only part within earshot. *Vermicelli?* What was it they were talking about? A frog's leg? Ah, they were discussing Erasmus Darwin, she realised.

'A man's leg? Imagine!' Claire screwed her face up with revulsion. 'What would you make it do? *Hop?*' The image was as absurd as it was horrifying and she covered her mouth to stop a spluttering laugh.

'In point of fact, I don't see why not,' countered Shelley. 'The animating principle is the same.'

Mary frowned. If the principle were already understood in a frog, it seemed repellent to seek to establish the same in man by animating a limb. The more she thought about it, the more it troubled her. Where would a man's leg be got from? From a corpse, she supposed. But why would anyone want to effect such a thing? To take a man's leg – *his leg* – and, in Claire's example, make it hop? What grotesque circus that? Grotesque, yes, but also fascinating and disturbing. *No.* She shook the thought away. It was utterly abhorrent.

'*Imagine?*' said Shelley, as he picked up on what Claire had said. 'This is not a matter of conjecture and is in the realm of the possible. It is what Darwin sets out in his work.'

'Ah, but could *life* be made to begin in such a manner?' asked Albé, warming to the idea. 'With the vital spark provided by man? A corpse reanimated? Taking a leg, adding another and so on; a being created that way?'

A hideous thought. They fell into silence as they contemplated it.

'Life, as we know, *is* of man,' countered Shelley, at which Albé roared his approval.

But a child is born of woman, thought Mary. Such an obvious thing it was to say that she kept quiet, for fear of appearing foolish. Twice the experience had been hers and what, after all, could any man know of that? Of the carrying of a child within oneself; of the extraordinary force of gestation and birth? But a child born of man, which they proposed now – to move beyond hypothesis to creation? It was all very well to suppose such things possible, but there must be limits, she thought, to what was acceptable. The pursuit of reason had seemed to her unassailably good: a fundamentally and unquestionably *reasonable* act. But without mind to the consequences, she saw how readily reason might be perverted, how profoundly amoral and heartless it was.

'Perhaps God is necessary after all?' she said, but her question had come too late and went unanswered, drowned out in the rising from chairs and the replenishing of glasses that came after.

And still through the night the storm blew. Albé would not hear of their return and offered them room above the hall where they were gathered. Mary retired first. Though fatigued, she was not sleepy. She stood at the window, lulled by the sound of the men's voices as they drifted up from below. Even with the shutters closed, she could feel the push of the wind against the glass as though the storm were trying to force its way in. It was cold in the room so she went to bed, fully clothed, her eyes open to the dark, searching for the familiar in this unfamiliar room. Anything recognisable took on a cloaked appearance, the shadows of which leapt at her in the candlelight. Then, there by her side, so close she felt she could touch him, she saw a man on his knees, pale and hunched, bent on some hideous task. And, before him, the hideous phantasm of a man stretched out, the thing he had put together. Then, as if on the working of some powerful engine, it stirred with an uneasy, half-vital motion. *He sleeps; but he is awakened; he opens his eyes; behold, the horrid thing stands at his bedside, opening his curtains and looking on him with yellow, watery, but speculative eyes . . .*

Mary sat up, one hand clutched to her chest, her heart racing beneath it. Her thoughts tumbled one over the other as if to sprint away from her. She went to the window and flung open the shutters to light the awful visitation. But as the moonlight fell in it revealed not the phantasm she had seen, but the room in all its familiar, mundane detail. She held out her hands in front of her, studying them, appalled they were hers, as though they were responsible for fashioning the vile creature on the floor.

As the dream fell away, a strange triumph overcame her fear. It was frightful, she knew, a tragedy, but finally, finally she had a story to tell.

John

'I'M NOT PAYING to look at a grey day for the rest of my life, John. We have to live with the picture. Mrs Rebow has had quite enough of the rain.'

'Yes, certainly.' As soon as he had said it, John realised he was not sure what it was he had agreed to. Since the fateful dinner with the Bicknells, he had been endlessly totting up numbers in his head, stacking one on top of the other like a child might stack wooden blocks – careful, careful – to see how high a tower could be made of them. One hundred pounds – the allowance he had – to which he could add the annual interest from the sale of the family estate and proceeds from the corn mill: four hundred pounds, perhaps, in total. And now this Wivenhoe commission. A first.

Major-General Rebow was a man of abrupt, certain opinion and quick to find fault. John must not disappoint. If Rebow did not like this painting, it was doubtful he would consider a commission for anything of similar ambition. John would be back to portraits and the vexatious vanities that accompanied them. He gave a thoughtful nod towards his patron. 'It has been very wet, Mr Rebow.'

But Mr Rebow was not done yet with making his point. 'She does not want it. It would be a miserable thing to have on display. Is that what you want to be known for – dreary paintings of rain?'

In defence of the rain, it had made everything very green, but it was a pleasure John doubted Mr Rebow shared. He wondered the extent to which Mr Rebow used his wife as a proxy for his opinion, to hide thoughts that might otherwise be considered churlish, womanish, even?

They'd taken shelter under a young oak tree, but it afforded little protection against the cold wind that whipped around them. Mr Rebow had on a winter coat of heavy black wool with a brown fur collar that he wore turned up, having the effect of muffling his speech. John regretted not putting on a second shirt that morning. It would make for an uncomfortable few hours sketching; he would be cold to his bones by lunchtime.

'Unfortunately, I have no control over the season.'

The sharp look Mr Rebow gave him left no doubt that the thought would have been best kept to himself. Careful, John. How easily those blocks totter.

'But you could paint it different?'

'I'm sorry—'

'The weather. You're an artist. Art being an interpretation of what you see, you can paint the weather however you like, can you not? Artful-like?'

The observation so surprised John, he had no reply.

'Come off it, John. When you are painting in your room you must have to imagine what is before you?'

John had no need to justify his process to Mr Rebow and was desperate to close the discussion down so as not to give Mr Rebow ease of return. 'I paint, when I can, from nature, as I am now. It is true that in my studio work I use a combination of memory and imagination. But I refer to a library of oil sketches, captured on the spot, throughout. The imaginary—'

'The imaginary! There you have it.' Mr Rebow pressed his hands together as though John had confirmed his thoughts exactly. 'Memory, imagination. Close cousins, are they not? Imagine something brighter than this endless fucking rain is all I am asking.'

Damn it, the man was a test to his patience.

'I've made a few changes to the park since you were here last, John. A good many new trees have gone in to fill the area to the other side of the weir.' Mr Rebow pointed into the distance. 'And fencing put in to stop the deer escaping. It frames the park well, don't you think?'

John noticed a number of juvenile trees and the raw sawn wood of the fencing.

'I like a wild hedgerow as much as any man, but I think you agree that what we have offered up here is a vision of harmony, an Eden, if you will.' Mr Rebow blushed as he realised the extent of his boast. 'I admit our work here cannot be other than a pale imitation of God's intent. I could think of no one better to paint it than you. To capture its . . .'

'Design?' John offered, if only to assuage his host's embarrassment.

'Design. Yes. Exactly so.'

Good. A moment of understanding. Now that he looked, John noticed fences marking every boundary of the park. Did God's plan include such a quantity of posts and planking?

Mr Rebow lapsed into silence and turned his back on the view. 'I've said Mrs Rebow can visit you, as you paint, to be sure she is happy. Often as she likes. You don't mind?'

'Not in the slightest.' Mr Rebow could not have made a more wretched suggestion if he had tried.

'Good man.' At this, Mr Rebow cheered, like a glimmer of sunshine had finally peeped out from behind the clouds and he'd become the weather his wife most craved. As he walked away, he skidded on a patch of mud. He jabbed a finger at the ground. 'None of this fucking mud in it either.'

John raised a hand to show he had understood. He felt the cold seep of the mud come in at the sides of his shoes. Only with difficulty did he manage to extract one foot then the other. When he wrote to Maria that evening, he must do his best not to complain.

With peace returned to him, John stood for a while and let his arms go slack by his sides and his vision go in and out of focus. It was what he liked best, gaining the sense of what was before him, a way to absorb the movement and detail of light, of tone and colour. Then, and after some time, he closed his eyes to let what could not be seen impress upon him too. He heard the wind – the restlessness of it in the tree above him; felt it run through the weave of his shirt and steal the heat from his back. A freshening wind meant a palette at once bright and watery. He blinked his eyes open and rocked back on his feet as the scene before him veered up in all its detail. In the distance, and only just visible, Wivenhoe House. These past few months, the thought of it had occupied him almost entirely, but now that he saw it he realised it did not interest him in the slightest. To make it feature in any meaningful sense, he would have to be *artful* and ignore the trees that obscured it. Several disconsolate cows grazed nearby, their hooves sunk in the mire. The meadow had been grazed flat; brown scars had formed where the grass had been stripped away or been churned into mud. A degree of artistry would be required with that too.

An hour into sketching and he saw the unmistakable form of Mrs Rebow on her approach, a basket looped into the crook of one arm. Luncheon. Or it as excuse for a nosying visit.

He stood politely to one side as she considered what he had sketched. Although she said that she liked it a good deal, she frowned. 'Why are there no clouds?'

'I thought it best to omit them.'

'Why ever would you do that?'

'For the rain they contain.'

She gave a laugh then became quite helpless with laughter. 'Ah, John, John. Has my husband been berating you? It is simply that I do not want a painting forebodingly dark, all gloom and portent. Our new curate has us suffer enough of that kind of thing. A serious fellow he is and thinks us quite without hope. Might we not enjoy paradise *a little*, though we know of its fall? Nothing would please me more, John, than if you could capture the park as it is today. Bright and clear and fresh.'

'If you are certain?'

'Oh, yes. I am. Quite certain.'

But as the painting progressed, the Rebows grew increasingly displeased. It wasn't that it was too dark, or too grey, or too rainy; no protest was made at the sky he settled on – admittedly free of the bucketing showers that had sent him scurrying for shelter many times, but blustery none-theless, showing the rain recently passed through. No. It was the scope of the painting that troubled them.

'It's a little' – Mr Rebow rubbed his chin as he thought – 'little. Smaller than I expected.'

'We do so want Mary included.' Mrs Rebow gave John a hopeful look. 'And the hunting lodge.'

'Is it fixable, Constable?' Mr Rebow arched an eyebrow in question. 'To have the hunting lodge here' – he waggled his fingers in the space to the right of the canvas – 'and some addition that includes our little Mary here?' His hands formed a vague shape to the left of it.

Constable looked from his canvas to the expectant faces of the Rebows. His immediate response was to dig in his heels and object. He could understand why they would want their daughter Mary included but she would be little more than a half-dozen brush strokes at most and recog-nisable only to them.

Mrs Rebow took his silence for reticence and gave an impatient tut. 'We are doing what we can to help you. You know the regard with which we held your father and we sympathise deeply for your loss. In proposing this commis-sion we hoped it would ease matters as regards your marriage prospects . . .'

John managed a weak smile. The friendship with his father had been occasion for discussion of his personal affairs, he saw now. 'Yes. And I thank you for your generous support. Let me think what I can do.'

He could attach a canvas strip to either side and extend the painting that way. But it was not an ideal solution and would require skill if the joins were not to show. There were risks to extending it. It would take the painting in an uncertain direction, away from a format typically expected for this subject.

Typically expected? The devil with that. He would give the Rebows what they wanted.

And so he added a canvas extension to each side and painted, frantically, in snatches, as fat raindrops dripped heavily down on him through the last week of August.

And when he was done, he left with full payment and the happy sound that a weight of guineas could make in a leather purse. In his other pocket, he carried a letter from his friend John Fisher telling him to stop his shilly-shallying around and get on with it. *Marry her!* If he must come to London to conduct the service himself to ensure it, then he would.

As John was driven away from the park, he thought back to Mr Bicknell's dismissal of him. Short of John's election to the Royal Academy – and God only knew when he might expect that – he knew he would be in no better position than he was now. Perhaps it was the rattle of guineas in his purse, but something wilful had grown in him these past few weeks – like a small shoot pushing up through the cold earth and into the light.

Then he remembered how ill the season fared. Not a small shoot then. He cast about for another analogy but was at a loss to find one that would do.

Hope Peter

THEY FOUND THE Cock on Grafton Street without difficulty. Peter shook the rain from his clothes and ordered
ale for him and Willie. Through the thick fug of tobacco
smoke, he could just make out the man who'd addressed
the crowd at Billingsgate, sitting at a table at the far end of
the room. Three others were seated with him, but not one
did he recognise. All the candles were lit though it was
afternoon, the shutters bolted against the rattling storm.
Though the room was warm, the damp of his clothes clung
to him and a deeper cold gnawed at him. He felt a heavy
weariness come on, to be here at all, chasing after what
likely would turn out to be a rat.

'Just sup your ale, while I figure out what's what with
this lot,' Peter said as he and Willie made their way over.

'We need pikes,' said one of the group in an urgent
whisper, turning sharply as Peter came up.

On seeing Peter, the man from the market reached out
a hand. 'Welcome, brother.' He rose to his feet with an
eagerness normally kept for good acquaintances. From his
surprise, it was clear he'd not expected Peter to come.
'Please, come join us. Our table is yours.'

Two of the men, at first seeming reluctant, shuffled their
stools sideways to make room for Peter and Willie to sit
down. Peter nodded his thanks and stole a look at them

both as he did. All wore the same hungry look, though it was clear from the dishes piled up that he'd caught them at the end of a meal.

'As I was saying, pikes—'

An older man, easily with twenty years on Peter, held up his hand to silence what was being said. From how they looked at him, his was the word that was listened to. 'You're ahead of yourself, Preston.' He turned to address Peter. 'Are you here to join us?'

Peter took the ribbon from his pocket and laid it on the table, 'My name is Peter Dunn and this here is Willie Hutchen. I am back from the war with nothing. I want to know what it is you are for.'

The man extended a hand to him. 'Name's James Watson and I am glad you decided to find us. This is Arthur Thistlewood. Seems you know each other already. This here's Thomas Preston.' He cocked his head in the direction of the man so vexed about pikes. 'And John Hooper.'

'Take it you're here for the same reason as us?' asked Hooper.

Before Peter could reply, Thistlewood spoke for him. 'He was a soldier.'

'So?' Hooper appraised Peter with a heavy suspicious look. ''Tis only you thinks that is important.'

'John . . .' Thistlewood's voice wore an edge of caution, suggesting he'd had cause to have the same words before. 'Let's not chase away our friend before he has chance to know us.'

The men called themselves Spencean Philanthropists. These were bad times and they would do something about it. Willie took a noisy sup of froth off the top of his ale.

'So what brings you two to town?' asked Watson.

'This and that,' answered Peter. He never was easily brought into a stranger's confidence and wasn't letting this be the start of it.

'Looking for work,' said Willie at just the same time.

'This-ers and that-ers?' Watson's eyes were bright with amusement. He turned to Peter. 'A soldier were you? At Waterloo?'

'I was.'

'Thought as much. I've an eye for such things.' Watson drank up what was in his cup. 'If it's work you're after, we can find you something to do. We have plenty of money for everything.' He lifted his hand and ordered a pitcher of ale and another of porter. Perhaps it was a way to show the truth of his word, for he dug in his pocket and brought out a fistful of coins, guineas among them, Peter saw.

'For many, death would be relief, such is their distress.' Watson picked through the coins in his hand. 'The Tories care only for their own. Abolishing taxes for them that are best able to pay them. The land is our farm, that's what we believe. There is land enough in this isle for six or seven acres to be given to every man, woman and child. Would there be starving then?'

'No,' said Preston, 'there fucking would not.' He filled up his cup till it overflowed the top and drank deeply.

Watson pushed his half-eaten plate of pie towards Willie. 'Hungry, are you?'

Willie looked to Peter, who nodded. Not a wink of this missed by Watson. 'The boy yours, is he?'

Without a moment in which it could be doubted, Peter

replied, 'Yes.' He watched Willie shovel up the pie. Once was he'd have had it off him and eaten it himself.

'New to London, are you?' When Peter gave no answer, Watson went on, 'Isn't one among us who hasn't made their way here the same.'

'Can't say I care for it. Weren't by choice.'

'Oh?' Watson raised an eyebrow.

This man and his questions, thought Peter; worse than the lad on a quiet day. He felt Watson's eyes on him, studying him; could feel his story being drawn out of him without need for words.

Watson nodded slowly. 'You'll find London has a generous cloak for those wanting to be hid.'

Peter shrugged. 'I need work and then I will be right.'

The door clattered open and a constable came in, accompanied by two yeoman guards. As Peter huddled down, so did the others, their voices dropping low too. He saw the same wariness in them that had dogged his every step since leaving Corringham. Perhaps he was among his own kind after all.

Seemed the constable was only after sheltering from the storm and having cast an eye about the room to see who was most likely to pick his pocket, he settled at the bar, happy to share the cheer of a beer and a pipe in the dry.

Peter's gathering closer to Thistlewood and the others brought them into a necessary confidence. Watson told of the time he had been an apothecary in Lincolnshire and the prosperous times he'd had with it too. John Hooper hailed from Yorkshire. It was hard to glean much from what Thomas Preston had to say. He was a shoemaker, but not much else of sense could be had from him. The man was pissed to begin with and then only more so and seemed there only for the ale. Thistlewood, he determined, was a man he could trust after all. He'd been a soldier too, good with a sword, rising to lieutenant in the Royal Lincolnshire before he was sent out to the West Indies. Peter had respect for him for that. It added up to a deal more than the first impression he'd had of him standing on a box in the rain, haranguing the good folk of Billingsgate.

Another jug of porter was ordered and fetched.

'Cheers,' said Peter and took a sup. Oh, it was tasty. Dark, treacly sweet, with a rich, liquorice tang. He drank in big gulps, grateful for it. Had to stop himself downing it in one. By his fourth cup, he was no longer so caring about what should be kept to himself and what he would tell of and it came out then how the war was a terrible infliction not just on him but on all soldiering men. He told of his return home and the fucking idiocy of the hares. He thought it might raise a laugh because there was grim humour in the telling, but they only shook their heads. At the end of it, he closed his eyes, beyond tired. The truth of it was this: the fear was back in him, the fear he'd be shot or run through at any moment. A Frenchie there, or a constable here, what difference did it make? Either way, if he wasn't careful he'd end up fucking dead.

Watson took a moment before he spoke. 'We've come by different paths, but we are met here in the same place.' He raised his cup and touched it to Peter's.

They agreed they would meet again in a week's time. Before that, and if it pleased him, Peter could find Watson the very next day at 9 Greystoke Place where work would be found for him and an advance paid.

Watson emptied his glass and set it on the table. 'Until then.' And before Peter could answer, he'd turned his attention back to Preston and the matter of the pikes.

He and Willie left not long after. Out in the street again, Willie heaved up the pie in the gutter.

'Next time, don't gobble it up so fast.'

Willie gave a sorrowful nod, lifted one leg, and let out a fart.

That night, they slept under a narrow arch. It provided scant shelter but Peter was too knackered to look for anything else. Tomorrow, he'd have coin in his pocket, enough perhaps for them to find part share of a room. As the wind changed direction, hail funnelled through without regard for those huddled there or the curses they threw back at it. Peter hunched his back to it, feeling it pelt against his shoulders, the cold burning his ears and neck. The hail crusted on his jacket and froze, stiffening like a gibbet about him.

Willie let out a cry. Ah, for fuck's sake. Peter sank to the ground and drew the shivering lad to him, to give him the warmth he had. It wasn't just this summer that seemed lost; at that moment he could well believe there'd never be a summer again. 'Here, lad,' he said and he drew a memory towards him as if on a thread. He told Willie of when he was his age and larking about in the shallows without a stitch on and the sun burning his arse red. Not that he'd cared. It had been worth it for the feel of it, for his knackers jiggling free between his legs. And the afternoons he'd spent, staring up at the sky and the thick heat of August on him, watching dragonflies dart by his nose and swifts in black flashes and their mad cavorting about in the sky. Stories. Only stories. What part of it was true no longer mattered. It was comfort for him too. This fucking weather would chase every bird from the sky; dragonflies would drop out of it, frozen like sticks.

Peter woke in a puddle of slush with Willie still clung fast to him, his head tucked into his chest. Peter eased out one leg, but was too stiff to move any of the rest of him. The lad weighed nothing, might only have been made from thin pickings gleaned from the wind, but had him pinioned to the ground the same. A weakness had come into Peter that night; he had no strength to lift the lad, as if a thief had been and had robbed Peter's bones from out of him. When he coughed, his chest cracked with pain.

'Willie? Willie, lad?' Peter ruffled the boy's hair. 'Willie?'

Not a peep.

'Willie?'

Then he knew.

Peter let out such a cry and the lad still on him. But no cry, no matter how loud, could wake the dead.

A woman, sheltering nearby and hearing the din, came running over. She eased Willie off, rolling him sideways into the gutter.

'Poor mite,' she said when she saw what had passed. She reached out her hand so as to help Peter to his feet. But Peter could not. He covered his eyes with one hand. He'd fancied himself father to the lad. What kind of father would bring a child here and expect shelter? Why had he brought him to London at all? Precious little hope for a grown man, never mind a boy. He should have picked up that stone and shooed him off when he'd had chance to. But no, he'd brought him into the bedlam of his life and his own selfish disregard. What bastard would do that? What kind of man would let a child die?

'Was the boy yours?' the woman asked, still with her hand held out. She spoke with an Irish accent, but the gentle lilt of her voice was unbearable to him.

Twice he'd been asked that, in less than a day, but this time he shook his head. 'No, he was not.' It near broke him to say it.

She told him her name was Róisín. *Róisín*, it fell upon him with the same gentleness as her voice. 'Come on now. We will take the child to Father O'Cuinn. He will know what to do.'

'His name was Willie, so I reckon he was no Catholic.'

'There is nowhere else I know of to take him. He had no say in his name. We'll take him and God will be waiting for him there.'

This time he allowed her to help him to his feet and between them they lifted the lad on to his shoulder. Out from under the arch they went, through a narrow cut and on to Bond Street. Each road they turned into she told him the name of it so that Peter would know: Bond Street, Burlington Gardens, Vigo Street. The rain came at a savage slant as they crossed Regent Street. They dodged between the carriages and carts and the chancing touts selling ha'penny bets and a girl pressing a rabbit's foot charm on him. All of life pushed past him regardless, uncaring or blind, and he knew not what was worse: those who saw and looked away or those who did not look at all. He hated the city the more for it. Then they were on Warwick Street and stopped in front of a plain, red-brick building. 'Here it is,' said Róisín. 'St Gregory Church.'

Once inside, they laid Willie down on a pew at the back. Peter felt Róisín's hand rest on his shoulder and her solemn stillness go into him. 'I'll go find the priest now.'

The lad should never have put his trust in him. Peter had no home to shelter him, how could he have hoped to keep the lad dry? He had no hearth, how had he hoped to keep the lad warm? He had no employ, so how was the lad ever to be fed? He'd fought for this country, but for what? So a poor lad, who had nowt to begin with, could die in his lap in the gutter?

As he saw Róisín and the priest approach from out of the gloom, Peter held his head in his hands. For the first time in as long as he could remember, he wept.

Sarah

SOME SAID WE should have gone home then, after taking ourselves round the town, and giving them a good shouting at. Showed them, hadn't we, the long and tall of what we had to say? But what did that give us other than summat to tell each other when we'd crawled out hungry again from our beds? Stories never filled anyone's belly that I knew. Besides, farmers were bastids. They'd remember them of us who'd shouted the most. We needed a magistrate to agree to what we wanted, same as the magistrate had at Downham Market. But there was none such here, other than Vachell, to take our appeal to, and what sympathy would we have off him? The other magistrates lived in Ely with the other fine to-dos. Until we had a magistrate's say-so on the matter, spit on his hand and shook on it, then we had nowt. Worse than nowt. For, further besides, as mole catcher George were then keen to remind us, hadn't Vachell gone to fetch his pistol? Were we to let him? And be afeared of him ever after? When this got talked of it caused such a ruckus, same as a storm had twisted up in the midst of us all. No, we'd not stand for it. We'd have that pistol off Vachell and face him up fair. Then we'd find a magistrate who'd listen and get his word off him.

We found Vachell stood on his step, pistol in his hand,

waiting for us. Next to him stood the others of the parish board and Henry Martin and his wife. It were getting dark a little and some held torches above them. Shadows danced on their faces, making boggarts of them all.

Vachell would be heard first. 'There being more than twelve of you—'

'Aye, aye, we can count—'

There being more than twelve of you,' he shouted, drawing hisself up tall. He stuffed his pistol in his belt and pulled a scroll from his pocket. 'And your intentions *being clearly riotous*—'

Booing at this when he said it. 'Oh, the Riot Act, is it?'

Tessie pushed forward. 'We've come to speak with you, is all.'

'*And being unlawfully, riotously and tumultuously assembled*—'

'Will you not hear us?'

Vachell gestured for a torch to be brought close so he could read what was on the scroll. 'Our sovereign lord the King *chargeth* and *commandeth* all persons, being assembled, *immediately* to disperse themselves, and *peaceably* to depart to their habitations, or to their *lawful* business, upon the *pains* contained in the Act made in the first year of King George, for preventing tumults and riotous assemblies. God save the King.'

God save the King? Weren't no one threw their hat up at that.

Vachell's hand rested back to his pistol. 'Well, then. You have had your warning. I'll blow the brains out of the first man who crosses my step. Take yourselves off. I'll not warn you again.'

A roar went up as the crowd heaved forward; aye, he

might shoot one of us, but he could not shoot us all. Three men rushed at Vachell from the side and had the pistol off him quick.

'Oi, Martin, give us a try on of that shirt!' A man grabbed Martin by the shoulder, looking to have his coat off him. Martin shoved back. Well, he might as well have shoved us all for the cry that went up. *Bread or blood! Bread or blood! Bread or blood!*

Vachell and Martin and the rest of them turned and were in through the front door but hadn't chance to shut it behind them. The man who'd taken a fancy to Martin's shirt followed after, then just as soon was back. 'They're on their way out through the scullery and are headed to Ely.'

'Cowards,' shouted Tessie. 'Hope they run all the way.'

Thomas gave a broad grin and held the door wide open. 'Gentlemen and ladies, do come in.'

And then we saw, with them gone the house was ours. So that's how I found myself in Vachell's front parlour, pressed to the wall, gone meek. Weren't proper to be stood there not invited, expecting the maid to come in and tell me to get my filthy feet off the rug.

I stood by the dresser. It was taller than me and had glass in it, same as all the windows had. I saw the dint of my reflection and, behind, all the pretty pots in a neat arrangement. I reached in and picked a dog with blue eyes and white curls and a red collar with a tiny gold buckle all painted on. I turned the pot in my hand and wondered about who had painted it and how there was work like that so different to mine and I wondered if they ever got hungry too. Prettiest thing I had ever seen. My throat ached because

I knew my grubby hands shouldn't be on it. I touched a finger to its black nose and then put the pot back where it was.

Thomas came up next to me and yanked open a drawer. In it, lined up neat as the Sunday folk on Vachell's pews, though many more plentiful, silver cutlery of all kinds, large and small, knives on the left, forks on the right, spoons in the middle.

'Blimey! The Royal Mint.' Mole catcher George went to scoop up what was there. 'I'll have some of that.'

'No you'll not.' Downham Tom stepped in between them and shut the drawer.

'That fucker owes me.'

'Owes us all,' said Thomas. 'Ain't right he has this and you know it. Damn all the parsons to hell, they don't subscribe anything towards the maintenance of the poor. They abolish taxes on themselves then says we have to accept our place. Five pence off the parish a week I get. And they suppose me to live on it?'

'We're not here to thieve. But that don't mean we can't show him what we think.' Downham Tom picked up a dish from the dresser and lifted it above his head. He let the pot drop and it splintered to bits at his feet. 'Oops. That was clumsy of me.'

Half of us went *oh* and the other half went *ah*, and all of us giddy like our manners had jumped out of us and were rolling about on the floor.

Tessie passed Thomas a plate from the dresser and, *oops*, that got dropped too. Then she took two plates for herself and threw them against the wall.

'Tessie!'

'It'll learn him, that's all. Come on, your turn.' She reached behind her and grabbed hold of the pottery dog. 'Here . . . Well, go on then,' she said, when I'd not take it from her.

I looked at the pot. It weren't real. Not a real alive thing. I'd never do harm to anything like that. Just a pot. A daft pot dog. So, with that, I grabbed hold, brought my arm back and hurled it from me and it smashed to bits in the grate.

'Right,' said Tessie, as if that had it decided. She swooped her arm around my shoulders and steered me out of the door. With her other hand, she grabbed a fancy glass bottle off the side table, knocked the stopper off the top and took a swig. 'Let's see what's upstairs.'

As we went out, we passed a man taking a piss on the rug. I turned to see Thomas pull the drawer out that Downham Tom had shut and tuck what spoons he could in his pockets.

What followed that night was the same. I woke, topsy-turvy, with my feet on the pillow on Mrs Vachell's bed. I had Tessie by my one side and Downham Tom on the other. We'd dressed ourselves in Mrs Vachell's fancies. Downham Tom had a corset on over his shirt and red rouge on his lips. Lilac ribbons tied about his head and I remembered that was my doing. He was the bonniest man I ever saw.

'Hello, Tom,' I said when he opened his eyes.

'Hello,' he said, surprised to see me, and red as his lips when he saw the corset he had on.

We picked our way downstairs, past them still asleep on the stairs and them in the kitchen, ferreting after a breakfast of sorts. A fire had been set in the grate and was being fed with a kitchen chair leg and sermons. Shutters hung from the window. I had to be careful where I stepped because anything that could have been broken was broke. Across the floor, splinters of pottery, like seeds thrown across it, but who'd want the harvest this would make?

Tessie covered her mouth and turned to me with a *did we do this?* look.

Well no, not the all of it, but it had started with us and we knew it. Tessie still had on a blue skirt and an orange bodice off another dress: three sizes too large and hanging down off her shoulders. I suppose I looked no better: pink and green with feathers and my same old feet sticking out the bottom.

We'd made a mess all right, showed Vachell what we thought of him, but what good was that? Vachell would come back and see it and then what? We still did not have a magistrate's word on anything.

Downham Tom was thinking the same thing. He wiped his mouth on his sleeve. 'We need to press on and get more on our side. Take our case to the magistrates. Just as we did at Downham Market.'

'Why would the Ely magistrate listen to us?' asked Tessie.

'If we go to Ely and get Ely folk on our side, they'll have to listen. We're hundreds here, but we'll be thousands there.'

And then the jesting was gone from us. We roused the rest and fetched carts and fixed on punt guns both sides to show that we meant it. As we made our way out of

Littleport the tumult of our night was plain to see: the butcher's and the baker's and other houses all broken up the same.

'We showed them,' said mole catcher George. But nothing got said at this. We had no bread and now we'd no baker to bake it.

The road to Ely had ditches either side to drain it so though it was wet our carts could make their way with us sat on top and not needing to get off and push. The Bedford Level Commissioners had not reckoned with that, they had not, when they sunk their ditches in. Water stood in lakes on the fields they had drained. We sore needed a plentiful year, but how would we get one with the land being so drowned? What could grow up through that? The geese seemed happy enough. Great numbers had gathered and they stretched and beat their wings. Here and there, a heron, stern upright, stabbed at the water, mistaking its shadow for a fish. All there was to see was everywhere around, laid out flat and Ely Cathedral ahead and all our attention fixed on it. For anyone looking back the other way, what would they see? Us, clear as anything. Same as we could see them: a line of men on horseback, blocking the way. Twenty or more, all in their best. The morning's light on their sabres and the horse brass rattling made them no prettier a sight. There might have been twenty of them but there were more of us. So, they had sabres. Well, we had punt guns. I looked back in the direction we had come, at the line of our carts stretched halfway to Littleport and when I saw us all, the fear I had in me gave way. And though it were yet cold, a fire had took up in my heart.

'Well then, this is it.'

'How did they know to expect us?'

'Vachell and Martin come this way, did they not? Must have given them good warning.'

One man rode forward. 'I'm Reverend William Metcalf. What is your business in Ely?'

'You're to stand out of our way and let us go where we are headed.'

The reverend straightened hisself in the saddle. 'That I shall not. I have had word you intend a riot in Ely.'

I were up on my feet at that. 'We want the magistrate's say-so.' I saw his eye go across me and the wondering it had in it.

'The magistrate's say-so on what?'

Then Tessie was up on her feet beside me. 'We're starving! It's not right that we are.'

'Our demands are not for you,' said Downham Tom. 'We will put them before the Ely magistrates.'

'I am an Ely magistrate,' he thundered. A funeral bell could not have got us to hush up quicker. 'But if you think that I, astride my horse, in the middle of the Fen, am in a position to agree to anything with you then you are seriously mistaken. The Ely magistrates sit once a quarter—'

'If they're not sitting today then we're not interested. We're not waiting for your convenience. Seeing as you are here, you will listen.' Downham Tom turned to us. 'Will you tell him what it is we're after?'

The price of bread cheaper.

'*A living wage!*'

'*Our children are starving, give us a living wage.*'

'*I work and still do not have enough.*'

'*The price of a stone of flour per day, that's what's needed.*'

Metcalf scowled. Clear enough he had no understanding of what it was we meant. 'I do not consider that under the existing conditions an increase in wages is reasonably required—'

'You don't, don't you not?'

We were all shouting now. Tired of trying to get them that should know better to see how it was. But how could you make someone see when they was happy not to? When they had a hand in tying their own blindfold on? Even our ponies were tired of it and had started to nudge their way in the direction of Ely again.

When he saw we weren't for stopping and would push through his line, Metcalf stood in his stirrups, his face flustered red. 'I will take what you have said to the other magistrates, but only on condition that you return to Littleport.'

'Oh, you do that,' said Downham Tom, same fire in his eyes as I had in me. 'But we've come this far. We're not going back. Now, you will stand out of our way . . .'

As we passed him by, the reverend pulled a scroll from his pocket and read us the self-same words we'd heard the night before. But his words were no more than nuisance flies about us and we had hardened ourselves to that. 'Shame on you,' I said as we went by.

He didn't wait to see us all go past. He turned his horse around tight on itself and headed on ahead of us at full gallop for Ely.

Mary

IF SHE STARED hard enough, for long enough, she fancied she could see something other: a haze, a chimera; as pure a vision of nature as she thought possible. A place, un-peopled – apart from the tourists who had made it here before them, their footprints evidence of their giddy delight. Thankfully, she and Shelley and Claire had left their companion group further behind and had this spot to themselves. Having made the effort to be here, she would not want to share it with those whose desire was only to gawp or express themselves by way of wild exclamation. As she drew her scarf from her face, a cold, like no other, shocked her breath from her. Their guide motioned urgently that she should wrap her scarf around her again, which she did, feeling foolish. Below, the Mer de Glace heaved up into vast ice peaks. From somewhere beneath the glacier came the sound of creaking and cracking as the ice pushed forward with a force and violence she could barely imagine. Their guide had told them that it gained a foot every day. Yet what struck her was the fragility of it too. Above the crevices, ice crystals lifted in white smoke; marbled streaks of shadow ran quickly across the plateau, thrown down by the snow clouds above, as if looking for escape. Beautiful, dreadful; relentless in its desolation; the most desolate place in the world. Mary blinked slowly, as though afraid that this slight movement might shatter the vision apart.

They had come up the glacier by mule, as far as they could, then clambered the rest of the way over boulders, brought down by a recent avalanche. The dull thunder of avalanches had accompanied them on their ascent. They had narrowly avoided being caught in a smaller fall and it was only at their guide's insistence that they were held back when they had wanted to press on. And then came the snow's sudden drop, the sound of it conjured from nowhere, it seemed. Though it had not reached them they were rattled nonetheless. For some time after their voices wore the nervous edge of a near miss. Just a small fall of snow, the guide had laughed, dismissing it, but enough to have swept them off the path, through the shattered pine trees and into the valley below. Finally, they reached a point where they could go no further, boulders completely choking the way. Further progress from this vantage point was impossible. This was it: she had come as far as she could, to the edge of what was possible. She sat down abruptly on a rock, exhilarated by the notion.

She had thought she would write a little and had tucked a pencil and notebook into her pocket for that very purpose. But what loon would suppose that could be done? It was far too cold to contemplate. She felt the tug of the story she had begun nonetheless; a restlessness that would have her off the mountain and writing it if she were to concede to its importuning demands. Begone! Wretched thing. She closed her eyes and thought of her monster, *her Prometheus*. She blinked her eyes open and searched the landscape before her, as though she might find him hidden there.

Her attention was drawn to Claire who, it appeared, was waiting for her reply. At Mary's smile, Claire reached out her hand.

'Dear Mary, I think you are quite deaf. Come here, by me, and look at the view from here.'

'I shall. I shall.' But as she went to join her, Shelley came and sat down by Mary's side. 'Claire is looking better, don't you think? A deal better than she has in days. The altitude is good for her.'

'I didn't realise she was ailing.'

She watched Claire raise a hand to her brow and stare into the same inscrutable distance.

'You know how she is,' Shelley replied. This was said in a way that seemed to suggest otherwise; that hinted at some confidence between them of which Mary had no part.

'No? How is she?' Mary kept her voice steady though, truly, it pained her to know that Claire went to him first. 'Tell me then. Why should I always be the last to know?'

Shelley took a breath but even then did not speak.

'Well?'

'She is expecting a child. She says it is Albé's.'

'Oh!' Mary's shoulders fell at the news. It was both a surprise and it was not. She had supposed this would happen, it being only a matter of when. This whole sorry escapade was bound to carry them to this point sooner or later. As certain as the sun's route across the sky from sunrise to sunset. The only surprise, it seemed, was that Shelley had chosen to tell her here, in Chamonix, when they were just the three of them. Perhaps he had needed time away from Albé too. Yet any surprise she felt was quickly replaced with concern. 'Has Albé been told?'

Oh, how timid these men, she thought, when she saw first his discomfort and then his relief at being able to share the burden with her.

'Yes,' he said.

'How long have you known?'

'A little more than a week.'

A week? And yet he had said nothing? 'And Albé's opinion?'

'I spoke with him. It was difficult. He denied it. Then accepted. Oh, Pecksie Maie, do not give me that look. He is his own man. Charming. Stubborn. Brilliant.'

'Selfish. Unreliable.' She might have added more besides.

'She knew that. The risks.'

'Do not speak of risks, as if these are borne equally.' Really, she thought crossly, as if she need remind him. 'And so?'

'So?'

She turned away from him, exasperated by the need to explain. 'What now? If he knows and admits – what arrangement will be made? For her? For the child?'

He gave her a blank look, momentarily confused. 'There is provision for Claire in my will . . .'

'But, my love, that requires you to die!' It seemed incomprehensible that no arrangement would be made. Her thoughts ran ahead as a sudden fierce need to protect Claire overcame her. 'But you must talk with him. He will listen to you.'

Shelley shook his head. 'The will is my affair. It is hardly my business then to tell him anything—'

'You must! What else should she do? *Vanish?* Are we to erase these last few weeks, this adventure; pretend it did

not happen? There will be a child! A child!' It was preposterous they had not discussed what next. 'It is easy for
him . . .'

'Easy is not the word I would—'

'No, I expect not,' she interrupted, losing patience. 'What
man ever does?' It was a heartless thing to say, she knew.
But what position was Claire in? What position any
woman? She had been Claire once, coming to him with
news of their child and now Claire was her. And as for the
infant child? Poor mite. To be so discussed before it had
drawn its first breath. 'You must talk with him again.'

Mary would not leave him until she had secured his
agreement on this, which he gave, albeit reluctantly. He
rose to his feet under some pretext to be away from her
and seemed glad to be so. Mary rose too and went to Claire's
side. She threaded her arm through Claire's.

Claire rested her hand on Mary's and gave it a squeeze,
then grew pensive. 'I saw you two talking. He has told you,
hasn't he?'

'Yes, he has.'

'Are you angry with me? Think me stupid? I am stupid.'

'I'm not angry with you. Nor do I think you stupid.'

Claire brought her hands to her belly and held them
there. 'He doesn't hate me. At first, I thought it some small
consolation. But it's not. Because I am nothing. Nothing
to him. Hatred, at least, requires passion. Sometimes, when
he looks at me, it is as if I am not there and I have to pinch
my arm to remind myself that I am. I was fully and freely
and happily his, as if that should make him care. But now
I see he does not. Not in the slightest. He cares only for
himself and little else. I do love him. I do. It's desperate

really. Without hope.' Claire spoke quickly, her words in a tumble as though she had not breath for them all. 'Why can't he want me as Percy wants you? I'm afraid, Mary. What a fool I have been. You won't tell, will you? Mother? *Godwin?* Oh, God. I thought I'd not mind who knew, but I do. I mind more than anything. You bear it so well, Willy, that is. Not caring what people say. I admire you so for that.'

Mary blinked. She crossed her arms in front of her to hold herself in. *Whore.* That's what Godwin had called her when she had first taken up with Shelley. The memory still had the capacity to sear her, to bring indignant tears to her eyes. And no word from him other than several requests for money. If she were whore, then what did that make him? To revile her and her beloved, but not his money? *Whore.* So he had disowned her, but she was still her mother's daughter. She had tried to be generous, to understand her father's motives, but it exhausted her. She had, with all childish innocence, believed him good, fervently so, as any child would. *Whore.* So be it. She was not a child any more.

'Shelley will talk to Albé. We cannot assume his reply. You should not, in any case, rely on him. We will find somewhere together on our return.' Return? Here she was, discussing it as though it were certain when in fact this was the first time it had been mentioned in anything other than vague terms. Shelley, she knew, would be preoccupied with publishers on reaching England, so this – this matter with Claire – would fall to her to resolve. 'Of course, you will live with us, or close at hand, until your confinement is over. We will cope somehow. And Albé?' she asked, sounding more tentative. In all this, how he might be part of their future had been quite forgotten.

Claire slumped. 'Perhaps, in time, he will care for his child.'

Perhaps, Mary thought, but she was not confident of it. What was this summer to him but a brief sojourn before reaching the place he most wanted to be? And who were they but a useful, slight distraction, to beat back against boredom and loneliness?

When they had returned to their hotel, they thanked their guide and bade him farewell. They stood for a moment so as to see him off, but the guide made no sign of leaving.

'I think we are expected to tip him,' said Shelley. He patted his pockets. 'I brought nothing out with me, I'm afraid.' He looked hopefully at Mary then shook his head in an exaggerated manner, a degree of foolishness being required in pursuit of a weaselling attempt to escape the tip.

'Really,' said Mary. 'No.' And, with that, she went in.

Perhaps it was the cold, perhaps it was Claire's bleak joyous news, perhaps it was but one small remembered part of Godwin's unkindness, but something had hardened in her. It had been lodged in her for a little while now, she realised, hard and unyielding, like a small stone trapped in her shoe.

Two days later, they were back at Diodati. Perhaps Albé only did it to provoke Claire, but he did so want Mary's attention.

'Tell me, how is that story of yours coming along? When it is finished, shall we publish our stories together, side by side?'

Well then, hers would be published alongside a blank page, she might have retorted, remembering that he had given up on his. 'It progresses. Slowly. But it progresses. Thank you.'

'Not quite writing itself?'

No more than *Childe Harold* had written itself. 'It is not what I first thought it was, that is all. I found something larger inside.'

Albé widened his eyes. It was a way he had, that made one feel immediately and fully his, no less beguiling or disarming for knowing it a habit he had perfected through practice. She took time in answering him so as first to enjoy the effect and then to dismiss it.

'Shelley encouraged me to think more on it.'

At the sound of his name, Shelley looked up from the book he was reading and gave her a warm smile.

'Well then, there it is. But I suspect the cleverness is yours, *dear.*'

She let this remark pass over her. It might have charmed her once, but now she saw it for what it was: facetious, winnowing. 'Whatever it is, in the end, it must have worth.'

'*Worth?* So not a story at all, then?' He laughed. 'And its theme?' he asked, by now a little perplexed at the coldness of her tone, at her resistance. Mary touched a finger to her collar to show how flattered she was to have been asked and lifted her eyes to meet his. 'Selfishness, I think. A life lived in pursuit of the self without regard.'

'Without regard to what?'

'And responsibility,' she continued, declining to answer his question. 'Or rather, its abnegation. A moral tale, I think.'

Not a flicker at that. 'Do send it to me when it is finished. I should be delighted to read it.'

'But of course. It would give me great pleasure if you did.' Her heart beat furiously at her audacity, but it was he who looked away first.

'And how fares my dear Shelley – atheist, lover of humanity, *democrat*? I am glad you are returned to me safe.' He brought his arm around Shelley's shoulders. For the briefest of moments, Mary thought she saw her dear love cringe.

A gloomy letter arrived from Fanny; quite the gloomiest letter that had come from her and sufficient to stall thoughts of a hurried return. England, by her account, was grim and grey and famished.

> They talk of a change of Ministers; but this can effect no good; it is a change of the whole system of things that is wanted. Mr Owen, however, tells us to cheer up, for that in two years we shall feel the good effect of his plans; he is quite certain they will succeed. I have no doubt that he will do a great deal of good; but how he can help to make the rich give up their possessions, and live in a state of equality, is too romantic to be believed . . .

Mary skipped ahead, looking for what she knew would be there: not words, but numbers.

You seem to have forgotten Kingdon's £300 . . .
Oh, goodness, no, she had not! –

Papa has had a great deal of plague and uneasiness about it, and has at last been obliged to give Kingdon his promissory note, payable on demand, so that every hour is not safe. Kingdon is no friend, and the money Government money, and it cannot be expected that he will show Papa any mercy. I dread the effect on his health. He cannot sleep at night and is indeed very unwell . . . Taylor of Norwich has also come upon him again; he says, owing to the distress of the country, he must have money for his children . . .

Mary touched her hand to her brow. The world could not be shut out, their troubles would find them even here.

It was growing increasingly difficult to find what they needed too; prices for the most basic commodities leapt ahead of their dwindling purse. More than anything, they were tired. One stubborn grey day followed another, until their mood bruised grey too. And the rain, the rain – the optimism and hopefulness she had arrived with seemed irrecoverable, washed away with it. The mountains that had so made her spirit soar when she first saw them, were lost in cloud. It was a bleak thought when she realised she might not see them again, that in some way she was already gone from this place with only her memory of it to rely on. Even the brightest, wittiest moments dulled as though they too had been shifted into the shade. Albé wrote a poem, all darkness, heaving his depressed soul on to the page. *Seasonless, herbless, treeless, manless, lifeless. The bright sun, extinguish'd. Morn came and went – and came, and brought no day.* Although she thought it overwrought, this summer, the season, knocked out of kilter, pressed down on them all. Their new-found friend in his four-shouldered house on the hill had tired of it and of them. He spoke more of going to Italy, reaching towards it, as if to the sun.

Claire's presence at Diodati grew intolerable to Albé and she was no longer welcome there. He visited their chalet less, wary of meeting her there too. His was a simple, abrupt unkindness. The poet, for all his fine words, had a cold heart.

It could not continue. Even Shelley now spoke of return and when they were together they made whispered plans to do so, as though a ghastly betrayal were being fomented between them. Mary wrote in snatches when she could, at night, when worry about Claire and Godwin and their future in England kept her from sleep. But it was an ungainly work, all knuckles and shins. It would not yield and yet heeled in and refused to quit her either. Sometimes so occupied was she by it, it seemed utterly habited within her. Trespasser or tenant? Both, she decided. Other days, she kicked it away, mongrel that it was, furious at her inability to write.

Then came time to pack their books, Shelley's papers, Willmouse's toys. A kitten they had adopted was settled in a basket and packed to come with them too. Shelley had Albé's *Third Canto* in his safekeeping for delivery to Albé's publisher, John Murray, in London. Mary's was the smallest load. She packed her notebook in their trunk along with several pages of loose notes. Not very much, she thought, as she patted the pages flat and closed the lid of the trunk over them. Very little indeed and yet it was all.

And now, with nothing to keep them and with Albé's errand to fulfil, they could go.

Charles

HE PRAYED ALL morning and all afternoon and then, feeling no better for it, he took himself for a walk, thinking it would help. But the path from the house was the path he had avoided for weeks: the path that took him past the field where the foal had been lost. He stood there, caught between going anyways or scuttling back inside, when the sun came out, warm on his back, as if to mock him. What had happened had happened and nothing could be done to change it. He could not live his life confined in contrition, turning over each wherefore and why and polishing his every regret. He would go.

It had been near two months since the snowfall. Though the snow had thawed, branches brought down by it still littered the ground. Leaves, hard hit by the frosts, had heaped in strange green desiccated drifts. Fall had arrived early, clothed in high summer colours; unlike any leaf fall he'd known. They'd left the corn to rot. Neither he nor Laurel had the strength of heart to dig it back in, even if the earth had been soft enough to turn over. Charles drew his jacket tight around him and pressed on, hunkered down as if against winter.

He knew not of any combination of misfortune like it. Not locusts, not flood, not frogs. The troubles they faced gathered about them as if God, undecided, had yet to make up his mind and had thrown down one test, then another, and another at their door. The drought, the snow, the frosts, the continuing lack of rain, this slow, slow starving.

'Shhh,' he said, as he reached the paddock and Bella came to his call, hopeful, he knew, for hay. The pitiful creature was all ribs, the flesh on her haunches and neck sunken in. She veered up against his touch with a panicked whinny, a wildness crept back into her nature. She knew he had nothing, that they were starving together. He took the rope that fastened the gate and fashioned a short bridle from it. He couldn't leave her here, to starve in the open. Was no food for her in the barn either, but the shame of it would at least be hidden away.

That evening, Laurel fetched him supper: a small mound of yellow-grey grits and chopped greenery that might have been nettles. A pickled onion rolled about, lost on the plate, the very last of them, she said. He'd noticed the empty pickling jars lining up one by one on the sill in the kitchen, the light that come through them, punched flat and yellow as dust gathered on them. Nothing growing to fill them with this year either.

Charles was appreciative, but ever since they had eaten the foal, whatever he ate burned like a slow poison in him.

'I'm not much hungry, Laurel.' He gave her the most gentle smile he could muster to reassure her it was nothing she had done.

Laurel looked at the plate as though to chastise it. 'You got to eat.'

'Perhaps Seth will have it.'

'Well then. Perhaps.'

He heard her go out, her light tread on the stairs and the

door to Seth's room open and close. Muffled voices, then a long stretch of quiet that hung above him, reproachful. He raised his eyes to the ceiling, imagining what passed between them, the silence worse than any reprimand. A sharp ache seized in him. He leaned forward, doubled over, his hands over his face, surprised to feel tears.

A meeting was called in the town. With the winter fodder gone and the continuing drought having stopped the pasture, there was urgent need to know how the livestock would be fed over the months ahead. The snow and the frosts had killed what hope there was of the harvest amounting to much; what had looked likely to be a miserable harvest to begin with was now one of despair. How would they make it through the winter? And as for next year, with nothing to carry over from this? As Charles went to take his seat at the front, he felt worry stir in the room and the flit of eyes across him. He raised a hand in greeting to those he knew and ministered to, but only a few raised a hand back to him, the rest seemed not to have seen.

The meeting had been called by the mayor. Charles took a seat to his left on a low platform, together with Dr Casey Brown, the doctor, who eased the ailments of those with means to afford his care. Charles looked out on row after row of pinched faces, everyone bundled in winter coats. Though the room was filled to capacity, the air hung against his cheek, cold as any day in November.

The mayor stood up first to speak to say that the meeting was open. The object of them being there was this: to hear from those gathered – and as much time as necessary would be given to know the full extent of the suffering. To ascertain need – with a view to identifying the most needy – then to decide what could be done about it. These were calamitous times indeed. None worse. He sat down abruptly and looked to Charles and the doctor. 'Did either of you have anything to add at this point?'

Charles said no, he had not. Dr Brown took to his feet and mumbled a few words.

'Speak up,' came a voice from the back.

'I said, the immediate effects of starvation are most severely felt by the very young and old. No one wants to die before their time, but the old have had a good life, or a long one at least, but to see a child, a babe suffer for want of food is a heinous thing. And no man or woman here is exempt from the ill effects of starvation. Without nourishment, a young man will soon lose his strength – same as a sapling deprived of water. Likewise, can a young woman defend the needs of her children, if she too is starving? The wealthier have the means to keep hunger at bay. But should these parlous times continue, hunger will reach them too.' He turned to Charles. 'I am sure the minister can support me when I say I have seen nothing like it in my time – and I have witnessed great suffering in our community on my travels about.'

Four rows back, Teddy Spalding rose to his feet. He considered Charles with cold regard. 'I've seen nothing of our good minister for some weeks. He knows his reasons. No doubt is suffering, same as the rest of us.' He paused before he went on. 'Some might say he's been avoiding us, avoiding being asked why he got so many of us to stay. He can't avoid that here. Perhaps he could tell those that trusted him what we should eat?'

The room cleaved down the middle as some turned to stare at Teddy and others turned their attention on Charles. More nodded their heads in agreement than did not and folded their arms and hunched into themselves more.

Seth rose to his feet with difficulty. 'When will it ever end? That's what I want to know.'

Charles reached for words that might be of some consolation, but wherever it was they were held in him – his soul? – had hollowed out. He looked at his hands. 'That I cannot say, Seth. God is testing us.'

At this, half the room were up on their feet and the air filled with the clamour of questions. *Do we stay and face it, is that what you're saying? Are we to die? My daughter? My son? Is everywhere suffering the same?*

'It has been uncommonly dark,' said the mayor, addressing Charles directly. 'Many fear God is extinguishing the sun.'

'No, no—'

'*No?*' said Teddy, the word seeming to choke in him. 'How do you know there will be plenty again? Is your name Joseph? Are your dreams his? Do you pretend to know what God intends? You've hurt us enough, is what I think. I'll not stay here to listen to this. I'm leaving this town while I yet have a horse that can carry me. Them with any sense will do the same. I ask the minister for God's blessing on us as we depart.'

Try as he might, the words would not come. Charles closed his eyes and gave a small nod. He heard the sound of chairs being pushed back, of feet on the floor as they made their way to the door. When he opened them again, he was alone on the platform. Seth and Laurel and a half-dozen others were all that were left. They sat looking at him, then to the side, then, finally, at the floor.

The Spaldings were the first to go and their leaving unstopped the reticence any others had. Thereafter, not a day went by without word that another family had gone or was thinking of it. Strangers passed through with news of whole communities on the move and the trickle became a steady stream. But this river did not head seawards, as a river is ought to, it flowed westwards, thinning, thinning the further inland it reached. By drips and drops, a small hole could empty the largest pail. All of Vermont would empty that way.

Charles took a scythe to the corn. The stalks had dried out to sticks, the leaves peeled away in long papery tatters; chopped up, it could provide a short week of fodder for Bella. Then a thought seized him that the ground must be cleared, for if the ground was not cleared, then nothing could grow. He managed to cut back half a row before he stopped, made faint with the effort. He felt an uneasy lift in the wind; darkening cloud threatened a storm. Thunder, far off, confirmed it. He counted in his head until he heard it again, reckoning it to be over Lake Champlain. *Rain?* He picked up the scythe and though his hands stung from the blisters on them, he now had the swing of it, using its weight to his benefit. The next stalk he struck with a firm, clean blow. It fell, like that, like it was no more than a blade of grass. A gust of wind carried the hat from his head. He watched it tumble across the field, but hadn't the strength to run after it. And then, the slap of rain on his bare skin, scalding almost. *Merciful God!*

The rain turned sharply to hail, scattering like stones across the hard earth, chased into white ribbons by the wind. He turned from its direction, to shelter himself from the stinging assault. Then came a deafening crack of thunder, so close he felt it go through him to his feet. All around the field, fir trees and hemlock pine shivered and thrashed, their branches whipped about in a frenzy. Birds scattered into the sky and were lost.

'*Charles!*'

He saw Laurel come running towards him, one arm raised to protect herself from the hail. He dropped the scythe and ran to her.

'Are you mad? Are you trying to get yourself killed?'

They cowered as lightning flashed above them. And again it came and again, tearing the sky apart. A piece of hail, the size of an egg, caught his hand, drawing blood.

Laurel pulled herself free of his hold and set off running.

'Come on,' she called.

On reaching the field's boundary, he realised he'd forgotten the scythe. *Christ.* If he left it out, it would rust. He told Laurel to carry on without him and turned back up the slope to fetch it. But only an idiot would run with the scythe on his shoulder, so he walked, quick as he could, careful as he went so he did not trip.

Each crack of thunder sent his heart leaping with fear. Impossible to brace himself against it. From the field's boundary came the sound of a tree falling and the crash and splinter of smaller trees brought down with it.

Then he smelled burning. He stopped, turned in a circle, all of him alert. *Smoke?* It was impossible to tell from which way it was coming with the wind in such a frenzy about him. He listened, but what could be heard above the riot of the storm? Then, from between the trees, he saw a lick of orange flame leap up from the base of a tree. It ran up the bark and the leaves went up like paper, then the lot extinguished in a sudden down-draught and a choke of grey smoke pushed through the branches. He dropped the scythe and ran.

'*Laurel!*'

Months of no rain and it all dry as tinder. Grasses crackled and fizzled, sending sparks in spirals in the air. And the wind, the wind, demented it seemed, threw the fire from tree to tree. A sudden violent draught sent the heat down on him, carrying the air away and sizzling up most of his hair. He dropped to his knees then fell flat on the ground for the air that was there.

It was the end of times; he knew of no other reason for it. He lay there, prostrate, for the hand of God to pluck him up, or for the fire of hell to consume him. But neither one nor the other came. The wind spared him and pushed the blaze away.

Somehow he found strength to stand and make his way on down the path to the farm. As he came round the next corner, he saw Laurel curled up like a child, ahead of him. Reaching her side, he was relieved beyond reason to see she was not burned.

'Laurel?'

As he touched his hand to her back, he felt the small lift of her breath. He eased her over, seeing soots crushed into the folds of her clothes and thick black lines in smudges around her nose and mouth. The breath she had came quick, as if she had not breath enough. He saw then how the smoke had overcome her even as the flame had left her untouched.

The lightning had started it. The fire had run up the hillside, narrowly missing the farm. It took out acres of forest and, with nothing to stop it, it ran on unabated. For nights, the sky held the grim orange glow of it. Wolves and deer and any livestock that had been set loose were driven into ravines, or were found drowned in the lake.

Beneath the soot, Laurel's skin took on a waxy sheen, no pink in it at all. Her eyes, same as when he'd found her on the path: half open, half closed. Every so often she gave out a shudder that had him clutching her hand, but no sign, no sound suggesting she knew he was there. She'd gone from herself, walked away from him and not come back.

And then, in the night, she was gone.

'Laurel?' But even as Charles said it, the question became a terrible certainty. He touched his hand to her cheek, then felt for her breath. No. It couldn't be.

He went to the door, flung it open and called for Seth. Then back to the bed and his darling, darling Laurel. Love of his life. His only.

They buried her at the end of the day as dusk came on, slipping its shadow over the hillside, as if joining them in mourning. He tried to dig a grave, but the ground would not yield and he and Seth had no choice but to heap up rocks over her.

When it came time for words, he had none. No words good enough for the consoling needed, none strong enough for the hardships ahead.

Charles knew, heart of his heart, that the blame was his. He should have let her go to Ohio. He should never have tried to keep her for himself. All he had to do was step himself backwards; step himself back far enough and it was plain to see. Vanity and arrogance had been his mission. To have a congregation and keep it. A church? What right did he have to break ground? Who was he to presume?

And if he knew all this, then God had it known before him.

In the end it was Seth who spoke. *'For dust thou art, and unto dust shalt thou return. Amen.'*

The next morning, Charles took Seth's pistol off the wall. He filled his pockets with shot from the drawer and turned and went out and crossed the yard, heading towards the barn. Inside, he lifted the loop of rope that held Bella fastened and dropped it free.

'Yarhh! Yarhh!'

The pony looked at him, reluctant. He slapped one hand on her haunch, to get her to shift and when she didn't, he kicked her hind leg.

'Out of here.' He followed her into the yard and watched her trot about into the middle, dazed by the light.

Bella, seeming regretful, turned and was on her way back to the barn. He lifted the pistol and took aim. That first shot near lifted him off his feet; the force of it cracked his arm back. He saw birds rise in fright from the trees. Bella staggered then fell forward on to her knees, blood running down from a wound on her shoulder. She blinked at him, not believing it, as though he might yet help. Charles loaded more shot into the pistol. As he did, Seth came out on to the step. 'What the—?'

Coming up close to Bella, Charles brought the pistol close to her head and shot again. This time she went down, crashing on to her side. Charles's chest heaved with a terrible elation.

'Charles!' Seth was out over the yard, hobbling as quick as he could. 'That was Laurel's pony you filthy, good-for-nothing . . . Why would you do that? Is the devil got in you? You bastard! She weren't yours to kill.'

Charles felt the weight of the shot he had left in his pocket. He levelled the pistol at Seth. 'You leave me be to do what I have to or, damn it, you will be next.'

Seth stopped up, his face gone slack with shock.

'I'm warning you, stay back.'

An inch up or down, that's all it took, the difference between life and death. The difference between a day that could be lived through and a day that could not.

Charles lifted the pistol to the sky, arm out straight, high as he could. He brought his finger to rest on the trigger. He thought of God looking down on him from up there and how he had willingly and gladly laid himself down in His service. He squinted up one eye to be sure his aim was true. The shot tore out, splintering sharp. This one, with nothing to stop it, seemed to split the sky apart. He heard the sound go away from him and its thunderous echo return.

One last shot. He packed it into the barrel. Then, turning the pistol to him, he heard the sound come again. But this time it passed straight through him and the sound never did come back.

John

'A CLOUD IS a visible aggregate of minute particles of water suspended in the atmosphere. In the more extensive signification of the word, smoke, and all the visible effluvia of volatile substances, may be considered as clouds: meteorologists have, however, confined this term to aqueous particles . . .'

Fisher closed the book and held it out to John. 'Well, my dear friend, a small gift to you, from Dorothea and me. I knew it would be exactly your thing, but did take the liberty of reading it first. Second edition, but published just this last year.' He turned to Maria. 'I do hope you know what a *tête dans les nuages* you have married.'

'Do you think? On the contrary, I think John has his feet firmly on the—' Maria covered her mouth as a racking cough gripped her.

'Dear, dear. Here . . .' Dorothea passed the jug of water to John, who filled Maria's glass.

'Maria has been so badly afflicted this year.' He rubbed her back until the cough had subsided then brought the glass to her lips so she could drink. He felt her hands shake under his as he steadied the glass.

'Such terrible air in London; a wonder anyone can breathe.' Fisher pointed to the book. 'Howard, who's quoted in there, calls London a volcano with a hundred thousand mouths. Well, there's none of that here.' He took a deep breath in and exhaled with satisfaction. Pushing back his chair, he rose to his feet. He reached for his glass and raised it high. 'To Mr and Mrs John Constable. A long, happy and hopefully not too *cloudy* life together. May God protect and shelter you from life's storms, though we do appear to have a month's worth arrayed across the Channel right now.' He give a quick nod to the window where the rain battered the glass. 'And reward you with rainbows instead.'

'No rainbow is possible without rain,' said John.

'Or sunshine.' Maria smiled and in that instant John felt a balance restore, a state of being that had been utterly lost to him in recent months. The realisation was so sudden, so profound, that for a moment he was stunned. Maria held one hand to her chest, as she fought the urge to cough again.

Dorothea rose to her feet alongside her husband and lifted her glass to his. 'To rainbows! And to Mr and Mrs John Constable.'

'Thank you, and I shall treasure the book.' John leaned towards Maria. 'Fisher knows me too well.'

'An assumption to think the book is only for you and I shall not want to read it.' She took the book from him and turned through several pages.

The Fishers took their seats again. 'Forster draws heavily on Howard. You've read his work, I presume?'

John nodded. 'Yes. I know it well.'

'Of course you do.'

'Cirrus. Cumulus. Nimbus,' said Maria, reading aloud. 'Even clouds must be named. A new lexicon.'

'Oh, please put the book away for later and tell me about

the wedding.' Dorothea brought her hands together, all attention.

Fisher gave his wife a warning look. 'Is it not enough to say these two are wed? I saw to it myself. Here we have the happy proof, married and on honeymoon and seated at our dinner table.'

'Really, Fisher, please do not berate me. You were there. I was not. I should like to know.'

Maria placed her napkin neatly by her plate. 'And I am happy to remember it for you. We were the first in church that day, so eager were we to be married, so afraid was he that I might change my mind.' This, a whispered aside to Dorothea, who gave a startled laugh before realising it was a tease.

'It was quiet, serious, perfect in all ways. Your husband, Dorothea, was generous and kind and understanding in the face of such a nervous bride.

'As for the ceremony, it was a small affair. My family did not attend. Disappointing, but not unexpected.' She looked down and swallowed. 'A disappointment, if anticipated, can be more easily borne than one which catches one unaware. We have had some time to prepare ourselves against the campaigns of my family – seven years, in fact. During which time my grandfather exercised his control in myriad ways; threatening this, threatening that; mostly concerning his property. If that is how he would show his love for me, then I should rather not have it.' She reached for John's hand and laid hers over it. 'We persisted and here we are.'

Dorothea brought one hand to her breast. 'Oh – you are brave.'

Maria lifted her shoulders and let them drop. Any defiance seemed lost.

'Well, I never did think that my good, *kind* friend here could be the source of such consternation. *Constable*,' Fisher chided gently.

Relieved laughter at this, and by means of which, John saw, the conversation might be steered on to other, less painful, matters. A good time to tell him about the Wivenhoe commission. 'I came away with an absolute aversion to gentlemen's parks. But at least the final result was pleasing to all.'

'You cannot bite the hand that feeds you. All art must yield to the patron's taste; every purse, a compromise.' Fisher gave a knowing wink. 'But it is good you were properly rewarded.'

Dorothea rose from the table. 'Well,' she said, 'come and sit with me by the fire, Maria. We'll leave the men to make their plans.'

When they had gone, Fisher outlined to John the preparations he had made. Paints, canvases, new brushes from Exeter. It was not Suffolk, but there was Osmington village and the White Horse, a chalk folly on a nearby hill – both interesting subjects in their own way.

'And the coast?'

'In easy reach. A half-hour's walk to Osmington Mills will bring us down to Weymouth Bay. We can walk along the tops if you prefer and come back to Osmington that way.' He leaned in to John and dropped his voice. 'She is a delight, your Maria. You did well. As she said, patience rewarded and all that.'

'I have to remind myself it is finally done. I can't give her what she had, but in time perhaps. There is the return on my father's legacy and the mill continues to provide. I can't see us starving as long as there is a need for flour.'

'And how is your brother, Abram? These can't be easy times for him, I imagine? Has the Corn Law provided some guarantee?'

'From what I know of it, it protects the landowner farmer from foreign competition. But it is a blunt instrument and the season so poor that prices have risen sharply.' The last he'd heard from Abram was of wheat stood in sheaves covered over in snow. Barley, left in the vain hope of ripening, beaten down by the wind.

'Bread is more expensive for us all. We'll all need to sell a painting or two to afford a loaf at this rate. It has been a wretched year all round. We had the smallest crop of strawberries I can remember. Not one of my peas germinated. I had erected a glasshouse to try my hand at melons, but all that effort was rewarded with fruit the size of crab apples! I tried bees. Three hives and not one attracted a swarm. No honey, no mead. Gah! My congregation looks up at me in despair. The parish provides what it can – but the pressures are many and acute. Simply put, there are too many after too few resources. Malthus is right on this.'

'Malthus?' Fisher's admission surprised John.

'He speaks a deal of sense. I'm sure Abram would agree. Malthus is for the Corn Law, is he not?'

'I believe so.'

'Do I sense some equivocation on your part, Constable? Do you not think the country should be self-sufficient in corn and some means of protection is required? Cheap imports are the farmer's bane, threatening ruination. The papers are full of it.'

Yes, he thought, then no. He had no truck with Malthus, whose philosophy he deplored. 'Equivocation? Perhaps. On the issue of sufficiency, is starvation to be the regulatory control? Malthus cloaks his argument in velvet. How many should starve? Half the country is starving, and the papers tell of that too, yet by Malthus's reasoning, more must do so. He'd starve us all to prove his point.'

'It is a matter of balance.'

'*Balance?*' The suggestion was as offensive as it was preposterous. John flushed, suddenly piqued. He had not expected such an abrupt turn in the conversation. 'Who should starve to redress the imbalance in the order of things? Me? You? *Malthus?*'

'You're being silly now. Malthus does not name names.'

'No, he does not, and nor does he include his own. But if we took a moment to consider not numbers, but faces, and saw among them those we recognised, we would reject his argument in an instant.' He remembered the boy with the rabbits and hare and wondered how he fared; and the beggar under the arch he had barely a coin for. His *Wheatfield*, tacked up high on the Royal Academy wall. He thought he had captured perfectly all that was fine and honourable about the harvest: labour and its reward. But the more he thought of it, the more the scene took on the substance of a dream, slipping away further from him with each moment. This year had upended so much of what he thought true.

'I profess, I do not have the answer, Fisher. Last year's peace has not brought the dividend we expected. Only today I read a report in *The Times* of a man of thirty found dead in a field in Islington. A most wretched and emaciated fellow, barely shoes on his feet, who had died from the want of food. A soldier last year, a vagabond this? It is shameful. Our world this past year has taken a turn for the worse.'

Fisher shifted uncomfortably. 'I cannot speak of the wider world; however I am faced with the harsh realities, the practicalities of providing relief. There are people from Wales who have made their way here. Wales! What they think I can do, what help they expect, I do not know. The world, as you said, is changing. It is hard to stand still against the storm.'

Is that what Fisher thought he was doing? Standing still? 'Perhaps so.'

'I didn't think you cared so much, John.'

John shook his head, weary of it. He hadn't the answers. He did not wish to fall out with his friend who, on most other matters, talked good sense. 'I am as much a hypocrite as the next fellow, Fisher.'

Fisher pushed back in his chair. 'Well, my dear fellow, do not go so hard on yourself. These are vexatious matters to which no easy answer can be found. We must do our best. And besides, all this politicking very nearly made me forget . . .' He got up from the table and came back with a decanter from the sideboard. 'I have a Madeira wine new arrived from a merchant in Bristol. Forget Malthus. I'd much rather your opinion on this.'

John broke into a smile and held out his glass. 'Nothing would please me more.'

He would paint every day. No matter the weather. Cirrus, cumulus, nimbus. A new lexicon, as Maria had said.

As their first week with the Fishers gave way to the second and then the third, a routine was established which saw Maria's time increasingly monopolised by Dorothea. Fisher only accompanied him when he wasn't busy with parish work. It meant that John, oft times, found himself on his own.

He set his paint box down on his knees and rested a rectangle of millboard on the top of the lid. He worked quickly, using the sparsest amount of paint, stippling the brush out on a rag until it was practically dry. This way, it allowed the colours underneath to show through and he was able to build up paint quickly before the next drenching shower landed on him. He found it exhilarating; a race against time to capture the scene before the weather piled in from Weymouth Bay. One day, it was too blustery to paint from the vantage point of the cliffs. John made his way down to the beach to Bowleaze Cove where a group of women and children were scavenging seaweed from the rocks.

'What is that, that you're doing?' asked one little girl after he settled on a position nearby.

'I'm making a sketch.'

In the time it had taken him to come down from the cliff to the shore, the sky had darkened to a thunderous grey. On the far side of the bay, the sunshine fell through it, lifting an extraordinary vivid green where the light chased across the grass. Rising above and bright in the sunshine too, gulls tilted giddily over the beach. When he next looked up, the girl was still there, studying him with serious intent.

'What do you think?' he asked.

'It looks very windy.'

'That's because it is.'

She frowned. 'How do you paint the wind?'

'Like this.' He stippled the brush clean on a rag, touched it in a dark charcoal-grey paint then added the smallest amount of white to the tip. Working quickly, he brought the brush to the board in a series of rapid strokes, lifting it away with a sharp twist of his wrist. The harder he pressed, the more the colours would combine, creating a lighter, pewter grey. But he wanted a separate effect too, when the white streaked through the darker grey, standing out in bright flecks; the more he worked the paint, the less this effect showed.

'Is the wind all you paint?'

'I sometimes paint people.' He pulled a face to show he did not care for it, which lifted a small giggle from her.

'What would you do that for?'

'Because that's what some people like. And they pay me for it.'

'They pay you for that, do they?'

The surprise in her voice made John laugh. 'They do. I could draw you, if you like.'

She shook her head and took a step back.

How old was she? he wondered. Seven or eight? He removed the half-finished oil sketch from the paint-box lid and weighted it under a stone to stop it from blowing away then pinned a fresh piece of paper in its place. He sketched quickly, in pencil, and held it out to her when he was done.

'What's that?' she asked.

'It's you.'

'Oh no. I could never afford any of that.'

'Don't be silly, I don't want paying. Here, it's yours. Go on, take it.'

Reluctantly, she took the sheet from him.

'Are you from the village?' he asked.

The girl shook her head.

'Where then?'

'Wales.'

'Wales? That's a long way to come.'

She nodded and dug her toes in the sand. 'I walked it. All the way. My brother's in London. But Ma said that was too far for us to go to so we come here instead.'

'I'm from London.'

The girl looked at him, her eyes as wide open as they could be. 'Are you? Did you see my brother then? His name's Davy.'

'Well, I might have, but London's such a very big place . . .'

'Oh.' Her shoulders fell.

'Davy,' repeated John solemnly. 'If I meet him I'll let him know we had this talk.'

He closed his paint box and set it to one side. 'I'm hungry. How about you?'

She shook her head. 'A little bit.'

'Here.' He dug in his shoulder bag and brought out the lunch he had been given, a chunk of bread and two slices of cold ham, left over from their supper the night before, and wrapped in a cloth. When he offered it to her, she would not take it.

'It's yours,' she said.

He opened the cloth, tore off a small piece of ham and bread and ate both; a mouthful, at most. 'There. That was plenty for me. Thank you.' He held out the rest for her to take.

She took a mouthful of bread and chewed. 'I like the picture you did of me.'

He watched her eat. Poor child was half starved. 'Oh good. Thank you. I'm glad that you do.'

'Well, I have to be off now.'

He watched her make her way over the beach with the bundle of food in one hand and the sketch in the other, to the rocks where a small huddle of people were gathered. One woman – the child's mother he presumed – looked over to him and raised one hand in thanks. He saw the girl sit down and share the food out, and the sketch get passed around, then left to one side as they ate. But the next gust had it and the paper tumbled away over the sand.

'John?'

He turned to see Maria making her way towards him, hat ribbons flying, framing the most beautiful smile he had seen. Her progress was erratic against the wind. She had one hand pressed to her hat and the other bundled in her skirts to preserve her modesty. Her skirts billowed around her as she fought to contain the turbulent, wilful cloth. He needed no imagination to grasp the shape of her figure beneath.

'I came to see how you were doing.' She leaned down and kissed him slowly on the lips, then brought her mouth close to his ear. 'Actually, I made good my escape! Please do not send me away.'

He looped an arm round her, bringing her close against him, suddenly serious. 'We'll have children, won't we?'

'John . . .' She laughed, pushed against him a little then

saw he was not joking. 'But yes, of course. As many as you would like.'

He laid his head against her breast and she brought her arms around him to cradle him there. 'John. My dear. Whatever's the matter?'

He closed his eyes wanting no more of the world than this, of being held in her arms and the sound of her heart against his ear. 'I do love you.'

'Oh, my love, I know that you do. And I love you too.'

After a little while, she eased gently away from him. 'Well, can I see what you have done?'

'It's not finished.' He reached for the oil sketch and tacked it back on to the lid of his paint box. Already, the scene had darkened; the air alive with the approaching storm.

Maria cast a doubtful look at the sky. As he picked up his paintbrush, she smiled at him, all encouragement. 'You will have to be quick!'

With that, he set to again, working with furious concentration. A well-dressed couple had brought their dogs to the beach to exercise them. They walked seaward of the high tide mark, where white-capped waves rushed towards their feet. He sketched their forms in loosely. The girl and her family had scattered over the rocks in front of him, searching for limpets – the girl's ragged form barely distinguishable from the rocks on which she clambered. He added the faintest touch of red for a shawl. A Welsh shawl on a southern beach. Like Rebow's daughter, he had fixed her there in the moment.

When he was done, he threw his brush down, exhausted, as though he had wrestled some part of the storm from the sky and pressed it to the paper. He remembered his earlier oil sketches: their dense, dreary tones; his leaden, plodding touch. This was nothing like that. He had captured, truly, what it was to paint outside – nature's urgent force – and had brought colour fully into its service.

Maria leaned in to see. 'So it's not just Suffolk you have in you after all.'

She sounded surprised. But she also sounded proud. Her approval soared in him.

And then came the rain, a hard, pelting rain that put a stop to any thought of him painting another. Maria shrieked. John clattered the lid shut on his paint box, trapping the sketch inside, and reached for her hand.

A ridiculous, ruinous day to be out in. If they were to get back without a soaking, they would have to run.

Sarah

WE WERE A tansy bunch, hooting and hollering at the sight of Metcalf ahead on his horse, full gallop back to Ely. It was early when we came into the town. Word had got ahead of us and in twos and threes and threes and fours, they came out to see what we was about.

Oh, the folk that greeted us, as many as when the news come that Napoleon was done for. We had the most part of Ely following along beside us and hadn't needed Napoleon for it either.

'See?' said Downham Tom and I did see, I did. And the most hope I'd ever felt filled me up brimful. It had only been me before against mutton chops, Mairster Cook, Reverend Vachell. Me on my own, never knowing what to do. They could easy say *boo* to me. Let them try to say *boo* to us all.

Word was that Metcalf was in the White Hart Inn, holed up with the other Ely magistrates, parleying what had gone on. Downham Tom turned to us. 'What do you say that we help them along with their considerations?'

'Aye!'

'Certain of that, are you?' He cupped a hand to his ear, pretending he'd not heard us.

'Aye!'

And so, with that, we continued on our way to the

market square and the White Hart Inn, the carts with the fowling guns at the front to show them we were serious in our intent. And if they thought that because we laughed and were in a high spirit we were just the same fools as always, then they hadn't listened close enough. Our laugh was hard as Norfolk flint.

When we reached the square, a deadly hush came over us, as when winter pulls the snow up to the sills and the frost comes down over it. They knew we were there even if they pretend'd not. Metcalf got spotted upstairs at a window. He darted out of sight, like a fat grouse hid behind a reed. We leaned in, at a whisper, as though to catch their words from the air. Time went by then a window opened and Metcalf peeped out. He had a piece of paper clutched in his hand and proceeded to read from it.

'The magistrates agree, and do order, that the overseers shall pay to each family two shillings per head per week, when flour is half-a-crown a stone; such allowance to be raised in proportion when the price of flour is higher, and that the price of labour shall be two shillings a day, whether married or single and that the labourer shall be paid his full wages by the farmer who hires him.'

What a lot of words they'd wrapped round the words that were needed. *Two shillings a day? Two shillings a day? Wages paid in full by the farmer?* That meant the farmers could no longer rely on the Parish to top up the miserable pittance they paid. A cheer went up and our hats went up after it but none waited to catch them again for we was all running around like chickens after corn.

Downham Tom raised his arms in the air, his fists in a clench. He threw back his head and roared. And I thanked the good Lord on high for giving us a sky big as that for all of our cheering to go into.

But some there weren't done with Metcalf yet. A man pushed forward to the front. 'Yer a coward, Metcalf. Come out. Come out and tell it to us here.'

A chant started up, pitchforks hammered on the ground. 'Come out! Come out!'

'Bring the rest of them too! The lot of you!'

'Don't be shy!'

'Come out! Come out!'

As the door opened, the crowd surged forward and Metcalf stepped out. Somewhere up behind, a window shattered. I was too small, too short to see Tessie anywhere about.

I went on to tiptoe. 'Tessie?'

I saw Metcalf, one, two, three hands under his arse, get jostled up on top of a donkey cart.

'The Ely magistrates have agreed to your demands and have set it out on these handbills to show that you can count on our word.' He threw out a great sheaf of papers and their promises tumbled down on our heads. I caught one from the air. Not that I could read it, but it made it certain seeing their words fixed out flat in ink.

'Now, I really do think you ought not—'

Whatever got said next was swallowed up in a kerfuffle about me.

'Beer!'

'Aye, beer. We're thirsty!'

'Now, now.' Metcalf patted the row down with his hands. 'I do not think—'

'What do we care for what you think?' yelled a woman

next to me. The more he shushed her, the more vexed she got. 'Are yer ears stuck in yer pants to yer arse? You'll listen to us for a change. A number of us here have walked a long way and we want a sup! If we want beer we shall have it!'

'No. No. Absolutely not. No beer.' He shook his head to a chorus of jeers and low whistles.

A clog came flying over and hit him square on the head. He went to say something then thought better of it and bent down to the other magistrates stood at a clutch at his back. Meek as mice they were – a sight not to be forgot.

Metcalf cleared his throat as he straightened up. 'I can confirm that in addition to meeting your demands and being generous in every respect of them, we have granted an allowance of beer to everyone as a sign of—'

Well, what a hullabaloo at this. No one seemed much interested in what else he had to say.

'As a sign of our good will, and would ask you, in return, to show us your good will also and then to quickly and quietly disperse yourselves home and put a swift end to these, er, *lively events.*'

As barrels were rolled out into the square, I pushed my way out of the crowd and went and sat down on a step. I needed to sit. Then up stepped two feet before me in scuffed boots. Knew who they was belonging to before I even looked up.

Mutton chops.

'Bugger off.'

'There's a nice greeting.'

Only then did I look at him. 'You're a bad 'un.'

'*Me?* A bad 'un?' How he laughed at that, doubled right over, hands on his knees. When he had breath enough again he said, 'So what's that you got there?' He pointed at the handbill I still had in my hand.

'The magistrates' say-so.'

'Is it now?'

'Here, then. If you're not believing me.' I held it out to him.

He took it off me, shaking his head before he'd even read a word. 'Do you see what it says here, at the end?'

I shrugged, pretending I wasn't minded.

'*No person to be prosecuted for any thing that is done at the present time, provided that every man immediately returns peaceably to his home.* You think there won't be a reckoning for this?' He swept out one arm to where a shop window was in bits and hats and bonnets lay trampled on the ground.

'Weren't me done that. I have my own bonnet.'

'I suppose you'd rather Mrs Vachell's wardrobe?'

What did he know of that?

'Vachell had a gun and we took it off him, that's all.'

'And who was it chased the reverend and his good wife off? And then took the liberty of inviting themselves into his home and wantonly destroying what was there?' When I said nothing, he went on, 'Sarah, Sarah. I always thought there was summat to you. But what d'you reckon if everyone got their way? Maybe I fancy a pound a week rise from Cook—'

'That'd be greedy, that would.'

'And went about smashing windows and frightening folk until I got what I was after?'

I folded my arms against him. 'We got what was fair.'

'I could take you back to the farm with me, out of the way.'

'Out of the way of what?' I weren't going anywhere with him.

Just then, Downham Tom came over with two tankards of beer. 'Who's this?' he said, when he saw mutton chops stood by.

'No one. He's off now.'

'No? Not coming?' said mutton chops, still looking at me. 'Can't be persuading you?' He shook his head like I was the saddest thing that had crossed his path in a long time. After a couple of steps he turned back and patted his pocket. 'Still have that knife. Keep it safe for you, shall I?'

'Knife?' Tom looked from him to me.

'It's nothing,' I said. 'No one and nothing.'

As mutton chops wandered off, Tom handed me my beer. 'Drink up. You'll be needing it for the walk home.'

So I drank it straight down and then had another to get the thought of mutton chops off out of me and only then did I feel myself better.

The beer was strong but I wasn't minded. Aye, the day would come soon enough when I'd be working again, and paid properly for it, but today was not it.

'Well then,' Tom said after we had supped up a third. He held out his hand to help me to my feet. 'We got what we come for and now it's time for us to get back.'

For the most part, folk were in agreement, but others weren't ready to go back and said so. Some were tipsy-side out but didn't want free beer to go to waste. The most of us made our way out of Ely and over the Fen. Even the sun had come out to cheer us; first sight of it in weeks. We ambled our way home with the warmth of it hung against our backs, our bellies full of beer and all of us gone quiet with the thought of what we had done and what we had got.

As we came into Littleport, lolling our drowsy way up Mill Street towards the George and Dragon, Thomas and Tessie, who'd been some way ahead, came running back.

'They're coming!'

'Who's coming?'

'The fucking dragoons. *Fuck!*' Thomas spun in a circle, hands gripped to his head.

'*Where?*'

Tessie threw out her arm and pointed back the way they had come. Never had I seen such a fear in anyone as was in her then. 'Coming over the Hemp Field. With their sabres in the air.'

Then came the holler of them and a terrible clattering of hooves. People scattering, like hens with a fox among them. As many of us as could bundled into the pub and pushed what was there up against the door. Tables, chairs, all of it heaped in a pile. One man grabbed a poker from the fireplace. 'Find summat to defend yerselves with.' I picked up a tankard and gripped it hard. Tessie did too. And we stood there, like winter had us frozen to the spot.

The din of them as they came thundering past. I shut my eyes tight against it.

Downham Tom turned wildly about. 'Anyone have a gun?'

Mole catcher George pulled out a small pistol from his belt. 'It's just for crows.'

'Ah, hell,' said Downham Tom when he saw it, but he took it anyway. 'Anyone else?'

'Two rifles, kept upstairs, in case of trouble,' said the publican.

'And shot for them?'

'Some. Not much. It's Littleport, not London.'

'It'll have to do. Stay here, defend the door. Don't let them in. The rest of you, keep back from the windows and do what you can.'

Downham Tom gave a last desperate look about the room then legged it up the stairs. Even stepped back from the window I could see the soldiers circling about on their horses outside, rounding up those who'd not run away quick enough, or got themselves home or hid in time; children for the most part, wailing after their mothers. When an old woman went to comfort one, a soldier raised his sabre against her and brought the grip down on the top of her head.

Then came a hammering at the door, so hard even the man with the poker jumped.

'Open up! We know you are there.'

The hush that followed, like every sound in the world had been frightened out of it.

Bang, bang, bang!

'I command you to open this door.'

They came running at the windows, some with sabres, others with guns, shattering the glass to bits and clambering in after. The man with the poker dropped it to the floor. Then, from above, came a shot. In fright, I let out a yelp and dropped the tankard in my hand.

More shots, this time from outside. Then some scrawny

shit of a soldiering man was before me, one hand in my hair, his other hand tight at my throat. He dug in his fingers deep as he could. My knees went from under me and he dragged me out. Thrown down I was with the rest and given a hard kick. Then Downham Tom was thrown down next to me. Before we could speak, up rode Vachell, high on his horse. He squinted at us and prodded each in turn with his whip so he could get a good look. Round he went, clip clop, clip clop, prod prod poke, till he got to us.

'You,' he said, when he spotted Downham Tom sat by me. '*You fucking bastard*. This one here and the girl with him.'

As Vachell turned to get the captain's attention, Tom sprang to his feet. He grabbed my hand and kissed it. 'I'll be back, I promise.'

And with that he was off. Quicker than a hare over the Fen; his fair hair like a rabbit's tail in the sun.

Then came a crack that split open the day and sent him tumbling forward. His feet went from under him and his knees folded in and he was falling, falling, falling.

'*Tom!*' I screamed, up on my feet and after him. '*Tom!*' The sound of my cry gone ahead of me, to catch him, catch him before he fell.

Mary

ALL SHE WANTED was a place, some lone place, with a garden, a river, a woodland to walk through, and she would be happy. But the only growing things were great tufts of dandelions that forced their way into every nook and crack, and dank stinking mosses that clung in patches to the walls. The River Avon was a short walk away, but it ran in full spate, an angry torrent of water that had scoured away the bank. Only a fool would walk there. Bath provided neither peace, nor privacy, their accommodation being on a busy corner across from the abbey and readily looked into from the street. Sitting in the window, where the light was best, she felt herself on display; sufficiently scrutinised for it to have a quite debilitating effect.

In truth, there was nothing glorious about the rooms she had secured. She had found them herself shortly after their return from Cologny, rehearsing all that was good about them before Shelley's return from London; prime among them being their temporary state. They were shabby and worn; filthy, in fact. She had made herself look beyond this. They were situated above a reading room, a proximity that had seemed fortuitous, a good omen, and that decided it. But the sound of chairs scraped back on the floor beneath them all day was wearying and made her cringe. How could reading make such a racket? A stale smell of tobacco rose from between the floorboards and hung in the air. Most days, she could taste it, becoming aware of the reek with a grimace. The kitten they'd brought back with them from Switzerland grew into a cat. It ate the rose Shelley fetched from London for her, the only dash of colour on that grey day – perhaps as transfixed by the scent as she was. She had laughed at the cat's antics, until it pissed on the wall and ran off. She wanted her own Cwm Elan, she realised, the Welsh idyll Shelley had shared with Harriet before her. If the hateful Harriet had enjoyed that with him, then why couldn't she have the same?

There wasn't room for Claire to be with them together, despite her protest, and a room was found for her separately nearby. It made little practicable difference. She arrived most days after breakfast and only departed again after their evening meal, when Shelley would escort her home. Mary knew she should not complain. With Elise put to errands and Claire occupied most days playing happily with Willmouse, Mary could work. She had two chapters now, almost a third, and was working on an account of their travels too. This had prospect of selling; at least it was her sincere hope it would.

Papa had had the most of their money, yet still Fanny sent panicked letters, as though the blame for his pecuniary difficulties were theirs. What more could they do? Shelley's father was an obdurate old goat, who fed Shelley his estate teaspoonful by teaspoonful, an estate with a worth of six thousand pounds per annum too! Mary had only the vaguest understanding of how, when, or if, any of it could be released. Until then, they were caught in the middle: money withheld on one side and pulled from them on the other. They had Claire in their keeping too, for now, though none of the family could know of it. Word from Albé, there had been none, not even in reply to the letter Shelley had forwarded to Italy to let the poet know his manuscript was safely delivered to John Murray. Fanny's letters hinted at wanting to leave home, but she could not come here for the risk of Claire's condition becoming known. All in all, the worry kept Mary from a good deal of sleep.

Another letter came from Fanny to which Mary's answer was an abrupt *no*. There was no more money. They, too, had to live. Everywhere about her, from the moment she stepped out of the door, among the full skirts and lavishly hand-embroidered shawls of pretty patrician wives come to Bath to tourist and rest, she saw the pale drawn faces of people rushing to their employ. Mary was startled to realise that she recognised something of herself in these poorer folk.

That night she wrote in her journal: *Walk out with Shelley to the South Parade; in the evening work.* For this is what writing was: *work.*

Yet another letter came from Fanny, by return, which Mary had expected. God knew, her sister was persistent. Anticipating its contents and already infuriated, Mary slotted it behind a candlestick on the mantel. She would read it later when she was in better mood.

It wasn't until that evening that she remembered it was there. She frowned as she saw the postmark was from Bristol. Bristol? What was Fanny doing there? She broke the seal and sat by the fire to read it. She had only read a couple of sentences, when she sat forward in alarm. Fanny had left home: *I depart immediately to the spot from which I hope never to remove.*

'What is it?' Shelley, who had been reading a draft of her work, looked up.

She held out the letter to him and saw the frown deepen on his brow as he read.

They agreed she had likely taken herself off to Bristol to escape the gloom of the family home on Skinner Street. But it was concerning, for she was certainly on her own. Shelley left immediately to see what he could discover, but when he returned in the small hours he brought no news of her. Again the next day to Bristol, but nothing. No other letter had come from her either, which troubled Mary more. If not Bristol, then where?

'Swansea?' A desperate suggestion, she knew, but she reasoned that Fanny might have sailed from there to Dublin, where their aunts Eliza and Everina had found work. A proposal for Fanny to join them had once been mooted but like so much else in Fanny's life, it had stuttered and stumbled and was quietly forgotten. But even as it came to her, Mary realised it made little sense. Fanny almost certainly would have written to her with news of that. But knowing no other place she could be and at Mary's insistence, Shelley agreed he would try Swansea too.

He came back a day later, shattered by what he had

learned. He had terrible news. The worst news of all. A young woman, found dead.

'It was her, Maie.' Shelley closed his eyes. It was several moments more before he could speak again. 'She killed herself by her own hand. Laudanum. A bottle was found by her side.'

And then it was as if the avalanche that had missed Mary that day had come down upon her after all, sweeping her into oblivion.

He told her then how she had been found. Each horrific, banal detail, which had guaranteed her anonymity to strangers, but carried such terrible charge to anyone who loved her: her brown-berry necklace, a favourite of hers; the Swiss watch they had so recently gifted her; her stays and stockings, carefully embroidered with their mother's initials, MW. She had dressed for a journey, that was certain, but must have decided against it.

Shelley took a letter from his pocket and held it out. 'There's this too . . .'

I have long determined that the best thing I could do was to put an end to the existence of a being whose birth was unfortunate, and whose life has only been a series of pain to those persons who have hurt their health in endeavouring to promote her welfare. Perhaps to hear of my death will give you pain, but you will soon have the blessing of forgetting that such a creature ever existed as . . .

There was no signature. Fanny had torn away her name at the bottom. Mary ran her finger along the edge of the tear and brought it sharply away as if from a knife. This, the most heartbreaking detail of all, to spare them the shame of her suicide. She had been thinking of them, even as she died.

Letters were sent to and received from Godwin at Skinner Street.

Do not expose us to all those idle questions, he wrote, *what I have most of all in horror is the public papers, and I thank you for your caution, as it may act on this.*

And so between them they agreed that the truth of Fanny's death would be concealed. Her body would be left in Swansea, unclaimed, for anonymous burial. And come the time when, finally, poor Fanny's absence was noticed, they would repeat the story they had prepared: that she had died of a fever while sailing for Ireland. Poor, poor Fanny. Not wanted in life, nor in death either.

Were the circumstances of her death not sufficiently pitiable without them dressing it in all propriety so as to spare themselves shame? Who was she, when her sister's love, so casually disregarded, was lain, mortified, at her feet? When this last note could be returned to her, but poor Fanny's body could not? That she would need to grieve her here and never at her graveside?

Mary thought of what she had agreed with her father. Why so readily compliant of morals she otherwise sneered at and eschewed? Her hypocrisy was deplorable. She despised herself. She sat for hours, staring into the street, rubbing away tears until her eyes were red and sore. Dearest Fanny. What had they cared? They had despised her, pushed her away, ignored her pleading. They'd abandoned her for their summer jaunt. And even as they had done so, they had laughed.

This life they had made for themselves: a hideous, selfish conceit. Did they believe poetry could inure them from tragedy, that clever conversation could hold life's harsh realities at bay?

When finally she returned to her work, she was seized by the futility of it and swept the papers off her desk. Wretched book. She loathed it. What was it for? Life was struggle enough as it was without stupid, stupid words. She picked up the papers and bundled them into a drawer, slamming it shut with the heel of her hand, so they were hid. As well they were out of kindling because if she'd had the makings of a fire she would have burned the lot.

The days passed. And there came a day when she took out the papers again and smoothed them flat. She read what she had written, striking out words until she was satisfied with it:

She died calmly, and her countenance expressed affection even in death. I need not describe the feelings of those whose dearest ties are rent by that most despicable evil, the void that presents itself to the soul and the despair that is exhibited on its countenance. It is so long before the mind can persuade itself that she, whom we saw every day, and whose very existence appeared a part of our own, can have departed for ever – that the brightness of a beloved eye can have been

*extinguished, and the sound of a voice so familiar, and dear
to the ear, can be hushed, never more to be heard. These are
the reflections of the first days; but when the lapse of time
proves the reality of the evil, then the actual bitterness of
grief commences . . .*

That night, she brought Willmouse to their bed and
made a nest of all she held dear. As Shelley and the babe
slept, she lay there, sloughed by grief.

The rain fell. A drowning sleep overcame her from which
she surfaced the next morning with the shock of life, startled to be awake, startled to be alive.

The world that had cast her from it so suredly, had
returned her to it anew.

Hope Peter

RÓISÍN TIERNEY CAME from Barleycove, a nip of land between Bantry and Skibereen. Her voice lifted up as she told him – had he heard of it? Cork, then, had he? No? Ah well. So it was. It made him no worse than any other Englishman she knew, but was it not a curious thing that insisting Ireland was theirs, not a one could tell her the first thing about it? She'd fetched over on a boat after the Feast of St Francis, hoping his blessing would carry her safely across. A storm had come down hard on them in the night. Terrible it was. Many times the wind near drove the rail under, threatening to pitch them over. If milk could be churned into butter, then it was a wonder the butter on board had not become cheese. They had been bound for Milford but the gale fetched them south to Bideford. The men there were a rough sort. Said that if she wanted supper, she'd have to take her chance up on the moor with the sheep and get a nibble of clover with them.

All the fishing boats there, tied up on account of the weather. She could mend nets and lobster pots and maybe there was chance of a coin doing that. *Show us what you can do with a shuttle*, they asked her, so she did. She knotted two rows of a net, neat as neat. Why, the fish would jump into it just so they could see. *Well then*, they said, *that is right pretty*, but they could do mending themselves and it didn't cost them nothing if they did.

'Then why did you ask me? I asked them. *We wanted to see what you could do with yer hands,* they said. *A lass with hands like that,* well, that set them laughing and I told them I would not, that I never would behave myself ill. So I came to London the next day with the butter, back of a cart. And that's how I am ended up as I am now.'

She lived by ferreting through waste carts at the back of hotels, after any scrap fit to be had. She went to the priest only if she had to, because there were too many now at his door, most like Peter, if he did not mind her saying so, with not a clue what to do.

Barleycove was a pretty place, with a beach where her father's boat used to go out from. If you stood in the water, even up to your knees, you could see your toes and all of the freckles on them. But the butter was for England and the water was not fit for drinking and sand could not be ate.

She knew how to make butter – of course – and take the bollocks off a calf, not that there was need for it in London. She told him about the buzzards above Mizen cliffs. Watching them circle, up and up, till her neck ached. Was there an end to it, did he reckon, to the sky? She imagined them so high, as far up as any living creature could go. But not to heaven, because then they'd be dead.

Peter listened. He offered no opinion, no story of his own. She was only trying to help carry his thoughts off elsewhere, away from resting on the lad. *Willie*. Guilt prickled across him. He felt a sore pain, and it pierced him through.

'Well, then,' she said, quiet now, 'here's me going on.'

'Will you ever go back again?' he asked, words finding him at last.

Her mouth pulled down. 'Did you not listen to what I said?'

He spent the next weeks with Róisín. And though he could bear the days better with her, the grey bore down on him like stone, smutching his shadow at his feet. Leaves came down from the trees. Rain clattered through the branches. Cold set a curve to his spine.

He did not go back to the Cock and he would have forgot all about them had he not found a leaflet on a bench.

Break open all Gun & Sword shops, Pawnbrokers or other likely places to find Arms. Run all Cunstables through who touch a Man of us.

No rise of Bread etc! No Castlereagh off with his Head! No Nationall Debt!

The whole Country waits the Signall from London to fly to Arms.

Stand firm now or never!

N.B. Printed Bills containing farther Directions will be circulated as soon as possible.

John Dyall Chairman, Thomas Preston Secretary,

Seale & Bates Printers Tottenham Court Road.

Thomas Preston? He knew that name. He told Róisín about them, Thistlewood, Watson and the others and she said she would come with him if he went. 'No Castlereagh?' she repeated. 'An Englishman put that?'

But he was ashamed to go, to be seen as he was, the tatters these weeks had brought him to. His whiskers grown long and no means to cut them. Most shameful of all was to have to tell about the lad. But Róisín did insist. Who were these Englishmen who knew so much about Ireland? She wanted to know.

'An unnecessary death, a tragedy,' said Thistlewood when Peter admitted to Willie's fate. 'And we shall have our revenge for it.'

Revenge was not what Peter wanted. Nor, either, did he want to eat. When food was divided between them: mutton and turnip and gravy, Róisín ate most of Peter's share. He wasn't used to such any more. His stomach griped and clutched at the mouthfuls he had. He felt a brush of cold against his cheek as he forced another mouthful down, fearful that the hand that had grabbed Willie away would soon come for him too.

Thistlewood launched himself into a long parley about what had gone on and what Peter had missed by not being there. A throng of thousands at Clerkenwell's Spa Fields. Ten thousand, by his reckoning.

'How d'yer reckon that?' asked Róisín, not afraid of asking the questions he'd have looked daft to.

Thistlewood explained how a crowd could be figured by taking a small number and seeing what space they took up. He asked her how many, standing up, it would take to fill the room they were in.

'Twenty of you; thirty of me. So it depends on how many women were there.'

'As many women as there were men.'

He said they'd gathered a petition to go to the Prince Regent. Three times they'd tried to fetch it over, but it could not be got through.

Watson scowled. 'The Prince Regent won't be moved. The man receives one million a year public money and gives five thousand pounds to all of the poor. Can he rightly be called the Father of the People? He'll not listen to our petition.'

'A petition? What for?' asked Róisín, her hunger for knowing greater even than for the meal they had shared.

'Universal male suffrage, an end to child labour, relief of the poor—'

'If plenty enough women are with you, then where is their vote?'

'I'm not against it. But most don't think the same way as I do. Some want to know, what would a woman do with it?'

Róisín fixed him a hard look. 'Same as any man.'

Then they were back to the fine deliberating points of it all. Peter had no patience for it again. His thoughts took him back to standing Willie on the wall and the poem that had come to him. *Blake*. That was it. The name of the man who wrote it. But what use the moon once daylight had come? And what use remembering that name now? Now he never could tell the lad?

'So, are you with us?'

Peter looked up to see Thistlewood's attention on him.

'We intend to muster two thousand men by Saturday week. Men who will act. That way raise the whole population to arms against all that is rotten and corrupt. You know how to handle yourself. We need men who are not afraid. Are you with us?'

The last thing Peter wanted was ever to hold a gun again. But he could not go forward, he could not go back. There was no way out of where he had got. He was stuck.

'I am,' said Róisín, though Thistlewood had not asked her.

Fuck it. What world was this for any lad? Peter looked about the table. Jerusalem, was that what they were building here? He gave a sharp nod. 'Aye, I am too.'

Thistlewood poured out the gin and they drank on it.

On gathering at Spa Fields, the crowd would go on to the Old Lady and Gentleman – *the Bank and the Tower* – and on persuading the soldiers there to stand down, take command of them both. Arms would be seized on the way. They needed guns and, damn Lord Liverpool and the rest of them, they would be got. Two hundred and fifty pike heads were hid in Watson's privy. But what use a pike head without a shaft to mount it on? Could a shovel be made to turn the ground with no foot to dig it? The doubts Peter had, he shook away. If what they stood for was an 'insane malignity' as he had heard some say, then what was the government and all those who ruled over them rightly to be called?

Saturday came and when he arrived at Spa Fields, Peter was admiring again of Thistlewood. There were military guards on horseback but, surprised by the numbers perhaps, they kept themselves well back. It had all seemed like talking when they had met at the Cock. Never had he imagined it would lead to this, to a crowd so big he'd not the numbers in his head to count it. He tried to figure it as Thistlewood had said, but it was impossible for more were arriving all the while. From every which way they came: women, men and children, some with red, white and green ribbons and others with tricolour cockades. Peter had hold of one end of a banner: *The Brave Soldiers are our Brothers, Treat them Kindly,* and Róisín had hold of the other. All those feet had churned the field to thick mud and it was a job to keep upright. He had to admit, heartened as he was, it was no day for standing in the cold, clartied up to his neck in it.

A man, wearing a white top hat, clambered up atop a cart and pulled himself straight to start the speeches.

'Henry Hunt, that is. Henry *Orator* Hunt,' said a man by Peter's side, as if he should know who he was. As well that may be, but from where they were standing and not a long way back, he could not make out a word of it.

'Let's move forward, I want to hear,' said Róisín. But the press of people was such, he was not confident they could gain any more than a dozen steps in that direction.

But Róisín was like a cat and squeezed her way through. Gripped tight to the other end of the banner, it left him no choice but to follow.

'At a soup meeting in Wigan, in Lancashire, a weaver went from his work, and told them that for three months, himself, his wife and four children had not eaten an atom of meat, and that they would all die before they would taste their soup. He was asked what he wanted. *"Want?"* said he, *"I am an Englishman and I want my rights!"*

A roar went up from those around him. Others wanted to know what an atom was.

'Those who fatten themselves on the people, telling them charity is the only way to relieve their distress, deserve no other name than that of a cheat.'

The crowd cheered again.

'Give us bread, or the Regent's head!'

A man leapt up on the cart and waved a flag. 'Fellow citizens. Ye want bread, ye want employment. Do ye want a leader?'

'Aye!'

And then all manner of bedlam broke out. He saw Thistlewood head off one way and Watson another and the crowd cleave apart as though a gale had run through it, chasing it away in a tumble. He saw a number of the guard come charging through, heading for him and the banner. One wrestled the banner from him and when he tried to break the pole over his knee but could not, he threw it down in the mud and trampled it underfoot.

He was no more than a spotty lad, but Peter had only his bare hands to all the metal he sported. He knew how that ended. Then he and Róisín were running. Legging it out of the fields, with a crowd of two hundred or so, out along Corporation Row and on to Skinner Street.

'Come on,' said a man at the head, an Irishman who went by the name of John Cashman. 'Beckwith's shop is here. We'll have his guns off him.'

By now they were down to twenty and Peter did not fancy their chance of success. But they rushed into the gunsmith's with such a holler that the men at the counter dropped themselves behind it and would not come out.

They took whatever was there, fowling guns and pistols, and powder and shot and ball for them. But Beckwith was not going to be so easily relieved of his livelihood. He came at them from the back of the shop with pistols.

And now soldiers were in the shop and upon them. They were no different to him, but a year before. Doing what they were told to and blind to what was before them.

'The soldier is our friend!' Peter raised a fist in the air, in a desperate bid for their fellowship, but was rewarded with a clout to the side of his head. A dizzying blow that sent him crashing backwards, away from the day he was standing in and into the blackness beyond.

Sarah

THEY KILLED HIM. My Downham Tom. Shot him in the back of the head as he ran off.

Weren't the soldier that shot him got took away, but us, back of a cart, tied up like pigs and trundled off to Ely where they locked us in gaol. Me and Tessie and the others all shut up together, eighty-two of us, when counted. The gaol was not made for that number of us. Only just room to stand and one small window, too high to see out of, that the wind blew and blew through. It were a very hard place to be.

Though we could not see out, folk come up on other side of the wall and could just be heard through it.

You done well.

Be brave.

Have heart.

They let Tessie go, there being no reason to keep her. That left me the only girl there. What was it I had done that were so bad?

One evening, a voice I knew.

'Sarah?'

'Ma?'

I was up on my feet, ear pressed to the wall, then trying my best to climb it. 'Ma?'

'Sarah? Lovey?'

'Oh, Ma . . .' I was so happy and yet so sorrowful to hear her. 'I'm sorry, Ma.'

'It's them should be sorry.'

'They shot Tom, Ma.'

'I know they did. A terrible thing that was to do.'

Panic beat in my chest like a small bird trapped in there. 'Will I be shot too?'

'Oh, lovey. My dear, lovely girl. You didn't rob no one. You didn't hurt no one. You were a part of it, that's true, but nothing you done was harmful. When the time comes you must say so.'

I held my arms flat to the wall as though to hold her through it. I wanted my ma more than anything. 'How are you keeping, Ma?'

'Mrs Vachell is making soup again. No one will have it off her. She can sup her own soup.'

Made me smile, it did, though sorrow shook in me. Me and Ma, the same. That's who I had it off.

'It's tomorrow, I've heard. The court.'

I let out a sob as the panic flew up in me again.

'Me and Tessie will be there. You tell them, Sarah. You tell them.'

'Yes,' I whispered and wiped tears away with the back of my hand. 'Yes, Ma, I will.'

The judges were Mr Justice Abbot, Mr Justice Burrough and Mr Edward Christian Esquire, Chief Justice of the Isle of Ely. Mr Gurney was prosecuting counsel. A Mr Hunt would speak for us, but he didn't look none pleased that he had to. He took a long hard look at the scraggle of us and scowled.

'Gentlemen of the Grand Jury,' said Mr Christian as he started, 'you have been called together at this unusual period, and with the present solemnities, in consequence of some very daring acts of outrage committed by various misguided individuals in this town and its immediate neighbourhood, which must still be fresh in your recollection. In contemplating the nature of these atrocities, it is impossible to consider without commendation the conductors of those prompt and efficacious measures by which, after it had domineered for several days together, the spirit of tumult and devastation was finally subdued . . .'

Next, Mr Hunt got asked to speak. He stood up then sat down again, said he had nowt to say. What was the good of that when it was for us he was supposed to be speaking?

Mr Gurney got to his feet and I was told to do the same. 'Sarah Hobbs, you stand accused of putting Reverend Vachell in bodily fear and feloniously stealing from him property to the value of ten pounds. How do you plead?'

Ten pounds? I thought of the pot dog I had smashed to splinters and all the days earning it would take me to pay for it.

Mr Christian cleared his throat. 'Guilty or not guilty?'

I looked at him and he looked at me. A few strides apart we were, but I might as well have been stood on the moon. 'Not guilty.'

I glanced about the court. There they were: Mairster Cook, mutton chops, Reverend and Mrs Vachell. Not a one of them with a good word to say for me.

I was a thief, said mutton chops. He brought out Mairster Benton's knife to prove it.

Ohh, went Mr Gurney and the jury men narrowed up their eyes.

I was a scallywag, disrespectful, insolent, said Mrs Vachell, challenging my betters by sticking out my tongue and other gestures too offensive to mention.

Reverend Vachell was full red in the face even before he were asked up to speak. Hadn't I invited myself into his house and look what had happened to that? Hadn't I been at the forefront of those who had bawled at him from the step, then been seen on top of the cart with the fowling guns tied to it? In his book, that made me a ringleader, did it not? He stabbed his finger in my direction so they was in no doubt it was me that he meant.

'Are you sorry for what you did?' Mr Gurney rocked back on his heels and stared at the ceiling, as though my answer were waiting for him up there.

'I am sad for what happened to Tom.'

I saw his back stiffen. Not a peck of kindness he had in him. He turned to the jury. 'This is the only case in which a girl, *a young woman practically* – little difference, I suggest – has been indicted. She must understand that she cannot engage in things of this kind – *acts of great violence* – without being responsible for the consequences. She was very active in persuading the mob to go to Reverend Vachell's and assisted in breaking the windows of the house.'

'I did not!' I cried.

'Quiet!' Mr Christian gave a look to frighten the words back into me.

'The violence committed had been preceded by some

threats and excesses in another part of the country, under
the pretence of the lowness of wages, and the high price
of provisions—'

'*Pretence?*' shouted a woman from the back. 'You try living
as we do!'

Mr Christian banged a hand down. 'I shall not have this
court disrupted and will tolerate no further interruption.
You will be quiet. Any disturbance will be treated as
contempt and the perpetrator will join these miscreants
in Ely gaol. Do I make myself clear?' Mr Christian nodded
at Mr Gurney for him to continue.

Mr Gurney gave his papers a brisk shake.

'And the high price of provisions. Some pressure,
perhaps, arising from the peculiar circumstances of the
season, had fallen on the lower classes of the community,
but it was considerably magnified by tumultuous assemblies and great excesses were perpetrated.

'Let me be clear. When offences are carried out by a
mob, it is the whole mob that is guilty, not just the person
doing the deed.' He raised one hand and pointed at me. 'It
is of the highest importance to the peace and safety, not
only of this isle, but of the surrounding country, that all
who are present on this solemn enquiry, and all who read
the account of its proceedings – and there are few parts of
the kingdom in which it will not be read – may be convinced
by the awful lesson which may here be taught, that whatever wild or chimerical notions may prevail of the power
of an armed multitude, the law is too strong for its assail-
ants; and that, however triumphant or destructive their
sway for a few days, those who defy the law will ultimately
be compelled to submit either to its justice or its mercy.'

With that he sat down and the jury told to consider their verdict on me. The men leaned in together and mumbled. After a short while, for there were many of us to be got through, one of them lumbered to his feet.

'You have a verdict?' asked Mr Christian.

'We do.'

'The defendant will stand. Stand, Miss Hobbs.'

As I got up, a whistling set up in my ears like the wind is on the Fen in winter.

'What is your verdict? Is the defendant guilty or not?'

They all turned to look at me.

'*Guilty.*'

Their judgement fell on me. If it weren't for the gaolers holding me up, I would have dropped to the floor like a stone. A cry went up but I hadn't a chance to see who it was as they led me straight the way out.

When Tessie came to visit me later, she said twenty-three others had been found guilty the same, including her Thomas, William and John Beamiss and mole catcher George.

'Oh, Tessie,' I cried, 'what will happen to us now?' Terrible things were said of Mr Christian. He were a hard, harsh man, who thought kindness an encouragement to bad ways.

Tessie went quiet. 'I don't know, Sarah, that I don't.'

Two days later, they brought us back to face the judge.

'Prisoners at the Bar,' he said, 'you stand here, twenty-four persons in number, a melancholy example to all who are here present. It was suggested abroad that you had been induced to perpetrate these violent acts by hard necessity and want, but after attending closely and strictly to the whole tenor of the evidence, there has not been any reason to suppose that you were instigated by distress. The preservation of not only the good order and peace of society, the preservation of life itself, imperiously calls upon the court to declare that many of you must expect to undergo the full sentence of the law.'

He stopped talking so that what he'd said could weigh on us.

'It now remains for me to pronounce on each and every one of you the awful sentence of DEATH; and that sentence is that you and each of you be taken hence to the place from whence you came, and from thence to some place of execution, where you are to be hanged by the neck until you are dead—'

Such a tumult at this as chairs were kicked over. And those stood there with me cried and shook.

'Shame! Shame!'

One man had Gurney's wig off his head and stamped on it. Scuffles as papers got thrown in the air. The justices were shooed out of a side door, escorted by a guard.

My breath had gone from me and my hearing had too. My ears could not take any more violence upon them. The room fell down on me and I saw a bog dog's black mouth open, ready to swallow me down.

They took us out the next morning and all of Ely was there and all of Littleport too and they reached out their hands as we went by, to give us their strength. Whispering, whispering: *Be brave, be strong.*

Up to the gallows we were took, where the ropes had been strung in a line.

Mr Christian came out on to the platform. On seeing him, a hissing set up in the crowd, then a low murmur: *shame, shame, shame.*

'William Beamiss. John Dennis. Isaac Harley, George Crow, Thomas South step forward.'

As they did so, Mr Christian stood them to one side. 'These five are to be left for execution.'

A sob came up in me. My legs shook so hard I could bare stand.

'No, *Thomas!*' Tessie screamed. She rushed forward but got held back.

'Mark Benton, John Easey, John Walker – sentences commuted: you are to be transported for seven years. Richard Rutter – sentence commuted: you are to be transported for fourteen years. Joseph Easey, Aaron Chevell, Richard Jessop, John Jefferson, James Newell – sentences commuted and transported for life.

'All remaining to be taken from here and imprisoned in Ely gaol for twelve months.'

Thomas and William and John and Isaac and George were then stood on over the drop and a noose placed over their heads. Tessie wrenched at her hair.

'*Be strong!*' came a shout from the crowd.

'No person here would give the rope that will hang you!' shouted another.

'God Almighty bless you.'

Then prayers were said and the church bell sounded eleven. Then the worst quiet as the drop opened and the men fell to the terrible sound of our gasp.

After they'd hanged them, they took me back to the gaol. Half dragged, half carried I was, sobbing and screaming and kicking for what they had caused to be done. To my Tom, to Thomas, to the rest.

As I come in, mutton chops was stood there, waiting. He shook his head at me. Like I was the bad 'un and he'd had it known all the while.

Hope Peter

PETER DUNN. OF Corringham parish. Brave soldier, poacher of hares. Never married, nor a father, nor likely ever to be so.

On learning of his parish, the constable of Corringham was fetched: *Johnson*. Peter remembered the innkeeper's warning the morning after the business with the hares. How Johnson cared only for the law when it was for his reward.

As Johnson came in to where Peter was held, Peter tensed himself, ready for a beating. But it was not the matter of the hares Johnson had come to discuss, nor even him being found in Beckwith's shop.

'You was seen at Spa Fields. Some says you was seen holding a banner. Big banner at that. Must have took some holding. Who else had hold of it with you?'

When Peter said nothing, Johnson rubbed at his knuckles. He stretched his fingers then balled them into a fist, perhaps considering thumping Peter after all. 'Who'd you have the banner off? Give me their names, the place of their meeting and *if they are got* I will see to it that the matter of the hares is let go.'

Oh, aye, thought Peter. He folded his arms. The look he gave was clear: he would not tell what he knew, not even if Johnson was a man he could trust. Not even if he was the last fucking man in the world left to talk to.

'Arthur Thistlewood. Do you know the fellow? James Watson?'

Peter shrugged. 'Watson's a common enough name.'

'Thistlewood's not.'

When Peter shook his head, Johnson let out a sharp laugh, in no way amused. 'The hares it is then. Think I care about where you are headed?' On his way out, he gave Peter a punch in the guts after all.

And so later that day, Peter was brought before the judge.

'What makes you think you had a right to the hares?'

He knew where he would be going and would say what he had to. If crime this was, he would not disown what he had done. 'God made all men equal and the world for men equally to use.'

If the judge seemed to be weighing Peter's words, it was only the better to scorn them. 'Don't be ridiculous. Have you no understanding of private property?'

'I do, but why should I respect it when those at the Hall showed none such for us who had lived there for generations past? My mother, hastened to her end because of it.' But, as he spoke, it was not his mother's face he saw but the lad, rolled on his side in the gutter.

'Then there is the matter of the affray at Beckwith's shop for which, from your countenance, I judge you to be not one part remorseful.'

Peter fixed the judge with the last of his courage. 'I would do the same if I had to.'

'Had to? *Had to?* Do you seek to place the blame for your wickedness elsewhere? On circumstances without you? Look within. Look within. There alone will you find the source of your folly.'

The judge had no qualm, no hesitancy, would shew no mercy. Peter would be sent immediately from that place, seven years for affray, and, with the hares, transportation, for life.

He saw Róisín, at the back, leap to her feet. 'There never was a just English judge! You are the thieves, for you thieve our lives away—'

They were the last words he heard from her. And as she was jostled out, it was the last he saw of her too.

Róisín

THISTLEWOOD CAME TO tell me. He promised he would, if he ever heard. But months had gone by and nothing and perhaps, I thought, that was him only forgetting. But now he was here, with a stillness that was all sorrow. He brought out a newspaper and showed me a rectangle of words marked around with black. And I knew, with no word said between us, that this was a coffin, brought to me at last.

I had gone to that court every day, a witness to so much strife and misery, in the hope I'd see him, so that whatever his fate I would know it. They sent him from me. And now, this was him come back.

'Will you read it?' I said, my voice but a whisper.

Thistlewood took a breath:

It is reported that the Albion has been lost while crossing the Bay of Bombay. Of the captain and crew, nothing is known. Three of the prisoners survived, by dint of their wits, clutching barrels that came up to the surface. They recounted that they were under full sail when the ship went under, subsumed in moments, as if snatched by a hand from the deep. Being in sight of land, a rescue mission was launched. Of a hundred and twenty-two souls, all perished save for the three already mentioned. It is not known why the vessel foundered, but a

*vast raft of pumice that has plagued vessels bound for Calcutta
is suspected.*

He folded the paper in half and slipped it into his pocket.
He shook his head. 'I'm sorry. His name is not one of those
that lived.'

He never was mine, but he was mine enough. I thought
of him that day and the fat, square judge who had never a
day's starving in him. 'They may as well have hanged him.'

'No,' said Thistlewood. 'You're not to say that.' He
crouched down and took my hands in his. 'Listen to me,
Róisín, listen. James Towle, of Leicester, Harwood and
Thody of Norwich, John Dann of Nottingham, Joseph Bugg
of Ipswich. Five good men in Littleport – all put to death
for wanting the same. Hundreds more thrown in gaol or
transported. Are we to let their deaths pass in vain?'

I looked at him and he told me again of how it could be.
'We cannot be afraid to make the world we are after.'

It was hard to imagine how it could be different. Never
had there been such a bad year as this.

I gave a small nod. The time for words was over.

Sarah

WHEN IT IS dark, I touch my fingers to the hull so I know it is there and that way my breath comes back to me.

I haven't ever hope of an 'oss but I have my two feet and when I get home again I'll walk the Ten Mile Bank, end to end, even if it is all four-cornered fields going that way. Hard to imagine what insult they will have caused to be done to it; the corners they'll have made, where none was before. No place for a bird to perch nor anyone who knows me; just me and my thoughts looking back.

I wouldn't mind it, to see it again.

Oh yes you would . . .

I sit up and reach out my hands in the dark. *'Tessie?'*

But no answer comes and I close my eyes for the crying that is in them.

They is supposed to take us up once daily but most times they leave us where we are below. Who'd want sight of us? Skanky and rottid and half eaten by lice.

* * *

When they forget us, we press our fingers into the cracks, seedlings after light. And when a storm comes and the sea heaves below, we go in a huddle so it won't break us. Annie, Edie, Hetty and Molly are the ones closest. We're all wrong 'uns together but hold each other like we are the dearest and most precious.

On whose say-so was it that I was sent away after all? And Ma and Tessie kept from me so I could not bid them farewell and they never knew?

Botany Bay. Sounded pretty when I first heard it, but Edie says it's not.

'Are you sorry for what you did?' she asks.

'I am not.' And I kick at the hull with the flats of my feet, trying to push a plank out of place.

When I get that way and pulling my hair, they chuck water on me to get me to hush. Seven hundred and eight pounds and nine shillings that reverend got given. *Bastid.*

Sometimes they sit us on deck, sit us there for so long that dusk comes on and the moon rises, heavy and pink. The stars are the same but when I next get a look someone's shuffled them about for the mischief of it.

The sea leaps with fishes and when whales get spotted we are stood at the rail so we can look. *Anyone fancies swimming the rest, they're welcome,* the bosun says and holds out his hand to see who will jump. When one lass steps up, he pushes her back with a laugh.

Other days, the sea is as flat as the Fen and the boat stopped still upon it. Such a hush falls on us and all lost in thinking.

If the Fen were the sea, no one could fence it or burn it or chase the wild creatures away.

One day, the bosun spies a great, silvery patch of water, like silver poured over the sea. But when the boat fetches near it is all timber, a tangle of trees, the trunks worn smooth as our shins. We go quiet, for it is a terrible sight. Not silver. Not treasure. Nothing green grows, nor ever can.

A girl like me, sending me here to put an end to it? For me to be sorry?

No. For I am learning the size of the world.

I am every mile that's gone under me and I am every mile yet to come.

The sun has a burning in it I never felt before. No shelter can be had. I shut my eyes against it. Meadowsweet, meadowsweet, to my waist.

Oh, Tom. It's all imagining. I will not die on this ship. I will not.

Afterword

THE TAMBORA ERUPTION of April 1815 remains the largest volcanic eruption of modern times. A 'super colossal' explosion, it measured 7 on the VEI (Volcanic Explosivity Index); by contrast, the Krakatoa eruption of 1883 was a 6. Twelve thousand people are thought to have perished immediately on Sumbawa. Across the region, between 80,000 and 100,000 died of starvation or disease in the following weeks. Tambora is believed to have stood at 13,000 feet. Some 4,000 feet were lost from the summit, leaving a crater approximately four miles across and 3,000 feet deep.

Tambora's impact, beyond its devastating local effects, was not understood at the time. It took more than a year for the event to be reported in British newspapers – most poignantly reported the same week as the death of Golding Constable, John Constable's father. Thanks to research of volcanologists such as Clive Oppenheimer and climatologists such as Hubert Lamb, we now know that the effects of the Tambora eruption were profound and far-reaching and led to sudden cooling across the northern hemisphere, crop failures, famine and social unrest. Summer temperatures across western and central Europe were around 2-4°C cooler than average in 1816. These effects were felt most acutely in 1816, but led to cumulative hardships in 1817 and 1818 and devastating cholera and typhus epidemics triggered by the failure of monsoons. The year became known as *The Year Without Summer* and in North America as *Eighteen hundred and froze to death*. Snow fell in June and August; weeks of incessant rain seemed to foretell the end of times. But whereas large parts of Europe suffered floods, North America experienced a sustained period of drought and wildfires. In the longer term, the Tambora eruption is credited with social change through the nineteenth century and with the pressure for political reform.

In addition to Clive Oppenheimer's work, there are two excellent studies of the Tambora eruption: Gillen d'Arcy Wood, *Tambora: The Eruption that Changed the World*; and William K. Klingaman and Nicholas P. Klingaman, *The Year Without Summer*. Dr Lucy Veale and Professor Georgina Endfield have analysed, with painstaking detail, a large number of primary sources of the period as evidence for Tambora's impact on the UK. Recent research by Dr Genge at Imperial College London has suggested a link between Napoleon's defeat at Waterloo in 1815 and the Tambora eruption, which brought weeks of heavy rain to Europe, bogging down troops on the battlefield. This novel draws on these works for research purposes, and on biographies, art histories and literary studies of Mary Shelley and John Constable which acknowledge the impact of the Tambora eruption on their work, especially in the genesis of *Frankenstein*. But this novel is also in part a telling of these places as I have known them. Some years ago, I worked at the University of Essex, situated in Wivenhoe Park. On lunchtime walks around the lake, I used to wonder about Constable working on the Rebows' commission. Today, I live not far from Littleport, the scene of such unrest at the time, the legacy of which is commemorated vividly on the village sign.

A plaque in Ely names the five men who were hanged for their part in the riot. The story of Sarah Hobbs is based loosely on a woman of the same name. She was the only woman condemned to hang but her sentence was commuted to twelve months in Ely gaol before, it seems, she was transported to Australia after all. In fictionalising her story, I made the decision to make her younger and a resident of Littleport – the real Sarah Hobbs was married, came from Ely, and took part in the riot there. Downham Tom is based on the story of Thomas Sindall, the only person known to be present at the riots at Downham Market and Littleport. He was shot and killed while trying to escape arrest. Lord Liverpool's and Sidmouth's brutal suppression of the Littleport riots in many ways fore-shadows their response to the protesters who gathered in Manchester in 1819, demanding reform. Those notorious events are now known as the Peterloo Massacre.

The University of Cambridge Library, Cambridge Central Library and Cambridgeshire Archive hold a good collection of local maps of the Fens and the Bedford Level Commissioners archive, which show in stark terms how land use was changing as fenland was enclosed and drained. Other research took me further into the Fens to Wisbech, where I discovered, quite by chance, William Godwin's birthplace. I had not expected to find a connection to Mary Shelley there. Mary would later write that the 1816 summer was the time when she 'first stepped out from childhood into life'. On her return to England, she worked to complete

Frankenstein and it was finally published in 1818. That year also saw the Shelleys leave England for Italy, again with Claire, and again to meet Byron. By now, Mary had two children: William and Clara Everina. Neither child would survive these travels. Clara Everina died of dysentery in 1818 and William, a few months later, of malaria. Mary, now childless, fell into despair.

Art critics have described 1816 as the year when Constable moved from tone to colour. His oil sketches provide vivid evidence for that. Landscape painting was deeply unfashionable at the time but Constable painted it regardless. He was no fan of enclosure or 'Gentlemen's parks' as he called them. Whatever your opinion of Constable's art, there is a defiance to it, I think, and he was acutely aware of what was being lost. He had to wait until 1829 before he was finally elected to the Royal Academy.

After the Spa Field riots ended chaotically, Thistlewood was arrested but later released. Undeterred, the Spencean Philanthropists regrouped. In 1820 Thistlewood was found guilty of treason for his part in the Cato Street Conspiracy, a plot to kill Lord Liverpool and his Cabinet. Widespread public revulsion at the brutal manner of his execution – Thistlewood was hanged and then decapitated with a small knife – provided impetus to calls for reform against such barbaric practice.

I have based the story of the Tambora eruption on the account of the captain of the *Benares*, who was sent to investigate several explosions. He set sail, expecting to encounter pirates, but instead found himself sailing into the immediate aftermath of the eruption, a catastrophic event, without precedent. Sumbawa Island was then under

British rule and governed by Stamford Raffles. As D'Arcy Wood notes, Raffles responded to the eruption both as modern bureaucrat and scholar, requesting reports from across the territory. These reports were collected together to form a *Narrative* of which the captain of the *Benares'* account is one part. It was not until four months later, in August 1815, after reports of famine on Sumbawa, that Raffles sent a relief vessel with rice, a response that D'Arcy Wood describes as 'pitifully inadequate'.

We live at a time of climate crisis. Although the Tambora eruption was a natural event and its impact limited to a handful of years, it provides a clear example of the devastating effects of climate breakdown. The poor were hit hardest, creating large numbers of famine refugees and dislocating many more.

1816 was a year of flood and fire, of popular protest and revolutionary struggle, of Constable's art and Mary Shelley's *Frankenstein*. A famine year, when protectionist policies were enacted to protect landed wealth and benefit those never at risk of going hungry. It was a year dominated by strikingly similar debates and concerns about national debt, poor relief (welfare) and protectionism as those in austerity-ravaged Britain and in Trump's America.

Historical fiction often presses history into the service of the present. The story of Tambora is not just the story of then, it is a story of now. But in writing this novel, I was also interested in how fiction might be used to interrogate the past. How should we understand Constable's art, Mary

Shelley's writing and what might the novel reveal about their lived experience of that year, and their response to it, at a time of undeniable crisis?

Writing *The Year Without Summer* took me to the heart of what it means to be a writer and to question what fiction is for at a time of man-made climate change, when we are living through the sixth mass extinction event.

For where should fiction take us? Towards comfort? Towards hope? What is a story for, if not to propel us? To provide, above all, urgent impetus to act?

Acknowledgements

MY THANKS GO to the following people for their support and encouragement: Anni Domingo, Siobhan Costello, Maartje Scheltens, Cressida Downing, Todd Johnson and Kaddy Benyon. The staff at the University of Cambridge Library, Cambridgeshire Archives and Cambridge Central Library, and the staff at Monadnock History Centre in Peterborough, New Hampshire.

Thanks also to Dr Harvey Osborne, who kindly commented on the novel as a draft and answered my questions on rural history and poaching. Harvey and I were history research students together at Lancaster University many years ago. What a treat that this book enabled our work to overlap all these years later. He's the historian, and I am not. This is a work of fiction and any errors are mine. My thanks also go to Professor Clive Oppenheimer for reading the *Afterword* and for his invaluable feedback on it.

Thank you to the MacDowell Colony Foundation who awarded me a six-week Fellowship in 2017/18. Thanks also to the Society of Authors for the award of a Foundation Grant which kept me afloat financially as I worked to complete the first draft of this novel in early 2018.

Thank you to my publisher Lisa Highton, and all at Two Roads and to my agent, Veronique Baxter, without whose hard work and expertise this book would simply not be.

Finally, to my husband Damian and my daughter Saskia, whose love and kindness sustained me through the everyday of writing this book – I thank you most of all.

About the Author

Author Guinevere Glasfurd was born in Lancaster and lives near Cambridge with her husband and daughter.

Her debut novel, *The Words in My Hand*, was shortlisted for the 2016 Costa First Novel Award and Authors' Club Best First Novel Award and was longlisted in France for the Prix du Roman FNAC.

Her second novel, *The Year Without Summer*, written with support from the MacDowell Colony Foundation, tells the story of the 1815 Mount Tambora eruption and the catastrophic events that followed. Awarded grants from the Arts Council England and the British Council for her novels, her writing has also appeared in the *Scotsman*, *Mslexia* and the National Galleries of Scotland.

She is currently working on her third novel, a story of the Enlightenment, set in eighteenth-century England and France.